The Girl ⸳ ⸳⸳m Eureka

Cheryl Adnams

16pt

Read How You Want
LARGE PRINT BOOKS, BRAILLE & DAISY

Copyright Page from the Original Book

TABLE OF CONTENTS

The Girl from Eureka

Cheryl Adnams

On the sun-drenched goldfields of Eureka, a wild colonial girl and an honour-bound soldier will break all the rules to claim a love worth more than gold...

Ballarat, Australia 1854

Gold miner Indy Wallace wants nothing more than to dig up enough gold to give her mother an easier life. Wild and reckless, and in trouble more often than not, Indy finds herself falling for handsome, chivalrous British Army Lieutenant Will Marsh. But in the eyes of immigrant miners, soldiers are the enemy.

Will has been posted to Ballarat with a large contingent of Her Majesty's Army to protect the Crown gold and keep the peace. But once he meets rebellious Indy, he doubt's he'll ever be at peace again. As Will and Indy's attraction grows, their loyalties are tested when the unrest between miners and the military reaches breaking point.

On opposite sides of the escalating conflict, can their love survive their battle of ideals? And will any of them survive the battle of the Eureka Stockade?

About the author

Cheryl Adnams lives in Adelaide, South Australia. She has published four Australian rural romance novels and this is her first Australian historical novel. Cheryl has a Diploma in Freelance Travel Writing and Photography, and has lived and worked in the United States, Canada and spent two years with a tour company in Switzerland and Austria. Her passion for Italy, volcanology and cycling have made their way into her stories and her favourite writing retreats include Positano on the Amalfi Coast and Port Willunga Beach just south of Adelaide. When she's not writing, Cheryl is still creating in her busy full-time job as a trainer and learning designer.

If you'd like to know more about me, my books, or to connect with me online, you can visit my webpage cheryladnams.com, follow me on twitter @cadnams, or like my Facebook page http://www.facebook.com/cheryadnamsauthor.

Acknowledgements

I enjoyed researching this important moment in time and want to especially thank Clare Wright for her incredible Stella-Award-winning book *The Forgotten Rebels of Eureka.* Her insights and untold stories of the women who were at the Eureka Stockade, and in Ballarat during that time, were vital to the creation of Indy and the other female characters.

Thanks also to the amazing work of Sovereign Hill, the Gold Museum and the MADE Museum in Ballarat for keeping the history alive. I urge you to visit Ballarat and see this incredible historical site and gorgeous city for yourself. Researching this book was truly a wonderful experience and I am happy to say that I know just a little more about Australia's foundations as a democracy and our interesting and all too often overlooked history.

Huge thanks to Kate Cuthbert at Escape for taking on Indy's story, and to all the crew at Escape for their efforts in bringing it to readers. Thank you to my editor Chrysoula Aiello for being so easy and wonderful to work with. Thanks to Belinda Stevens for your design expertise and the beautiful cover.

And last but not least, thanks to all my faithful readers who have stuck by me through the highs and lows. Writing can be a challenging business and it's only when you face the struggles that you understand exactly what having a passion for it means.

To all the feisty Indys I've known who stood up for what they believe in

Chapter 1

August 1854

The strange murmur grew louder.

As their journey stretched on, the travelling party had settled into an exhausted silence. They were no longer able to find the energy or desire to converse. The coach that carried the lady creaked and groaned as the wooden wheels crackled on the dirt road. The horses struggled to pull the coach up the hill, they too were tired. This was the final hill, the old coachman had assured them. It was nearing sundown and a huge flock of large, white parrots with the sulphur-coloured crests flew overhead, screeching their departure.

While the travellers ascended the hill the murmur became a rumble, deep, with no discernible qualities in the otherwise peaceful countryside. The two escorting soldiers crossed glances as the din increased in volume. In silent agreement, they rode ahead of the carriage to the top of the hill to inspect the way forward, wary of danger as always.

Reaching the crest, Lieutenant Will Marsh shaded his eyes against the bright sun perched low on the horizon. Only when the golden orb became obscured by a cloud was he able to take in the full effect of the vista below. And he knew he would never in his life forget his first look at the mining town of Ballarat.

The unmelodious symphony of so many humans in such a dense space was near deafening now, as he cast widened eyes across the expanse of the messily erected township below. From his elevated vantage point it seemed to him as though an army of ants had moved in and turned the place upside down and inside out. Barely a patch of green was visible, despite the supposedly abundant winter rains. Mineshafts and their resulting conical-shaped piles of dirt were strewn haphazardly, interrupted only by the canvas tents erected in, around, between and sometimes over the top of the shafts. It reminded him of military camps he'd been stationed at, although somewhat less ordered. Flags representing different countries flapped and snapped on top of tent posts in the cold wind, clearly stating the nationality of those living in proximity. Even in this mottled together township, folks seemed destined to congregate like with like.

It was easy to distinguish where the Irish camp ended and the Canadian camp began. The American Stars and Stripes flew above yet another grouping of tents. But it was the Union Jack that was most prominent amongst them, and there were many flags he did not recognise at all. What lay before him in this busy makeshift metropolis was a map of the world.

Humans of every kind—adults and children, men and women—could be seen moving about the place on foot or on horseback. Will watched with bewildered amusement as bodies appeared and disappeared in and out of the ground, reminding him of rabbits back in the wilds of England. Men shifted dirt from here to there and back again and the dust that rose into the air from all this industry left a gritty haze, hovering like a gauzy blanket over its busy inhabitants.

Industry. Yes, that was the word the view conjured for Will. Gold mining was an industry of epic proportions.

'Welcome to the Ballarat Goldfields, Governor Hotham,' Will said, as the important man rode up beside him on his impressive-looking stallion.

When the Fortieth Regiment of Her Majesty's army had been relieved in India, Will had expected to be sent back to England. Instead, he'd found himself on a ship bound for one of the latest acquisitions of the British Empire.

Victoria. So named for their Queen, it was a settlement in its infancy, having split from New South Wales and formed its own government only three years prior. And for the small contingent of a rather war-weary regiment, the town of Melbourne had been the port where their ship from Calcutta had landed. Alongside them, boatloads of immigrants arrived on the shores of Victoria seeking not only gold, but a life free from the famines of Ireland, the economic ruin of England and the

European continent and the wars of Africa.

Will and his comrade, Lieutenant Cedric Timmons, had been sent on to Ballarat ahead of their comrades, as the newly appointed Victorian Governor Sir Charles Hotham had required a guard detail for him and his wife to visit the goldfields.

Staring out at those goldfields now, Will shared a bemused smile with the new Governor. The coach that had paused upon reaching the summit began to move again, breaking Will out of his trance.

Leading the way, he and Timmons rode slowly down the hill and into the bustling township. Gunfire rang out as the coach trundled through the centre of town. Twisting quickly in his saddle, Will's hand went to his revolver by instinct, his eyes sharp on the man he protected.

'Gold!'

He stared astounded as a man, covered head to toe in dried mud, danced an ungainly jig before firing his weapon into the air once again, whooping and cheering as he went.

'Another lucky strike,' Timmons said lightly, his relaxed manner surprising Will.

'And what? They're shooting it out for it?' he asked, baffled by the reckless behaviour.

Timmons chuckled. 'No, I believe when someone gets a strike, they fire off their weapons. Actually, as I understand it, they fire off their weapons for any damn thing.'

Will removed his hand from his gun, but did not relax completely. 'Interesting place this Victoria.'

The party passed through one large campsite and then another. While the men still toiled in the mines, women bustled about by campfires preparing the evening meal. People stopped and took note of the carriage and its entourage as they travelled by, but didn't seem to know the importance of its passengers. Will kept his eyes peeled, but the residents of Ballarat were more interested in getting about their business than the arrival of more people.

A veritable trooping of the colours topped the timber buildings that lined the main road into the town proper. More British standards flew, and even the red flag of the Chinese sat atop what appeared to be a food stall. An assortment of languages could be gleaned above the relentless noise of gunfire, barking dogs and mining apparatus. Will recognised the tongue of his homeland and a few Eastern European dialects were also evident. The sing-song of Celtic Ireland blended together with the clipped sounds of the Africans, making for a dazzling assault on the senses.

'They say the world has moved to Victoria,' Timmons said.

Will turned his head to follow the path of an oddly dressed Asian man as he scurried across the road, carrying on his shoulders a long piece of wood with two huge bags of rice tied to each end. In his haste the man almost collided with a very large, bullish black man.

'Watch it, Chinaman,' the black man grumbled loudly in a strong American accent.

'Whoever "they" are, I'd say they're right,' Will responded.

'Do you suppose we'll find any chunks of the gold stuff?' Timmons asked with an almost boyish hope.

'We're here to protect Her Majesty's Governor until he and his wife return to Melbourne, Timmons. Then we are charged with protecting the gold, not finding it.'

'I heard that in the first years of the rush you couldn't walk ten feet without tripping over a nugget,' Timmons said, his eyes filled with excitement. 'The gold was easy pickings for any man with a bit of determination and a good, strong back to dig out a nugget and change his fortune. If it happened to be just lying about on the ground, would you not take some? Take it and get out of the army? Get far away from any British garrison and start a new life. I hear of places in this colony that are unlike anything in England.'

'There were places in India unlike England too. Did you want to stay there and make a home?'

'Good Lord, no.' Timmons's pinched expression told of his disgust. 'Those Godforsaken places were war ravaged, overrun with disease, and peopled by savages. But this place, Victoria, I hear it is so big there are lands no man has even seen yet.'

'No white man perhaps,' Will said eyeing one of the dark-skinned natives who stood on a distant hill, watching. Will was distracted by a group of children chasing chickens across the road, and when he looked back to the hill, the native man had disappeared. Was the native keen for his own bit of the gold? Or perhaps he was wondering what had happened to his beloved homeland. Will had seen plenty of what invaders had done to foreign lands and their people for Queen and country. It was rarely a happy merging of nations.

Scrubbing his hand across his filthy face, Will shook off the unwarranted feelings of discontent. He enjoyed his life in the army. He was just tired from their long boat trip from India, and now this three-day journey to the goldfields had him worn out and saddle-sore. All he needed was a good feed, a snort of whiskey and a bed and he'd be his normal cheerful self again.

'Did you see the stretches of golden beaches as we sailed up the coastline into Melbourne?' Timmons went on, his voice filled with reverent awe.

'I did,' Will answered, barely listening anymore as he took in the massive spread of the diggers' camps. There seemed to be an organised chaos to it all.

'And the weather, Will.' Timmons leaned his face up to the sun, which had popped out from behind the clouds again for one last peek before it set. 'Evidently, this is what passes for an Australian winter. It's so mild. Until that blasted rain that met us earlier this afternoon, the sun has shone every day.'

'And that is why this place suffers with water shortage,' Will tossed back with a grin for his friend and comrade. 'You romanticise a place you know nothing about, Timmons. Give it a few weeks. I hear the summers are brutally hot, the snakes and spiders are copious and deadly, and the flies and mosquitos are large enough to carry a man away, boots and all.'

Timmons laughed heartily. 'A romantic I may be, Will, but you are a cynic of the fantastic kind.'

Will couldn't argue with that. He felt like a belligerent old man sometimes. He never thought he would feel so old at twenty-eight years of age. Then again, there were times he never thought he would live long enough to see his late twenties.

'You need to relax and enjoy our new posting, Will. This is no war-torn place. There will be no trouble here.'

A gathering of diggers had stopped working as the coach passed and were paying more attention to Hotham's arrival. Some of the men removed their hats and smiled as Lady Hotham waved at them. Other faces amongst them were filled with suspicion and it was those men that Will kept his eye on.

'There's always trouble. You just have to know where to look for it,' he murmured.

The travelling party arrived at the government camp without much fanfare and were directed to the Gold Commission Office. Will stood by while Governor and Mrs Hotham were introduced to the Gold Commissioner Robert Rede, his Assistant Commissioner James Johnston and Police Inspector Gordon Evans.

The minute the new Governor and his wife were led away to their quarters, the polite mood in the tent vanished. Ignoring Will and Timmons, the senior officers began to argue. It was easy to see that Police Inspector Evans was none too pleased at being forced to give up his comfortable quarters to the new Governor.

'If Hotham had to spend some time in the tents, perhaps he would follow up on the more permanent housing Governor La Trobe promised.'

'Evans, I am not going to trouble the Governor with our petty concerns on his first visit to the goldfields,' Rede dismissed. 'Nor will I put him in unsuitable quarters.'

'Then give him yours,' Evans murmured.

'If that will be all, sir,' Will interrupted, keen to get out of there. These two gentlemen were clearly not friends. 'Timmons and I would like to get settled in our tent.'

Commissioner Rede dismissed them with a distracted wave of his hand and they set off to unpack their horses and find their accommodations. Compared with others Will had been stationed in, the government camp was a relatively small garrison that sat on a slight rise surrounded by a fence with picketed posts. Behind the Gold Commission Office they had just left, where licences were sold to miners, Will noted several wooden buildings he assumed to be the homes of the Gold Commissioner and his assistant, and the recently put out Police Inspector.

Across the grassy compound stood the mess tent. His stomach made an embarrassingly loud rumble as he thought again about food.

'Your stomach reads my mind, Will,' Timmons said as they carried their saddlebags across the compound. 'Let's relieve ourselves of this gear and see what's on offer at the mess.'

They passed by several other wooden structures including the courthouse that boasted a wide veranda and a makeshift jail beside it made of thick logs of wood. Its current inhabitants numbered four, and Will wondered what the men had done to find themselves unwilling guests of Her Majesty. They appeared extremely worse for wear so he imagined drunk and disorderly to be the charge.

Reaching the northern border, on the edge of a small incline, the two men found rows of white calico tents, where soldiers, both commissioned and non-commissioned, were clearly housed. Even from a distance Will could see the shabbiness of the calico. The mould and mud of a long wet winter had taken its toll on the temporary housing. It didn't concern Will overmuch. He'd lived in worse conditions. Several campfires burned in a small break of land beside the soldiers' camp, and on the other side of the fires were more tents in even worse disrepair than the military accommodations. Policemen in dark blue uniforms, ill-fitting and equally as shabby as their tents, eyed Will and Timmons with contempt as they crossed to the soldiers' section.

A young corporal directed them to a tent at the rear of the garrison. It was barely large enough to hold two men. But Will observed the surrounding tents holding three or more soldiers, many of them sleeping on the ground. He wondered what poor souls had been evicted from their home to make way for two new officers.

Flipping open the tent flap, he was relieved to see two wooden cots with canvas strung for the mattress. He sat down on one of them and it drooped so badly his backside almost hit the floor. Stretching out, he closed his eyes and exhaled the day's exhaustion. The bed was rudimentary but functional.

'I'd heard they were supposed to have barracks erected by now,' Timmons said, frowning at the dirty and bedraggled state of the calico tent before him.

'Been saying that nigh on six months,' the corporal said with a grunt. 'Wouldn't hold your breath.'

Timmons stepped into the tent and just as quickly stepped back out again as the smell of rot and mildew greeted him. 'We may have to.'

'It will be fine, Timmons,' Will called from his flat out position, his eyes still closed. 'Stop your bellyaching.'

'At least you got here at the end of winter,' the corporal said. 'It was miserable. Never bloody stopped raining.'

'Well, that explains the mould,' Timmons said. Holding his hand over his nose and mouth, he reluctantly followed Will inside. Taking a seat on his cot, he let out a surprised squeak as it sagged dramatically with his weight, leaving his knees in the air and his backside touching the floor. Will didn't bother to stifle his laugh.

Timmons struggled for a moment to stand from his odd position and finally gave up with a frustrated hurrumph.

'And what of that?' Timmons asked, pointing at the jagged slice in the canvas above their heads where the breeze floated in.

Will finally opened his eyes and gazed up through the hole in the tent. 'Think of the unobstructed view we'll have of the beautiful southern stars,' he said, marvelling at the red and orange clouds moving slowly across the violet dusk sky. The day was coming to an end.

'Fine, but it's your buy when we finally get in there,' Timmons told him as he caught up.

Passing by another building to the side of the hotel, Will looked in the open door. A few fellows were tossing heavy wooden balls down the lane and he heard the clatter as the wooden pins were scattered. A bowling alley in the middle of the goldfields? Strange place this Ballarat.

As they rounded the rear of the hotel, another cheer went up and intermingled with some grumbles and groans. From what Will could see over the tops of the heads of men squatting, hovering in a circle, it looked to be some sort of game of dice.

One of the men spied Will and Timmons and, taking in their red coats, his eyes widened in panic. He stood up from his squat and yelled, 'Blimey, it's the traps!' before running in the opposite direction.

Following their friend's lead, men jumped up and began to scarper away.

'What's a trap?' Will asked Timmons as they stood by innocuously watching men scatter like ants on a disturbed hill.

'Haven't the foggiest.'

A young man tried to rush past them and Will reached out and grabbed the boy by the collar. The fellow struggled and kicked and managed to get Will directly in the shin.

'Ouch, you little rotter!' Will complained angrily. He took the boy and pushed him up against the back wall of the hotel. His shin stung like the blazes, but he bit down on the pain. 'That bloody hurt. Where are you running to, boy?'

A moment later, two uniformed policemen rushed around the corner.

'Traps!' came the call again.

'Ah,' Timmons let out a sound of understanding. 'I assume anyone in uniform gets this moniker of a "trap".'

'And what do they call you?' Will asked the boy he held against the wall. The hat obscured his face so Will tried to remove it, but the fellow held tight.

'I asked your name, lad,' Will demanded. He managed to tug away the man's hat and blinked, shocked when miles of long blonde hair tumbled out in loose curls all the way to his waist—her waist. He was most definitely a *her.*

'You're a woman?'

'Well, aren't you the smart one,' she answered bitingly, the Irish in her voice unmistakable.

She continued to struggle against his restraining hands, and as the shock of discovering her a woman wore off, he belatedly released his grip.

'I beg your pardon for seizing you, madam. I did not realise you were a lady,' Will apologised, stepping back.

'She ain't no lady.'

'Shut up, Jackson, you pig-faced moron,' the girl spat back at the trooper.

Will's eyebrows shot up in surprise. 'Not a lady, indeed.'

It was obvious the girl was well known to the local constabulary. A troublemaker perhaps.

'Can I go now?' the girl asked, her chin jutting out in defiance.

'Well, I don't know,' he said, gracing her with a severe frown despite the fact he was enjoying himself immensely. What a firecracker this girl was—not to mention how remarkably pretty she was beneath the wicked temper and masculine clothing. 'You were playing an illegal game of dice, were you not? I really should let these police officers arrest you. What is your name, Miss?'

Smiling coyly now, the girl stepped towards him and Will's war-honed instincts heightened. Gone was the sturdy Irish temper, and in its place was a demure, helpless woman. It was an act, he was sure, but her suddenly female vulnerability was so effective he almost fell for it.

'Indigo Wallace, sir' she said demurely, running her index finger down his uniform before tugging lightly on one of his tunic buttons.

He took her by the shoulder and, more gently this time, pushed her back a step.

'Why do you pretend to be a boy?'

'Oh, I weren't doing no harm, sir,' Indigo pouted, putting on an accent of the uneducated.

It seemed the girl was a chameleon. Entertained as he was, he wasn't buying it. Crossing his arms and exhaling an impatient breath, he simply stared her down.

'I'm not pretending to be anything,' she said, the short moment of helplessness gone and her diction once again more articulate.

'Then why do you wear boy's clothing?'

'Have you ever worn a dress, Captain?'

'It's Lieutenant actually,' he corrected her. 'And no. Of course I have not ever worn a dress.'

'And a corset? Have you ever worn a corset?'

He cleared his throat. 'I beg your pardon?'

She smiled slowly, devilishly, 'Does it embarrass you, Lieutenant? Talking about a lady's underwear?'

'There are some who would say it is improper to discuss a lady's undergarments in public.'

'Well, a corset is a torture device created to strangle the life and vitality out of a woman. They pinch and they ache and they throttle the breath right out of you. All so a woman can look how fashion, and a man, deem she should look. And I for one, sir, will not be strangled for any man.'

And with that, the girl grabbed her boyish hat out of Will's hand and stormed away.

'Should we arrest her?' One of the policemen who had stood by during the exchange began to follow her.

'What for?' Will asked with an amused shrug as he watched the girl disappear around the side of the hotel. 'I didn't see her doing anything wrong. Did you, Timmons?'

'No, Lieutenant,' Timmons answered, biting back his smile as the policemen left to join their colleagues.

Will glanced down at the gold buttons of his tunic that the woman had played with. She'd had such long, delicate fingers. But he hadn't missed the dirt beneath the nails. What would possess such a pretty, young girl to join the local rabble, playing illegal games of dice in the dirt behind the pub?

'A fascinating creature,' Timmons said, reading Will's mind. Perhaps they had spent too much time together these last few weeks.

'Yes, fascinating,' he agreed. He dusted himself off, straightened his red uniform jacket and followed Timmons through the rear door of the hotel.

'I imagine men would be lining up to strangle the fascinating Miss Wallace, with and without a corset.'

Timmons laughed heartily.

'I believe I owe you a drink,' Will said, pushing the interaction with the girl aside.

'I believe you do,' Timmons responded, and raised his hand to get the bartender's attention.

Chapter 2

More bloody soldiers. Just what they bloody needed.

Indy dragged her feet as she headed back to camp. It wasn't bad enough they had to contend with the new Victoria Police, its ranks now swelled with any vagabond and ex-convict who needed a job. No, now they were bringing in replacements, fresh soldiers to settle in for the duration. The soldiers who had been in Ballarat throughout the winter had nigh on self-destructed by the end of their campaign. They'd seen war, yes, but a Ballarat winter could test the mettle of the strongest of men.

She knew why further regiments had been called in, though. Since the Gold Commissioner had increased the taxes on mining, the diggers were more resentful than ever. And they had a right to be, Indy thought indignantly. Thirty shillings for a miner's licence? It was double what they used to pay. And it covered no more than it had before: the right to stake a claim, water usage and wood to shore up a mineshaft. Those who could afford it paid the exorbitant taxes, but had very few basic rights. The miners had no voice in the legislature and were not permitted to own land. They were angry, and becoming much less frightened to speak their minds on the matter. To make matters worse, the Assistant Gold Commissioner Johnston was calling for more regular licence hunts to track down those who refused, or couldn't afford to pay, the licence fee. Johnston had quickly become the most hated man in Ballarat.

Indy was irritated too but she kept her head down and paid the blasted fees. Calling undue attention to herself would only cause her more grief. As one of only a hundred or so women who worked a mine on the goldfields, she was unpopular enough. Most women stayed in the camps, taking care of children and feeding their men when they came home from the mines. Indy had no intention of sitting on the sidelines while all the gold was ripped up and carted away by men.

Now that the sun had set, the cold was beginning to seep in. She increased her pace but it wasn't only the cold that had her quickening her steps. When she'd first arrived at the goldfields it had been relatively safe for a woman to wander around the township and camps unaccompanied. But in the last year, with the continuing influx of new inhabitants and the rise in drinking—thanks to newly licensed hotels—it had become dangerous for a woman to be out alone after dark. Alcohol had become one of the biggest social problems on the Victorian goldfields. Not that she minded a tipple or two herself. She was Irish after all. But there were dangers for a woman in a man's world. Especially when that man was three sheets to the wind.

Other miners were heading back in to camp as well, filthy and exhausted from digging dawn to dusk. Some were drunk already, others just tired and anxious to get home to family. Indy had given up the digging early to join her usual game of dice behind Bentley's Eureka Hotel. She'd been doing well too until those soldiers in their red coats and shiny brass buttons had walked in and broken it up.

She chuckled as she recalled the uneasiness of the tall blond one as she'd flirted with him. Men were so easy to disarm. They went weak as newborn puppies in the presence of a pretty lady. Some remained gentlemen, others lost their heads and felt it was within their rights to touch and take whatever they wanted.

'Well, I for one, am not for the taking, soldier boy,' she said out loud, kicking a stone down the road.

But this soldier had proved himself to be a gentleman, and a good-looking one at that. He'd been considerably taller than her. His blond hair pulled back and tied in the usual way of the military at the nape of his neck. Strong hands had held her fast when he'd thought her a boy, but then turned soft as a caress when he'd discovered her a woman. Eyes the colour of treacle had changed from commanding to apologetic as she had done her best to unsettle him. Yes, his eyes were most expressive, and he'd been confused by her masculine garb.

When gambling, she chose to hide her gender and outfit herself as a man. She owned dresses, practical dresses mostly, but she preferred trousers that allowed ease of working in the mine. All the regular dice players knew who she was. It was the ring-ins who didn't like a woman being there. They said she was bad luck. And she was. But only because she was better at the dice and card games than most of the men, and often left with their share of the shillings.

Bad luck for them indeed!

She smiled as she pulled those shillings from her pocket and stepped into one of the tent stores.

'Good evening, Mrs Murphy,' Indy said to the buxom woman behind the table.

'Indy love, how are you?'

'I'm well, thank you. I was hoping you may have one of your lovely pies left.'

Mrs Murphy had recently purchased a Yankee cooking stove and her apple pies and cranberry tarts had become somewhat legendary about the goldfields. She was just one of the hundreds of women who had travelled to the fields with their husbands. The smart ones found occupation in setting up stores to support their families, while their menfolk gambled their day away in dirty, wet mines in search of the promised return of gold.

The selection of little tent stores sold everything from eggs and cheese to bonnets and baby clothes. Many were known to sell sly grog from their back rooms. The stores were as much a booming industry as the goldfields themselves, and often more profitable. It was a strange thing to see the women making a living for the family while the men brought home nothing. Some husbands took it in their stride. Others felt emasculated and drank to deaden the shame.

'Well, normally I wouldn't have any left come this time of night—you know how popular my cakes and pies are. But, you're in luck. I was just trying a new recipe,' Mrs Murphy said excitedly, wiping flour from her pudgy hands. 'Young Allen Fisher found some fig trees not far off the road from Geelong. He's been selling them to all the stores, for an inflated price naturally.'

Indy laughed at the storekeeper's suddenly grim expression. 'Mrs Murphy, everything in Ballarat is at an inflated price. Are you telling me you have fig tarts?'

'Fig and apple. I had to try and make those expensive figs go further.'

Indy eyed the tarts cooling on the rack behind Mrs Murphy and her mouth watered. 'I'll take two please.'

'Two?' Mrs Murphy asked with a surprised and delighted chuckle. 'Did you strike gold today, Indigo Wallace?'

'Of a fashion,' Indy said, smiling at her good fortune at dice.

She handed over the required shillings and stuffed the rest into her boot for safekeeping. Then taking the still warm pies, she moved out of the tent and continued for home.

As she made her way through the Eureka campsite it seemed to pulse around her like a living organism. Tents of all shapes and sizes swept up the slow rise, interspersed with fires now burning strongly again in readiness for the evening meal. The sea of white canvas glowed orange, beating like a heart by the light of lamps and candles. The beating heart of the Ballarat goldfields.

The rich smell of burning wood and cooking food permeated the air and Indy breathed deeply. It didn't always smell so good here. Over the winter just passed, the incessant rain had reduced the campground to a muddy, festering sty. The putrid stench of dysentery had wafted regularly amongst the tents as disease spread thanks to filthy sewage pits that overflowed and mixed with drinking water. But now that winter was almost done with them for another year, soon the ground would dry up and once again life would be infinitely better. At least until the stinking hot summer arrived.

Passing through the Chinese section of the camp, she bowed to the men. They ignored her as usual and she chuckled quietly to herself. She'd break them one day. Until then she would continue to smile and bow until they acknowledged her. She wondered how they fared living in a faraway land, so different to their own. It was common knowledge that their wives never travelled with them as the Europeans or Americans did. They did not mix with other cultures either as many of the other immigrants did. They cooked for themselves and laundered their own clothes, and did a mighty fine job as far as Indy could see. She sniffed at the unusual aroma of spices as they fried their food, all mixed together in the wide black cooking pans they'd brought with them from the Chinese Empire. And after dark, by the light of their fires and paper lanterns they played their funny game of tiles—mahjong she'd heard it was called. Or they'd partake in their version of checkers, played with little round balls instead of flat pieces.

Indy crossed the little creek into the busy campsite where the Irish diggers lived. Somewhere a tin whistle played a jaunty tune and Indy let a genuine smile cross her features. She was home.

'Now, there's a smell to warm a working woman's heart,' she said, as she reached the tent she shared with another Irish woman and her son.

Not a day after she'd arrived in Ballarat with Annie and Sean in the early days of the strikes, she'd bought her gold mining licence and gone into partnership with Sean. Together they had staked a claim and spent long days working their small patch of Victorian soil, hoping that one day they too would find their slice of wealth.

She'd made some good finds already. But unlike others who'd struck, Indy had kept her good fortune to herself. It was too easy to find yourself looking down the barrel of a gun in the middle of the night, whilst thieves rustled up your hidden riches and ran off into the bush with it. If you were lucky you got to keep your life, but never your gold. Bragging was a bad idea and she rolled her eyes to heaven whenever she heard the gunfire celebrating another strike. It was akin to advertising to bushrangers and thieves that you were a mark to be taken.

In those first few months, Indy had sent much of the gold she'd found back to Melbourne. It had been hard to leave her mother in the city and make the journey to the goldfields, but the lure of striking it rich and providing a better life for them was too strong. Mary now lived only a thirty-minute walk from Ballarat, just off the Melbourne Road. The proceeds from Indy's first big strike of gold had gone towards renovating a little shepherd's hut she'd discovered in the bush. She visited her mother as often as she could, but it had been more than a week since she'd last been out to the little cottage. Perhaps it was time for another visit home.

She took a hefty inhale of the wallaby stew that simmered in the pot over the fire.

'I'm fully starved.' But when she went to dig a spoon in for a taste, she felt the swift rap of Annie's wooden spoon across her knuckles. 'Hey!'

Annie's auburn-coloured hair was swept back in its customary bun, giving her a school marm look about her, especially with the current glower she aimed at Indy. As she stirred the stew, her cheeks glowed red from her exertions over the campfire, working hard to provide dinner for them all. Annie was like a surrogate mother to

Indy, a wonderful friend and an even better cook.

Making a show of it, Indy opened the little box she carried and watched her friend's face light up.

'Pies?' Annie gushed. 'Oh, but they must have cost a fortune, Indy.'

'Mrs Murphy got her hands on some figs. She was experimenting with recipes and had some spare so she gave them to me.'

'She just gave them to you?'

'Yes,' Indy lied. Her friend didn't need to know she'd spent on a few sweet tarts the equivalent of what Annie earned in two weeks doing washing for miners. Annie carefully placed the pies by the fire to keep them warm.

'Find any gold today?' It was the same question Annie asked every day when Indy and Sean returned from the mines. And Indy gave her the same response she did just about every day.

'Not today. But I have a feeling we'll strike it tomorrow.'

Sitting down on a long log, she took off her boot and emptied her sock, handing Annie the remaining shillings she'd won at dice.

'Been gambling again, missy?' Annie raised an eyebrow full of disappointment. How a woman's eyebrows could say so much, Indy would never know, but Annie's eyebrows could depict many emotions.

'Me? Gambling? No, of course not,' she denied, feigning insult, but had to chew on her lip to suppress the grin that threatened. 'I got that money selling my body to the butcher man in town. We had a right cracking time of it behind the store until his wife found us.'

'What?' Annie's horrified look had Indy chuckling, killing all pretence that she'd been serious. 'Oh, Indy, the devil will take your tongue for speaking so.'

Indy laughed as she pulled her boot back on. 'I love how you see gambling as such a sin when there are so many other more colourful sins going on under your nose here every day.'

'I choose to turn the other cheek to certain goings-on,' Annie said. 'But you are in my care here, young missy, and I will not have you breaking the law. Sean! The stew is on the table!'

Sean stepped out from the flap in the tent and grinned at Indy. He was a tall and gangly lad. Although, hardly a lad anymore at nineteen years of age. His bright red hair, fairer than his mothers, was long over his ears and sat on the collar of his working man's blue shirt.

'What table, Ma?' he asked, his Irish brogue as strong as his mother's. 'We've eaten dinner in our laps since the day we got here.'

'Don't sass me, my boy. You're not too old for me to take a strap to your backside.'

Sean sat beside Indy and they playfully dug elbows into each other like proper siblings. Indy loved living with Sean and Annie, but she was reminded again how much she missed her own mother.

'It seems the new Governor Hotham and his wife are a big hit,' Annie said. 'Came wandering through the camps this afternoon, they did. Melly Jones's husband told her the new Governor actually listened to the miners' concerns and promised to see what he could do.'

'Really?' Indy tried to hide the cynicism in her voice.

'And Mrs Hotham had all the men removing their hats and helping her through the fields,' Annie went on as she served the stew into bowls. 'Her expensive dress was all muddied at the hem but she seemed so unconcerned about it, laughing even when her boot got caught in a mud-puddle.'

Indy ate heartily, dipping a hunk of bread into the thick gravy and taking big bites as she listened to Annie talk on about the new Governor and his wife.

'Do you think they'll drop the licence fees?' Sean asked Indy.

'I doubt it,' she said with a shrug. 'Why would they? They're making a fortune off us.'

'But maybe this Hotham fellow will make some changes,' Sean said with all the naivety of youth on his side.

Indy smiled. He was such a positive boy, always seeing the good in people and situations. She only wished she were more hopeful that things could change for the better.

Chapter 3

Having escorted the Governor and his wife safely back to Melbourne when the time came, Will found himself making the trip to and from the city frequently over the next month. The journey was always hazardous. Thieves would often try to attack the convoys of supplies coming from town or gold being sent to Melbourne. More than once, he'd had to enter battle with highwaymen on the road. Most were poorly armed, and even less capable of fighting, but occasionally men with guns would try their luck. He had heard they sometimes got away with goods or money. But not on his watch.

By luck or good management, he sustained no injuries in any scuffles he'd been involved with. It could not be said for several of his comrades. One soldier took a bullet to the leg and was left in Melbourne to recover while Will and Timmons made their way back to Ballarat with the supplies for the government camp.

A terrible late winter storm pelted as they traversed the ravine, and the trip to reach Ballarat took them hours longer than it should have, as the road became waterlogged and muddy.

'Still loving the weather in this land, Timmons?' Will yelled over the thunder and teeming rain, as they walked their horses back into camp in the early evening.

Timmons glared across at Will, a waterfall of rain running down his shako and onto his face. 'I'll thank you not to toss my own words back at me. This place is the soggy armpit of hell.'

'I don't believe hell to be soggy,' Will returned with a laugh. 'I fear you might enjoy the weather there wholly better.'

'At least it would be warm,' Timmons responded through chattering teeth.

They handed off the dray full of supplies to other soldiers to unload into the storage tent and were then dismissed of duty for the rest of the evening.

'I need a brandy,' Timmons insisted sulkily.

'But how sad, there is no liquor in camp,' Will teased as they stood by a fire to dry off. The rain had finally slowed to a sort of misty spittle.

'I'll bet there is in the Commissioner's tent.'

'Come, Timmons.' Will slapped his friend heartily on the back, forcing water to spray out of Timmons's sodden jacket. 'I shall shout you a brandy at the Eureka Hotel.'

He brightened instantly. 'I say, you make my day.'

The men changed out of their sodden uniforms and into dry ones before mounting their horses and heading into town. Braking in front of the hotel, they hitched their horses and headed inside.

Stepping into the front bar, Will noticed the mood had most definitely changed since the last time they had set foot in the Eureka Hotel. He was all too aware of their red coats. When they had visited a few weeks before, there had been many other soldiers in the bar. This time all of the men wore the miner's uniform of the blue or checked flannel shirt and hard-wearing trousers of corduroy or moleskin. Even without the army uniform, Will and Timmons would have stood out for their shocking lack of facial hair.

Will scanned the room. He had been too tired the last time they'd been here to take much notice of the décor. The green wallpaper shot with gold and the bright red velvet cushions in the booths gave the room a regal look that felt in complete contrast to its less than royal patronage. The sconces were painted gold and an elegant chandelier hung overhead, its glowing candlelight softening what was essentially a working man's pub. The long wooden bar was masterfully carved and polished to such a high sheen, Will found himself staring at it between the legs of the men who leaned against it. He had only ever seen the like of it in the more fashionable hotels of London. It seemed very much at odds here in the mud and dirt of the Ballarat goldfields. Through a nearby door, an elegant dining room hosted ladies and gentlemen at long tables set with gleaming silver cutlery and tall brass candlesticks. The Bentleys were clearly doing very well for themselves.

Following Timmons up to the bar, they were greeted with more scowls and turned backs. One man even spat on the floor near Will's boot.

There were many hotels licensed to sell liquor around the town. In fact, Will had read a military report to Governor Hotham stating there were more hotels per person in this small settlement of Ballarat than anywhere else in the world. Commissioner Rede had concerns about the effect of alcohol on an already discontented population.

In hindsight, Will thought they perhaps should have chosen a pub that was a little more hospitable to soldiers. But they were here now, it had been a long day, and he was thirsty. The barman didn't seem to care who he served as long as they had the shillings to show for it.

Will lifted his beaker to Timmons. 'What shall we drink to?'

'Mother England?'

Will rolled his eyes and surveyed the room full of miners who were still sending them looks of abject disdain. Then he raised his glass and his voice with it. 'Good luck to you, gentlemen.

May you find the wealth and prosperity you seek.'

A cheer went up from some of the men and they drank, accepting of Will's toast. Others continued to scowl and grumble and there were even a few insults tossed their way.

Like the rain outside, it was all water off Will's back. He'd grown up in the boys' home where antagonism was the national sport. There he'd developed a thick skin and an even thicker head thanks to numerous beatings—and not only by the other boys.

But his keen eyes continued to scan the room. It had become habit for him from a young age to study any place he walked into. To know where the exits were, to understand where the threats may lie. A good portion of these men would hate him simply because he was a soldier in Her Majesty's army.

He hadn't been in Ballarat long enough to understand the full extent of the reason for the dislike of all government officials by miners. Only that they were unhappy about the mining licence fees. But he did know that wherever disgruntlement and alcohol shared space, no doubt there would be some form of disturbance.

Catching sight of a face amongst the crowd, he thought it familiar. But when he looked for it again it seemed to have disappeared.

'You aren't wanted in here,' a voice grunted from behind him.

Will sighed, but didn't turn around to face his challenger.

'Ten minutes,' he said to Timmons. 'I believe that to be a new record.'

'Indeed, it usually takes at least twenty minutes for someone to get up enough front to take on the uniform.'

'Now, don't you go starting anything, McCracken.'

Will glanced at the barman who had moved in to try and settle things before they got going.

'You start another fight in here and I'll ban you for life, you hear me?' the barman threatened, before turning to them. 'That goes for you two as well.'

'I have no desire to begin a brawl in your fine tavern, sir,' Will assured him and turned to face McCracken. However, he found himself having to tilt his head back to see into the eyes of the giant who stood before him. 'We shall finish our drink and be gone in one moment.'

'You'll go now,' McCracken said and cracked his knuckles, making Will wonder if McCracken was indeed his real name, or just a moniker given thanks to his exceptionally loud joints. He was about to try to placate the fiery McCracken, when to the left of the big man's shoulder, he once again saw the face he recognised.

It was the girl. The tough young girl from the dice game out the back of the pub all those weeks ago. Her hair was piled under the hat again, but he could not mistake those large blue eyes looking out from under the brim of her hat and directly at him. Yes, he was sure it was her. Miss Indigo Wallace.

Distracted, he made a move to cross the room and approach her, although he had no idea what he was going to say. An apology perhaps for the first time they met? Or maybe he'd ask why a young woman should be in a pub full of men. A bar was no place for a girl. As though his thoughts of danger foretold the future, his forward movement was misunderstood as one of attack and he caught McCracken's defensive elbow in his cheekbone.

Timmons moved in to avenge him, despite his yells not to, and then it was on. Men jumped them from all sides, punches were thrown, kicks were doled out and Will found himself face down and crawling along the filthy, stinking, wooden floor of the pub. A forest of fast moving legs were laid out before him, their owners fighting above him. Receiving a few kicks to his ribs, he somehow made it to the wall where he was able to stand upright again, only to come face to face with the girl.

'Miss Wallace,' he said with a cheeriness that belied the situation. 'I thought that was you. How do you do?'

'I do quite well, sir,' Indy said, dodging a pannikin that was thrown her way. It bounced off the wall and back into the crowd. 'And how do you do?'

'It seems my friend and I are rather unpopular in this tavern,' he answered with a sheepish grin. 'You should not be in here, Miss Wallace.'

'Neither should you,' she said. Grabbing his arm, she pulled him out of the way just as a chair smashed against the wall where he'd been standing, showering them both with splinters of wood.

Will dusted off his coat. 'Thank you. Now leave.'

'Absolutely,' she said without question. 'After you.'

'No, I must get back in there and help my friend.'

'Then I'll help you.'

'Like hell you will,' he argued, and taking her hand, he pulled her towards the bar where he put her behind the relative safety of the long wooden bench top.

'Stay here.'

'Like hell I will,' she threw his own words back at him.

Will just scowled at her and rushed off into the fray to assist Timmons. Finding his friend being held by two men while another laid into him, Will managed to drag them all off his comrade, landing a few punches before together they fought their way through the throng of humanity, who seemed as intent on fighting each other as they did at fighting them.

'Let's get out of here,' Timmons suggested, but Will surprised him by heading back into the thrashing mass of bodies and up to the bar. 'Where are you going? I think our drinking here is done, Will.'

'I have to get the girl!' he called back over the noise.

'What girl?' Timmons yelled.

Standing before the bar, Will couldn't see Miss Wallace anymore. He was grabbed from behind, and struggled to fight the unseen attacker before the hold was suddenly removed. Turning, he found McCracken sprawled unconscious at his feet and Miss Wallace standing on the bar with a broken bottle in her hand.

He smiled up at her, impressed. 'Again, I thank you.'

'Again, you're welcome,' she replied, grinning as though she were having the time of her life. 'And just whose neck do I continue to save, sir?'

'I'm sorry. How remiss of me. Lieutenant Will Marsh at your service, Miss Wallace.' He gave a quick formal bow.

'I think it is I who is at your service. That's twice I've saved your neck now.' She held up a full bottle of brandy she'd collected from behind the bar. 'Want to buy me a drink, Willy?'

'Perhaps at a more opportune time.' He lifted her off the bar by her legs and threw her over his shoulder, before rushing through to a rear room of the hotel, a kitchen it seemed.

She slapped furiously at his back, struggling to be released. 'Put me down!'

Dammit, there was no exit. They were trapped. Looking rapidly about the kitchen he hit upon an idea. 'I'm sorry, Miss Wallace, but you need to go.'

And with that, he tossed her into the wooden garbage chute and watched her slide down and out into the yard.

Collecting her dislodged hat from the floor, he didn't stand around to hear the rest of the quite inventive string of profanity that followed her departure. But he heard enough to decide that the lady had spent too much time with rough gold miners. Timmons joined him a moment later and the two of them managed to find their way out a side door of the hotel before anyone else could catch up with them.

To Timmons's surprise, Will began to run around to the back of the hotel.

'Will! The horses are at the front. We don't have time for you to pick up a girl!'

Regardless of Timmons's warnings, Will skirted the corner and stopped short as he saw a furious Miss Wallace standing at the bottom of the garbage chute in what seemed to also be the pigpen. She was covered in vegetable scrapings and was wiping the mud from her face when she spotted him.

'You!'

The fury in that one word had him hesitating to assist her. Instead, he stood back and watched her scramble first over the pigs, squealing now in their disapproval at being disturbed, before she climbed easily over the low wooden fence.

'Now, Miss Wallace,' he warned as she stormed towards him, dirty blonde curls flying about her furious face.

Her fists were clenched, her sapphire eyes blazing. 'How dare you?'

He took a wary step back as she neared. 'Stop. Do not do something that will no doubt hurt you more than it will me.'

She halted in front of him and took a deep breath, exhaling long and slow.

'That was uncalled for,' she said in a calm voice, belying her obvious rage.

'I'm afraid I have to disagree. That establishment, with or without the brawl, was no place for a lady.'

She opened her mouth to speak but he put up a hand to cut her off. 'Despite what your admirers in the local constabulary say, you are still a lady.'

'I can take care of myself,' she insisted, a mischievous glint coming into her eye. 'Do you want me to show you?'

'I have no desire to see how many ways you can hurt a man, Miss Wallace,' he told her and then frowned as he took in her appearance. 'I'm sorry, I cannot have a serious conversation with you with that cabbage leaf hanging from your hair.'

Furiously, she pulled at her hair, trying to find the leaf and failing dismally.

He shook his head impatiently. 'Please. Allow me.'

She lowered her hands and stood still. He went to take a step forward before he remembered his last run in with her. His shin had sported a bruise for a week.

'Do not kick me,' he warned. 'I was only trying to help you.'

With great care he removed the cabbage leaf from her hair and then smoothed the flyaway strands down. His fingers brushed together over a golden lock. It was so soft. A softness so at odds with her current temperament, that he found himself noticing again how pretty she was, even covered in mud and vegetable scraps.

Her high cheekbones were not pale and translucent—unlike that which so many English ladies took pains to retain—but showed a healthy tan thanks to the Australian sun. Deep blue eyes were rimmed with long dark lashes and were presently too bright, he realised. The anger was still there, but he found it added something. There was a fire in those eyes, a spark that sizzled as she stared unabashedly at him. And her lips—an Irish rose was never so pink. Remembering himself, he dropped his hand and cleared his throat.

Shouts permeated from inside the bar again, and a moment later Timmons rounded the hotel mounted on his horse with Will's stallion trailing behind him.

'Come on, Will. Let's go!'

He ascertained Miss Wallace was quite healthy, if her fury was anything to go by. She didn't require a chaperone.

'Good evening, Miss Wallace,' he said, bowing lightly before taking a running jump and mounting his horse in one quick movement. Giving it a sturdy kick, he and Timmons fled along the road back to the government camp, passing the police troopers who'd no doubt been summoned to break up the fracas at the Eureka Hotel.

'How was the girl?' Timmons asked as they raced along the dirt road.

'Angry,' Will said, but grinned broadly as he recalled how she'd looked covered in food scraps.

'Well, I guess that's the last time we'll be able to drink there.'

'There's always the Clarendon,' Will tossed back and they laughed all the way back to camp.

Chapter 4

The yawn was almost audible before Indy stifled it with her hand as the minister droned on.

She didn't attend Mass often. Only on the odd occasion when she felt the need to placate Annie. The woman could guilt an alcoholic into sobriety. Here, in the seventh circle of hell that was the Victorian goldfields, she wasn't completely convinced that God existed. With so much death, particularly children, she could scarcely believe a loving God could stand by and watch his flock suffer.

As Father Smythe completed his hellfire and brimstone sermon, Indy surmised there were more than a few passing similarities between the Victorian goldfields and Sodom and Gomorrah. It was no wonder God was less than eager to bestow his blessings here.

But even the fear of being struck down in God's house couldn't stop the giggle that popped out each time the priest used the word 'strumpet' when he spoke of the loose women of Ballarat. Annie's pointy elbow temporarily curbed Indy's uncontrollable mirth, but soon Sean was chuckling right along with her. Finally, Annie sent them a glare that had Indy and Sean fighting hard to keep a firm hold on their childish snickering.

When Mass was over and the communion taken by the faithful, Annie, Indy and Sean left St Alipius Church and followed the parade of parishioners up to the main street.

And because it was Sunday, ladies were at liberty to stroll down the high street, thrilled to show off their best churchgoing dresses. The Sunday stroll had become a market for unmarried men to shop for pretty wives, and for unmarried women to dress up and flirt with, or ignore, those men as they chose.

But on this particular Sunday, the spectacle wasn't in the array of styles and fabrics on show or the fancy bonnets purchased thanks to husbands who had struck gold during the week. It wasn't in the diggers eyeing pretty girls and hoping they would drop a metaphorical handkerchief in order for the gentleman to pick up and begin a courtship.

They heard them before they saw them.

Ratta tat tat. Ratta tat tat. A drummer rapped out the cadence.

Marching down the hard-packed clay road and into town were soldiers. Many, many soldiers. Their red coats, adorned with shining brass buttons, paired with black trousers that had red side-stripes, flashed in bright contrast to the dull brown tones of the wooden buildings and nearby mines. They paraded by in their black boots, still surprisingly shiny despite the long march from Melbourne. Ballarat had seen soldiers come and go for many years. It was nothing new.

'Oh, they look so clean, these soldiers.' Indy overheard Elena Gibson say. 'Look at those boots. I'll wager I could see my face in them.'

'Perhaps they shined them up on the outskirts of town,' Indy said, rolling her eyes at the women who stepped forward to get a better view. They waved their handkerchiefs and batted eyelashes as the soldiers marched solemnly passed. Most didn't blink an eye or take any notice of the crowd, but occasionally a soldier would give a sidelong glance at the ladies who would then giggle and make a fuss and sigh.

Indy could see the distaste and disgust of the diggers who had come to town in hopes of meeting a woman. But the women were now too distracted by the spectacle of the soldiers to care about securing a dirty, poor miner husband.

'They appear much more refined than those soldiers who were here over the winter,' Elena's mother, Gloria, added. 'These gentlemen are still fit and proud. They are, as yet, untouched by liquor and the squalor of the government camp. They hardly live in luxury over there, you know.'

'They must be the replacements for those poor exhausted soldiers,' Elena said.

Indy just shook her head at Elena's cooing and sighing. 'Those poor exhausted soldiers arrested your son and brother Freddy just last week. Or had you forgotten?'

'It was a misunderstanding,' Gloria hissed back, her quiet voice unable to hide her anger at Indy's dig.

'So Freddy wasn't caught drunk and disorderly beside the Melbourne Road rolling around in the bushes with a strumpet?' Feigning shock, she covered her mouth with her hand and whispered loudly. 'What would Father Smythe say?'

'Indy,' Annie said, in hushed reprimand.

Gloria and Elena gave Indy narrowed glares, before turning and moving away in the opposite direction to continue their ogling of the incoming regiment.

'Why must you be so prickly?' Annie asked, disappointment in her voice. 'Everything that comes into your mind flies straight out of your mouth.'

'It's a gift.' She honestly didn't care what the likes of Elena and Gloria Gibson thought of her. 'Besides, at least now you know I was listening in church.'

Turning back to the street, Indy had to admit the soldiers did cut a fine picture marching through town towards the government camp.

Unbidden, Lieutenant Marsh's face came to her and, in comparison, she thought none of these new soldiers as handsome as he. She shook her head at her own thoughts. She hardly knew the man. Had met him only twice. And both times he had been pushing her about. Arrogant. That was the word for Lieutenant Will Marsh. Arrogant. Not handsome.

Indy heard her name being called and looking around for the face that matched the voice, she spotted Mr Albert Lawrence cutting a hasty path in her direction.

'Miss Wallace,' he called again, waving as though she couldn't see him, barely ten feet away.

She liked Mr Lawrence—mostly. A gentleman a good decade and half again older than she, he was educated and personable, but she always felt he was a little too impressed with himself and his station in life. He'd been a barrister in London and, despite sinking a mine with his brother in the early gold rush days, Mr Lawrence had gone back to his occupation. He had discovered that, even here on the goldfields, there was far more money to be made from the law. His clientele were gentlemen mostly, in property and business disputes. He never seemed to be available to represent the lowly diggers when they got themselves into trouble. It was a character trait that grated on Indy. But she liked Mr Lawrence—mostly.

'Miss Wallace,' he said, bowing his head and touching his hat to both ladies. 'Mrs Sheridan.'

'Mr Lawrence,' Annie responded and elbowed Indy. She would have black and blue skin after all the elbowing Annie had been giving her today.

'Hello, Mr Lawrence. How do you do?' she asked as he shook hands with Sean.

'I had hoped to find you here today.'

'Then you are of good fortune, sir,' Indy said and began walking again. He fell into step beside them as they passed the Criterion store. Annie stopped to covet the lovely lace tablecloths.

'We have no table, Mother,' Sean reminded her, but Indy could see Sean

Will cringed. 'They were more than likely waving you out of the place. We are hardly welcome here, George.'

'Whyever not?' George asked, truly surprised. 'Her Majesty's regimentals are welcome, by the fairer sex at least, wherever we go.'

'I fear this place is going to be different from our other postings.'

'Quieter I'd expect.'

'No physical battles, I grant you. More of the clash of ideals type, I would say.'

Will made room for George in the tent he shared with Timmons, but most of the new arrivals would be relegated to sleeping under the stars as accommodations were already overcrowded. When his friend had squared away his belongings, the two men stood in the sunshine and caught up on their time apart.

'Well then,' George said. 'Are you going to show me around this place they call Ballarat? I've heard of nothing else but the Victorian goldfields for the last year.'

'It's a long ride from Melbourne. Are you sure you wouldn't rather take some rest?'

'I'm a little saddle-sore, but a quick trip across town won't kill me, old boy.'

Riding with George down the main street of town, Will was surprised at how rapidly the place had grown in the six weeks since his arrival. There were more tents in the campsites, more mineshafts and piles of dirt besides. More permanent timber structures were continually being built on what was becoming the budding township of Ballarat's high street.

Since the publican's licences had been offered, beyond a dozen hotels now graced the streets around the different goldfields of Ballarat and they were all doing a roaring trade. The number of stores that sold necessities, digging tools, food, and of course the ever present—but always hidden—stashes of grog, had doubled overnight.

'I was sure I was going to be exiled to the East Indies for the rest of my life,' George complained. 'Finally, we got orders to ship out, and then half the regiment came down with cholera and we were all quarantined for a term before we could sail. My word, there's a pretty looking lass.'

Will twisted in his saddle to follow George's glance. A woman with long blonde hair and a straw bonnet whispered and giggled with two friends as they passed by. He couldn't see her face but the long, golden curls had him wondering if it were Miss Wallace. When she turned and lifted her face to them and Will saw that it was someone else, he was baffled by his disappointment.

George tipped his hat at the ladies.

'Perhaps you can ask her to the Subscription Ball,' Will teased.

'Who is the ball open to?'

'Everyone.'

'Everyone?' George looked positively stunned.

'Careful, George, your breeding is showing,' Will teased.

George just grunted. Will was well aware that George didn't like to be reminded of his upbringing any more than he wanted to be reminded of his.

The son of a wealthy gentleman, George Preston's upbringing would have been vastly different to Will's. But a falling out with his father when he was a teenager saw George determined to prove to the old man that he could make his own way in the world. Joining the military had been a surprise to George too—he had woken one morning after a drinking binge to find himself enlisted. He met Will that same day and, whilst they were an unlikely pair, they had become firm friends during their first posting in Scotland.

'There seems to be no caste system here,' Will explained as they rode slowly through town. 'It's quite astounding. The working class and the upper class toil side by side in the goldfields.'

'I confess I did not expect to see so many women here in this outpost,' George noted, dipping his head in greeting at another group of ladies as they sauntered by. Some smiled and giggled up at him, while others turned their faces away. He smiled back cheerfully to both groups.

Will laughed at his friend's ability to attract pretty women with nothing more than a wink and a grin. George was a handsome fellow by anyone's standards.

His black hair and tanned skin showed the Spanish heritage on his mother's side. Long sideburns framed the high cheekbones and strong jaw that women seemed to flock to.

'There are many married women. But just as many, if not more, unmarried. You would think it easy for men to find a wife, but somehow the ladies have all the power and many choices besides. Women have jobs, they are allowed a licence to dig for gold and many do. They do not simply have to accept being someone's wife in order to survive.'

He thought of Miss Wallace again and wondered what she did for money. He highly doubted she was married. Married ladies didn't usually frequent the front bar of a working man's pub. Then again, neither did unmarried ladies. Not ladies of good breeding in any case.

'The women get to pick a husband?' George's shocked voice snapped him out of his distracted thoughts.

'Yes, more often than not. Surprising isn't it.' It still truly amazed him the way men would fall over themselves to secure a wife. Groups of men often made the trip down to Melbourne when a ship from England was due in. They would gather on the wharf, each man with hopes of meeting a woman who would agree to be his wife, if not for love and companionship then for safety and security.

'It's a brave new world.'

'And have you been picked?' George teased.

'Ha, not as yet old friend,' Will said with a wry laugh. 'Come now, George, you know we military men have no stomach for marriage. It would take one hell of a woman to entice me away from a life of travel and adventure.'

'Cramped accommodations, foreign diseases, terrible wages.' George listed all the less than attractive joys of being tied to Her Majesty's army.

Will laughed. 'Well, I never said it was perfect.'

Marriage wasn't something Will had thought a lot about. He truly believed that men of the military had no use for a wife. What was the point of marrying a woman you may never get to see again once you were shipped off to another part of the world for years at a time?

'Come now, let's head back to the high street, shall we,' George said turning his horse around. 'Women can wait, but my stomach cannot. Is there a place we can get something to eat that will save us from having to consume the slop masquerading as food the army rations out?'

They'd almost reached Main Street again when eight of the local constabulary galloped past, heading into the Eureka goldfields.

'What's all that about?' George asked as the dust raised by the horses enveloped them.

'No idea.' Will turned his horse back to the way they had just come from. 'Shall we take a look?'

Arriving at the Eureka goldfields mere moments behind the police, they could already see the mayhem as miners ran in every direction across the fields yelling 'Joe! Joe!', as they were chased down by the mounted troopers.

'Who's Joe?' Will asked a man who stood by watching, seemingly unconcerned by the ruckus.

'Traps. Local coppers,' the man grumbled in a strong Scottish accent around the pipe in his mouth. 'It's a licence hunt. The Assistant Commissioner has upped the hunts to five times a week now, to check for diggers who don't have licences. Ye ought to know this, ye work for the bastards.'

'Right.' He'd heard about the licence checks of course, and the penalty of fine or imprisonment for not having one, but this was tantamount to a stampeding convict round-up and it didn't sit well with him.

A policeman rode in their direction at a trot. Two men with hands tied were attached to a long rope and being forced to run alongside, or be dragged if they couldn't keep up. One man stumbled and the policeman leaned over and hit him across the head with his wooden batten.

'Constable!' Will called, moving his horse into the path of the policeman. 'You may have the right to arrest these men, but you do not have the right to treat them so inhumanely.'

'I'm just following orders,' the sour-faced policeman answered.

'Whose orders?'

'My orders.'

Will turned his head to see a higher-ranking police officer ride towards them. He stopped near Will and George and studied them with suspicion, and not a little bit of contempt.

'And you are?' Will asked.

'Doing my job,' the man said. He spoke with a cultured British accent that surprised Will. Most of the local police officers he'd met were largely uneducated.

'I'm sure the Commissioner would prefer you treat these men with more care. They are not murderers after all.'

'They're scum miners who don't believe they should pay for the right to dig for gold.'

'Perhaps they are digging for gold because they have no money to pay for the licence in the first place,' Will suggested.

'I have the feeling the irony is lost on him.'

The trooper gave George's comment no more than an irritated sneer before returning his attention to Will.

'Trooper...?' Will started, waiting for the man's name.

'Donnelly,' the man responded. 'Sergeant Donnelly. Do not feel sorry for these men, Lieutenant. They have broken the law. They're dreamers and vagrants and you, sir, have no jurisdiction here. You are nothing more than a guard sent to watch over Her Majesty's gold as it is shipped to Melbourne.'

Will's ire began to rise. This man was obviously from good breeding, his accent and his countenance made that clear. But he was also an arse. And he was also right. The army and the police were quite separate in their roles in Ballarat.

'So I will kindly ask you to keep your unwanted suggestions of leniency to yourself and to not interrupt my men in the fulfilment of their duties,' the Sergeant continued. 'Good day, sir.'

And with that, he rode away after his men and their human cargo.

'What a charming gentleman.'

George's sarcasm wasn't lost on Will and he bit back his own irritation. 'Hm, charming.'

'Come now, Will, he is right,' George said, playing the voice of reason. 'This is none of our business. Let's get back. I feel the lateness of the hour and before we followed this rabble back here, I saw a few of our comrades hovering about the Bath Hotel. I could use a feed and a whiskey, couldn't you?'

Will agreed wholeheartedly. But as they were about to turn their horses away from the patchwork of mineshafts, he saw her. She stood with one hand on her hip and the other shading her eyes as she looked directly at him. Apparently realising he had spotted her, she bent back down to the little cradle that sat before her. The fields were dotted with the little wooden contraptions, not unlike a baby's cradle, used to filter the dirt in order to find the gold that hid in it. He studied her as she shovelled earth into the top. Next, she tipped water across the sieve of the cradle before using both hands on the lever to rock the cradle this way and that.

Watching her, he remembered the dirt beneath her fingernails the first time he met her as she'd played with the buttons on his tunic. Miss Indigo Wallace was a digger. He wondered idly if she were licensed. Perhaps luck had been on her side and had spared her capture by the traps today.

Then he recalled the last time he'd seen her. Covered in vegetable muck and standing in the pigsty looking like a furious angel. He felt a little guilt settle in about the manner in which he had ejected her from the bar.

'Just one moment,' he told George and urged his horse forward through the diggers who were still reeling and cleaning up from the raid.

He'd have to have been blind not to the notice the looks of fear and suspicion from the miners, but he ignored them and focused on the girl.

She stood again as he stopped his horse at a respectable—and safe—distance from her.

'Miss Wallace, we meet again.'

Her irritation was palpable. Then again, he didn't believe he had ever seen her when she wasn't aiming some measure of anger in his direction. But her mood appeared much more sombre than at their previous meetings.

'I fear I owe you an apology for the last time we met.'

She stared at him for a moment, her expression set in stone. Most women would take his sincere apology with grace. It was becoming quite evident that Indigo Wallace was not most women.

'You part of that lot?' she asked, tilting her head towards the direction the troopers had gone.

'Not at all. We were simply curious as to what they were doing.'

He smiled a little to try to break the ice. 'Are you licensed to dig, Miss Wallace?'

'Are you going to arrest me if I'm not?'

'No,' he replied, surprised at the fury emanating from her. 'I would just warn you. I would hate to see you dragged away behind a horse.'

'But you are happy to see others go the same way?'

He frowned, his irritation rising at being likened to the viciousness of the police round-up. 'I do not believe in treating any man thus. No matter the illegalities he may have committed.'

She stared at him with narrowed eyes, as though she were trying to decide whether to believe him or not. 'Then I shall offer you a word of warning, sir. I'd stay away from the Eureka Hotel if I were you. Most officers drink at the Bath or the Clarendon. It's safer for you there.'

He allowed himself a small smile at her warning. 'Thank you, my lady. I shall take that under advisement.'

He knew he should turn his horse and leave her be, but he couldn't seem to make himself leave. He wanted to talk to her a little longer.

'So you are a digger,' he said, realising he was stating the obvious. 'Have you been successful?'

'I do alright,' Indy replied, the caution evident in both her voice and her wary eyes. 'Not found enough to buy that castle in England yet, but we poor colonialists make do with what we have.'

She was most definitely suspicious of him and his motives. Then again, if he'd struck gold he wouldn't be advertising it around the goldfields. It was a good way to get robbed.

Will scanned the area and across to the distant campsite where the diggers of the Eureka lead tended to live.

'You live in that camp?' he asked. A small twinge of concern poked at him. 'Is that not dangerous for a young woman like yourself?'

'No more dangerous than being thrown through a garbage chute by a soldier of Her Majesty's service,' she shot back, a dangerous twinkle in her eye.

'Yes, well.' He squirmed in his saddle and tried to ignore the questioning glance George sent him. 'I apologise again for my method of extraction.'

'And I do not live alone in the camp.'

He was surprised at the disappointment that flooded him. She *was* married.

'You have a husband?' The question was out of his mouth before he could stop it.

He thought he saw a hint of a smile touch her lips, but before she could answer, a middle-aged woman ran up to Indy, seemingly oblivious to Will and George.

'Indy, Sean just told me they arrested young Aidan O'Farrell. Mrs O'Farrell was hoping you could go and bail him out again and—'

Indy shushed the woman quickly and tilted her head pointedly at Will and George.

'Oh.' The woman smiled to cover. 'Begging your pardon, officers.'

'This is Annie,' Indy introduced. 'I live with her in the camp.'

'Lieutenant Will Marsh.' He introduced himself. He heard George clear his throat. 'Beg my pardon.' He'd almost forgotten his friend was there. 'Ladies, may I present Lieutenant George Preston.'

'A pleasure, ladies.' George dipped his head in greeting, then gave Will a pointed look that said he wanted explanations later.

'And what brings two of Her Majesty's finest soldiers to the digging fields?' Annie asked.

'Curiosity,' Indy tossed in, giving Will a glaring smile. The beauty of it nearly took his breath away.

'Yes,' he agreed, feeling his own smile broaden as his eyes stayed on Indy. 'Curiosity.'

Like lightning, Annie's demeanour changed from polite lady to fearless protector. 'Well, you can take your curiosity elsewhere, sir,' she spat, putting a proprietary hand on Indy's arm. 'I'd say if you've that kind of curiosity you should visit Miss Margaret's establishment just outside of town. The ladies there will fix all the curiousness that ails an officer.'

Only shock and good manners had Will stifling the laugh that threatened. George wasn't as polite and had to cover his chuckle with a cough.

'I see you are well looked after, Miss Wallace. We'll bid you good afternoon, ladies.' Will dipped his head in farewell and turned his horse away, following George slowly out of the goldfields.

'Did that woman just direct us to the town brothel?' George asked, both fascinated and delighted.

'I believe she did.'

'She has concerns for her young friend's virtue.'

'She does.'

George gave Will a sideways glance. 'Does she need to be concerned?'

'Don't be ridiculous,' Will scoffed. 'The girl is a good eight years my junior. A child at best.'

'No, she's older than that,' George said, taking a look back over his shoulder. 'And she's hardly a child, Will.'

'We're not here to fraternise with the women.'

'No, of course not,' George said, grinning across at his friend, a teasing glint in his eye.

'I mean what could possibly come from courting trouble. And, believe me, Miss Indigo Wallace would be trouble.' And that was the understatement of the year. He rubbed at the sweat that had begun to collect on the back of his neck. 'We shall do our duty and leave this place just as we have left every other place we have ever ventured to.'

'You don't have to marry a girl to have a good time, Will,' George said raising his eyebrows up and down suggestively.

'I guess that depends on the type of lady you wish to be involved with.'

'Well, by your standards, a lady should not be trifled with unless you are committed to her and you do not wish to marry. So what option does that leave?'

Will scowled but said no more.

'Perhaps we ought to take a look at this Miss Margaret's place she mentioned,' George said, a wry smile touching his lips. 'To be sure it is of a good health standard only of course.'

Will gave his friend a sidelong glance before he laughed heartily.

Chapter 5

Indy stepped out of her tent and into the cool morning. No frost, she noted. Winter had done its best to hold on through September, but finally they were beginning to get a taste of spring. She hefted the empty canvas water bags onto her shoulder and began the long walk to the river that ran beside Black Hill.

Sanitation had long been a problem in the campsites around the diggings. The closer creeks and rivers were becoming more and more polluted now that the Ballarat camps were full to overflowing with humans. People hadn't wanted to venture far for their ablutions during the harshness of the winter, and so the waterways nearby were foul with human excrement and food scraps. The uneducated folk still bathed in and drank from those waterways, but Indy knew better. She would happily take the walk upstream each morning to fetch their drinking water if it meant avoiding the wealth of diseases on offer in that lower creek. Dysentery and typhus were the biggest killers in camp. Childbirth came in a close third.

As she hiked the small incline along the bottom of Black Hill, she couldn't stop her eyes from wandering across the field to the cemetery; the scattering of makeshift crosses a sad reminder of the overwhelming loss of life on the goldfields. More than half of the crosses marked the resting place of children. Giving birth in an unhygienic tent in the pouring rain was hard enough. If you could afford a doctor to preside over the birth, you may be lucky enough to survive it. Of course, that depended upon whether the man was an actual doctor with the proper training or just an opportunist who had hung out a shingle, claiming to be a doctor for the shillings the occupation could charge. Midwives were scarce and cost money too. What didn't cost on the goldfields? Most women were left to fend for themselves as they struggled to bring their offspring into the world.

Indy shuddered as she recalled a night a few months back when one of the women in the Irish camp had laboured for almost twenty hours, finally giving birth to a son. Tragically, the baby boy had died less than an hour after his arrival. He had been the woman's sixth child and all six had died either in the womb, during birth or before they had reached their second birthday. During the funeral service for the boy, she'd watched the woman stare blankly, as though in a daze, at the hole in the ground where the tiny wooden box was finally lowered. Had the poor woman finally lost her mind?

A month or so after the funeral, the same woman had been found in the river having drowned. Grieving his loss, her husband said they had just found out she was pregnant again. The devout Catholics did not speak of the fact that when the woman had been lifted from the river, her coat pockets were filled with heavy stones. But when Indy heard that little bit of gossip at the Criterion store on Main Street, she knew the woman had taken her own life.

Indy had never really been interested in becoming a wife. She much preferred to control her own destiny. But if she had had any designs on becoming a mother, this one woman's tale had scared the idea right out of her. She never wanted to feel that kind of loss. That's not to say she hadn't had her fair share of proposals of marriage. But she had declined them all. It wasn't as though the men hadn't been good solid citizens who weren't half bad to look at. She just didn't think she needed to have a man to take care of her. Soon enough, the men stopped asking. She didn't care that the gossips thought her a spinster, or that she preferred the company of women instead of men. She had her mother and her friends. They were her family. She was in charge of her own life, and that was exactly how she liked it.

Of course, she wasn't silly enough to believe that marriage caused pregnancy. There were plenty of unmarried women who had found themselves with child. The girls who chose to keep their babies, born out of wedlock, were shunned by much of society. Others gave their children away, or worse, left them on the church steps in Melbourne. Hopefully to be found and cared for by someone before they died of exposure.

Reaching the top of the rise, Indy inhaled deeply the fresh air that drifted over from the dense scrub. The plains behind her had been laid to waste years before, at the beginning of the gold rush. So many trees had been felled to make timber posts to shore up mines or be used as firewood. And now the tree fellers were going further afield to collect timber to construct the shops and hotels in the main street. The post office and the auction houses had sprung up overnight. No one was leaving Ballarat or the goldfields any time soon.

She frowned at the remaining bushland laid out before her. There'd be nothing left but barren landscape if they continued to go on this way. And that would be a tragedy. The wildflowers were blooming in some patches that caught the early sunlight as she headed for the natural spring. Water bubbled from between the rocks, cool and clear, into the river upstream from where the soldiers were garrisoned at the government camp. Setting down the canvas bags she stretched her back before scooping a hand into the cold spring and taking a mouthful of the fresh-tasting water.

Above her head, a reflection darkened the water and she spun around so quickly she nearly fell in. With a giant sigh of relief, she laid a hand over her heart to calm its suddenly rapid beat.

'Why do you always have to sneak up on a girl like that, Whitey?'

He didn't speak, just moved to kneel beside her and drank as she had from the spring. She smiled as he sat upright again and grinned broadly at her, the whites of his teeth glowing against the black of his skin.

'I saw my mother last week,' Indy told him. 'She said to tell you to come by and try her kangaroo stew again. She says it's getting better, but I don't think it is.'

Indy had been living with Annie and Sean for six months before she'd finally saved enough money to bring her mother out from the city. The hut in the bush had seemed like a good base to build on, but her mother's appalled expression as they'd stood in front of the ramshackle wooden building had concerned her. Having seen it only once herself, she admitted she must have imagined it in better repair than it actually was.

'It's so run down, Indy,' Mary had said.

She wondered if she'd made a mistake bringing her mother out so soon from her comfortable bedsit in Melbourne. The violent storm that blew in that evening confirmed it.

They spent the night inside the little hut, huddled together, trying to stay dry as the torrential rain leaked through every gaping crack in the wooden structure of what was really nothing more than a broken down shepherd's shelter.

'I'm sorry, Mother,' Indy said, lifting the blanket further over their heads as the rain pelted the tin roof and the wind howled around them, rattling loose timber. 'I should have fixed it up a little before I brought you here.'

By morning, Indy had made the decision to send her mother back to the city until she could ensure the house's structure was sound. But as they had stepped out of the hut just after sunrise, they'd been shocked to see a native man, with the whitest of white hair, standing not a hundred yards away.

Terrified at first, Indy's mother had tried to pull Indy back into the house. But the man had lifted the dead kangaroo he held in his hand as though he were offering it to them.

Indy walked cautiously towards the native man.

'Indy, don't!' her mother cried in a panic. 'He's a native. A heathen.'

Ignoring her mother's pleas, she moved closer to him and reached out, prepared to take the kangaroo. 'Thank you.'

He spoke in his native tongue but did not hand over the animal. Instead, he walked up to the fire Indy had set, carefully removed the billy of tea she'd had boiling, and lay the full kangaroo carcass on the flames. Mary retched but Indy was fascinated. She stood by and watched as the carcass cooked, and when it swelled, the man pulled the kangaroo from the fire. Setting it down on the ground, he sat beside it.

Mary gasped when he pulled out a knife. 'Indy, come away.'

But Indy had just watched as he meticulously gutted the animal. Enthralled by his skill, she asked what seemed like a hundred questions over the next hour. He spoke no English but they used hand gestures to make themselves understood. Once the kangaroo was cleared of all its entrails, he scraped the remaining fur from the body and placed the kangaroo over the coals of the now waning fire. That day they had shared rare cooked kangaroo meat with the native man they called Whitey.

After they had eaten, Whitey had taken a quick look at the little hut and, without a word, had set about replacing the rotten wood. By nightfall, the holes in the roof had been patched and when another shower of rain came through they were thrilled to see it was waterproof. Mary made soda bread with the supplies they had brought up from Melbourne and they offered for Whitey to dine with them again. Afterwards, he disappeared and they didn't see him for a few weeks as Mary and Indy set about doing their best to create a proper home. But Whitey came back every so often with meat or more materials to shore up the hut. Mary quickly lost her fear of him and over the next months she began to teach him English words. In turn, Indy learned some of his native language, which entertained them all as she struggled with the difficult phonetics. Over the months, Whitey became a good and trusted friend.

Indy bent down to the spring to fill her canvas water bags.

'I think the winter is finally over,' she chatted away to him. Whitey was never much of a conversationalist, so she just rabbited on about the weather and other menial goings-on. 'More soldiers arrived yesterday too. Did you see them?'

'Mm hm,' he murmured his agreement. 'White feller dead in Ballarat.'

'Oh yeah?' Indy asked, unsurprised. Death was hardly news. It was more a daily occurrence.

'Man they call Scobie.'

She didn't know James Scobie personally but she sure knew him by reputation. He was a Scotsman with a love of drink and a greater love of causing trouble.

'What happened?'

Whitey ran his thumb across his throat as a sign that someone had killed the man.

'Murdered? James Scobie was murdered?' The shock of it had her fumbling and she nearly dropped her water bag in the river. Righting herself, she turned to look back towards the campsite in the distance. 'Murdered how? By whom?'

He shrugged.

Knowing she wasn't going to get much more information out of Whitey, she said goodbye to her friend and rushed as quickly as she could carry her heavy water bags back to camp.

News had obviously spread through the camp like an outbreak of the measles, because people were standing in groups talking about the alleged murder of James Scobie.

'It were Bentley and his cronies. I know it were,' she overheard one man say as she made her way back to Annie and Sean. Why would a well-reputed businessman like James Bentley have cause to murder a man like Scobie? she wondered.

'Oh, Indy, I was worried when you weren't here when I woke,' Annie said, catching sight of her.

'I went to get the water,' she said, dumping the heavy canvas bags at her feet.

'Have you heard?'

She wiped the sweat from her forehead and sat down, trying to catch her breath.

'About Scobie? Yes. Whitey told me up at the spring. Was it really Bentley?'

'No one knows.' Annie shook her head.

'Well, it's not the first time someone's gotten themselves killed here,' Indy said with a shrug. 'Probably won't be the last.'

'How can you be so calm?' Annie asked, clasping and unclasping her hands.

Indy placed her own hand over her friend's to stop the fretting. 'Just wait until we hear the whole story. No doubt

Scobie was drunk and it was an accident. Or he got into a brawl and lost.'

***

The next day, rumours circulated that James Bentley and his mates were about to be arrested for the murder of James Scobie. It was the talk of the goldfields. Everywhere Indy went, people gossiped about how Bentley and several of his friends had chased Scobie down and knocked him over the head with a shovel from outside someone's tent. There was apparently a witness. A young boy had evidently seen everything. But each time Indy heard a version of the story it became more fantastic.

In front of the Criterion store, she heard Mrs Tavistock tell Wilhelmena Krick that Scobie had sexually assaulted Mrs Bentley. At the California Tent Maker, while she was purchasing a new windsail for the mine, she listened to the Italian Raffaello Carboni, a friend of Scobie's, saying Bentley had all but beheaded Scobie with the shovel.

By the time she and Sean were sitting down to dinner with Annie that night, gossip had Scobie painted as a saint and Bentley headed for the gallows for certain.

'He broke a window at the Eureka Hotel,' Sean said through a mouthful of food as he read from the newspaper.

'Who did?' Indy asked.

'Scobie.' Sean flipped the page of the paper and read on. 'They say he was drunk, broke a window trying to get into the pub after midnight, and then he called Mrs Bentley a whore.'

'Sean!' Annie reprimanded. 'You will not use that foul word in my presence, do you understand?'

Indy smiled at Sean. 'He called her a "lady-who-rubs-her-naughty-bits-up-against-men's-naughty-bits-for-money"?'

Sean chuckled.

'Not any better, Indy,' Annie warned.

'Sticks and stones, for goodness sake.' Indy rolled her eyes and broke off a hunk of soda bread to dip into her gravy. 'You don't kill a man over a bad-mouthing. If that is indeed why he was killed.'

'You do here,' Sean murmured putting the paper down to concentrate on the roasted meat before him.

The mutton joint Indy had bought that day from the store was surprisingly cheap, but the butter had cost her four shillings, the sugar a hefty nine shillings. Food was becoming more expensive as the coach companies and transport lines cashed in on the import trade to the goldfields.

After dinner, Indy left Annie and Sean to clear up while she prepared for her latest group of students. Johannes Gregorius, Father Smythe's young Armenian servant boy was the first to arrive. He was shortly followed by Joaquim the Spaniard and Jonte the German. All three men had English as a second language, but she also had a few students who spoke English well enough, but were simply illiterate. That evening there were five students in all, once Brie Flanagan and Teria O'Hara joined them. Indy was proud of the progress the two married women were making. She knew they intended to teach their own little ones to read when they were old enough. She habitually borrowed books from the lending library for her classes. Children's books mostly, which had some of the men grumbling at reading stories meant for the kiddies. But Indy insisted it was the best way for them to learn the language.

'We didn't learn to walk by running marathons,' she told them when they'd complained.

Some of her more experienced students had worked up to reading the local newspaper. Of course, with all the recent excitement over Scobie's death, reading from the paper started more discussions and arguments between the miners in her class than Indy could bear to listen to. But she didn't want to discourage their excitement at finally being able to understand the print on the pages.

Only half listening to Jonte's strong German accent as he took his turn with a paragraph from the paper, Indy slapped at the mosquito that bit her arm. Once the summer came, the horrible little biters would swarm in and help spread the diseases around camp once more.

She said goodnight to her students and watched them walk away, back to their own camps. The moon hung high in the dark sky above her and instead of going straight to bed she sat by the waning fire and listened to the night sounds of Ballarat.

Dogs barked ferociously, defending their master's mine from a claim jumper or simply at the night animals that scurried around after dark picking up scraps. In a tent nearby, a man snored loudly and somewhere in the distance a fiddle played a slow, wistful tune, its strings wafting on the light breeze. Indy sighed with rare melancholy.

Three years. Three years she'd lived in this commune of contradictions. So much wealth and so much poverty existing side by side. It had been an adventure for sure. But, like any adventure, it had provided its fair share of challenges too. And, despite so many people living so close together, it could be a lonely place. The thought made her uncomfortable. She wasn't exactly lonely. She had Annie and Sean. Although, she did miss her mother terribly, and worried about her being out there in the bush by herself. Trusted friends looked in on her from time to time but Indy promised herself, once again, that she'd go to her mother soon.

Glancing across at the Bentley's Eureka Hotel, thriving with late night business, she thought of James Scobie. Did he have a family back in Scotland who would miss him?

Rumour was rife about who had killed him. There had been murders on the diggings before. It was hardly a new phenomenon. Miners had shot other miners for their claim or their gold. Drunken men had been stabbed in brawls and the perpetrators arrested and tried. Some were even now languishing in Her Majesty's prison in Melbourne. Others had been acquitted due to lack of evidence and shoddy work by a corrupt and often inebriated police force.

But Bentley's supposed involvement meant this particular murder was different. A wealthy English businessman being accused of the murder of a troublemaking Scottish miner was a different kettle of trouble altogether.

Ballarat was already a place struggling with an imbalance of justice.

As she finally slipped into her tent to find her bed, Indy had a terrible feeling the real trouble was only just beginning.

Chapter 6

'Joe! Joe!'

The panicked shouts rang out across the goldfields. Men scattered. Running, hiding, trying to escape the troops as they descended on horseback from all directions. Those who were licensed got out of the way and held up their hard-earned parchments for the police to see.

Indy stood by, fuming as men were hit with batons and dragged away, tied behind horses. She wished she could do something, but risking a split skull was hardly going to help anyone.

'Indy!'

She turned to see Annie running towards her. 'Annie? What is it?'

Annie panted, puffed and collapsed against her weeping. 'They've got Sean! They've taken my boy.'

'But he's licensed.' Indy searched the mayhem of clashing police and miners, until she spotted Sean across the creek. He'd gone to fetch more wood to shore up their mineshaft that had begun to come loose with the last rains and was now arguing with the policeman trying to tie him to the horse.

Together, Indy and Annie ran across the shallow waters of the creek towards Sean.

'I left my licence in the tent!' Sean was yelling, the wood he'd collected now in a pile at his feet.

'Then you've no right to collect wood, nor to dig today,' the trooper told him and landed a baton to Sean's legs.

'Stop!' Indy shouted. 'Annie, go back to the tent and get his licence. Run!'

Annie turned and ran back towards the Eureka camp.

Reaching the group of diggers and the trooper who was hitting them, Indy threw herself at the policeman, grabbing the baton from his hand before he could land another blow on any of them.

'Wretched wench!' the trooper yelled. 'Give that back.'

'You bet I'll give it back!' With all her might she landed the baton against the trooper's arm. He screamed in pain. 'Not so fun when you're on the receiving end, is it?'

As she swung again, the policeman grabbed the baton in one hand and Indy in the other.

'No!' Sean demanded. 'Let her go!'

Despite his tied hands, Sean threw his weight into the trooper and they all tumbled to the ground. The sound of horses' hooves echoed around them.

'What's happening here, Constable Stone?'

Indy's fury doubled as she tried to get up off the ground and out of the trooper's grip. She knew that voice.

The trooper stood and dragged Indy up with one arm and Sean with the other.

Turning slowly, Indy faced the man she hated with every inch of her being. Sergeant Warren Donnelly.

He glared down at her from his horse, an equal amount of hate emanating from him as he recognised her too. His dark hair showed some grey around the ears, his nose was broad across his face and his skin was pink and blotchy. Premature ageing, Indy thought. Or too much alcohol. He was slim of stature, but had the beginnings of a pot belly beneath his dark blue police uniform.

'I should have known,' he said, his voice full of quiet revulsion.

Indy gathered herself. She refused to let him know she thought any more of him than she would a bug caught under her shoe. 'This man is licensed,' she said holding Sean's arm. 'You've no reason to arrest him.'

'I saw him attacking one of my officers,' Donnelly said, a sort of bored calm about him. 'Licensed or not, he struck a law man.'

'He was only defending himself.'

Donnelly leaned down from his high position on his horse and grabbed her upper arm, squeezing hard. 'I don't give a damn. The sooner we rid this place of scum like you the better.'

'If I'm scum, it's the part of me I owe to you that will be the cause of it,' she shot back in a low voice, before spitting in his face.

He let go of her arm and she tried not to flinch when he raised his baton, but her eyes closed of their own accord. So she'd get that cracked skull after all.

And then she heard another voice she recognised.

'Strike that woman, sir, and I can guarantee you'll regret it.'

She opened her eyes and there was Lieutenant Marsh on his steed. His expression was serious, quietly dangerous even. His dark eyes appeared almost black, his mouth a thin, straight line. She'd only ever met him when he'd been in good spirits—teasing her usually. She'd never seen him as the threatening and commanding warrior. A little tremor of excitement ran down her spine and she shook it off. Since when did a dominant man turn her to water?

Stupid girl, she reprimanded herself.

But then his dark eyes flickered to hers momentarily and the tremor returned. She was unnerved by the conflicting emotions whirling through her.

'Lieutenant, I've warned you about interfering in police business,' Donnelly said, slowly wiping Indy's spittle from his face with a handkerchief.

'The beating of women is not police business. It's no one's business, and if you do not let her go this instant, there

will be consequences.' Will's voice
remained calm and measured but Indy
could hear the underlying rage, could
see it in the tightening of his jaw.

'The boy is unlicensed and he and
the woman struck one of my men.'

'Who, no doubt, deserved it.'

'And the boy is not unlicensed, you
rum-soaked pig,' Indy aimed furiously
at Donnelly.

'Miss Wallace, will you kindly keep
a civil tongue in your head,' Will
warned, his eyes blazing down at her,
before he turned his attention to Sean.
'Are you licensed, boy?'

'I just said—' Indy interrupted, but
was silenced by Will's impatient scowl.

'I have his licence here, sir!' A
flustered Annie ran towards them,
waving the paper over her head and
puffing frantically as she collapsed
against Indy.

Indy consoled Annie as Will took the
parchment and read it. 'It seems you
are mistaken, Sergeant. This gentleman
is licensed.' He turned to the young
constable. 'Untie him.'

'But, sir—'

'I said,' Will interrupted in a raised voice that made even Indy jump, before he calmly added, 'untie him.'

The constable turned back to take his direction from Sergeant Donnelly. After a moment's hesitation, his nostrils flaring, Donnelly gave a sharp nod.

Sean was released, but Indy couldn't help but cast a worried glance at the diggers who were still tied to the constable's saddle. She watched helplessly as Constable Stone mounted his horse and rode away with the men scurrying alongside.

'This isn't the end of it, Lieutenant,' Donnelly said, turning his horse to go but not before giving Indy one last glare. 'I should have had you drowned at birth when I had the chance.'

Indy stuck her tongue out at Donnelly as he rode off, and when she turned back to the Lieutenant she saw the whisper of a smile on his lips before he collected himself.

'Sean, is it?' he asked.

'Yes, sir,' Sean answered cautiously as he rubbed his rope-burned and bleeding wrists.

'Carry your licence with you from now on and avoid an unnecessary beating.' He handed the licence paper back to him.

'Yes, sir, thank you, sir.' Sean nodded, putting the valuable document in his pocket.

'See to his injuries.' Will dismissed Annie and Sean, who collected the scattered wood and headed off down the road towards camp.

Indy stayed where she was. 'Thank you, Lieutenant.'

'Miss Wallace, is there any possibility you can stay out of trouble for more than five minutes?'

Indy's lips twitched into a smile. 'Doubtful, sir.'

Eventually, he smiled too. 'Are you injured?' He seemed relaxed now that Donnelly had disappeared and she wished she knew how he was able to shift so quickly from anger to calm. Her mother would love someone to teach Indy that trick. Her foul temper was rarely tamed once it was let out.

'Just a bit scratched up.' She lifted her wide pants leg to her knee and saw the shallow, but bloody, scrapes left behind from her scuffle with the constable. When she glanced back up at the Lieutenant, his eyes were fixed on her bare leg. A strange warmth washed over her at the intensity of his gaze. She let the pant leg drop and his eyes came to hers again.

He blinked and shifted awkwardly in his saddle. 'See you get those cuts properly seen to. I hear infection is rife in the camps.'

'I'll be fine,' she said, shrugging it off.

She turned and began to walk away. But after a few steps, she couldn't help herself and looked back. He was staring after her, a strange expression on his face, and she felt that little spark of excitement run through her again. Smiling timidly, she turned away again, irritated with herself for being such a ninny around a man.

***

Will had never known a woman to get herself into so many scrapes so often. It also mystified him how often he happened to be in the vicinity when she found herself in those scrapes.

As she walked away from him, she turned her head, peering coyly back over her shoulder, and something deep in his belly twisted a little. The smile she gave him was unusually shy for Miss Indigo Wallace. She was normally so strong and in control. Pig-headed, was a word he'd use to describe her. This coyness was at odds with his original summation. He found he liked the subtle softening.

A crowd had gathered to watch Will's confrontation with Donnelly and something bothered him as he watched Indy walk away, back to her claim site.

'You, sir,' Will called to a man who had stood by so close throughout the altercation he was sure to have heard the whole conversation. 'What was all that blathering about the Sergeant drowning Miss Wallace at birth?'

'Well, he's her father, ain't he,' the man answered matter-of-factly. 'Not that he'll admit that official like, but all and sundry knows.'

Will's head snapped back to Indy who had now reached her mine site once again. Sergeant Donnelly was her father? The man had treated her with so much detestation. He could scarcely believe it. 'Does she know he's her father?'

'Well, if she didn't, she do now,' the man responded with a raspy chuckle, before moving back to his own mineshaft.

Will's head reeled with this revelation and he was lost in his own thoughts until suddenly George appeared beside him. Turning to his friend, he was baffled by the ear-to-ear grin George wore. 'Where did you come from?'

'I was passing, saw the fracas and was surprised to see my old friend dive into the fray. It seems Miss Indigo Wallace has a personal protector.'

'Don't be ridiculous. It's not my fault that she's always getting herself into trouble and that somehow I am always there to witness it.'

'Coincidence?' George asked, a teasing glint in his eye. 'Or fate?'

'Fate?' Will huffed. 'If it's so, then the fates are plotting against me.'

'She's a pretty girl, Will. And despite that ability to find trouble, and shrew's temper, I'd say she's a good match for you.'

'A good match? For me? Don't be absurd.'

'Come now, Will,' George said with a laugh. 'What will it take for a woman to steal away with your heart?'

'A lot more than a pretty teenage girl with a foul temper, I can assure you.'

George barked out a laugh. 'If she's a teen, I'm a geriatric.'

Will gazed out across the goldfields again. Miss Wallace was back at work, despite the good roughing up the Sergeant—her father—had just given her. He frowned at the mess the troopers had left in their wake. What would have happened to her, had he not come along and intervened?

'I think it's time we spoke to the Commissioner about these licence hunts,' Will said changing the subject.

'Be careful, Will. You've never challenged authority before. Why now?'

'Licensed or not, the police should not be permitted to hit women or boys. This isn't a war zone, George,'

'Isn't it?' George asked, but didn't wait for an answer before turning his horse and riding off ahead of Will.

***

Indy was careful not to get caught as she snuck a peek at the Lieutenant. He had that little furrow between his eyebrows that said he was unhappy about something. When he waved old Harold Smee over, she wondered what the drunkard was telling him. The Lieutenant's head shot up, his dark eyes scanning across the fields and that furrow in his brow was now a deep trough of displeasure. What had that old bastard Smee said? Whatever it was the Lieutenant didn't like what he'd heard one bit. She wondered if he had been astute enough to ascertain from that little exchange between her and the Sergeant that the man was indeed her father. It wasn't the first time she'd had words with the man who'd apparently sired her, and she had no doubt it wouldn't be the last. But she'd promised that she would do her best to stay away from the wretched man and wasn't about to upset her mother by going back on her word.

Indy turned away from the Lieutenant at Sean's call from the bottom of their pit, determined to put both Sergeant Donnelly and the Lieutenant out of her mind, but for very different reasons. Having shored up the mine with the timber he'd collected, Sean sent up another bucketload of dirt and Indy got back to business. Upending the bucket into the sieve of the small mining cradle, she sorted the coarse stones from the soil. Once it had all been separated, she poured the water slowly across the dirt to wash it away, in the hope that some shiny little nuggets would get caught in the cleats. She looked into the bottom of the cradle where the water shimmied off, back into the creek. Nothing. Moving back to the pit she lowered the empty bucket, and dragged up the new one filled with dirt and rubble that Sean had scraped off the walls. It had been a long time since they had seen any good colour in the ground.

Unable to stop herself, her gaze moved back across the fields. But this time her eyes didn't find their mark. The Lieutenant had moved on. She gave up any pretence of working and leaned against the windlass. What was he playing at? The soldiers were as much the enemy as the traps, the Commissioner, and even Governor Hotham, depending on who you listened to. The Governor had made promises to the people when he'd visited with his wife in August. Promises he didn't seem intent on keeping, now that he was back in the safety and luxury of Government House in Melbourne.

Twice now the Lieutenant had intervened in a raid, telling the traps to go easy on the diggers. It baffled her. Okay, so he wasn't exactly stopping the raids—they were the law after all—but he also seemed to abhor the violence with which they were carried out. A soldier who disliked violence? Who'd ever heard of such a thing?

She thought back over her encounters thus far with the Lieutenant. He'd mostly ordered her around and man-handled her. Nothing to like about that, she scowled. But he had also gently teased her in his interactions, even when he was trying to save her from a bar brawl. Which, of course, she had not needed saving from. Today she had seen the first signs of the serious man behind the carefree façade. Strong and unwavering, he was not a man to be trifled with when he chose to speak out.

She chuckled to herself. Even her darling daddy had backed off at the Lieutenant's hard line. And wasn't that a first! She'd kiss the Lieutenant's feet for that alone. She frowned at the errant thought. Kissing the Lieutenant? When she'd thought him the enemy, he was just a soldier, another redcoat. Now that he had shown this other commanding, yet humanitarian, side to his character, he somehow seemed more attractive to her. His sideburns may have been a tad too long for her liking, but his face was quite pretty.

She grunted at her wayward girlish thoughts, tossing away the little rocks she still held in her hand, and got back to work as Sean sent up another bucket. Lieutenant Will Marsh was not to be trusted. He was getting beneath her skin and the barriers she'd built up against such pretty men. He was confusing her and that had to stop. She determined to put him out of her mind and get on with the job at hand.

As the end of the day drew near, Indy called Sean up out of the pit and the two of them secured their mine as best they could. Some miners had big, vicious dogs kept chained to their mines to ward off claim jumpers. Indy had seen those dogs turn on their masters more often than not and decided they'd take their chances with the claim jumpers. Big Lenny, the six-foot-five, dark-skinned American could see Indy's mine from his tent, and she knew he kept watch over their claim when they weren't around. She waved to him now as she passed by and he grinned and waved back, holding up the book he was reading for her to see.

'Got it from the lending library.'

'You'll have to tell me if it's any good,' she called back.

Lenny had been her first ever student. Although, it hadn't exactly been his choice. He'd paid her to go to the government camp to buy his licence for him. But when she'd returned with his licence in hand, she'd given him back his shillings and told him it was about time he learned to read and write for himself.

'It's either the school with all the kids, or me,' she'd given him the ultimatum. 'Take it or leave it, Lenny.'

He took it. And two years later Lenny was a proud literate man, a voracious reader of novels, and Indy's staunch ally.

On arrival at their tent in the Irish camp, Annie launched even before Indy had a chance to sit down and remove her boots.

'What a surprise that man was today,' she gushed. 'He's not at all like the other soldiers, is he? The way he saved Sean and yourself from a beating. What a gentleman.'

Indy unlaced her boots, and tipping them up, watched half the Ballarat goldfields pour out onto the ground. 'Annie, you know nothing about him.' Removing her woollen stockings, she wriggled her toes in relief as the fresh, cooling air hit them.

'I know he saved your rock-hard head,' Annie said, tapping Indy's head for emphasis. 'That Donnelly. He's pure evil.'

Indy just grunted. She was too tired to go down that particular mineshaft again.

'He's quite handsome, isn't he,' Annie said and Indy screwed her face up at her.

'Donnelly?'

'No! Of course not Donnelly,' Annie scoffed. 'The Lieutenant. And most imposing when he chooses to be.'

'Do you want an introduction?' Indy snapped. Her fatigue, and her own disconcerting thoughts about the Lieutenant, were making her irritable. 'Perhaps you can go with him to the ball next week instead of Walter O'Shanahan.'

'Mind your manners, Indigo Wallace. I'm just saying it's nice to see a soldier who's a true gentleman. He has an officer's commission so he must come from money and breeding.'

Indy moved to wash her hands and face in the basin of water Annie had already prepared for their return from the mine.

'Do you see how all those other redcoats hang about in front of the saloons cavorting drunkenly with loose women?'

'And how do you know he doesn't?' Indy wiped her hands roughly on her hips. 'He's a man, is he not? He no doubt has the same desires and drives and lecherous thoughts as other men.'

'My word, Indy, aren't you harsh on the man who saved you from a head splitting.'

'No. I'm just not about to pretend he's some sort of hero. He's a soldier. It's us, and them, remember? And you're the one who directed him to Miss Margaret's house of ill-repute when you met him the first time.'

'I'm humble enough to say when I am wrong,' Annie said clasping her hands in front of her. 'Perhaps you ought to be the same. Next time you see him you should thank him properly.'

'Next time? There won't be a next time.'

'Don't forget he stepped in when Sean would have been arrested. For that alone he'll be in my good graces until he proves himself otherwise.'

Indy didn't wish to hear anymore. It'd been a hell of a day. Licence hunts, a near head bashing. It was hot, she was tired and the turn in her own thoughts and feelings about Lieutenant Marsh were nagging at her. She didn't need Annie singing his praises as well.

***

Sean and Indy were working on their mine the next day when Annie came rushing across from the campsite.

'Did you hear?' Annie said bursting with excitement as she reached them. A calico bag was slung over her arm and Sean went straight for it. Their lunch, Indy guessed.

'They arrested Mr Bentley for the murder of James Scobie?'

'The gossips predicted true then,' Sean responded, already shoving food into his mouth.

'It won't hold,' Indy said, putting down her little rock hammer and taking the sandwich Annie handed her. She took a bite. Corned beef again.

'And what would you know about it, missy?'

'Bentley plays cards with Police Magistrate D'Ewes.' Indy gave a dismissive shrug. She took a long drink of lemonade and swallowed. 'There is no way the magistrate will convict a prominent business owner over a drunken Scottish miner.'

'But there'll be a jury no doubt,' Annie surmised. 'Even here in the bush the law is upheld for murdering a man.'

'From what I hear they only have the word of a child over Bentley and his co-conspirators,' Sean added.

Indy nodded. 'And the boy and his mother only *heard* the murderers' voices outside their tent. They didn't see anyone.'

'Well, I still believe in justice,' Annie told them. And taking the remaining food from Indy and Sean, Annie packed up her lunch bag and stormed back to camp.

'I didn't get my pudding,' Sean sulked, gazing longingly after his retreating mother.

Indy handed him hers and he brightened instantly, biting heartily into the piece of teacake. She wished she believed in justice too. But she feared there would be no justice for a murdered miner when the accused was friendly with the local authorities. She wouldn't be surprised if Bentley was also lining the pockets of those authorities to ensure the ongoing ease of obtaining his liquor licence for the Eureka Hotel.

***

Despite her scepticism, two days later Indy found herself squeezing into the hot and tiny courtroom in order to watch the case against Bentley and two of his staff. The makeshift courtroom in the grounds of the government camp only held about thirty people, but many other miners gathered outside the courtroom, all anxious to know if Bentley would indeed hang for the murder of a fellow miner.

As court was called to order, Indy saw that she had been right to be dubious. There was no jury. Only Commissioner Rede, Assistant Commissioner Johnston and Magistrate D'Ewes presided. The grumbling of the miners who had made it into the courtroom showed their dissatisfaction at the whole proceedings, but order was called and the trial began.

The trial lasted two days as the witnesses were called, and by the end of the first day Indy had seen enough. She'd guessed from the start it would amount to nothing and it hadn't taken long into the trial to realise she had been correct. Frustrated, and unable to listen to anymore so called 'cross-examining of witnesses', Indy left the courtroom to make her way back to her mine.

Along the road, she came across Father Smythe, and couldn't stop the grimace that formed on her face. It had been a few weeks since she'd last been to Mass and while she liked the young priest she always felt guilty whenever she saw him. Knowing she couldn't avoid him, she took a deep breath, put on her best smile and prepared herself for the lecture she knew would come.

'Hello, Father Smythe.'

She was surprised when he didn't acknowledge her, and taking a closer look, she noticed he appeared most anxious. Unable to watch someone in such obvious distress, she put a hand on his arm before he could pass her by.

'Father Smythe, are you alright?'

He blinked at her, as though just realising she was there.

'Oh, Miss Indy,' he said, his accent strong with the Irish county he hailed from. 'I beg your pardon. I did not see you.'

'Are you well? You seem a little upset.'

'Oh, I am well in body, Miss Indy, though I am at sixes and sevens in mind.'

'I am sorry to hear that. How is your young servant fellow?' she asked, hoping to lighten his mood. 'I didn't see him at my English class this week.'

He sighed heavily. 'This is why I fret so. He was arrested on the Gravel Pits diggings a few days ago.'

'What? Why?' Johannes Gregorius was a sweet Armenian man who had a physical disability. He was dedicated to Father Smythe and did not belong in the horrid holding cells of the government camp.

'He was running an errand for me and was picked up in a licence hunt.'

'But he is not a digger.'

'No, but the police officers did not care. They arrested him anyway,' Father Smythe told her. 'When I went to the government camp to see him, they would not let me in. They said I had to pay the five pound fine for his being unlicensed on the goldfields. Then they said he had to go to court. But his court date had to be put off in light of the current Scobie case being brought to trial. They struck him during the raid. I fear for his safety in the jail. He is not a criminal, Miss Indy.'

'No, of course he isn't. Father, I'm so sorry,' she said wishing there was something she could do.

The justice system of Ballarat was breaking down before her eyes. The licence raids were abhorrent and carried out by overzealous, and usually drunk, troopers who secured a cut of the fine paid by those arrested. Of course they were going to be enthusiastic with such a reward on offer. But assaulting and incarcerating poor invalid servant boys was stepping way over the line. Before she could utter any more words of comfort to Father Smythe, he had once again become lost in his own grief and moved on up the road towards the church.

Chapter 7

On the day of the Subscription Ball, the town was abuzz with excitement. Diggers left their mines early to wash up and women prepared their finest gowns, purchased especially for the ball if money allowed it. As the sun, half a golden orb now, tucked under the horizon in the west, hundreds of men and women, many with babes in arms or children in tow, were walking the short road to the Adelphi Theatre.

Mr Lawrence had collected Indy from her tent and she, along with Annie, Sean and Mr Walter O'Shanahan, joined the throng as they entered the large theatre tent.

The theatre's long wooden pews had been moved to transform the space into a makeshift ballroom. A large area was clear for the dancing, and the heavy pillars supporting the tent's roof were festively wound with pink bunting and colourful garlands. Lanterns were hung about the tent adding a slightly oriental feel. Smaller tents surrounded the large theatre and served as ladies' dressing rooms and safe havens where mothers could leave their children with carers, should they wish to dance. Refreshment tents were in abundance to provide libations and a quieter space to chat.

Indy glanced around at the thickening crowd. Gentlemen diggers mingled with civil servants. Even Commissioner Rede and Assistant Commissioner Johnston were in attendance with their wives all gussied up in their finest ballgowns. Several of the commissioned officers of the regiments mixed and mingled with single ladies, and Indy wondered if Lieutenant Will would make an appearance.

Up on the stage, a band warmed up their instruments readying for the first reel. It wasn't long before lively music filled the tent and drew couples onto the dance floor.

'Miss Indy would you like to dance?' Mr Lawrence asked.

She cringed before turning back to smile prettily at him. 'Perhaps later.'

She had absolutely no intention of prancing about like a horse at dressage, but she didn't wish to be rude to Mr

Lawrence so early in the piece. His disappointment was evident, but he soon became engaged in conversation with several gentlemen in his acquaintance, leaving Indy to wander the room alone. She said hello to people she knew, declined more requests to dance by eligible bachelors, and some not so eligible. She spotted Sean dancing awkwardly with a young lady she recognised as one of the new school teachers. He sent Indy a nervous and shy smile. She returned an enthusiastic two thumbs up.

As she stood in a corner watching a high-stakes card game at one of the tables in the games room, she felt someone sidle up to her. Irritated at the invasion of her personal space, she gritted her teeth.

'Listen, I'm sure there's plenty of room for the both of us without you hovering over my—' she began and turned into the broad and cheesy grin of a familiar face.

She laughed out loud and slapped his shoulder heartily. 'Jack Fairweather! What in the name of Victoria and Albert do you do here?'

'What?' he asked, holding on to the lapels of his coat and raising his nose high in the air to give off the appropriate amount of snoot. 'A man of the highway cannot attend a ball?'

'A man of the highway by any other name would spell bushranger.' Indy kept her voice low, so as not to be heard by the crowd.

'And being so, I have money to burn,' he said as they wandered back into the main tent. 'Granted most of the money was theirs once,' he said, waving a hand at the crowd. 'But let's not quibble over a small technicality such as that.'

'And where did you get that suit?' she asked, chuckling again as she looked him over. Jack was a handsome fellow, a year younger than herself. Pale brown eyes were topped with long lashes, his russet hair hung longer than current fashions dictated, but Jack Fairweather would care little for that. His inability to grow a decent beard meant his baby face gave him an edge on the highway. Who would believe such a fresh-faced young man could be a dangerous bushranger?

'I liberated this fine article of clothing from an American gentleman coming in from Melbourne for the ball.'

Indy struggled to contain her laughter as she saw that the suit pants didn't quite reach his ankles.

'So it's a little small.' He shrugged against the tightness of the jacket. 'I couldn't exactly measure the man while I was robbing him, could I?'

'No, because that would be rude.'

'Indeed,' Jack said with a nod and a wink. 'Watching all this dancing is making me thirsty. Shall we get a drink?'

She looped her arm through his and smiled. 'Let's.'

They walked arm in arm through the crowd and Jack nodded to folks, who frowned at the man they didn't know, or simply said hello out of politeness. Indy had to stifle her giggles. He had no shame.

Indy had met Jack briefly after her arrival in Ballarat. He had been a miner on the Golden Point fields and, although he had made some good finds, his impatience saw him seeking a less exhaustive and more immediate way of making money. He'd started with petty theft, stealing gold and money and items from other miners. But once he began to hear stories about the highwaymen of New South Wales, he turned his hand to bushranging and had never looked back. He robbed drays and coaches along the Melbourne Road with his two partners, and moved around the towns of Victoria's goldfields so as to elude the lawman. He popped in and out of Ballarat every few months and always dropped by to see Indy. He would never have thought to steal from her, or any of her friends or family.

Once out of the theatre, and into the cool, fresh night, Jack steered Indy towards one of the many refreshment tents. At the bar, he handed over his shillings and ordered two whiskeys.

'So, who did you come with?' Jack asked, as they moved back out of the tent. 'Never thought I'd see the day Indy Wallace would attend a dance.'

'Annie backed me into a corner,' she said, her sigh full of regret. 'I'm here with Albert Lawrence.'

Jack choked on his drink. 'That old peacock? Whatever possessed you?'

'Oh, he's not so bad as some of them,' she argued, but it didn't sound convincing, even to her.

'Not so bad?' Jack repeated. 'Well, there's glowing praise if ever I heard it.'

Indy just shrugged.

'No. You, Miss Indy, need a man who will give you trouble and lots of it.'

She snorted, 'Who? Someone like you perhaps?'

'You could do worse than the likes of me,' Jack answered, taking offence.

'Really? Worse than a thief?'

He looked offended. 'What's your point? I may not be rich, but I have enough. I'm handsome, I have all of my own teeth—almost. What more could you want?'

'I'd rather the man I end up with not end up with a bullet in his gullet,' she stated.

'There's just no pleasing some women,' Jack said with a huff and swallowed the rest of his whiskey.

'I have no desire to marry anyone, Jack,' Indy said and tossed back her own drink, feeling the delicious liquor warm her from the inside out.

They moved back inside and watched the dancing increase in energy. Alcohol was beginning to loosen bodies and lips, and all sense of propriety was quickly disappearing. A fight broke out in a corner of the tent and the three miners involved were quickly removed from the theatre by nearby and, as usual, overzealous policemen.

'But you don't want to end up like those old spinsters, do you?' Jack asked, nodding in the direction of a row of older women seated along the wall. 'You're not getting any younger, Indy.'

It was the same thing Annie had said to her. 'Christ almighty, when did everyone become so concerned with my ageing?' she asked, talking to herself more than him. 'Do I have that many wrinkles about my eyes?'

'No, indeed. You are still the prettiest miner on the goldfields.'

'Considering I am one of only a few women who still work a mine, it's a thin compliment, but I'll take it anyway. Besides, there are worse things than being alone.'

'Perhaps,' Jack conceded. He turned to face her. 'But you deserve better than that.'

The rare seriousness in his expression sent a little niggle of unease running through her. 'Jack, you can't really mean you and me? You're like a brother to me.'

'And what man doesn't like to hear *that* from the woman he's courting?' Jack stepped back, focusing again on the couples on the dance floor.

His heavy, frustrated sigh had Indy staring up at him, stunned at the turn of the conversation. She and Jack had been friends for years. Regardless of how handsome he was, she had never had designs on him as a potential partner. She really did see him as a brother figure, and had thought he felt the same about her. Apparently not. How long had he been carrying a torch for her?

'Are you courting me, Jack?'

'Evidently not very well if you don't recognise the signs,' he responded, but gave her one of his patented crooked smiles anyway. 'Oh well, mustn't dilly-dally.' The old relaxed and devilish

Jack was firmly back in place. 'There are pockets to be picked.'

He lifted her hand and kissed it. 'I bid you goodnight, Miss Indy. Tell Mr Lawrence that if he so much as touches you inappropriately, he'll be facing guns at dawn with Jack Fairweather.'

'I can look after myself, Jack.'

'Of course you can.'

'Stay out of trouble,' she called after him as he began to move away.

'Of course I won't,' he called back, and threw her a wink before the crowd swallowed him.

***

Indy was leaning against a tent pole feeling decidedly bored when Mr Lawrence approached her and asked again for a dance.

'I may as well tell you, Mr Lawrence, I have no intention of...' She stopped short of saying she had no intention of dancing, when across the dance floor she spotted Lieutenant Marsh. He was with Elena Gibson, who sashayed elegantly in a blue silk gown embroidered with gold thread. The dress sat daringly off the shoulder and was cut very low in the décolletage. It was no doubt the latest fashion out of London and her mother must have spent a fortune on it, hoping to catch Elena a good husband, no doubt.

Watching Elena dancing in the Lieutenant's arms, left Indy with a strange feeling she did not recognise, and a bitter taste in her mouth that had nothing to do with the cheap whiskey she'd been drinking.

As Mr Lawrence was about to give up and walk away, Indy grabbed him. 'On second thought, I would love to dance.'

He grinned with obvious delight, allowing her to lead him into the crowd that was in the middle of an easy polka.

Mr Lawrence was a fine enough dancer, and she allowed him to lead her about the floor for a while as she watched the Lieutenant and Elena over his shoulder. Indy could dance; she just never saw the point of it. She didn't need the exercise and wasn't looking for a husband, so what purpose did it serve? On a mission now though, she manoeuvered Mr Lawrence in the direction she wished to go and he fumbled a little on his feet.

'Keep up, Mr Lawrence,' she scolded, not taking her eyes off her destination.

'Miss Indy, I know you aren't much for dancing, but it is generally the man's position to lead.'

'Huh?' she asked, not paying him any attention. 'Oh, yes of course.'

***

Will did his best to stifle the smile that threatened. While he pretended to listen to Miss Gibson prattle on about her last visit to Melbourne as they danced, he found himself immensely entertained by Miss Wallace driving her poor partner across the floor. He wondered what she was up to. From the little he knew about Indigo Wallace, she didn't strike him as a woman who liked to dance, and rarely did anything she didn't want to without a good reason.

He turned his attentions back to his current dance partner. Elena Gibson was a pretty dark-haired woman, whose mother had all but thrust her daughter at him, urging them to dance. Trapped,

Will had obliged the young woman, and her mother, and taken Elena to the dance floor. But the moment he'd spotted Miss Wallace, his attentions to Elena had waned. Out of the corner of his eye, he made a good study of Indy Wallace. Her long flaxen hair was wound into an intricate braid with wildflowers woven through it. The dress she wore was a dull purple, it had some lace, but it was plainer than the fabrics, colours and flounces of the other women's ball gowns. It didn't matter a damn though. She was still, by far, the most beautiful girl in the room.

He felt the less than gentle bump in his side and knew instantly that it was Miss Wallace and her partner.

'Oh, I am terribly sorry,' Indy apologised as soon as he turned to acknowledge her. 'I told Mr Lawrence I am a dreadful dancer, didn't I, Mr Lawrence.'

'Quite,' Mr Lawrence agreed, bending to rub his aching toes where she'd trod, more than once, in her rush to get across the dance floor.

Will extended his hand to her rather embattled looking partner. 'Lieutenant William Marsh.'

'Albert Lawrence,' the man returned, shaking his hand.

'Miss Wallace.' Will turned his attentions to her and dipped his head cordially. 'You look lovely this evening.'

'Thank you, kind sir.'

He took her hand and bowed to kiss it, but he couldn't quite stop the smile on his lips as he noted that she still had dirt beneath her fingernails. You could dress her up but you couldn't quite clean the digger out of Indigo Wallace.

She must have seen him notice her nails, because she pulled her hand back rapidly and hid them both in the folds of her skirts. He was thrilled to see the flush in her cheeks. So there was a self-conscious young woman under all that bravado after all.

'Indigo, it's good to see you out of your manly workpants,' Elena said, her smile belying the cattiness barely hidden in the words.

'Elena,' Indy greeted her with a nod and glanced across the room to where

Gloria Gibson was keeping an eagle eye on her daughter's progress. 'I see your mother has been hard at work. I have no doubt your dance card is filled already.'

'Naturally,' Elena said haughtily. 'I do enjoy a good dance.'

'And enjoy a good man more,' Indy murmured. But Will had heard, and put his white gloved hand to his mouth to cover the chuckle that was leaping out unchecked.

'Shall we take some refreshment?' Mr Lawrence suggested.

The foursome walked out of the tent and into one of the beverage tents. Mr Lawrence ordered whiskey for himself and Will, and lemonade for Elena as she requested before turning to Indy.

'Lemonade, Miss Indy?'

Indy frowned at him like he'd gone mad. 'No. I'll have a whiskey.' Then added a belated, 'Please.'

Will looked away to hide his smile. Two minutes in Indy Wallace's company and he'd been more entertained than fifteen minutes in Elena's.

Mr Lawrence's expression showed his disapproval at Indy's choice of drink, although he did not argue. He handed over the required shillings to the barman and passed the drinks to Will and the ladies as they moved back outside for fresh air.

In front of the tent, drinking nobblers of brandy, were several of the civil servants from the government camp. If Will were honest, he didn't particularly like the two gentlemen, but he politely introduced Indy, Elena and Mr Lawrence to the men he knew only a little from occasional interactions.

'May I present Mr Errol Mathews and Mr Colin Simons.'

Mr Lawrence shook hands with both men. 'A pleasure, gentlemen. Isn't it nice to see the diggers and the peacekeepers mingling together,' he stated raising his drink in toast before he downed it.

Will saw Indy give the man a sour look.

'Only the gentlemen diggers of course,' Mr Lawrence added. 'Have to keep some degree of decorum at the ball.'

'That depends on what you consider to be the actions of a gentleman,' Indy tossed back lightly.

Will choked a little on his drink at her quiet, but very pointed, slap. It went over Mr Lawrence's head, however, and he ploughed on talking politics with Mathews and Simons. It didn't take long before Will realised Albert Lawrence was trying to ingratiate himself with the government officials.

'And what do you feel about the miners' requests for a voice in the legislature?' one of the men asked Lawrence.

'Ridiculous,' he answered, rolling his eyes heavenward. 'How could an uneducated man be expected to make decisions of government?'

'Who says all diggers are uneducated?' Indy demanded. 'You're a digger, Mr Lawrence, and you're educated.'

He looked uncomfortable then, almost embarrassed, Will noted.

'I'm a barrister, Miss Indy,' he corrected her, his back straightening.

'Only because you didn't find any gold,' she said. Will had to bite his lip to quell the smile. She really was untamable. Poor Mr Lawrence. One more word from him and all hopes he had for himself and Indigo Wallace would go up in flames.

Will couldn't help himself. He decided to add fuel to the man's already smoking hopes. 'And the licence hunts, Mr Lawrence, what do you think of those?'

'A necessary evil, I'm afraid, Lieutenant.'

At least he'd aimed for contrition, Will thought. He let his glance slide sideways to Indy and saw her big blue eyes narrow and her lips press together. Will knew that look. Poor Mr Lawrence was about to get the tongue-lashing of a lifetime.

'And do you believe the beating and trampling of an invalid servant was justified?' Indy asked.

'You mean the priest's servant man?' Mr Mathews asked.

'He was caught unlicensed on the goldfields,' Mr Simons added.

'He was unlicensed because he is not a digger, sir,' Indy explained. 'He was visiting someone on the fields at the direction of Father Smythe. And your Assistant Gold Commissioner stood by and watched with never a care for the poor fellow.'

'He would not explain himself,' Mr Simons added.

'He is Armenian and barely speaks a word of English.' Her tone was getting sharper and Will could see she was struggling to hold on to her temper.

He was surprised to find he admired her lack of timidity in the face of powerful men. A woman with strength *and* intelligence was a wonderful thing. Simpering women, who thought of nothing but the latest dress styles, did absolutely nothing for him. He enjoyed a good debate and why shouldn't a woman have an opinion of her own? But he could see Mr Lawrence didn't feel the same. The man was more interested in putting himself in good stead with the government gentlemen. He was already puffing himself up ready to respond.

Don't do it, Albert, Will warned the man silently.

'I heard it was Gregorius who attacked the trooper,' Mr Lawrence said, nodding at Simons and Mathews. The men just shared a glance, neither agreeing nor denying.

'That's a lie!' Indy threw back, her face reddening with her barely suppressed fury. Will had to give her credit though. He'd expected her to explode by now but she was keeping surprisingly calm—on the surface.

'So by your estimation, Mr Lawrence,' she began again, 'should you be wandering the goldfields, they would have the right to beat your thick head in as well.'

'Indy, please! There's no need to be crass.' Mr Lawrence's face turned a sickly puce, before it coloured up to a nice crimson as embarrassment took over.

'I'm afraid Miss Wallace is quite right, sir,' Will added, schooling his expression into a severe soldier's scowl. 'If I were to see you on the goldfields and you were unlicensed, I would have no choice but to arrest you. Now I, myself, would not take to beating a man for anything as simple as not having a gold digging licence,' he said with a pointed look at the two government men. 'But arrest you I would.'

'Well, then it's a good thing I am a barrister,' Mr Lawrence said. 'I have the money to bail myself out and the wherewithal to represent myself in court.'

Lawrence, Mathews and Simons had a great laugh, but Will could see that like a kettle ready to boil, Indy had hit her limit. He decided to intervene before poor Mr Lawrence ended up with a scratched face. He turned to ask Elena if she would excuse him, but discovered she had already gone, having obviously become bored with the conversation. He was not the least bit upset.

Looking back at Indy, her clenched jaw and heavy breathing showed him the extent of her anger towards Mr Lawrence and his new friends.

'Miss Wallace, would you care to dance?' he asked.

'No.' Without even looking at him, her answer was rapid and definitive as she prepared to launch into a full out attack on the three laughing men.

He sighed, and hoped it wouldn't be he who ended up with a scratched face.

'Please, Miss Wallace?' Not bothering to wait for her answer, he took her arm and spun her forcibly away from the group.

***

Inside, dancers were engaged in quite a vigorous reel and the tent was beginning to steam with so many bodies in locomotion. The room's aroma was getting a little ripe, and lantern and cigar smoke hung thick in the air, making it hard to see, let alone breathe. But Indy's breath was coming fast as she fought against her temper. She didn't know who she was more furious with. Those three stuck up, ignorant men belittling her views on politics as though she were nothing but a ... but a ... woman! Or the Lieutenant for interfering and insisting she dance with him.

And he still had hold of her arm.

'Stop steering me around. I'm not a bloody bullock dray.' She wrenched her arm from his grip as he stopped on the edge of the dance floor.

'Shall we attempt to join the revellers in this wild country dance?'

Full of venom, she spun towards him. 'Why did you drag me away?'

He leaned in close, his dark eyes fixed on hers. 'Take a deep breath, Miss Wallace,' he said, his voice emanating strength, 'and dance with me.'

Fighting her annoyance with him, Indy took his first suggestion and some of her anger leaked out with the exhalation. But she still continued to scowl, even as Will took her in his arms.

The music shifted and without missing a beat he led her into the slow waltz. After a few minutes of quiet dancing, Indy felt the rest of the tension slowly leaving her. She began to relax, allowing herself to enjoy Will's strong hands holding her confidently as he moved about the room, using only the slightest pressure on her back to guide her.

'Is it a requirement for soldiers to be able to dance?' she mocked, finally breaking the silence.

'Yes. It is included in all basic training. No man can become a soldier unless he masters at least the waltz, and the reel.' His eyes scanned the dance floor without emotion, his tone serious. But then he looked down at her and grinned broadly.

She couldn't help but chuckle at his attempt at humour. It felt so comfortable to move with him to the slow cadence of the orchestra's music. His gloved hand was warm on hers, and she remembered again his teasing smile as he had noticed her dirty fingernails. She flushed again. He had been kind not mention it. That made him more of a gentleman than Mr Lawrence would ever be.

Albert Lawrence. What an arse he turned out to be. Falling all over himself to snuggle up to those government officials. She wondered if he really meant what he'd said about the licence hunts and poor Gregorius. It didn't matter. She would never again be dancing with the likes of Mr Albert Lawrence.

'Is it true what you said about that poor servant being beaten?' Will asked, breaking into her thoughts.

'You doubt me, sir? You doubt the priest who told me so?'

'No.' His reply was quick. 'I simply ask to ascertain the facts.'

'The facts are that the poor lad, a servant to Father Smythe, was sent into the goldfields to deliver a message for his master. Servants do not hold licences. Everyone knows that. Johnston knows that. But he stood by and watched that officer beat Gregorius about the head.'

His calm composure slipped a little. 'Johnston saw?'

Indy nodded. 'That's what Father Smythe said. And those men back there, Mr Lawrence included, just laughed at the expense of a poor disabled boy. Gregorius will stay in the jail until the pounds can be raised to release him.'

'Miss Wallace, you are breaking my hand.'

'What? Oh, sorry.'

Releasing the grip that had tightened as her fury had resurfaced, she expelled her aggravation with a long breath. Gazing about the room, Indy could feel the Lieutenant's eyes on her. It was unnerving, the way he studied her. She'd caught him doing it before.

Looking at her as though she were a puzzle he was trying to solve.

'Mr Lawrence is not the man for you, Miss Wallace.'

His comment surprised her and she tilted her head back to meet his dark eyes. There was no mocking in his expression, or in his tone.

'No, I should say not,' she agreed in earnest, and the last of her anger dissipated at his understanding. She licked her lips as she took her turn to study him. He really was very handsome, so tall and solid. It was a pleasure to be in his arms. She had to fight a sudden urge to run her hand into his hair and pull the tie away to let his blond locks fall free.

'And who, pray tell is the man for me, Lieutenant Marsh?' she asked, hoping to shake the errant romantic thoughts from her head. But looking back up at his face, she could see he was no longer focused on her. His eyes were hard, his jaw clenched and it was his grip on her hand that had tightened. Confused, she followed his intense glare and saw what had caused his demeanour to change so rapidly.

Sergeant Warren Donnelly leaned casually against one of the huge tent poles. Drinking from a pannikin, he had such menace in his eyes she physically shivered. She forced herself to turn away from him. She was used to ignoring her estranged father. But when she looked up at Will, he could no longer meet her eyes. He too had turned away from Donnelly, but he also made sure he looked everywhere else but at her.

Dread was an icy wave flowing through her body.

He knew.

The Lieutenant had somehow discovered she was the bastard daughter of the Police Sergeant. And the fact that he wouldn't look at her told her he was disgusted by it. Disgusted by her. She didn't know why it mattered to her what he thought, but suddenly she felt ill and dizzy. The room was too hot, the cigar smoke too thick. She gritted her teeth against the rising nausea. No. She was not this weak woman. She would not faint in the arms of a man like some swooning fool.

Gathering her pride, she pushed back out of Will's arms and he finally met her gaze with a confused frown.

'Miss Wallace, are you alright?'

'I am. Thank you for the dance, Lieutenant,' she said, the strength in her voice belying the sickness she felt. Turning away from him, she ran out of the tent as quickly as she could manoeuvre through the crowds.

Once outside, she took in huge gulps of crisp night air and tugged at the tight bodice of her dress, fighting the tears that threatened to fall from her eyes. Would she never be free of the torment of Warren Donnelly? The dress was strangling her. She had to get out of it.

'Indy!'

She schooled her face, wiping her wet eyes, then turned and smiled with all the enthusiasm she could muster. Annie was rushing towards her with Walter O'Shanahan following along, holding her hand. Indy was surprised at the intimacy of his clasp on her.

'Having a good time?' she asked, struggling to keep her voice clear.

'I am having a ball,' Annie said, then laughed at her own little joke. 'A ball!'

Annie's rare exuberance was astonishing. It appeared the O'Shanahan knew how to show a lady a good time. Walter laughed along with Annie, not taking his eyes off her. The man was clearly smitten.

'Where have you been?' Annie asked, still breathless with joy. 'I have hardly seen you all night.'

'Actually, I was just on my way home.'

Annie's face fell. 'No. Not yet. It's only just gone midnight.'

'I know. I'm tired.'

'Where is Mr Lawrence?' Annie questioned, looking about. 'He should escort you back to camp.'

'No, thank you,' Indy said, keeping her thoughts about Mr Lawrence to herself for now. 'I am quite capable of getting home alone. I'll see you in the morning, Annie. Goodnight, Mr O'Shanahan.'

'Goodnight, Indy.' And taking Annie's hand again he dragged her away, thankfully before Annie could ask more questions.

Taking a deep breath, Indy walked away from the noise and the smells and the disappointments of the Subscription Ball and back to her place with the diggers in the camp.

Chapter 8

Strong hot winds were stirring up dust from the goldfields and whipping Indy's hair haphazardly about her face. She tied it back again and pulled her hat down to secure it. Her skin stung from the dry heat and she crunched down on dirt that blew into her mouth when a dust devil swept through the goldfields.

Sneezing up her own storm, she cursed the spring squalls, as more dust and flower pollen got into her nose and eyes. It was downright awful out on the fields, and she was desperate to wash away the filthy sweat that had congealed on her body and in her hair. A vision of her favourite swimming hole in the river sprung to mind as she took a long drink from her water bag and watched Sean climb out of the pit.

'I'd wager there's more soil coming down the blasted hole than I'm digging out,' he said, dropping onto his back and puffing from his exertions and the heat.

Indy tipped the water bag up so that a stream of liquid trickled slowly over his face.

'Ahhh,' he sighed, a goofy grateful smile crossing his young features. 'Keep going.'

'I'm not wasting good water on the likes of you,' she teased. 'Now get back down that hole and keep digging, you lazy git.'

'Can't,' he said sitting up and looking far too serious. 'Ma says I've got to go to the meeting on Bakery Hill to join the protest over that Gregorius feller that got his head cracked last week. He's still in custody at the government camp and Father Smythe is hoping to raise some funds for his release. Ma's expecting you there too, Indy.'

Indy screwed up her face. As much as she wanted to be there to join the protest against the disgraceful treatment of a handicapped man, the idea of a wash in the river had taken root, and she wasn't keen to let it go. She figured she could do both as Bakery Hill was on the way to the river—in a roundabout way.

Reluctantly joining Sean, she dragged her feet the short distance to Bakery Hill and stood amongst the large group made up mostly of the usual Sunday Mass Catholics. She listened to Father Smythe preach, again. Wasn't once a week enough? As the meeting went on and on, Indy lost interest as the protest turned into a sermon. Slowly and quietly, she crept backwards, away from the crowd, and using a passing bullock dray as coverage, made a run for it.

Feeling a new sense of freedom, she followed the barely discernible path through the dense bushland beside the rise of Black Hill. Twenty minutes later she was standing in front of the glorious shimmering river. Here, the mostly narrow Yarrowee River widened and deepened enough for a good bathe and a relaxing swim.

She scanned the trees around her. It was the most secluded spot she knew. Quickly stripping off her filthy working dress, she waded into the water, huffing and swearing as the freezing water bit at her ankles. Just because spring had arrived, didn't mean the rivers had warmed any. But the feeling of grit and filth that seemed to be entrenched in her skin, long outweighed her delicacy at the cold. Wading in far enough, she took a deep breath and dove headfirst into the water. Coming up for air, she exhaled audibly the breath she'd held. She wanted to scream out loud with the luxury of the icy water washing away what felt like months of grime from her body. So scream she did. She whooped and laughed and duck-dived, enjoying the shocking deliciousness of the cool liquid across her naked skin.

After swimming awhile, her aching muscles looser, she turned and floated on her back, gazing up at the perfect, cloudless blue sky. She remembered being in awe of it when she'd first arrived in Australia. At seven years of age, she had wondered how it was possible that there was so much sky. No clouds, no mist and such a bright blue, it seemed unnatural. There was none of the drabness that she remembered held England in its grasp at least eight months of the year.

Time meant nothing as she floated in the river, looking up at the tall trees that waved overhead, listening to the parrots fight over the sweet nectar of the honeysuckle. They almost sounded human. She frowned, straining her ears.

Dammit!

They were human.

Her peace was about to be shattered. She was too far from the bank to make a swim for it, so she stayed in the river, treading water quietly. Hoping that whoever the voices belonged to would bypass the river, and her, and continue on their way.

As the voices grew louder, she remembered her clothes. They would see her clothes, even if they didn't see her. She hoped and prayed that they were too busy talking to notice.

'Hey! What's this?'

'Bollocks,' she murmured.

She never had believed in the power of prayer.

***

Will rode his horse slowly through the bush. He'd needed to get out of the camp for a few hours. Since the arrival of the contingent of the Fortieth regiment, the camp was claustrophobic to say the least and he was slowly going mad. He needed air. And there was plenty of fresh air to go around, if you knew where to look for it. Many of his colleagues preferred to stay in town during their leisure time, playing cards or visiting their whores at the camps on the edges of the goldfields. He knew the non-commissioned soldiers certainly spent a lot of their free time at the many bars, drinking their meagre wages away.

'What else is there to do?' Timmons had baulked when Will had questioned him about the recent upswing in his drinking and whoring ways.

Will couldn't understand why they wouldn't want to explore this incredible landscape. To take the roads less travelled, out of the squalor of Ballarat, and into the untouched countryside. So much space for the taking. He didn't think he would ever get used to all the space. He could ride for miles and never come across another soul.

Bright yellow flowers exploded from a tree as he passed through a narrow section of the path. Wattle he'd heard them called. Not a flower you would pick and give to a woman like roses or carnations, but it was pretty and pungently fragrant, even if they did make him sneeze.

Jovial jeering and catcalls reached him before he could see who the perpetrators were. As he moved his horse into the clearing, he spotted the group of soldiers standing beside the river where it widened into a small lake. So it seemed some of his cohorts had ventured out of camp and into the bush as well. He was almost sorry to have his peace shattered. Then he noticed that one of them had his bayonet out and on the tip hung some sort of billowing fabric.

'Carter!' Will called out to the corporal he recognised.

The soldiers turned towards the voice then quickly stood to attention at the sight of an officer.

'Sir!'

'What have you there?' Will asked as he walked his horse closer.

'Ah...' Carter held up his bayonet again.

'Give me back my dress you English pond scum!'

Will shaded his eyes against the sun and peered out across the water. His shock was quickly replaced by knowing resignation and he rolled his eyes heavenward. 'Miss Wallace. Why am I not surprised?'

She was hidden up to her neck by the water but he had absolutely no doubt the girl was bathing naked. Will climbed lithely down from his horse and took the dress from Carter. 'Gentlemen, if you would be so kind as to make your way back to camp and leave Miss Wallace to retrieve her garments.'

The soldiers did as he said, but not without a chuckle and a last look out to where the girl was now swimming towards shore.

'Have fun, Lieutenant,' one brave soul called back.

Once the soldiers had gone far enough, Will walked towards the sandy little beach beside the river.

'Are you completely out of your mind or just mildly insane?' he asked her as she continued to swim closer.

'Why? Because I like to bathe?' she returned.

'Despite it being a lovely sunny day that water must be freezing. But that's not what I meant. There are many who would take advantage of a girl alone and naked. What if I had not come by? I cannot guarantee my colleagues would be so gentlemanly as I.'

'You have that disapproving line betwixt your brows again, Lieutenant Marsh,' she teased, as she reached the shallows. 'I much prefer it when you smile.'

His face remained rigid. He was angry at her ridiculous lack of self-protection and not in the mood to joke about it.

'I bet I can remove that stony look on your face,' she called out.

Too late he understood the devious grin she sent him. He could only gape as she stood up out of the water so that her entire naked body was his for the looking. Frozen with shock, he couldn't help but stare before good sense returned and he spun on the spot to put his back to her. Not only had she knocked the stony look off his face, she'd blown the top of his head off.

Although no longer facing her, he could still see her in his mind's eye. Her skin glowing in the midday sun, droplets of water glistening on small breasts before running down the curves of her body. Had he really thought her a child once? Just now she'd looked like a siren. A siren sent to taunt brave men and call them to their deaths. Oh, and he would follow blindly along behind them, without question. He already knew the vision of her perfect naked body would torment his days and nights.

Then she was next to him, taking the clothes he still held in his hand. But he dared not look back from where his eyes were firmly fixed on the odd red flowers that reminded him of the brushes used to clean bottles. He only glanced at her when she had taken the last piece of clothing from his hand and he could see in that quick peek that she was once again properly attired.

'Do you not wear undergarments?' He'd noted the lack of it in the pile of clothes.

She gave an unladylike snort. 'My mother can't get me to wear undergarments, what makes you think you can? And haven't we already had this conversation? You seem to have a healthy regard for what's under my clothes, Lieutenant.'

'I have a healthy regard for propriety, Miss Wallace,' he said. But, proper or not, there was no way he would ever get the image of her beautiful, pale-skinned, naked body out of his mind. It was fixed there for all eternity.

'What's the big deal? It's just my body, not my soul. Whether I wore thirty layers or none, a man would use me if he wished to. Men believe it is their God-given right to use women for their pleasure and walk away. Do you not see how many unwed mothers there are in the camps these days? Men are happy to take their pleasure, but not so happy to take on the consequences of a progeny, nor to make an honest woman of the girl in question.'

'That's quite a speech, Miss Wallace,' he said, unmoved.

'Come now, Lieutenant, I'm sure you've taken women to your bed. You are too handsome a fellow to be a monk. Perhaps you have even slept with women who take money in exchange for the pleasure?'

'I am not a monk, Miss Wallace,' he agreed. 'And I would be lying if I pretended not to be affected in the general way of men by the fairer sex. But I believe in control, Miss Wallace, in all things. I also believe making love should be consensual and pleasurable for both parties. A woman is not just a receptacle for a man to use and then leave after dropping shillings on the night stand.'

'Now who's making speeches,' she mocked. 'And do you believe that a man should marry a woman if he got her pregnant? Were you, for instance, to have an affair and that girl found herself with child, would you make an honest woman of her?'

'Yes,' he said with an easy shrug. 'I would marry the woman should she find herself in trouble.' She graced him with a look of utter disbelief and it irritated him. 'It takes two to tango, as they say. And, considering my own parents abandoned me as a babe, I would take care of any child I fathered and raise it in as loving a home as I could possibly give it.'

Disbelief turned to shock at his revelation. Pity usually came next, whenever he told anyone the sad tale of his birth. But Miss Wallace's expression now held nothing more than surprised interest. He wished to hell he'd never said anything, and walked to the water's edge hoping to change the subject.

***

Indy mulled over his revelation as the Lieutenant paced along the small sandy beach by the river. He'd been abandoned as a child? But he was a soldier. A commissioned soldier. It took money to buy a commission. An orphan couldn't possibly have afforded it. She wanted to ask him about it, but his turned back and shuttered expression told her that this particular conversation was over.

Though she was now dressed, the excess water on her skin soaked her clothes. The thin cotton clung and her nipples, tight from the cold, were clearly visible. Feeling unusually shy, and surprised by his recent honesty, she crossed her arms to cover herself.

'Well, it's not always a blessing to have two parents. I see you've met *my* darling daddy?'

Will turned his head and gave her a wary look. 'So you do know he's your father?'

'Of course I know,' she said, with a shrug to show him it didn't bother her. 'I've known for years. My mother does not keep secrets from me. She thought it better that she tell me than if I were to find out from someone else.'

'How is it that you have such a hatred for one another? He's your father.'

She sat down on a flat rock. The spot caught the sun and she closed her eyes, lifting her face to revel in its warmth. 'He raped my mother back in England. That is how I came to be.'

He stayed silent for so long that Indy opened one eye to peek at him. He was looking at her so oddly.

'I see,' was all he said, but the war of emotions on his face had her staring at him, captivated.

'Do not concern yourself, sir,' she said, smiling to make him feel better. 'As I said, my mother does not lie to me. She told me everything. She was a kitchen maid in a house in London, and Donnelly was a friend of the master's son. She'd catch him watching her when she served meals to the family in the dining room. Made her skin crawl like a thousand spiders, she said.' Indy spread her dress out to catch the sun's rays in hopes of drying it. The shiver she felt was not from cold, but from the memory of the story her mother had told her on her eighteenth birthday. 'Late one night, Ma was finishing in the kitchen. She took the vegetable scrapings out to the compost pile in the rear courtyard and he followed her. He dragged her into the little garden shed and assaulted her.'

Will turned and strode away from her then, and she watched perplexed at his sudden animation. She sighed. Clearly, he did not wish to hear her sad story. She was about to stand, when he turned again and walked back to her.

'What girl needs to hear that? Why did your mother find it necessary to tell you that?'

The judgement emanating from him irked Indy. 'Because he found us. He already knew I had been born in London before we left and, according to my mother, he knew I was his. I was only seven years old when we left England. We took assisted passage to this new colony of Victoria to find a better life, and lived in Melbourne happily for ten years, with my mother thinking we had left that ugly history behind. I don't think he deliberately followed my mother and me to Australia. Too many years had passed. In all honesty, I don't know why he ended up here and I couldn't care less.'

He was listening intently so she went on. 'Then, on my birthday, I came home from the market to find Warren Donnelly just leaving the boarding house where we rented a room. I didn't know who he was of course, but when I got inside Ma was there, shaking and crying. That's when she told me who he was and what he'd done.' She took a cleansing breath as the old anger flooded through her. 'Not long after that, the first gold was found. I hitched a ride out to Ballarat with a mother and her son, whom I'd met at the boarding house.'

'Annie and Sean?'

Indy nodded. 'They were headed to the goldfields, along with the rest of the city it seemed. I remember the mass exodus from Melbourne. It was like Moses leading the Jews across the Red Sea. People just up and left their jobs at the post office, the ship docks. Teachers abandoned schools, farmers gave up their properties and cattlemen and shearers left stations to travel to these rural fields to stake a claim.'

'The lure of the get-rich-quick fantasy.'

Indy heard the sarcasm in his tone and smiled. 'It wasn't a fantasy. But I didn't need to get rich. All I really wanted was to give my mother a life where she didn't have to work so hard. I wanted to get her out of Melbourne, away from Donnelly and into the country. She'd always dreamed of a country home.'

'So you, like everyone else, came looking for gold.'

She smiled, but said nothing more.

'Your mother is lucky to have you.'

She blinked, surprised at his compliment. 'Donnelly doesn't agree.'

'From what I've seen of Donnelly he is not fit for anything except being buried up to his neck in bullock waste.'

Indy chuckled, delighted. 'And I've no doubt that is exactly where he will end up.'

They sat in companionable silence a moment before Will's horse whinnied.

'I should go,' he said and made a move to his horse. But he suddenly stopped and turned to face her again. 'It may have been calm and friendly when you first came to the fields of Ballarat, but these are dangerous times, Miss Wallace. Please have a care where you bathe.'

'My name is Indy,' she told him, smiling softly. 'And I thank you for your concern, Lieutenant.'

'But you will ignore it just the same.'

She was amused at the resignation in his tone, but said no more, just grinned and stood from her rock to watch him mount his horse with no effort at all. She enjoyed watching him. A strong man with long muscular legs he sat a saddle well, she noted, his uniform trousers stretched taut across his thighs.

'Good day, Miss Wallace, Miss Indy,' he said, dipping his head in that polite way of his.

She chuckled at his fumbled farewell. It was obvious he didn't quite know what to call her. She curtsied poorly. 'Good day, Lieutenant.'

Her eyes stayed on him until he and his horse disappeared into the towering forest of eucalypts. She exhaled heavily, and her smile fell to a frown. She had just told the man her most secret history. A story she'd told no one else in such detail. What was it about him that had such a calming effect on her? Made her feel comfortable in a way that allowed him to glean truths she would normally keep hidden deep down inside? It was disconcerting and dangerous.

Then again, he'd also told her a moment of his life story too.

An orphan boy. It made him seem human and not just the tight-arsed, strict soldier she had originally thought him. It still didn't mean he could be trusted.

'Stupid girl,' she admonished herself aloud.

As she grabbed up her boots and headed back to town, she decided she needed to be on better form around him.

'Next you'll be telling him where your gold is hidden.'

***

As was often the custom after dinner, Indy joined Annie and Sean and their neighbours in a good sing-a-long. Wonderful Irish folk tunes filled the air as Walter O'Shanahan played his fiddle in accompaniment.

'You ran off so fast from the meeting this afternoon, you never heard the amazing story of that soldier friend of yours,' Sean said to Indy during a break in the music.

'I have no soldier friend,' she denied quickly, not wanting any of the other miners to hear that she'd been conversing with the military.

'That Lieutenant Marsh fellow,' Sean went on regardless. 'Father Smythe went to the camp again to see his man, Gregorius, but they wouldn't let him in. He said at the meeting today that the Lieutenant saw him at the gate and approached him. He took the priest to the jail personally to see that his servant boy was safe and well.'

'He did what?'

'Father Smythe said he was terribly generous and kind and promised to look out for Gregorius until Father Smythe could raise the second lot of pounds for his release,' Sean went on. 'The bastards are charging Smythe double the usual fine since they say Gregorius attacked that policeman.'

But Indy had stopped listening. The Lieutenant had already proved himself to be a fair man in his disapproval of the violence carried out in the licence raids. Now it seemed she could add generous and kind to the list of astonishing personality traits piling up against the Lieutenant's name.

She knew him to be a gentleman since their encounter at the river. A gentleman he may be, but her whole body warmed as she recalled the look on his face when she'd stood up from the water. Even in that split second before he'd turned his back on her, he couldn't hide the desire in his eyes upon seeing her fully naked. And once she was dressed, his eyes had kept wandering to her breasts where the cotton dress clung to her with the water still on her skin.

While his interest was clear, his upbringing had her baffled. How did a man change his fortunes so dramatically? How did he go from being a poor orphan boy, to becoming a gentleman in both station and nature? By the time Indy fell into her bed at the end of the day, she was determined to learn more about the mysterious and intriguing Lieutenant Marsh.

Chapter 9

All night long Indy listened to the man in the tent next door abusing his wife. Becoming more and more agitated, she tossed and turned in her bed. There was no privacy in the camps. You could hear all manner of things from domestic arguments and beatings, to crying babies and the screaming tantrums of children. Not to mention having to listen to the making of those babies.

Sexual activity in the camp was rampant. Entertainment was light on, but you'd think the men were competing to see how often they could get their wives to have sex with them, or to see how many babies they could make. Indy would lie there listening to the animalistic groans and grunts from the tents around her. It was agony most nights, but occasionally an ache would grow low in Indy's belly and she'd wonder what it would be like to have a man she loved hold her close. To kiss her and touch her in such intimate ways as to make her moan and, as her neighbours often did, scream out in ecstasy.

Indy had fashioned some earmuffs made of rolled up calico that she held to her ears with a strap. It helped in the winter to keep her ears warm but it also kept the constant ruckus of camp life from keeping her awake all night.

But it was the arguments between husband and wife that were the hardest to take. Occasionally, someone from another tent would shout out at them to keep it down, but no one moved to intervene or help the woman.

The next morning Indy woke to hear the couple still arguing. The man's words were slurred as he yelled at her to get his breakfast ready, to stop the kids from crying. It was obvious he had been up all night drinking.

Indy was exhausted, the lack of sleep making her irritable. When she joined Annie and Sean outside the tent they all exchanged tired, knowing glances. None of them had slept particularly well.

Taking the cup of tea from Annie, she glanced across at the tent where the man was now grabbing his wife by the arm.

'I told you to shut those bloody kids up,' he yelled. 'I've got an aching head and I don't want no lip from you and no cryin' from them bleeders.'

The woman tried to answer him in a quiet tone and he lifted his arm and slapped her so hard she went flying across a log and into the dirt.

'Right,' Indy said putting her cup down.

'Indy, don't,' Annie warned.

Ignoring Annie, Indy stormed across to the nearby tent and helped the woman to her feet.

'Get the hell away from her,' the man boomed at Indy.

'Go sleep it off, you drunken eejit,' Indy tossed back at him as she moved to help the woman to sit down. She appeared dazed and her cheek was red but that was nothing compared to the split lip and bruised jaw.

Indy felt the vice-like grip of the man as he grabbed her by the arm.

'Stay out of my family business.'

'Get your meat hooks off me,' Indy said pulling away. 'You have no right to beat your wife, just because she is your wife.'

'Law says otherwise. Now bugger off before I give you what I am about to give her,' he said, grabbing his crotch lewdly.

Indy barked out a contemptuous laugh. 'Please! You're so drunk there is no way you're getting that thing up enough to do anything to anyone.'

She turned again to the woman, so missed the backhanded slap that caught the side of her face. The pain shot up her cheek and her eye watered madly where he'd struck her. Losing her balance, she staggered and fell to her knees. Crawling back to get away from him, she saw the feet of the man as he headed towards her. She braced for the kick, but before he could land one, she saw him stumble backwards and land on his behind clutching his crotch again.

Confused, Indy raised her head to see the man's wife standing over him with a frying pan in her hand. She had evidently used it to whack him in the scrotum.

Struggling to her feet with the help of Sean, who was suddenly now beside her, Indy looked down at the man. Agony was stamped across his pale features as he huffed and panted, trying to regain his breath.

Indy smiled through the pain in her cheek and nodded at the woman. 'Do that every time he goes to hit you and you'll be just fine.'

Gingerly wiping her weeping eye, she went to finish her breakfast with Sean and Annie, feeling considerably better than when she woke up, despite her throbbing face. Annie just shook her head as Indy returned and, without taking much care, she grabbed Indy's face between her hands and surveyed the damage.

'Will you never learn to mind your own?' Despite the harsh reprimand in Annie's tone, Indy heard the pride beneath it. 'Sean, get me a washcloth.'

'We've got no water.'

'I'll go,' Indy said, and removing herself from Annie's hands, she picked up the canvas bags they used to collect water from the spring upstream.

'Don't be foolish, girl. Sean will go.'

'Nope, I'm fine,' Indy insisted. Truthfully, she needed to slink away alone and cry for a moment at the pain. 'I'll be back soon.'

***

Indy examined her face mirrored in the clear flowing waters of the spring. A mighty bruise was flaring and she winced as she pressed at the darkening purple skin. Her tiredness had made her rash. She should never have interfered. But at least the wife had learned to stand up for herself. If that continued, it was worth the shiner she'd sport for a week.

'Miss Wallace?'

Startled, she lifted her gaze from the water, relaxing again as she spotted Lieutenant Marsh on his horse appear from the trees. She really must be tired if she'd allowed him to sneak up on her.

'I heard about this place,' he said as he dismounted and began walking towards her with his own water container. 'It has the only fresh water nearby, I believe. The water in the river closer to town is unsanitary and not for human consumption. Though people still drink it I noticed. You learn quickly after your first bout of dysentery. The government camp has started getting its water transp—'

He stopped dead in his tracks and dropping the container rushed forward, leapt easily over the narrow section of the spring and had her face in his big hands in seconds, concern etched on his handsome features. 'What happened?'

She tried to turn her head away but he held firm. 'I'm fine,' she said, trying to push him back. 'Don't fuss.'

'I'm not fussing. Women fuss.'

It was hard not to smile at the insult in his voice. He had a good hold on her and she gave up the struggle and let him examine her. While he did, she took the opportunity to examine him as well. His lips were quite full for a man; his cheekbones high and striking. Her hand itched to reach out and brush at the long lock of pale hair that had fallen across his forehead. His long fingers stroking lightly against her aching cheek sent delicious shivers across her skin. She inhaled his masculine scent and nearly closed her eyes, revelling in his tender touch.

'Who did this to you?'

He was completely oblivious to how his touch was affecting her it seemed. She breathed in and out slowly, desperately trying to ignore her body's unwanted reaction.

'A man was beating his wife in camp. I talked him out of it.'

'You ... *talked* him out of it?' A look of realisation crossed his features. 'You mean you stepped in between them as he was hitting his wife?'

'Well, I wasn't going to stand there and do nothing,' Indy fired angrily. 'Just because there is no law against a man smacking his wife around, doesn't mean people should stand by and let it happen.'

The slow smile of admiration changed his face completely.

'What are you grinning at?'

'You'd try and save the world given half a chance, I'd wager.'

'Someone has to,' she tossed back, embarrassed at his obvious respect.

Will's eyes darkened as they met hers and held. The thumb of his right hand caressed the corner of her mouth and her heart jackknifed in her chest.

A bird let out a mournful cry atop a nearby gum tree. Coming to her senses, Indy stepped back forcing Will's hand to drop to his side.

'It's fine. I'm fine,' she said, fumbling around for her intelligence. 'Hurts like a horse kicked me, but I'll live.'

'Sshh.'

She frowned up him. 'Don't shush me.'

Will rolled his eyes and took her roughly by the shoulders. Her breath caught and her heart slammed against her ribs. He was going to kiss her. He was just going to grab her and pull her to him and kiss her. She should have been annoyed, or at the least concerned, but surprisingly she felt thrilled at the move. Until he spun her around and away from him.

'Look,' he whispered and pointed over her shoulder to where a kangaroo stood tall and proud and completely unperturbed by their presence.

Feeling like a fool, Indy shut her eyes and exhaled the breath she'd been holding. What an idiot she was. He'd had no intention of kissing her. The level of her regret astounded her and she did her best to shake it off.

'Stupid,' she murmured, forcing herself to step out of his grip and put some distance between them.

'Pardon?'

'He's stupid,' Indy said, pretending she was talking about the kangaroo instead of herself. 'Too trusting. It's a rarity to see them here now.'

'It's my first kangaroo.'

He had such a goofy, reverent grin on his face she couldn't help but smile too as they watched the big grey lean down to nibble some grass.

'Most of them took off when the forest began to disappear. Either that or they were killed for their meat and fur.'

'Killed? Who would kill such a majestic creature?'

'Hungry men and women.'

'People eat kangaroo meat?'

Indy shrugged. 'It's on the menu in most places in Ballarat.'

'I'm surprised I've not tried it then.'

'Who says you haven't? God knows what meat they feed you up at the government camp.'

The kangaroo took off, bounding away into the safety of the trees, frightened by something. Will pulled her protectively behind him as an aboriginal man appeared from the trees.

Indy shoved Will aside. 'Don't be silly. It's just Whitey. He went to get medicine for my eye.'

'He's a doctor?'

'He's Wathaurung tribe. They use native remedies. And they work.'

'Interesting outfit for a native.'

Whitey was dressed in trousers and a white shirt with a tan vest over the top but his feet were bare.

She chuckled. 'He struck gold early, before the rush. He says he likes the clothes, but despises wearing shoes.'

She waved Whitey closer, and with his dark eyes still cautiously fixed on Will, he stepped up to Indy. Without a word, he dipped his fingers into the shallow bowl made from the bark of a tree, and taking a handful of the rough medicine, he wiped it carefully on her eye.

'God, that stinks.' Will said, holding his hand over his nose.

'Aye, but it works,' Indy agreed, blinking against the sting and the smell.

'What's in it?'

'You don't want to know.'

'You should see a real doctor.'

'Ha! One of those quacks down there who say they are a doctor, though no one has ever seen their certifications? No thanks. I'll take my chances on Whitey's smelly medicine over leeches and bloodletting.'

'You've done this before?'

She gave him a sideways look. 'I seem to get injured a lot.'

'Meaning you get into fights a lot.'

'Maybe I'm just clumsy.'

The look on his face said he didn't believe that for a minute.

'Shouldn't you be getting back to the government camp?' She looked pointedly across at the discarded water containers.

He followed her glance. 'Yes, I suppose I should.'

But his eyes tracked to Whitey again and she read the concern in them.

'Don't worry about Whitey. He's a friend. He checks in on my mother now and again. She lives in a cottage not far from here and...' There went her mouth again. Lord, what was it about this man that had her so eager to tell him everything? She decided to change the subject. 'I heard what you did for Father Smythe.'

He stared blankly at her.

'Helping him to see his man, Gregorius, in the government jail,' she continued.

'It was nothing,' he said, his usual confidence now replaced with embarrassment.

'To Father Smythe it was everything,' she said, allowing admiration into her voice. 'And would, no doubt, have cost you dearly had you been caught.'

'I understand the fine has been paid and the boy has now been released into the good priest's care,' Will said with an easy shrug. 'So all's well that ends well, yes?'

But Indy refused to be distracted by his attempts to deflect her praise. 'It was a nice thing you did. I thought I had you all worked out, Lieutenant. Now I'm not so sure.'

He sighed heavily and met her eyes again. 'Then we are equal in our confusion, for I cannot seem to figure you out either.'

'Really? I thought I was easy.' She gave a delighted chuckle. 'Outspoken troublemaker and general pain in the arse is most people's opinion.'

He laughed too. 'True enough. But that's not all there is of you, deep down.'

An awkward silence fell between them.

'Why didn't you tell me yesterday about Father Smythe?'

'It slipped my mind,' he answered with a knowing smile. 'I was otherwise distracted by your lack of attire by the river. A priest, Miss Wallace, was the farthest thing from my mind.'

Indy stared at him for a moment, surprised by his uncommonly flirtatious speech.

The unexpected intimate moment had Indy remembering Whitey was still standing by. He had been quiet throughout the exchange, but as she crossed glances with him, she thought she saw a small mischievous smile touch his lips.

***

Will remembered the native man about the same time Indy did. He hadn't meant to be so forward with her. But he'd thought about that moment at the river so many times over the last twenty-four hours, it was etched indelibly into his brain. Shaking off the lingering memories, he steered conversation back to the safe.

'Why do you not live with her? Your mother I mean.'

'I prefer to be on the goldfields. I am a miner after all.'

'It's an unusual occupation for a woman.'

Will realised his mistake the minute he'd said it. But if he hadn't, the fire that sparked in Indy's good eye would have confirmed his blunder. Rather than get into another exhaustive argument with the enigmatic Indigo Wallace, he chose to retreat and live to fight another day.

'I apologise, Miss Wallace,' he said, raising his hands in surrender. 'You're right. I ought to be returning to the camp. They will wonder what became of me. Good day.'

He stepped over to the spring, and collecting his water containers, he filled them quickly. All the while aware of Miss Wallace and her native friend watching him.

Strapping the water containers to his horse, he mounted agilely.

'Take care of that eye,' he called out. 'And try to duck when the next fist comes at you.'

'Thanks, that's useful. I'll try to remember that,' she tossed back, rolling her eyes.

He winked, dipped his chin in farewell and turned his horse down the path to the government camp.

As he moved along the narrow trail, from his vantage point high on his horse, he was able to see over the scrub and down the hill towards the goldfields. A bugle call came and he watched yet another licence hunt cause chaos in the diggings. The traps were starting early today. This time it was the miners of the Canadian Field who were being subjected to the raid. Six hunts a week. Sometimes two in the same day. The Commissioner was really taking a hard line with the miners. The increase in raids was a tactic to try to settle and control the unrest in the mining community. Will had the feeling it was having the opposite effect.

And since the death of that Scobie fellow, the agitation of the miners had become more acute. He passed a sign posted on a notice board along the road nearest the Eureka diggings. It invited all who believed in justice to a public assembly in opposition to the recent trial, and subsequent acquittal, of Bentley, Hance and Farrell.

Trial? Even Will had to admit the whole thing had been a bit of a farce. Despite the severe lack of evidence, it was generally accepted, and plainly obvious even to him, that Mr Bentley and his friends had been responsible for the murder of James Scobie. But Magistrate D'Ewes was rumoured to be a friend, and financially in league with Bentley. The cross examination of all witnesses against Bentley had been tantamount to victimisation.

If Rede thought he was going to repress the miners with licence hunts and unfair trials, Will believed the Commissioner was going to be sorely mistaken.

***

A few days later Will found himself out riding on patrol around Ballarat with the Commissioner. Will knew Rede to be an intelligent and generally fair man, so he decided to try and talk with him about his concerns. The man was not, after all, his superior officer. The military, police and Commissioner's office all ran independently, with Hotham governing them all from the comfort and safety of Melbourne. Will had begun to believe it was this separation, and lack of regional leadership, that was causing issues in the government camp, and by extension Ballarat. Without order within their own ranks, how could control be implemented across the goldfields?

'Sir, have you seen how the licence raids are carried out?' Will broached the subject as they rode at a leisurely pace through the Golden Points campsite.

'Not firsthand,' Rede responded. 'But I believe them to be adequate.'

'The police are a little fanatical in their duties.' Will knew he had to tread carefully. He was not a whistleblower, nor did he wish to cause further friction in the already problematic relationship between Commissioner Rede and Police Inspector Evans.

'Fanatical? In what way?'

He seemed genuinely interested, so Will pressed on. 'The violence with which the arrests are carried out, sir. The men who are unlicensed are assaulted with a heavy hand before they are dragged away, tied to horses.'

'If the miners did not run from the police, they would have no cause to be assaulted, correct?'

'Yes, sir.' Will acquiesced reluctantly. 'But perhaps the aggrieved miners would not be so unreasonable should they know they were not going to receive a beating when arrested. I have also heard stories of the troopers demanding sex from the wives of miners in order to secure their release.

Or if they find the wives alone in camp, they simply force themselves upon them. The troopers are sometimes quite drunk when they carry out the raids.'

'Are these substantiated accounts?' Rede asked, seemingly surprised by Will's report. The man didn't live under a rock. Surely he had heard these accusations before.

'I have it on good authority,' Will said, unsure if he should mention the stories came from Miss Wallace. Whether he chose to say she was a miner or a woman would probably not hold much sway with the Commissioner. Regardless, he'd seen for himself how the boy Gregorius had been beaten. And he wasn't even a miner.

Rede looked thoughtful. 'I believe you. My understanding is that the police are more often drunk than not, but Inspector Evans has already stated that if he discharged or suspended all the men who were drunk on duty there would be no one left to do the job.'

'But, sir—'

'I cannot tell the police inspector how to run his company of officers,' Rede said, exhaling a frustrated breath.

'I have no power over him, mores the pity, but I shall have a word with him if you believe his methods to be too harsh.'

'Thank you, sir. Perhaps the miners will then settle down and calm can be restored once again to Ballarat.'

Rede smiled across at him. 'You are a gifted negotiator, Lieutenant Marsh. I believe you would be an asset on the battlefield.'

'I'm afraid my negotiation skills were not so often required in battle, sir.'

The two men had almost made it to the Eureka fields when a soldier on horseback raced towards them.

'Commissioner Rede, sir,' the soldier blurted, out of breath. 'There's a mob out front of the Eureka Hotel, sir. It began as a simple meeting, but some of the miners have been drinking and it's getting out of hand. There are police troops there, but they number only ten or so.'

'The Eureka Hotel?' Will was filled with dread. After having just taken the side of the diggers, and hoping that Rede would be more lenient in future altercations, he had a horrible feeling the miners in question had just undone all his good work. 'They're unhappy about the acquittal of Scobie's alleged murderers. They'll go after Bentley, sir.'

'Still believe the diggers are willing to be reasonable, Lieutenant?'

The Commissioner didn't wait for Will to respond as he took off after the mounted soldier, leaving behind a cloud of dust kicked up by his horse. Will should have known that the miners wouldn't just sit back and let the acquittal of Bentley and his friends go unanswered. He'd seen the placards all across the goldfields advertising the meeting today at the Eureka Hotel. The posted notices had read 'A meeting of the "Committee for the Prosecution of the Investigation into the Death of the late James Scobie"'. He had hoped the gathering would be a peaceful one. But it seemed they'd decided to take the matter of prosecution into their own hands.

With a swift kick to his horse's sides, he caught up with the Commissioner and they rode quickly towards the Eureka Hotel. There they found Police Inspector Evans with his men, struggling to disperse the angry mob. Will was staggered by the numbers. There had to be a few thousand people filling the street outside the hotel.

Rede turned to the mounted soldier. 'Race back to camp. Send for reinforcements.'

'Do you think a show of force is the best option here, sir?' Will put in. 'There are far more of them than there are of us.'

'Look at them,' Rede tossed back, clearly no longer open to negotiations. 'They're baying for Bentley's blood. We have to put it down before it turns violent. I will try to calm them, Lieutenant, but be prepared to do what is necessary.'

Will wished words would be enough to settle the crowd, but things at the hotel were already well and truly out of control. The huge crowd of men, women and even children hovered out the front of the Eureka. The afternoon heat was stifling, the hot wind kicking up dust and tempers as they chanted for the murderers to be brought out, as they chanted for Bentley.

Anxiously, Will watched as Rede fought his way through the crowd and stood on the veranda of the hotel trying to calm the aggravated mass.

'Please, gentlemen,' Rede began, holding his hands up in a defensive motion. 'This is not the way to get your point across. Petitions have been put forward by your representatives and will be addressed.'

'Bollocks!' someone yelled.

'Bentley's a murderer!' another man yelled.

'He and his men deserve to be hung!'

Cheers of agreement and yells for justice drowned out Rede's attempts to quell the angering mob.

Will prepared to dismount and step up to help Commissioner Rede when someone threw a bottle at the hotel. The sound of smashing glass was like the starters pistol at a horse race, a signal to the crowd, and all hope of control was lost. Some turned on the police and began pelting eggs—rotten of course, as no one on the goldfields would waste good eggs on the traps or the Commissioner—others began to pull apart the hotel. The door was off in seconds and men, maddened by the heat, the grog and their righteous anger, piled into the hotel. Soon kegs of beer were being rolled out to the cheering diggers. From upstairs, jewellery and clothes were flung from the windows to the waiting crowd below. It was a good old-fashioned mob riot.

Rede had no choice but to get out of the way when rocks began to fly. It seemed the eggs had run out. Hotel windows smashed and Will urged his horse into the crowd to try and break up the mêlée. But as he steered his horse to try to block the entry of the hotel, something hit him hard in the side of the head. Dazed, he lifted his hand to feel the warm sticky blood rushing down his forehead.

Spooked by the noise and the items being thrown down upon them from the second floor of the hotel, Will's horse bolted. He barely managed to stay seated as it ran panicked away from the raging mob. Racing down the road, the din of the destruction of Bentley's Eureka Hotel faded as the ringing in

Will's ears increased. He managed to rein in his horse and slow it to a brisk walk. His head pounded and he fought against the dizziness. Finally losing the battle, he slumped forward in the saddle, and darkness enveloped him.

***

Indy hated walking across town to the Gold Commissioner at the government camp to have her gold weighed. Usually she stashed her finds away in a secret hiding place at her mother's house. But when she was in need of actual shillings, and there wasn't a game of cards or dice available, she had no choice but to sell some gold. She did her best to ensure no one knew where she was going and what she was doing. Hence the late afternoon walk to the government camp in this fry-an-egg-on-her-head heat, when most sane folk were taking shelter inside the public houses or finding shade wherever they could.

An unholy ruckus could be heard as she reached the road. Curious townsfolk left shops and wandered in the direction of the Eureka Hotel where a huge crowd was assembled. Confused and concerned she began to follow them. But as she broke into a run towards the hotel, a horse bolted out in front of her. It reared a little before pulling up and she held out her arms to slow its forward course.

'Whoa there,' she soothed, cautiously moving closer to the man slumped over the horse's neck. Brushing at the blond hair that had fallen across the soldier's face, she gasped.

'Lieutenant?' She shook his shoulder. 'Will?'

His eyes opened momentarily and when he lifted his head, she saw the blood oozing down the side of his face.

'Sweet Mary and Joseph,' she muttered. She tore a strip of material from her dress and held it to his bleeding head, but she couldn't get it to stop. It just kept gushing. She needed help and fast.

Unsure of what to do, she surveyed the road ahead. The riot at the hotel was gaining momentum. They couldn't go that way. Striking upon an idea, she hitched herself up onto the horse behind the Lieutenant, grabbed the reins and with a good kick, they headed off, away from Ballarat.

***

'Mother!'

Slowing the horse to a stop in front of the little wooden house, Indy slid off its back and called again. 'Mother!'

'Indy?' her mother's voice came softly at first as the door opened a little.

Then it was wide open and Mary Wallace was rushing down the front steps, her lantern held high. The darkness had fallen quickly as huge, grey thunderheads rolled in causing the dry heat to turn thick and oppressive.

'Indy! What's happened? What are you doing here?'

Her mother's eyes widened as she took in the horse's unconscious passenger. 'Why do you have a soldier? Indy, what have you done?'

'Why do you always think I've done something? He's wounded.'

Indy reached up to the Lieutenant. 'Ma, I need help. He's heavy. I'll drop him.'

Mary put the lantern down and the two women struggled to pull Will from the horse without letting him fall to the ground. 'What's going on? Why did you bring a soldier here?'

'I'll explain later, Ma. He's bleeding. We have to stop the bleeding.'

Finally, they were able to get him down and together they carried him into the house to Indy's room where they laid him on the bed. Will murmured something incoherent before passing out again.

'Go see to his horse,' Mary said, fear and confusion replaced now with single-minded determination.

Indy stood staring at Will, reluctant to leave, but her mother was insistent. 'He'll be alright for the five minutes it takes to settle the animal with some water.'

Obeying, she went out to deal with the horse and when she returned Mary had removed Will's boots and tunic.

'It's beginning to rain,' Indy said, shaking droplets out of her hair. 'Going to be a rough night.'

'For him too,' Mary said pursing her lips. 'I need help with the rest of his clothes. He's a heavy weight and totally out of it now, poor lad.'

Not one to be shy, Indy helped her mother to undress him. She'd seen men naked before. You couldn't help it in the camps. There was always a drunken fool running about in his birthday suit. But seeing Will shirtless, Indy felt her heart rate increase and not from the shock of the evening. She'd stayed relatively calm in the face of his emergency but now...

His chest was muscular and pale, dusted with a few curls of fair hair. It would have been perfection if not for the scars that crisscrossed his torso. Injuries he'd no doubt sustained in the wars he'd seen prior to coming to Australia. Bullet wounds, she guessed, and gnarled, uneven slices in his skin from swords or sabres.

'This boy doesn't appear to make a very good soldier,' Mary said, noting the collections of scars just as Indy had. 'He's been wounded many times.'

'Will he be alright?' Her eyes were now fixed on the dark patch where his blond hair was matted with dried blood.

'The bleeding has stopped but I worry about the knock to his head,' Mary said, securing a bandage around it. 'He's been unconscious for how long?'

'I'm not sure. He was out when I found him.'

'I'll have to sit beside him, watch his breathing.'

'I'll do it,' Indy said staring at Will. She could feel her mother's eyes on her as she halted her medical care momentarily.

'Indigo,' Mary spoke, but Indy was transfixed and didn't look at her. 'Indy.' Her mother's voice was louder this time and Indy finally focused on her. The confusion and concern on her face was evident.

'I brought him here,' she said, her determination unwavering. 'He's my responsibility.' She sat down in the chair beside the bed where Will lay motionless. 'Thank you, Ma. You have done plenty. Go to bed. I'll see you in the morning.'

Mary hesitated, looking anxiously between Indy and the soldier. The only sound was the heavy fall of rain on the roof of the cottage. 'Very well.' She stepped to the door. 'I'll relieve you in the early morn and I'll be in to check on you throughout the night, you can be sure of that.'

Indy rolled her eyes but didn't say anything as her mother left the room.

'Alone at last,' she joked to the unconscious Will, but her worry for him ran deep. Deeper than she would have expected. She had known him only a few months, and in that time he had teased her, thrown her down a garbage chute, saved her from a skull bashing by her father, danced with her at the Subscription Ball and seen her swimming naked in the river.

Her heart warmed as she remembered his alarm when he'd found her by the natural spring, bruised after her altercation with the drunken husband. The Lieutenant was an honourable man, and she knew he would have been worried for any woman he'd found in her situation. But when he had touched her, when his fingers had brushed lightly over her cheeks ... There'd been something there. She felt it. She'd seen something in his eyes too. She shook herself out of her wayward thoughts. The very last thing she needed was to get involved with a soldier.

She sat by his bed as the hours ticked away, watching the rise and fall of his chest with his deep and even breath. It was hypnotising. And harmonised with the rain that had settled into a steady patter on the roof—it made her eyes droop.

But she stayed alert. She had to.

Chapter 10

Something was tickling her cheek.

Indy reached up a hand to scratch it, sighed, and tried to go back to sleep. The feather-light sensation returned, this time in her hair and she shifted, opening her eyes momentarily before they closed again. A second later they were wide open and she bolted upright in her chair from her position slumped over the bed.

'Ouch,' she said as her neck jarred. It ached from sleeping in the one position for too long. Sleeping. Dammit, she shouldn't have been sleeping. How long had she been asleep? She could see morning light filtering in through the small window. But her annoyance with herself was short-lived as she saw Will's eyes were open and he was smiling weakly at her.

'I'm sorry,' she said, stifling a yawn. 'I fell asleep. Are you alright? How long have you been awake? Are you in pain?'

'That's a lot of questions for so early in the morning,' he said groggily.

'You should have woken me. I was supposed to be watching you. Some nurse I make.'

'You looked too peaceful to wake,' he told her. 'Too beautiful.'

The intensity in his dark eyes and his unexpected compliment had her belly quaking, her cheeks heating.

'Well, you've had a knock to your head so I'm sure your eyesight is compromised. How is your head?' she asked leaning over to check the bandage. Blood from the wound hadn't seeped through so that was good. But it was the residual effects she was worried about.

'It throbs as though there were ten large artillery guns in there.' He groaned as she pressed at the lump there.

'Sorry. Sorry.'

Deep eyes sought hers and held and she realised she was inappropriately close to a half-naked man. She sat back quickly and he slowly pulled the fine sheet up over his chest.

'Um. My clothes?'

Suddenly mute, Indy pointed to his uniform, draped over the chair. She knew he only had his short underwear on his bottom half below the sheet. 'Mother took your tunic to soak in salt,' she said and Will looked baffled. 'It helps remove the blood.'

'Oh,' he answered and then blinked, surprised. 'Wait. Your mother? Where am I?'

He glanced about the unfamiliar room.

'You were barely conscious when I found you. I brought you to my mother's home in the bush. She took care of your injury.'

As though summoned, Mary Wallace opened the door and stepped in with a bowl of water and a sponge. 'Indigo, why don't you fix the gentleman some breakfast. Are you hungry, sir?'

'I am, thank you.'

Her mother gave her a look that brooked no argument and Indy reluctantly disappeared out the door.

Gingerly, Will pushed himself up in bed. 'I thank you for your help, Mrs Wallace, but I should be getting back to my regiment.'

'Hold your horses there, young Captain.'

'It's Lieutenant,' he corrected her. 'Lieutenant Will Marsh, madam, and I am most indebted to you, but I really must be going.'

He lifted the sheet to get out of bed, but realising just how thin and revealing his undershorts were, he pulled the sheet back across his lap.

'I beg your pardon,' he apologised. 'Perhaps I could have some privacy in order to dress?'

'Boyo, you've nothing I haven't seen before,' Mary said and urged him gently back against the wooden bedhead. 'Now you'll stay put until you at least have some food and I can see that you can hold it in your system. You've had a good whack to the head, and you need to be careful. It would injure more than you, should you suddenly drop dead.'

Warily, he met her gaze.

'My daughter is very fond of you, Lieutenant Marsh,' Mary said as she unwrapped the bandage around his head.

'As I am of her, Mrs Wallace. She is a sweet child, and I see where she gets her tenacity from.'

'A child is she?' Mary asked with raised eyebrows. 'And tenacity is just a polite word for stubborn.'

'I promise I have nothing but the utmost respect for your daughter. You have no need to worry about her where I am concerned. Miss Indy and I are different creatures from different worlds.'

Mary gave an elegant grunt that reminded him of Indy. Squeezing the excess water from the cloth, she carefully wiped the dried blood from his head. 'Is that your way of saying you're too good for her?'

'No,' he said, unperturbed by her sudden irritation. 'If anything, it's my way of saying she is too good for me.'

Will examined Mary as she tended to his wound. Fair of hair like her daughter, she had similar eyes of the same shape, but the colour was a little more sky blue than the deep blue-purple of Indy's. She still had a young woman's beauty. She could not have been much more than a teenager herself when she'd given birth to Indy. Thinking of Donnelly, and how Indy had come to be, it wasn't something he wanted to dwell on as her mother's gentle hands worked to heal his wound.

'I couldn't help but notice the old scars on your body,' Mary said nodding towards his bare chest and breaking him out of his thoughts. 'Are you sure that soldiering is for you?'

Will pushed himself further into a seated position and winced a little at the pain and dizziness.

'I'm not dead yet, am I?' he asked with a wry smile.

She didn't return his smile, just continued dressing his wound. 'But not all the marks are from the wars I'd wager.'

She was an observant woman. 'No. Not all, madam.'

'Some of those lashes, particularly on your back, are almost as old as yourself.'

Will said nothing. He'd come to terms with his upbringing years ago. It didn't mean he enjoyed discussing it.

Mary took a deep breath and changed the subject. 'My girl has a mind of her own to be sure, but I worry about her, living there in the diggers' camp. Lord knows, I tried to raise a lady. I failed. But bless her, she takes care of me.'

'May I ask, why did you name her Indigo? It's an unusual name.'

Mary smiled. 'When she was born, her eyes reminded me of the bluebells from my native Ireland. Despite being called bluebell, in the fields where I grew up, they were more of a blue-purple hue. Indigo.'

Mary's expression softened as she fell into memories. 'She was a babe born out of a violent act and I cried for nine months before she came.'

She stopped then, looking flustered, as though she'd said too much.

He laid his hand on hers to put her at ease. 'Indy told me of her unusual family situation. And unfortunately, I have seen firsthand how the man who fathered her treats her.' His jaw clenched at the thought of that horrid man assaulting such an angel as Mary Wallace. 'He is the lowest of men.'

'He is, yes,' Mary agreed solemnly. But then she smiled and Will saw where Indy got her inner light from. 'It was a terrible time for me, I'll admit. But the day she was born, I saw her sweetness and realised she was an innocent. An innocent just as I had been. I chose then and there to stop acting as though it was I who'd done something wrong. I chose to not let her live her life as an unwanted child, as a victim. We left England because I was afraid he would do something to her. I was afraid he would hurt her. He had political aspirations you see, and if anyone found out he had a child out of wedlock, and to the kitchen maid no less...' She paused and took an unsteady breath. 'Anyway, assisted passage was gained and we sailed on the *Isabella Watson* bound for Victoria. I raised Indy not to be ashamed of having no father. Finally, when she was old enough, I told her the truth. It was necessary at the time when I discovered that Donnelly, too, had arrived in Melbourne. Then, when he found his way here to the goldfields, and wearing a policeman's uniform no less, I knew I had done the right thing by telling her. But I'll not let her suffer for something she had no control over. I taught her to ignore the gossip and the wretched things people say.'

'People say things to her? As far as I see most people like her, and she is good to everyone in the camps. Her parentage shouldn't come into it.'

'I wish everyone had your good sense and good heart, Lieutenant. Most people do like Indy and look past her unfortunate lineage. But she is still what most would call a bastard child.'

'She's far from alone in that. After all, I knew neither of my parents.'

'An orphan boy?'

'Yes, madam,' Will confirmed. 'Brought up in a boys' home. And you have seen for yourself the results of that upbringing.'

As she again wrapped his head in the bandage, Mary's eyes went to the scars on his chest. 'Then you are an especially exceptional lad. To come from where you have, to be where you are now. You are a survivor.'

'As are you, madam. You and your daughter. You're both extraordinary women. I am proud to know you both.'

She smiled. 'She is my light, my Indigo. And she has grown up strong of mind and strong of heart.'

'She is all those things and you should be glad of it,' Will said, but his conscience pricked at him. 'I wish she would be more careful in the goldfields, though. Despite how strong she thinks she is, there are dangers for women. Can you not keep her here?'

Mary graced him with a sceptical look. 'You've travelled oceans, Lieutenant. Ever tried to hold back the tide?'

Will sighed wistfully. 'I fear I move my jaw in vain when I speak to you Wallace women. I shall keep my unsolicited advice to myself from now on.'

'Don't,' Mary said in earnest. 'You are a wise young man and my Indy needs that counsel. Whether she decides to take it or not will be her decision. You like my girl, Lieutenant?'

Will's face heated with his discomfort at the turn of conversation.

Mary sighed. 'I'm sorry. I have embarrassed you. I believe it's better to speak plainly in these strange times.'

'I like your girl, Mrs Wallace.' His admission worried him though.

She took his hand and squeezed it. 'Please keep an eye on her for me. Trouble follows her.'

Will laughed. 'Don't I know it?' He put his other hand over Mary's. 'I shall watch over her for you. Though I won't be telling her that for fear of my life.'

'You know her well already,' Mary said, chuckling along with him just as Indy re-entered the room. She looked from Will to her mother, clearly annoyed that she had missed something.

'What's so funny?'

***

By the afternoon, Will was strong enough to move out of the tiny bedroom and Indy helped him onto the porch to get some fresh air. Dizziness swept over him occasionally but he was happy to be out of the tiny house.

'It's a beautiful day,' he said, stretching his arms above his head and arching his back. He was glad for the opportunity to move his muscles, stiff from too many hours laid out in bed.

He took his first real look at the little homestead. It was such a sweet little wooden cottage that appeared to have been well-restored and shored up with mud. He found the workmanship quite impressive given the obvious isolation of the place. Turning to look about the property, he glanced up at the trees, stringy bark hanging loosely from their trunks like a half-peeled banana. They stood tall like sentinels, allowing only a little of the blue sky to peek through their towering branches, providing wonderful shade for the house. It was so different here to the dry, treeless Ballarat, and he wondered how far from town they were. To the right he could see his horse in an open stable, comfortable and safe from the elements. On the other side of the house appeared to be a small vegetable garden and he could make out tall green beanstalks, and tomato plants tethered to wooden stakes. The Wallace women were quite autonomous here it seemed.

Stepping down from the porch, he took a deep inhale. He'd never seen a natural world like it. The countryside of his English homeland was much greener and denser in its forestry. Even at the end of a winter season, this Victorian bushland was so dry and the earth so brown. Indy had said there was a road nearby but he couldn't see or hear any traffic. No beating of horse hooves, or shouting of voices as they passed between Ballarat and Melbourne. The little wood and mud cottage was hidden from the world.

'It is a lovely place, this Victoria.'

'It is a hard place, made for hard people,' Indy said, leaning on the veranda post. 'Speaking of which, what happened at the Eureka Hotel, Will?'

Taking a deep breath, he exhaled it heavily as he thought back to the riot of the day before. 'The miners went after Bentley. But it appeared he had run off to the government camp already. The last thing I remember was the mob looting things from the hotel rooms and stealing anything that wasn't nailed down. Then they began throwing things. Bottles, rocks.'

'Good God!' Indy exclaimed.

He wondered how things had ended up. Had the police and soldiers been able to control the situation? 'Did you see anything?'

'I saw you on your horse unconscious and bleeding. Other than that, I just heard a lot of noise and destruction. You needed medical help. I didn't hang about to see what was going on.'

Will nodded and looked back into the house where Mary worked at the kitchen bench. 'How is it that you and your mother have an actual home here when most diggers and families live under canvas? I myself share a tent with two other fellows.'

'How cosy!' Indy raised her eyebrows.

'I assure you, it is not.'

She chuckled. 'On one of my trips back to Melbourne to see my mother, our bullock coach broke a wheel. We were stranded for many hours on the road out there and I decided to go for a walk. I came across this old shepherd's hut. It was long abandoned and had only one small room but I thought it would be a good solid place to build onto.'

'That country home your mother wanted?' He remembered her story about wanting to bring her mother to the bush and for her to have her cottage.

Indy nodded. 'Whitey helped us fix it up so it was at least livable. I made a few lucky strikes of gold in the early days and as more and more people came out to the goldfields, they brought their skills with them. I paid a carpenter and his son to build on the two bedrooms and the veranda.'

She ran her hand down the timber post she leaned against. 'I bought some cheap furniture and, together with Whitey, we finished up the place. The carpenter struck gold and headed for Queensland before he'd completed the task. Hard to find good help these days. Anyway, the local tribe sold me some of their skins for the floor and we've made ourselves quite the little home.'

'Skins?' Will was horrified. 'Whose skin?'

'Kangaroo skins,' Indy chuckled. 'To lay on the floors. They're mighty warm.'

'So you have found gold then?'

Wariness came into her eyes. 'I have. Small amounts.'

'You don't speak of it often.'

'You'd just as soon walk down Eureka Street with pounds hanging out of your pockets if you want to lose your money. Telling folks you've found gold would have the same effect.'

'Clever girl,' Will agreed.

They fell into an awkward silence for a moment as neither of them could think of anything to say.

'Oh, look,' Indy said, pointing up into the tall trees.

Will craned his neck in the direction she was pointing. A long way up, in the vee of two tree branches, he could see what appeared to be just a ball of grey fluff. Until it moved. He blinked.

'What is it?' he asked intrigued, but wary at the same time.

'Koala,' she said.

'I've never heard of such a thing,' he said eyeing her suspiciously.

'It's another of the native animals, like the kangaroo or the wallaby.'

'Wallaby?' Will said laughing. 'What a ridiculous name? Who comes up with these names?'

'It's what the aboriginals call them.'

He was looking up again when the koala shifted slightly and its baby moved onto its back. Gingerly, he stepped out of the shade of the veranda and down the steps to move in for a closer view. He stopped suddenly and turned back to Indy.

'They're not dangerous are they?'

She laughed. 'No. Well, not unless you try and take their young. Then they'll scratch and bite worse than Elena Gibson in a catfight.'

'It's like a giant teddy bear,' he said, grinning at her like a schoolboy when she moved to stand beside him. 'It's wonderful.'

He breathed deeply. The overnight rain had left everything looking and smelling so fresh. He liked the earthy scent and took another deep inhale.

'Smells different here, doesn't it,' Indy said and, one by one, she pointed to the trees surrounding the little cottage. 'Eucalypt, casuarina, honeysuckle.'

'Fresh air is a rare commodity in the government camp.'

She nodded in sympathy. 'I've seen the government camp. Your conditions aren't much better than the rest of the goldfields.'

'I think they're worse. And with so many soldiers being brought in, we've scarcely room to breathe, even if there were fresh air.'

'Things are tough all over,' Indy said with a wistful grin.

'I'm not complaining,' he said and then laughed. 'Or maybe just a little.'

She laughed too, and he found he enjoyed the relaxed sound of it. She didn't laugh enough he decided.

'But imagine living out here away from town in the beauty of this bushland,' he said, turning on the spot to take it all in. 'And to think we sent our convicts here. Not sure who got the better cards in that draw.'

'I don't think you would want to come here as a convict.'

'No, I suppose you're right.' It may well have been a fate he faced if the army had not given him a new life. He began to feel light-headed and must have swayed because Indy took his arm to steady him.

'It's alright,' he said, annoyed at his feebleness. 'I'm not about to swoon.'

'Of course not. You're a big tough soldier,' she said, but led him back to the house.

'No, really I'm fine.' But not completely sure he wouldn't swoon, as he'd quipped, rather than make a fool of himself, he allowed her to help him back into the house and the bedroom. He dropped down onto the bed and lay back, his eyes already closing.

'I'll just lie here a minute until the dizziness passes.'

He was asleep again in minutes.

***

She stood by his bed and watched the even rise and fall of his chest as he fell into slumber. He looked so peaceful. His face softened in sleep, his pale hair left to hang loose about his shoulders. Broad shoulders. In his thin undershirt she could see the bulge of biceps usually hidden by the heavy cloth of his red coat. He looked wonderful in that coat. And he looked incredible out of it now. Little shadows formed beneath his eyes where long, dark lashes lay against his pale skin. One had come loose, she noted, and sat on his cheek. Holding her breath, she leaned in, her finger lightly touching the stray eyelash and collecting it. She closed her eyes, made a wish and blew the lash away.

How close had he come to being killed in the attack on the Eureka Hotel? How had the fight ended? Suddenly feeling like a foolish little girl making wishes on eyelashes, she wondered whether she should head back into town while he slept. Perhaps she could find out what had gone on. Had anyone been arrested during the attack on the hotel? Or worse, killed?

She couldn't believe the miners had been so violent in their attack on Bentley's Hotel. Yes, it was unfair and unjust that Bentley and his cronies had been found not guilty, but looting and property damage wasn't going to change anything. Had the miners been drunk? It had been a very hot day and tempers had no doubt sizzled along with the temperature. Until the disturbance at the Eureka Hotel, the miners had simply voiced their concerns and issues, signed petitions and held rallies.

Indy believed in democratic solutions, and the miners were putting together regular deputations to talk with Commissioner Rede. Surely he was not an unreasonable man. Talking and negotiation were the way to democracy. She just wished democracy moved faster than the glaciers.

Chapter 11

Will didn't stay asleep for long, and when he rose, Mary and Indy were preparing the evening meal.

'Would you like a brandy before dinner, Will?' Indy asked, reaching up on tiptoes to grab a jug from the top shelf.

He moved in to help and as he did, his body brushed against hers. Hearing her sudden intake of breath, he looked down at her. Warmth radiated from her and her face was flushed, from the heat of cooking perhaps, but when she licked her lips it sent waves of desire rushing through his body.

Oh, he was well healed. Head and body were more than well enough that he was thinking about what her lips would taste like. He took the brandy jug and to save his sanity walked in the opposite direction to where Indy had moved to stand by the fire. He poured the brandy and drank the entire beaker in one quick gulp. Unfortunately, the warm liquor did not douse the fire in his belly as he'd hoped it would.

'Mrs Wallace, can I pour you a drink?' he asked, trying to take his mind off Indy, and concentrating on the more important fact that her mother was standing not three feet from him.

'Please, call me Mary.' She deliberated for a moment. 'Go on then. Just a small one.'

Indy chuckled at her mother, and moved in to take the drink that Will had poured her. He'd been careful enough to leave the beaker on the table so their hands would not accidentally touch when he passed it to her.

He poured himself a second drink and a beaker for Mary. 'What shall we toast to?'

'To your health, Lieutenant. May your head continue to be made of brick.'

'Indy!' Mary reprimanded while Indy tossed down the liquor. 'I swear there's a lady in there somewhere, Lieutenant.'

Will laughed. 'A lady may not have been so bold as to try to save my life, so I shall be thankful for Miss Indy and her wild ways.'

He toasted her in return and drank.

An hour later, with their dinner consumed, they sat by the light of candles that burned low on the table and talked. Will found he liked Mary Wallace immensely. She was a strong, intelligent and caring woman. Having learned what she had been through, he knew she could have turned bitter and angry with her lot in life and the world itself. Instead she chose to look ahead and forget the ills of the past. She loved her daughter—that was obvious. And although Indy was unladylike and untamed in many ways, her mother still held her in check with her iron will. Indy loved her mother unconditionally too. He could see it. She had inherited that strength and integrity from someone. And it certainly wasn't Sergeant Donnelly.

'Well, I'm for my bed.'

When Mary stood, Will stood too.

She smiled and reached out a hand to his cheek as she passed. 'Such a gentleman. I'll leave you two to clean up after dinner.'

'Goodnight, Mrs Wallace,' Will said. 'Sleep well.'

'You just won't call me Mary, will you,' she said, shaking her head tiredly.

'Goodnight, Ma.'

Taking one of the candles from the mantle, Mary went into the bedroom she was currently sharing with Indy since Will had arrived.

Will sat again and watched intently as Indy cleared the plates from the table. In the glow of the single candle, she was breathtakingly beautiful and looked frighteningly young. The skin of her face, tanned by hours of working outdoors, glowed golden, while flecks of sun-streaked red flashed in her ash blonde hair.

Indy met his eyes, and for a moment they just looked at one another with secret wants unspoken.

Finally coming to his senses, Will cleared his throat and stood.

'Shall I help you clean up?'

'Well, I'm not doing it all on my own,' she scoffed, but her voice had lost its usual bite.

Indy washed the dishes in a large metal bowl, topping it up with water heated in the heavy kettle over the fire, and Will dried the crockery with one of

Mary's hand-sewn cotton towels. They worked side by side, keeping to safe subjects of discussion such as Mary's vegetable patch or Will's time in India.

'You've seen such far-off lands I cannot imagine,' Indy said, wiping her hands on her skirt as they finished up.

'But only during war time,' Will added. 'Some of the places were so beautiful and I would have enjoyed exploring them when they weren't being laid to waste by war and disease. I much prefer this quiet land.'

'Quiet?' Indy baulked, moving to the door to toss the washing water out. 'With a murder every second day on the goldfields? Bushrangers and thieves pillaging and plundering. It's hardly quiet.'

'Hm,' Will mused. 'You may have a point.' He hesitated a moment before speaking again. 'Your mother worries about you being out there on the fields with all those men, with all those guns. I mean that Scobie fellow...'

He saw the determined glower that he'd grown to expect cross her face.

'James Scobie was a rabble raiser. He didn't deserve to be killed. But he was no innocent bystander.'

'Still, innocent bystanders get hurt. Look at me.'

'I can take care of myself, Lieutenant.'

'I know you can, Indy,' he said, his voice deep and low. 'That doesn't mean your mother won't worry, that I won't worry.'

She stopped what she was doing and stared at him. 'You called me Indy,' she said, surprise in her uncommonly quiet voice. 'You never call me Indy.'

'I apologise.' It was overly familiar of him to call her by her given name. He'd relaxed so easily into their conversation, it had been a simple slip of the tongue.

'No, I like it.'

He studied her expression in the muted light. The prickliness was gone, replaced by a softer look. The look of a desirable young woman with hope and want in her eyes. It threatened to undo him, so he forced himself to turn away.

'I should go to bed, too.' Hanging the tea towel over a chair back, he moved towards the second bedroom. 'And I should probably go back to town in the morning.'

'We'll see,' she said as though she were solely in charge of determining his fitness for travel.

Indy took the candle from the table and handed it to him. Their fingers touched lightly as he took it from her and they held the candle together for a moment. He watched her long lashes lower as her eyes dropped to his mouth. Her lips parted slightly and he felt himself stir at the prettiness of her full pink mouth. Oh, what temptation lay in those lips? He felt his hand lifting to her cheek before his brain registered what he was doing. Her skin was so soft, so warm, and he was momentarily distracted by the small grouping of freckles on her nose. How had he never noticed them before?

You've never been this close to her before.

That realisation snapped him back to his senses. Taking the candle, he placed it just inside the door on the bureau. When he turned back, Indy was closer again. He could smell her fragrant hair and skin and he swallowed against the pleasant assault to his senses.

'Indy,' he whispered in warning.

'Shh.' Going up on her toes she leaned so close it would take only the slightest shift to close the gap between them.

His body burned. Every part of him ached to touch her. She laid her hands against his chest and looked up at him questioningly. Passion-hooded, dark blue eyes nearly broke him and her heavy breathing was doing wonderful things to her décolletage above her dress.

No battle he'd ever fought had required the feat of strength it took to turn away from her warmth. It was physically painful, but he knew it was for the best. Before he lost his ability to think, he stepped back.

'Goodnight, Indy.'

And closed the door.

***

Indy stood staring at the door. Everything she wanted was on the other side of it. Will. His lovely dark eyes and full mouth. His unruly blond hair, his heart of gold. He was a gentleman to the most annoying degree. She would gladly have given herself to him had he asked, but a gentleman he was.

And her mother was in the next room.

Where had her good sense gone? She liked to be in charge, especially when it came to possible suitors. But somehow, when she was with Will, she lost her ability to think straight.

She was shocked to discover she had more than a passing desire to become Will's bed mate. Did that make her a wanton? Was it wrong for a woman to have desires of the body? Men did, and they gave in to it frequently. Was a woman supposed to wait until she was wed before she was allowed to enjoy the thrill of what the body of a handsome and strong man like Lieutenant Will Marsh could bring? If that were so, why did God give her these feelings that rushed through her system like she'd devoured a thousand raspberry drops from Spencer's Confectionary store?

It wasn't as though Will would be her first experience with lovemaking. It had happened in this very room. She and the carpenter's son. A handsome young man, he'd caught her eye as he'd worked with his father restoring the house. One day the father had travelled to Bendigo, leaving the son alone to continue work, and Indy had dropped by to check on the progress. They had both been nineteen and curious. Neither had had any sexual experiences prior and Indy remembered the fumbling and the pain of her first encounter with intercourse. She'd found it neither fun nor thrilling, and although young Simon seemed to have enjoyed himself, as he'd lay across her panting and bucking, Indy simply counted the moments until it was over. Simon had hoped there would be more between them and even proposed marriage. But being a young bride—or a bride at all—was not something that appealed to Indy. She had declined politely and they had parted as friends.

Thinking of that one encounter, Indy hadn't experienced the rush of feelings in Simon's arms that she got whenever she was within breathing distance of Will Marsh. Her skin prickled and her belly rippled low at just the thought of

Will's big hands skimming across her naked body. And she knew he would be no dull or selfish lover.

Reining in her imagination, now wildly out of control, she took one more look at Will's closed door then crept into her mother's room. She didn't want her mother to wake up and see the no doubt obvious flush to her cheeks. Will had put that flush there and it wasn't fading any time soon.

A candle burned low on the armoire, and Indy got undressed as quietly as she could before blowing it out and climbing into the small bed beside her mother. She would have preferred to be climbing into bed beside Will, but he was too much of a gentleman—damn him. And bless him. A smile warmed her lips as she cuddled down into the sheets facing her mother.

'Be careful, my girl.'

Her mother's voice surprised her and she opened her eyes to see her staring back at her.

'Be careful about what, Mother?'

'Don't go looking where you shouldn't be looking.'

'I don't know what you're talking about,' Indy said. She knew her voice sounded wrong, too high, but she had never been able to lie to her mother.

'I like him too, Indy.' Mary lifted a hand to push Indy's curls from her forehead, before laying it against her cheek. Would she feel how flushed she was? Indy couldn't help it, she blushed even more. 'But he is a man. A military man and a career one at that.'

'What are you saying?' The high she'd floated on from her stolen moment with Will disappeared along with her smile. 'You think he's only going to use me and toss me aside when he's done?'

'He won't do it on purpose,' Mary denied. 'He is a good man. But his life is in the service and we are but a short stop on his journey. I worry for you. Don't go falling in love with a man who will most likely be gone again by year's end.'

'Since when have you ever known me to fall in love?' Indy said lightly, trying to laugh off her mother's concerns.

'Never,' Mary said sadly. 'That's why I worry now.'

If she were able to think straight when it came to William Marsh, she would have agreed with her mother's logic. She'd thought a casual dalliance with the handsome Lieutenant might be fun and quite harmless to both of them. But having spent so much time around him over the last few days, her feelings had become muddled. Despite her best intentions, her heart seemed determined to rebel against her common sense.

Realising her mother was still watching her closely, she rolled over in the little bed so that Mary could no longer see her face.

'Don't concern yourself. I am quite immune to handsome gentlemen,' she said staring wide-awake at the wall that joined Will's bedroom to theirs. 'Goodnight, Mother.'

Chapter 12

Will woke to a strange thwacking sound. Forcing his eyes open, he squinted at the sunshine pouring into the bedroom. He'd overslept. Again. He could no longer blame the damage to his skull, for it was healing well. He was becoming much too comfortable in this house in the woods, when he really ought to be getting back to the government camp. And he should go today. Resigned he would do just that, he climbed out of bed and peeked out the little window.

'Blast her independence.'

Terrible images of Indy taking off a finger or a foot with the axe she swung filled his head. Moving quickly he pulled on his trousers and tossed his shirt over his head. Awkwardly hopping across the room, tugging on his boots as he went, he threw open the bedroom door and stalked determinedly out of the house.

The fierce heat of the sun hit him square between the eyes, and it took a long moment on the porch before he could adjust to the brightness and continue his forward motion.

'Hell's bells, this place gets hot,' he grumbled. 'How does it get so hot? It can't be eight in the morning.'

'Well, if it isn't himself.' Indy's exaggerated Irish brogue made its way to him. 'It's after nine actually, Lieutenant Lazy Bones.'

He moved towards her now that his eyes and his body had acclimated.

'I cannot deny I have become somewhat of a "lazy bones" as you say. It's your mother's fine cooking and the softness of your bed...' He stopped abruptly. 'I beg your pardon. I didn't mean to discuss your bed...'

He shut his mouth before he did any more harm.

'Lieutenant, if you continue to say you're sorry for everything you think to be improper, we will never get past apologies,' she said and swung the axe again, splitting a log expertly in two. 'And it's beginning to annoy.'

'Here.' Will stepped forward and put his hand over hers on the axe. 'Let me do that.'

'I am quite capable of swinging an axe,' Indy said, defiance radiating with every word.

'I can see that,' Will said, his grip on the axe tightening in case she got it into her head to use it on him. He was quickly learning how not to ruffle the feathers of one Indigo Wallace. 'But as I said, I feel I have become too idle. My body will be wasting away without exercise.'

'Your body looks fine to me.'

His eyes shot to hers. 'I beg your pardon?' It had been barely a murmur, but he'd heard her well enough.

'I said I'm happy for you to take over.' Batting her eyelashes and smiling coquettishly, Indy let go of the axe.

Surprised that she'd given in so easily, Will watched her move to a safe distance where she sat on the woodpile. He'd expected at least twelve rounds of arguing before she would deign to surrender.

Dropping the head of the axe to the ground between his legs, he gripped the hem of his loose white shirt and whipped it over his head leaving his chest bare. He tossed the shirt towards the woodpile. Indy's expression had taken on a hint of astonishment—her eyes were well and truly fixed to his naked chest, following his torso down to the waist of his trousers. He allowed himself a little chuckle and, since he had begun to enjoy her unerring stare a little too much, he figured he ought to get down to the task at hand.

***

Indy followed the flight of the flowing white shirt as it landed beside her on the woodpile, and tried very hard to muffle the little squeak of surprise. She was not a woman to shock easily. Slowly her eyes tracked back towards Will. Yep, his shirt had come off, and yep, there was his now bare upper body gleaming, a little too white and bright really, in the sun. She watched sinewy muscle ripple in his sides as he bent to pick up the axe again. The only reason she had acquiesced so quickly was because his hand had felt much too warm, and much too comfortable on hers as he'd reached for the axe.

'You need some time in the sun, Lieutenant,' she teased, finally getting a grasp on her intelligence once again. 'I've seen polar bears with more colour.'

He graced her with an exasperated smile, but when he lifted the axe over his head, her bravado took a nosedive and she nearly slipped off the woodpile. The bumps and grooves across his chest and abdomen that had appeared innocent enough in rest, flexed and contracted mightily as he brought down the axe again and again. That burn, low in her belly, returned with alacrity—she suddenly felt very thirsty. The only thing marring the perfection of his torso was the array of scars seared into his chest and back.

'How did you get those marks on your skin?' Indy asked before she could censor herself.

Pausing, he looked down at his body. Sweat was now starting to glisten on his chest and he was puffing a little from his exertions. 'Various battles here and there.'

He acted so unconcerned about them as he lifted the axe once more, swinging down to split the log into two large parts.

'How long have you been travelling with the regiment?'

Indy watched him closely, his eyes scanning the tops of the huge eucalypts as he did the mental calculations.

'Eight years,' he answered finally. 'Or thereabouts.'

The axe swung again. *Crack!*

'You haven't seen home in eight years?'

'What home? The Army is my home. I joined when I was sixteen.'

'What did you do before you joined?'

'I lived on the streets, stole food to survive,' he said, pausing to push his hair from his eyes.

Indy was careful to school her features to hide the heartbreak she felt imagining him as a young boy, orphaned and homeless. But he was too perceptive.

'Do not pity me, Indy.' He said it so firmly she didn't even try to deny that she had felt sympathy for him. 'I did what I had to in order to survive. When I was eventually caught stealing fruit at a market by an officer of the

Fortieth regiment, he and his wife took me in and fed me. I planned on running away with the silverware in the middle of the night. But over dinner the Captain talked of his time in the Army: the campaigns, the travel to faraway lands. He showed me maps of oceans he had sailed and countries he had seen. Places like Canada and Africa and others I had never even heard of.'

There was so much awe and admiration in his voice when he spoke of the gentleman that Indy smiled.

'He made it sound like an adventure,' Will continued. 'I was facing prison and possible transportation for the term of my natural life and he offered me a different direction in the ranks of the regimentals. I figured I had nothing to lose. If I didn't like it, I'd run again. No harm done.' He sliced another log in half. 'So I took the Queen's shilling and never looked back.'

'And you liked it,' Indy said, caught up in his story.

He let out a sardonic laugh. 'No, I hated it. Every damn minute of it. The camps were rougher than the streets I'd lived on. The higher-ranking officers treated us like dogs. But then our regiment was sent to war in India. At only eighteen years of age, it seemed I had a knack for battle.'

'From fighting on the streets?'

Will leaned the axe head down on the ground and wiped his forehead. She could smell his manly sweat, watched a line of it run down across his taut stomach and she had to swallow the excess saliva that had somehow come to pool in her otherwise dry mouth.

'I think I was a good soldier because I didn't really care whether I lived or died.'

His answer knocked the wind out of her and the smile right off her face. It had been said so pragmatically.

'Don't look so troubled, you pretty fool,' he said, stepping to her and rubbing the frown lines from her brow with his large thumb. 'It's been a long time since I have felt like that. I enjoy my life and I enjoy what I do. I'm not a martyr. I do not wish to die.' He tapped her nose and gave her a wink. 'Especially not right at this moment.'

She fought to slow her racing pulse. 'I'm glad to hear it.'

His touch had been light and teasing, and her heart had softened just a little more thanks to his candour. But something was still bothering her.

'How did an orphan boy afford to buy a commission?' It was a question that had plagued her since he'd first told her his parents had abandoned him.

'I couldn't afford it. I was promoted when I saved the life of a Major General in battle. On his recommendation and letters from my old friend the Captain they promoted me to Lieutenant. So there. Now you know all there is to know about me.'

Feeling unnerved suddenly, as though by telling her his life story he'd given her his complete and unerring trust, Indy stood and took the axe from him.

'I think we have enough wood for now.'

She was so close to his sweat-covered chest she could smell the perspiration, could feel the heat radiating from his body. He licked his parched lips and her eyes were drawn to his mouth. She wasn't about to make a fool of herself by attempting to kiss him again, so instead, she walked away, turning back as she reached the porch.

Smiling deviously she said, 'Why don't you go take a wash in the river, Lieutenant.'

'A wash?'

'Yes. A wash. You smell.'

He grinned and gave an exaggerated bow of obedience. 'Always the measure of politeness, Miss Indy.'

***

The night was stiflingly hot considering it was not yet summer. Indy tossed and turned in the small bed while her mother slept blissfully beside her. How could she possibly sleep? Their shared body heat was overwhelming. Giving up, she left her mother with the bed.

Quietly, she moved past the room where Will slept. She stopped at the closed door and listened, but hearing nothing she continued outside onto the porch. Even out of the house it wasn't much cooler. Not a breath of wind stirred the leaves of the eucalypts. Night bugs were chirping and a sliver of moon cast a small amount of light.

It took a while for her eyes to adjust as she moved down the steps. She was wearing her thinnest nightdress but even that clung to her body with perspiration.

Crossing to the large wooden barrel she dipped her handkerchief in the water, reaching deep to get to the cooler liquid in the middle. Her nightdress draped a little at the top and touched the water, making her gasp when she stood upright as the cool freshness transferred to her skin. She wiped her brow and her neck with the handkerchief but the accidental soaking of her nightgown felt so nice she craved more.

'Blow it all,' she said out loud. Wanting to wash herself properly, she reached down to lift the dress by its long hem. It made it up to her mid-thigh before she heard his voice.

'Please don't.'

She gasped and spun around, dropping the dress back down as she covered her chest with her arms.

He stepped out of the shadow of the house and she could see his wistful grin as he moved closer. 'I don't think my gentlemanly nature would hold out if I were to see you naked twice.'

'Will.' She exhaled in relief, but the thrill of seeing him as he stepped into the pale moonlight stole her breath again. 'You scared me. I thought you were in bed.'

'Surely, you jest. It's too hot to sleep.'

He too was scantily dressed. He wore his uniform trousers but his feet were bare, and there was something incredibly alluring about his large, naked feet. But it was his chest, covered only in the thin straps of the suspenders holding up his trousers, which had her mouth watering, as it had that morning.

He had taken her advice and gone to the river to bathe. She'd watched for him as she'd sat on the veranda scrubbing potatoes for dinner. When he'd returned, his pale hair had been wet and slicked back, his shirt dripped and clung to his body as he had obviously decided to take the opportunity to wash it while he'd bathed. Her mouth had dropped open at how appetising he looked. That was nothing compared to the man who stood before her now bathed in moonlight.

'Can I talk you into a swim in the river?' she asked.

'You test my resolve, Miss Indy.'

'Your resolve?'

***

Will stepped past Indy and leaned against the veranda railing. It was wrong on so many levels, these feelings he was having. This was her mother's house. He could not accept Mary's hospitality and then throw it back in her face by taking advantage of her daughter. He was not free to marry. He had no idea how long he might be in Ballarat, or even Australia, for that matter. So where could it possibly go?

But, dammit, he wanted her. He wanted to touch her and taste her. But taking what he wanted would give her the wrong idea. Was it fair to give her false hope that more was possible? No. It wasn't. It wasn't fair to either of them. He had to end it. Now.

'Indy, you are a lovely girl,' he said, turning back to face her.

'Girl?' Indy said and chuckled richly. She stepped into him again and he felt the touch of her breast through her thin nightdress against his bare chest. 'Will. Do I look like a girl to you?'

Certain he'd break teeth his jaw was clenched so tightly, he struggled against his desire to reach out and feel her breast cupped in his hand. To run his thumb across the taut nipples he could see through her nightdress.

A girl? No, she looked like an enchanted seductress sent to torment him in his every waking and sleeping moment. If he didn't do something soon, he would never be able to stop himself from pulling her against him and crushing his mouth to hers.

He would have to be cruel. He would have to be cruel to be kind.

'I'm not good for you, Indy.' It came out gruffer than he'd expected and she seemed to sense his struggle.

'I'm sure you would be very good for me,' she whispered back and leaned up on tiptoes until she was closer and closer.

'I prefer an older woman.'

She dropped back to her feet again with a thud.

'It's no reflection on you, Indy,' he added. 'It's about my needs, my character.'

She shook her head. 'What are you saying? It's not me, it's you?'

He thought about it. 'Exactly.'

But Indy was not so easily put off. 'I'm not a fool, Will. And I'm not a girl. I'm a woman. A woman who knows when a man is attracted to her. Can you honestly stand there and say that you're not attracted to me?'

Will's well-honed military instincts were flashing warning signs. Her hand brushed against his manhood and he gasped.

'Your body tells me otherwise,' she said, her voice soft and seductive.

He gritted his teeth, damning his body for its traitorous reaction to her. Lord help him, she was unlike any other woman he'd ever met.

Cruel to be kind, he reminded himself.

'You're very pretty and quite spirited,' he said, taking her arms and pushing her back a step to save his sanity. 'I'm sure you will make a man very happy one day and give him lots of children. But I am not that man.'

She stared at him a moment. The only light to see by was the moon, but he could see plainly the hurt that crossed her face as it dawned on her that he was no longer playing. He also saw the moment that she steeled herself. The hardness came into her eyes, replacing the doe-eyed temptress.

'You're the fool, Will Marsh. You're panicking, pushing me away because you think I'm trying to trap a husband. You bloody men! You think every woman is going to fall in love with you and you're so damn scared of love that you run from anyone who shows an interest.'

'Indy, it's not like that—'

'Or perhaps you're terrified that if you kiss me, *you* will fall in love with *me,* and then where will you be when you have to leave this place for the next? And trust me, Will Marsh, if you kissed me, you would fall in love with me. I'm that good.'

He blinked at her boldness and opened his mouth to argue but she was on a roll.

'Oh, and if you think me still a virgin, then I'm sorry to crush that fantasy. I've been with men.' She stepped closer to him again and put her hand to his chest. 'Women have desires and needs of the body just as men do. And you, Lieutenant, have just missed your chance to have mine.'

And with that, she turned and stormed back into the house.

He stared after her, completely and totally gobsmacked by her outburst.

'Bollocks.'

He'd deserved that tongue-lashing. But he also knew he'd done the right thing. So why did he feel like such a horse's arse? And why was it that the thing that stuck with him most, out of everything she'd said, was that she had been with men? He didn't need to know that. He didn't *want* to know that. Despite his reluctance to get involved with Miss Indigo Wallace, he hated thinking that other men had touched her beautiful body, had gripped a hand in all that luscious hair, had kissed her until she'd sighed. He shook his head hoping those thoughts would fall out and never return.

Groaning with frustration, he leaned two hands on the edge of the water barrel. Still feeling the residual physical effects of being so close to her, he leaned forward and dipped his full head into the water, staying there for as long as he could hold his breath. When he surfaced, he inhaled lungsful of air and slicked his long wet hair back from his face. His skin cooled, but his blood still boiled with the memory of her touch, her smell.

Indy Wallace was not a woman to leave a man's system easily. He tossed and turned in his bed that night as much from the smouldering—and subsequent scolding—midnight encounter with a certain high-spirited vixen as from the relentless heat. The two melded together to make one very sweaty and uncomfortable night.

Chapter 13

When Indy returned from checking her rabbit traps in the morning, Mary was cooking eggs and frying soda bread and Will sat at the table drinking tea.

He stood as she entered the house. 'Good morning, Miss Indy.'

Without a word, she tossed a dead rabbit carcass on the table in front of him and graced him with a look telling him she was still extremely displeased. But even the fire in her eyes couldn't stop Will's stomach from flipping, like the eggs Mary turned in the pan, when Indy leaned past him to fill her teacup from the pot. Her long braid brushed against his forearm, the hair tickling his skin and sending heat directly to his groin. He moved his arm away and saw a glint of a satisfied smile on her lips. The woman was diabolical. Even in her incensed state, she could still get him riled up and she knew it.

'Good morning, Lieutenant,' she returned tersely, and left him to help her mother plate up breakfast.

'Get that animal off my table,' Mary insisted.

Indy dragged the rabbit off the table and into the meat locker, slamming the door on it.

'My, but you seem to have brought the frost in with you this morning, Indy,' Mary noted.

Placing the breakfast in front of Will, Indy sat across from him and the three of them ate in an uncomfortable silence. She did her best not to look at him, and he did his best not to look at her.

'I thought I might take a ride into town today,' Mary said, breaking the stalemate. 'Perhaps we can accompany the Lieutenant back to camp.'

Indy and Will stopped eating and finally exchanged glances.

'I don't want you going into town just now, mother,' Indy said, chasing the last of her eggs around the plate. 'Perhaps we can just stay here. Will can help get those posts in so we can erect the fence around your vegetable garden to keep the kangaroos out.'

'Indy.' It took a moment but she finally looked up and met his eyes. 'I must get back to camp.'

'So that's settled then,' Mary said, giving her daughter a telling look. 'We can escort the Lieutenant back to town and I'll buy more supplies. We're almost out of sugar.'

'I'll get it for you,' Indy insisted.

'Indy—'

'I don't want you running into Donnelly,' she said to Mary, standing to dump her unfinished breakfast on the kitchen bench. 'Whatever you need from town, I will get it for you.'

'I won't hide from him,' Mary argued.

'Mother—'

'If you'll excuse me, I'll go and get my things.' Will stood to leave the women to argue in peace. He closed the bedroom door to give them some privacy, even though he knew he would be able to hear everything that was said through the thin wall. But before they could continue their conversation, he heard galloping hooves approaching, followed by yells and whoops.

'Hi, ho, Mrs Mary Wallace!'

Pushing aside the lace curtains on the small window, he saw two men ride up to the house.

'Bushrangers.'

He finished dressing quickly, throwing his red coat on in a rush as he nervously surveyed the events through the window. One of the men dismounted in a leap and kissed Indy's mother on both cheeks as she went out to meet them. So not a danger then, Will surmised and slowed his movement.

'Jack!'

Will was astounded as the man he assumed was Jack, let go of Mary to catch Indy easily when she threw herself at him. Watching her wrap herself around another man was like a kick to Will's gut. Was Indy involved with this man? Could he be one of the lovers she had alluded to? He moved out to the living room and continued to listen from just inside the doorway.

'Hey kid,' Jack said lifting her off the ground with ease. 'Geez, what have you been eating?'

'Shut ya mouth,' Indy shot back laughingly as she extricated herself from his arms.

'No, it's good. I like it,' Jack said, his eyes scanning her body before his eyebrows did a saucy little dance. 'You're filling out in all the right places.'

Indy gave him a good-natured slap on the arm. 'I didn't see you again at the Subscription Ball.'

'I joined a game of cards,' Jack told her. 'Won the pot, and then unfortunately a gentleman complimented me on my suit and went on to tell me how he'd had one just like it before it was stolen, along with many of his other belongings, by a bushranger. I decided it was time to take my leave at that point.'

Indy chuckled but Mary shook her head in disappointment.

'Ladies, I have missed you. I was hoping—'

When Will stepped out of the house, Jack's revolver was in his hand quicker than lightning and pointed at Will's chest.

'Explain yourself, sir!' Jack demanded.

'No, Jack!' Indy exclaimed and put herself between Jack and Will.

'Why are you here?' Jack asked, pulling Indy out of the way to ensure the gun had good aim at Will. 'Taking liberties with these particular women will see you full of lead. I don't take kindly to soldiers forcing themselves on helpless females.'

'I could say the same about bushrangers,' Will insisted, keeping his eye on the gun aimed at him. 'And Indy is anything but helpless.'

'Thank you, Will,' Indy tossed back, slapping at Jack until he let her go.

'The Lieutenant has been convalescing here after an injury,' Mary added quickly, in hopes of diffusing the situation.

'In the line of duty?' Jack asked. 'One of those wily miners get one up on you for a change?'

'In a manner,' Will said, rubbing the side of his head where the rock had connected.

Jack seemed to relax a little, but the gun remained in his hand just the same. 'What part of England do you hail from?'

'Surrey, originally,' Will replied, thinking it an odd question given the circumstances.

'A fellow countryman,' Jack stated surprised. 'Though I doubt we moved in the same circles. I was but a lower-class citizen. Unable to buy a commission.'

'I did not buy my commission,' Will said. 'I earned it.'

'But you grew up in the large estates of Surrey, did you not?'

'I'm afraid not. I grew up under the strict tutelage of one Mr Gainbridge,' Will said, but offered no more explanation.

Jack blinked, seemingly stunned for a moment, before he lowered his weapon completely. 'The boys' workhouse at Effingham?'

Now it was Will's turn to be surprised. 'You know it?'

'I do. Only too well.'

Will frowned at first but then understood. 'When were you there?'

'Until I was a lad of fifteen,' Jack said. 'Before I was sold to go work at the pig yards for a shilling. But while I was being transported, I escaped and made my way to London. A year or so later I gained employment as a deckhand on a ship to the new colonies.'

Jack holstered his gun in the waist of his trousers and smiled, causing two dimples to wink out of his cheeks. The lad looked barely older than seventeen at that moment.

'So we are two from the same wretched upbringing. You chose the regimentals and I chose the more lucrative, but less revered, occupation of bushranging. Jack Fairweather at your service.' Jack bowed deeply then stood straight again looking at Will expectantly.

Indy gave a derisive laugh and jabbed Jack in the side. 'He hasn't heard of you. See, you're not so famous as you like to think.'

Jack scruffed Indy's hair and squeezed her body close to his as he dug his fingers into her ribs to tickle. Will's jaw tightened. Talk about taking liberties! And wasn't Indy just lapping it all up. He had a feeling her over-exuberance to see this man, and her exaggerated flirtation, was mostly for his benefit. She was trying to make him jealous.

And, blast her, it was working.

Jack was closer to her age than he was. Was it possible the two of them had a romantic history? A recent history even?

'Oh, give it a rest, you two,' Mary scolded them. 'Come inside and have some tea.'

'Thank you, Mary,' Jack answered and he, and the friend he introduced as Bobby, strode up onto the porch.

Will stepped aside as Jack and Bobby, who Will decided could be no more than sixteen years old, followed Mary and Indy into the house. It was crowded in the little living area with the barely-of-legal-age bushrangers sitting at the small wooden dining table. Will stood by, trying not to get in the way as Mary set about making tea and Indy put out some ginger biscuits.

'What brings you by, Jack?' Mary asked, setting the pot of tea aside to steep.

'I heard there was excitement afoot,' Jack told them. 'I thought I would ride through town and see for myself the smouldering ashes of what was once the Eureka Hotel.'

'What?' Indy and Will exclaimed crossing glances.

'The diggers burned the Eureka Hotel to the ground a few days ago,' Jack said. 'You hadn't heard?'

'It must have happened after we left,' Will said.

'You mean after you took a rock to the noggin',' Indy said. 'And I dragged your sorry arse back here.'

He rubbed at his 'noggin' again where the rock had rendered him unconscious. She'd obviously remembered she was angry with him and spoke as though she wished she'd hit him in the head herself. He struggled to think back. 'They were protesting the death of that Scobie fellow. They accuse Bentley and his friends of his murder.'

'That was the rumour, now believed to be fact,' Jack said, shovelling yet another ginger biscuit into his already full mouth.

'Rumour or truth, you don't burn a man's house, his livelihood,' Mary argued. 'Mob mentality.'

'Yes, madam,' Will agreed. 'It's how I got this lovely mark on my head and came to be in your care. I thank you for that care, but now I must be getting back to the government camp, find out what's going on.'

'Are you well enough?' Mary asked, pouring tea for them all.

'I have not had a dizzy spell in days. I should have returned to camp yesterday.'

Indy nodded curtly. 'I'm heading back to town too.'

'No, it may not be safe.'

'You have no say in it, Lieutenant,' Indy shot back, blue eyes blazing.

Frustrated, but knowing better than to argue, Will turned and headed into the bedroom to collect the last of his meagre belongings.

'It's not safe for you here, lads,' he heard Mary warn Jack and Bobby. 'There is much unrest in the goldfields.'

'Ma's right,' Indy tossed in. 'They're cracking down on highway thieves too. More soldiers escort the gold and even some of the passenger coaches carry guns.'

'And since when have I ever walked away from a good fight?' Jack said with a confident laugh.

Will returned to the living room. 'Mrs Wallace,' he said, taking her hand in his. 'I cannot thank you enough for your help and hospitality. I have to get back to my regiment. They'll surely think I've deserted by now.'

Indy just stood in the corner and scowled.

He kissed Mary's hand and headed for the door.

'Help him with the horse, Indy,' Mary told her.

'I'm fine, madam,' Will declined, noting Indy's sulky disposition. It wouldn't be a day ending in y if Indy weren't irritated with him about something, but he thought a little distance between them was warranted just now. 'I can manage alone. I do not wish to break up your tea party.'

'Nice to meet you, Will,' Jack said, and stood to shake the hand Will offered.

Will gave Indy one last look and walked out of the house.

***

Indy stood in the kitchen for all of about thirty seconds before she lost the battle with herself.

'I'll be right back,' she murmured and rushed out the door to the stables.

Will was saddling his horse as she entered the small open-sided shed and he turned at her arrival.

'So you're leaving just like that?' Her disappointment lent a bitterness to her voice she wished she'd been able to hide. She hated sounding so desperate, but she couldn't help it. Despite their argument the night before, not knowing when she would see him again was the worst kind of torment.

'I had to go back eventually, Indy,' he told her. 'What would you have me do? Stay here and play house for the rest of my days? I have a job to do.'

'Yes, harassing miners.'

He gave her an exasperated look, but didn't take the bait, as he secured his horse's bridle. 'I'm thinking of your reputation, Indy, your safety. I am a soldier, the enemy in the eyes of over a thousand miners. They would be incensed to find out you're cohort with a soldier. They can't do much to me, but they will take it out on you. Can you trust this bushranger fellow and his friend not to spread gossip that I was here? That you aided me?'

'Yes, I can trust Jack. And you and I are not cohorts,' Indy argued, but she knew he was right. If the diggers knew she was even friends with a soldier, they would be furious.

'Will you be alright here with those two gentlemen?'

'Safer than I was having you here.'

'I didn't mean—'

'Jack is a friend. He would never hurt us.'

'Is he your lover?'

Indy blinked, so taken aback by his question that she found herself speechless for once.

Will shook his head, 'Forgive me. That was out of line. Forgive me.'

He turned and mounted his horse in one quick movement.

Wanting the connection one last time, her hand touched his boot in the stirrup. 'He is not my lover.'

He reached down to run a hand lightly across her cheek. The look in his eye as his hand caressed her skin gave her hope. Sitting upright again, he clicked to his horse to move off.

'Will!' she called after him. He twisted in the saddle to look back at her.

'You can fight it all you like, but I know you want me as I want you.' She saw his jaw tighten but he said nothing.

'One day,' she called. 'You will kiss me one day! You can't be a gentleman forever!'

And with that she watched him kick his horse into a trot and disappear into the stringybark forest.

Chapter 14

'Well, look who it is.'

Striding quickly across the government compound, Will looked up to see George shading his eyes from the harsh sun.

'I'd given you up for dead,' George continued as the two friends clasped hands in greeting. 'I couldn't find you after the fire at the hotel. The place was bedlam.'

'So it's true then? About the fire at the Eureka Hotel?'

'It is,' George confirmed. 'Once it was ignited the hot winds fanned it into a firestorm. We could see it from here. The police arrested several men for starting the fire.'

'Is that what those men are doing in the jail corral?' Will queried, looking across to where the crudely constructed prison held three men.

'Yes. Although how they determined who actually started the blaze in that riot, I will never know.'

'I don't think they care,' Will mumbled. 'As long as someone is seen to be held accountable.'

He could see Commissioner Rede and Police Inspector Evans in the doorway of the Commissioner's Office, arguing as usual. Playing a blame game of their own, no doubt. Rede would be accusing Evans of not doing enough to ensure his men protected the hotel from the raiding miners, and Evans would be condemning Rede for not having read the riot act. The two men could rarely see eye to eye on the running of things in Ballarat.

'I didn't know about the fire at the Eureka Hotel until today,' he said. 'The last I saw of it, the crowd were throwing eggs and then rocks at the windows. And then at us.'

He turned back to face George, lifting the hair from his forehead to show the small scar and bruise where the rock had hit him.

'You were struck?' George moved in for a better look. 'Have you been unconscious all this time? You should see the doctor.'

'No, I...' Will stopped. He wondered how much he should tell his friend about Indy and her mother. 'I had help from some local folk out in the bush.'

'Local folk?' George questioned.

Will could feel his face reddening as George stared at him. But then George smiled.

'Oh,' he stretched out the word. 'A local lady perhaps?'

'Two actually,' Will said before he could stop himself.

George's thick eyebrows shot up into his even thicker hair. 'You've been holding out on me, old friend.'

'No, I have not. I've met the girl before—on numerous occasions as it happens—as have you.'

George looked perplexed. 'I've met her?'

Will saw the moment realisation dawned on his friend.

'The digger girl? The girl you thought a child?'

Will groaned and ducking his head, he stepped inside the tent they shared. He sat down heavily on his bed. 'I'd thought her a child until I caught her bathing naked in the river.'

George took a seat across from him, his face a picture of surprised amusement. 'You saw her bathing?'

'Yes.'

'Bathing in the river?'

'Yes.'

'Bathing naked in the river?' George repeated.

'Yes! Good God man, did I stutter?' Will asked, irritated at his friend's rapid-fire questioning. 'I caught her bathing naked in the river.'

It was suddenly stifling inside the tent and Will stood and walked out again. But George followed hotly on his heels.

'What manner of girl is this?'

'I wish I knew,' Will admitted. And it disturbed him no end. 'I can't sort her out. Like I said, I'd thought her a child.'

'And now?'

Will thought back over the last few days he had spent with Indy: her obvious flirtations and her very un-childlike sensuality. Not to mention the image of her beautiful body glistening wet and naked in the river that played before his eyes repeatedly.

'She is most definitely not a child,' Will said, pinching the bridge of his nose as a headache began to set in. 'She is a woman. A very attractive, very alluring, very ... infuriating and confounding woman.'

'Show me a woman who is not infuriating and confounding,' George said with a snort before he grinned.

Will stared about the compound. The number of soldiers seemed to have doubled again since his little sojourn into the country.

'So what happened?'

Will gave George a bewildered look. 'What happened when?'

'Did you bed her?'

'What? No!' Will denied vehemently, catching up with the conversation again.

'You're losing your touch, Will Marsh,' George teased. 'Three days with a beautiful woman who likes to bathe naked in rivers and you weren't able to get her on her back.'

'We were at her mother's house.'

'Oh,' George said screwing up his nose. 'Well. That is a setback.'

'No,' Will said, shaking his head to clear his erratic thoughts. 'The girl,

Indy, she is a willing party, believe me. It was I who stepped away.'

George just stared at Will, his brow furrowed. 'I really think you should see the doctor. I believe that knock on the head may have dislodged something.'

Will couldn't argue. He hardly recognised himself since he'd met Indy. She knew how to mess with his head, and his body. The girl was trouble. Ask anyone in Ballarat and they could tell you a story to prove it. He just didn't know whether he wanted her to be his trouble or not. He'd rejected her advances, and it had seemed like the right thing to do at the time. So why did he feel as though he was the one who'd been rejected? His thoughts were jumbled when it came to her, and he didn't like that one bit. And all he really knew was that, dammit, he missed her already.

***

Over the next few days Will stayed close to the compound. As another unit of the Twelfth regiment had arrived from Melbourne, the police were kicked out of their tents and relegated to the horses' stables in favour of the soldiers, the horses having been moved out to hitching posts and fences. The police were not happy about the slight and fights broke out regularly between soldiers and the traps.

Since the attack on the Eureka Hotel, all government camp residents had been warned not to travel into town alone. The entire compound was unsettled by the fearmongering that miners would try to liberate the three men arrested for the Eureka Hotel fire. The women in the government camp were sent away to Melbourne or Geelong to wait out the trouble with family or friends. Police were being harassed in the streets and soldiers spat on. More meetings were being held on Bakery Hill and attended by thousands of miners. Democracy they called it. But more often than not the meetings ended up with the miners drinking to excess and becoming belligerent and violent. Regardless, when Will spotted one of the latest notices posted on boards about town, requesting the government camp sort out its own issues before Ballarat and the goldfields could be expected to do the same, he had to admit they had a point. It wasn't an accusation without cause.

In the dark of night, Will lay in the tent he shared with both George and Timmons. He stared out the jagged tear in the canvas that framed perfectly the bright five-star formation in the night sky. A deckhand had pointed it out to him on his voyage to Australia from Calcutta. It was a constellation seen most prominently in the southern hemisphere, hence the name, the Southern Cross. He'd marvelled at the Aurora Borealis in the north of Scotland and had been amazed by the assorted exotic animals during his time in India. The elephants in particular had captured his imagination. But there was something about this small grouping of stars, in this distant country, that had him looking wistfully to the heavens when the night was clear. On nights like these, he would happily sleep out of doors, the only canvas above his head dark blue and bespeckled with diamonds. He was surprised to find he was coming to love this new colony.

A snore from Timmons—at least he hoped it was a snore—cut into his peaceful thoughts. It was close quarters, for certain, but he had most definitely lived in worse hovels than this. Compared with the other soldiers though, they were the lucky ones. There were only three in their tent where many had four or five men sleeping in any formation possible. Top and tailing with another man was not his idea of romance.

Romance.

He thought of Indy and his eyes cast up to the navy sky again. Was she back in the Eureka camp? Looking up at the Southern Cross just as he was? Or was she still at her mother's? Sleeping in her bed. The bed he had slept in for the few days he was there. Was that beautiful body lying naked now against sheets he'd been naked in?

Becoming aroused at his wayward thoughts, he quickly turned his concentration back to Timmons's bodily noises. Sleeping in close quarters with men was no time to be dreaming of the supple breasts and silky skin of a certain feisty, smart-mouthed, sexually alluring woman. He was no teenaged boy with raging hormones that he couldn't control. He was an adult. A soldier. Able to quash his basic desires and deport himself like the disciplined military man that he was. He'd proved as much in his decision to push her away. What good could come of starting a courtship? She'd been furious with him for denying her, and yet, as he'd left her at the house, she'd tossed out a challenge.

'You will kiss me one day,' she'd called after him.

The grin split his face before he could stop it. What a terror she was. What a wholly uncouth, unladylike, brat. Absolutely not the type of woman he had imagined himself being drawn to. But oh, how she appealed to him, unlike any other woman of his acquaintance in his life. Her physical attractions were obvious to any man with a pulse, but he found he also enjoyed her company and her conversation. With her sharp intellect and biting verbal jousting, she was fun to be around and a match to any man's wit. She had strength and integrity in spades, and he couldn't help but admire her even as she drove him crazy. He would miss their debates should he be required to stay away from her. Perhaps they could just be friends.

It had been less than two days since he'd seen her.

Two days.

And he was in agony.

He rolled over in his cot and begged for sleep to release him from his torment.

***

Indy had returned from her mother's house the same afternoon that Will had left the cottage. She'd had to see for herself the devastation of the fire at the Eureka Hotel. For a good twenty minutes she'd stood in front of it, astounded that something so grand had been reduced to blackened ruins so quickly, and without remorse.

'Was a windstorm came through. She went up like a barrel of gunpowder,' old Alistair McTavish told her as she'd stood there staring. ''Twas nothing could be done.'

'Was anyone injured?' she asked, thinking of Will.

'A few miners were burned as they tried to loot from the Bentleys',' he said, puffing out smoke from his pipe. 'Drunken fools were lucky they came out alive.'

Back in her campsite with Sean and Annie, she listened to Sean tell the whole story again and he filled in some of the gaps left by Jack's rather stilted version. She in turn told them the story of Will's injuries and his stay at the cottage. Of course, she didn't tell them everything about his stay at the cottage.

'And he's back at camp now, is he?' Annie asked, handing Indy a bowl of rice she'd cooked to go with the vegetables Indy had carried back from her mother's garden.

'I believe so,' Indy said, sulking a little. She was still annoyed with him. He had tried to make her believe he was indifferent, but she knew when a man wanted her.

She slept fitfully that first night. The sounds of camp were loud but her thoughts were louder. He was but a few miles up the road at the government camp, but felt a world away. She finally fell asleep, engineering ways of accidentally bumping into him.

Chapter 15

The blasted cradle was jammed again. Indy knelt beside it and did her best to shunt the caked on mud from the cleats. With so much clay wedged between the gaps nothing could be washed through.

She used an old boot brush to dislodge the hardened debris while Sean stood by popping lollies into his mouth one by one.

'Want to give me a hand?' she snapped at him.

'You said you had it sorted,' Sean argued through a mouthful of sweets. 'Independence is a double-edged sword, missy.'

She squinted up at his tall frame where he blocked the afternoon sun. 'Lord, don't you sound like your mother.'

'Do not,' he said offended.

'Do too.'

'Do not.'

Indy chuckled and got back to work. She picked up the bucket of water and ran it across the apron of the cradle to clean it.

'Right,' she said standing up again and stretching her back. 'That should do it.'

'Well looky, looky here,' Sean said, as she tested the rocking of the cradle. 'The man's got giant potatoes for balls, I'll give him that.'

'What in the name of sweet Jesus are you on about?' Indy asked. Sean picked up his shovel one handed and pointed it.

Following the direction of the shovel, she spotted Will walking through the diggings. Alone. And in uniform. He did indeed have giant potatoes. Or perhaps the knock to his head was still clouding his judgement.

'Better not let your ma hear you talking like that, Sean,' Indy reprimanded with a smile. 'Balls indeed.'

'Do I look like I have a death wish? Unlike this one who comes a calling.'

Indy swallowed hard at the sight of Will as he moved closer. It had been a mere four days since she'd seen him last. And what a miserable four days it had been. Her pride had suffered most when he'd denied her. But as the days dragged by, pride gave way to another feeling. A feeling of loss and hurt she didn't quite understand. She'd been maudlin, she knew, and had snapped often at Annie and Sean who had not deserved it.

And now, one look at the man who walked towards her, tall and distinguished and roguishly handsome and her heart was fluttering like a traitor.

'Shall I leave you two alone to smooch?' Sean teased Indy with an elbow to her ribs.

'Why don't you shove some more of those boiled sweets in your mouth. Maybe when you don't have any teeth left you won't talk as much,' Indy said just as Will joined them.

'Good afternoon, Miss Indy, Sean.'

'Good day to you, Lieutenant,' Sean said in greeting and offered him a boiled sweet from his paper bag.

'Oh, thank you,' Will said taking one. 'These are my favourite.'

'Are you mad?'

Will sucked on his lolly and gave Indy a confused look. 'Because I like sweets?'

'You walk into the goldfields as though you wore King Arthur's armour,' Indy said incredulously. 'There are at least half a dozen men here who would kill you before they even asked your name. Not to mention the bad position you put me and Sean in just by speaking with us.'

'Would you like me to arrest you so you can protect your reputation?' Will's tone heated to match hers.

Indy took a deep breath. Sweet Moses. They'd been two minutes in each other's company and they were fighting again already. Giving Sean a look that he should disappear for a moment, he took the hint and gladly stepped away. Although ensuring he was out of listening range, Indy saw him stop where he could still see her.

'I didn't expect to see you again so soon.' Indy was proud of how calm her voice sounded, but her heart was dancing a reel of its own beneath her blue mining shirt.

He looked good. As usual. She shoved her hands into the pockets of her corduroy pants to stop herself from touching him. 'I wasn't sure I would ever see you again after you left the house in such a rush.'

His expression showed genuine remorse. 'Would you please convey my apologies to your mother when you see her next? I fear I left the cottage on awkward terms. You gave me a lot to think about.'

Her eyes flew to his. He'd been thinking? Thinking about what? Did she dare to hope?

He took a step forward. 'Indy I—'

A loud groan, followed by a crack, interrupted Will and had both of them turning to look back across the goldfields. They watched in horror as above a nearby mineshaft the wooden barrel of the windlass snapped in half, and the rest of the A-frame and winch crumbled in on itself. The large pieces of broken off timber plummeted into the shaft beneath. The yells of panic and pain that rang out from the hole had Indy and Will rushing towards the collapsing mine. The timber that had fallen into the mine had dislodged other pieces of lumber used to shore up the shaft.

The first to reach the mine, they found the miner desperately trying to climb out and he had almost made it to the top when the loosened dirt began to fold in on him, trapping his legs. Will fell to the ground on his stomach and extended his arm to give the man his hand. The miner was able to grab it and dangled heavily in mid-air for a moment until the earth caved in and acted like quicksand, trying to pull the man back down into the dark hole. No matter how hard Will tried to pull the man up, the deeper his legs were buried. He was losing his grip.

'Get a rope!' Will yelled, grappling to hold on to the sinking man's hand.

Indy pulled away some of the loosened rope from the damaged windlass and handed it to Will. He tossed one end of the rope down to the man.

'Loop it around your back and under your arms!' Will called.

'I can't!' the man yelled back. 'If I let go of you, I'll sink. Help me!'

'I'll have to go down,' Will told Indy.

Fear clutched at her chest. 'You can't. You'll be crushed too.'

Will looked around, and spotting two strong-looking men he called them closer. They came but with suspicion in their eyes.

'Tie the rope around my legs and lower me down,' he told them. 'I can get this loop around the man and then you can pull us both back up. Understand?'

'Let me do it,' Indy insisted. 'I'm smaller and lighter.'

'Never in a million years,' Will said in a tone that brooked no argument.

But Indy being Indy she argued anyway.

'Lieutenant—'

'Indy, please, we don't have time to have another of our legendary quarrels right now.' He turned back to the man in the mineshaft. 'What's your name?'

'Trevor!' he called back.

'Trevor, I'm coming down. Don't let go of my hand.'

With the rope tied firmly around his ankles, Will was lowered carefully into the shaft head first.

Another groan from the remaining wood had Indy's heart pounding in her chest, as she watched Will drop lower into the hole. More soil loosened and collapsed from the side of the mine and fell on Will's head. Trevor was now buried to his waist and he shook his head to remove the dirt that covered his face. Indy shimmied closer to try and see in but the edges were now unsteady as well. Many other miners had moved in to watch and help, but they had to retreat back as the edge of the shaft began to give way. What if the rest caved in and buried both men?

Pushing all the horrible scenarios aside, Indy moved in beside Sean and another man and grabbed the rope, preparing to winch Will and Trevor back out. She wouldn't stand idly by and watch while others did the work. She heard Will's call, and the group pulled back carefully while he held onto the rope now attached around Trevor's underarms.

Will came out easily but Trevor was a little tougher since his legs were well caked into the packed dirt. Finally, with one last slow tug, Trevor popped like a cork from his would-be grave, and Will and the other miners were able to drag the man up the side of the shaft. Like a landed fish, Trevor fell to the ground beside Will. A resounding cheer went up.

The man received pats on the back when he pushed himself into a seated position beside Will, both men fighting to catch their breath. A few men even shook Will's hand and it made Indy smile.

'Get them some water!' she called out and knelt beside him, dusting the dirt from his face and hair with her kerchief. 'How did you know how to do that?'

'We had to pull the pig out of the mud at the workhouse on a regular basis,' Will said, puffing from his exertions. 'You soon find out how to not get yourself muddy.'

She knew he was making light of a situation, which could have ended badly for both himself and Trevor. She didn't want to think about how that had made her feel—the panic that had all but debilitated her.

A woman came running towards them and threw herself onto Trevor, weeping. Indy knew exactly how she felt, and had to bite her own lip to stop the wave of unexpected emotion that came over her, as she took in Will's dirty but uninjured appearance.

'Come now, woman, get a hold of yerself,' Trevor reprimanded. But Indy could see the relief in his face as she kissed him. 'Don't be getting all soppy on me. I'm fine.'

There was some blood, but mostly just superficial cuts and scrapes from what Indy could see. He'd been lucky the falling windlass had missed him, or things may have been considerably worse. The rope burns on Trevor's hands were soothed easily by the water, when it arrived.

The woman turned and reached over to kiss Will's cheeks too.

'Thank you, sir, thank you.'

'Dry your tears, madam, your husband is fine,' Will said with a reassuring smile and handed her back to Trevor.

'He's not my husband,' she said, gripping her man for dear life. 'Not yet. We'll be married come Sunday.'

'Congratulations,' Will said taking the pannikin of water someone handed him. He washed the dirt from his face and mouth before he drank thirstily.

'You must come, sir,' she said. 'And help us celebrate.'

Indy could see the hesitancy in Will's expression.

'I'm not sure that's a good idea,' he said and looked to the husband-to-be.

Both men scanned the diggings and the untrusting glowers of the collected miners.

'I am still persona non-grata in my red uniform, no matter how filthy its current state,' Will added quietly, dusting himself off.

'Please, sir, I owe you my life,' Trevor added. He drank a mouthful of water before also using the water to wash his filthy face. 'The least Eliza and I can do is give you a drink and a slice of mutton or two. We don't have a lot but what we do have, we'd like to share it with you. Indy here is coming along, so you will be protected from the rabble.'

Indy bit back a chuckle.

'Well, if Miss Wallace will be there to protect me, how can I say no?'

He shook Trevor's hand in agreement.

'Lord bless ya,' Eliza said and leaned over to kiss Will's cheek again.

Indy watched him blush. It was such a cute trait he had. He didn't take thanks or compliments well. But she imagined he'd grown up without ever having been thanked or complimented, so it wasn't surprising he didn't know how to take either graciously.

Trevor's mates and wife-to-be, Eliza, helped him back to camp where he would rest up for a few hours. No one had any doubt he'd be back digging out and shoring up his poor collapsed mine before the end of the day.

When the noise had died down and the sightseers had seen enough, Will and Indy were left alone. She put out a hand to help him up and after looking at it a moment, he took it.

'Do you mind?' he asked, still holding onto her hand.

'Do I mind what?'

'My invitation to the wedding.'

'Of course not. You earned it. Don't worry, I won't make you dance or anything.'

'We've danced before,' Will reminded her. His thumb moved rhythmically back and forth across her fingers causing her tummy to flutter each time. 'If I recall, you complimented me on my dancing.'

She bit back her smile. 'Then I shall look forward to the first reel with you, sir.'

He smiled and let go of her hand.

As they began to walk back to her mine, she remembered he had started to say something to her before the mine had collapsed.

'Was there a reason you came by the diggings today?'

'I just wanted to see how you are,' he said with a light shrug, his eyes on the ground. 'I promised your mother I would check in on you from time to time. To see how you are.' He must have realised he had repeated himself, and she was delighted when she saw the red creep into his cheeks again.

She stopped walking and stared at him until he finally lifted his eyes to hers.

'And how am I, Lieutenant?'

He looked at her as though he were committing every inch of her to memory. She felt the depth of it in the heating of her blood. Then he smiled wistfully and shook his head.

'You look wonderful.' He let out a frustrated groan. 'And you'll be the death of me, Miss Indy.'

'Then I trust it shall be a good death, sir,' she said and then chuckled. Feminine wiles were not her thing. She just couldn't do it without giggling. 'It's good to see you also, Will.'

They were interrupted by a loud group of men heading their way, calling out to diggers and mates as they passed.

'What's happening?' Indy asked as they barged past, more than one of them giving Will a shove or an elbow, until Indy pulled him behind her.

'I won't hide behind your skirts, Indy.'

'I'm wearing trousers and shut up,' she told him before calling out to an

Italian digger she knew. 'Carboni! What's happening?'

'We're meeting to discuss bailing out McIntyre and Fletcher,' the Italian called back and kept moving.

'McIntyre and Fletcher?' Will asked.

'The men arrested for the fire at the Eureka Hotel,' Indy told him. The diggers who passed continued to give Will a suspicious glance as they followed the others up towards Bakery Hill.

'You should leave,' she said. 'It's not safe for you here.'

'It's not safe for *you* here.'

'I'm fine. I keep my head down. I don't get involved in all that male posturing. I'm not the troublemaker you seem to think I am.'

'Really?' Will mocked. 'And how many times had you been tossed out of the Eureka Hotel before they burned it down.'

'One of those times was by you, if I remember rightly,' she said, jabbing at his chest with her index finger. 'Now get out of here before you end up face first down a mineshaft. And they use the old ones as latrines, did you know that? Full of piss and shit. You want to be face down in that?'

Will laughed uproariously as they reached Indy's mine site. He turned to face her.

'Well, then I will be going. But do me a favour?'

'Depends,' she said, narrowing her eyes.

He smiled. 'Have a care, my lady.'

And with that he bowed lightly and walked away.

God, she loved it when he bowed like that. She loved it when he walked away from her. She could see the tightness of his uniform trousers around his arse. Her stomach clutched at the sight of him in retreat. Well, he could retreat all he liked. She was going to kiss him and kiss him soon. She had to. She was near to bursting with all this ... this ... stuff inside her. Then she'd get over this ridiculous fascination with him and life would go back to normal.

Chapter 16

He wasn't going to come. The wedding was already in progress and she hadn't seen hide nor hair of him. The minute she'd arrived with Sean and Annie, Indy had been on the lookout for Will. It was a large crowd that had gathered near the Irish settlement for the ceremony, and she'd left Annie and Sean to move about the guests in hope of finding him. But there was no red coat to be seen.

As the wedding progressed she stopped searching, told herself not to be such a silly woman and tried to concentrate on the ceremony. It had been ridiculous to think he, a soldier, would come to the goldfields where he was most definitely not welcome by ninety-eight percent of the population. And for what? A simple wedding? He'd made himself perfectly clear at her mother's house that he did not wish to be with her. But then he had come to see her at her mine. To see how she was, he'd said. Her brain was a muddle.

She sighed as she watched Trevor and Eliza smiling dreamily at one another. Eliza was lovely in her plain taffeta gown. The bodice was overlaid with lace and the full skirt unadorned, but Indy imagined that even this simple dress would have cost plenty. A halo, made of a selection of native orchids, matched the little posy she held. Indy thought Trevor's face might just split in half if he smiled any harder. His brown suit was not new, but it looked clean, which was no mean feat here in the dustbowl of the goldfields. It was not a society wedding, that was for certain, but the bride and groom radiated happiness and Indy found herself feeling a little twinge of envy.

She shook herself out of her reverie. Marriage was not on her list of things to accomplish in life, so the envy was misplaced.

After another long sermon about the virtues of marriage, Father Smythe proceeded to the vows, and that's when she spotted him. Will stepped out from behind a woman who wore a large, wide-brimmed bonnet, and Indy's breath caught. He was resplendent in his dress uniform. The brass buttons on his red coat gleamed in the afternoon sun. His trousers looked as though they had come direct from the tailor, their creases pressed to perfection. She'd never seen a man look so handsome as to steal her breath. When his eyes met hers, he winked. Her cheeks warmed, her heartbeat fluttered wildly in her chest and she knew she was in trouble.

'I now pronounce you man and wife.' The priest's voice broke through her daydream.

Loud cheers went up all around her, as Eliza and Trevor kissed with much fervour. She grinned and clapped along, while people moved in to congratulate the happy couple, before they all headed across to the open field where a reception feast had been prepared.

'Miss Indy.'

She started at the sound of his voice behind her, and her heart leapt again, not from fright but from joy.

'Lieutenant,' she said breathlessly, feeling shy all of a sudden. She didn't turn around for fear her face would give away emotions she had not yet come to terms with.

'You look lovely today,' he said, his warm breath touching her ear, sending delicious tingles along her skin, down her body, all the way to her fingertips and toes.

She'd made an effort. More of an effort than she usually did for the continuous stream of weddings that seemed to have overtaken the goldfields in the last three years. She'd been to more weddings than she could recall, and they'd become much of a muchness over time.

'And what a pretty dress,' he continued, as he stepped into her eye line. 'I like the colour. Indigo. Just like you.'

She knew she should say something, but all she could do was blush like a ninny, feeling foolish all of a sudden for the effort she had taken to look feminine for once.

He leaned in closer to her side and whispered conspiratorially, 'Don't worry, I won't tell anyone you're actually a girl.'

That did it. She elbowed him in the ribs, and he laughed. He'd known exactly what to say to get her to relax. He held out his arm and she finally looked up and into his face. His beautiful face.

'Come, Miss Indy, let us join the party, shall we?'

Knowing, without doubt now, that she was completely besotted, she hooked her arm through his and he escorted her to the wedding banquet.

***

Two long planks of flat wood had been joined together to make a wedding table, and guests sat around it on a selection of chairs, tree stumps and wooden crates. Even a wheelbarrow served as a seat for a rather tall miner nicknamed Shorty.

The table was filled with platters of food that had been brought by the guests in lieu of gifts. Damper, sweet apple tarts, pickles of all varieties were spread before them, along with the now shredded parts of the whole lamb which had been roasting on a rotating spit above a campfire. The aroma had Will's stomach rumbling loudly. The bride and groom sat close together in front of plates piled high with food. But neither seemed that interested in eating, Will noted, as they stared into one another's eyes.

'The lamb no doubt cost a pretty penny,' Will said, hoping to waylay the looks of carnal lust in the bride and groom's eyes. He was beginning to feel singed from mere proximity to the heat they radiated.

'I know a man,' Trevor said with a wink when Will questioned him on how he had acquired it.

Will opened his canvas carry bag that sat beneath his chair and pulled out a bottle of good brandy, handing it to the groom. 'A wedding gift.'

'Thank you, sir,' Trevor said and stood to shake Will's hand heartily.

'Share it later in good health. Away from this drunken rabble.'

Will turned to Indy to find her staring at him, one eyebrow raised questioningly.

'What?' he asked, confused by her expression. 'Why do you look at me that way?'

'Expensive brandy? A little pricey for a soldier's wages, wouldn't you say.'

Will shrugged a shoulder. 'I know a man,' he repeated Trevor's words.

Indy continued to stare at him until he gave in and explained. 'I may have appropriated it from the latest supply wagon. Those thieves on the road from Melbourne are notoriously sneaky.'

'Sneaky indeed.'

'The Commissioner had box loads of the stuff. He'll not miss one bottle,' Will said, glancing back to where Trevor and his bride were hiding the bottle away beneath the table.

'As I live and breathe.' Indy stared agape at him. 'Lieutenant Marsh, the most honest of all the men I know, pilfering from his own superior officer. Going back to the old ways?'

Will felt a niggle of discomfort at being reminded of his misspent youth, but he smiled and dug his fingers into her ribs, 'I blame your influence.'

'I don't steal, Lieutenant.'

He gave her a look of disbelief.

'No more than absolutely necessary,' she added and Will chuckled richly.

They began the feast and Will enjoyed the change in food. It was a thrill to his tastebuds after months of army rations.

'How did the two of you meet?' he asked Trevor and Eliza. 'Did you know each other in Ireland?'

'No,' Eliza said taking a delicate sip of champagne. They'd managed to rustle up one bottle for the wedding. 'Trevor came over with his ma and brother from County Clare. In fifty-one was it, Trevor?'

'Fifty-two,' Trevor corrected through a mouthful of food. 'My brother died on board the ship before we reached Melbourne. Caught the fever and just never recovered.'

'I'm sorry,' Will said, as he was about to take a bite of delicious lamb.

Trevor shrugged it off. 'It's the way of things on a long journey, I suppose. My mother only lasted here a year longer. She came down with influenza in the winter of fifty-three. Complete bastard of a winter, was that one. She's buried up there in the cemetery. Along with hundreds of other poor souls who've lost their lives in this stinking arse-end of the world.'

'Anyway,' Eliza said, bringing the subject back around to Will's question about how they'd met. 'I came in on the boat in October of fifty-three. A few months after his mother passed over, God rest her.'

'And I was down at the docks to find me a wife,' Trevor said, puffing himself with pride. 'There I stood in me Sunday best, along with hundreds of other poor buggers, looking to catch a bride. She didn't have to be pretty. She just had to take care of me, like my ma used to. I needed a cook, someone to do me wash, and darn me breeches and socks when they became holey. Instead, I see this vision of loveliness in a pale pink dress stepping down off the gangplank. I was sunk like the merchant *Madagascar* in August.'

'Interesting analogy,' Will put in. 'They still haven't found that ship.'

Eliza giggled. 'He was carrying a posy of carnations. Oh, he was handsome alright, but so were many of the other gentlemen waiting by the docks.'

'Hey now!' Trevor objected.

'But I was no fool,' Eliza said, a shrewd glint in her eye. 'I'd heard the rumours of men looking for wives, just so they had someone to do their cleaning and cooking, and to give them their wants in the bedroom after dark. I wasn't about to become some man's whore or whipping girl.'

'Atta girl,' Indy tossed in.

'I offered to escort her and her cousins to Ballarat,' Trevor continued where Eliza left off, and Will marvelled at the perfect synchronisation of their storytelling. 'And once she'd settled in, I set about courting Miss Eliza. I asked her to marry me after that first week, but she refused. And she continued to refuse me for nigh on nine months.'

'Nine months!?' Indy exclaimed. 'Eliza, you tease.'

Eliza giggled. 'Ah sure. But by then I knew he loved me. I'd made him fall in love with me, and in doing so, I fell in love with him too.'

Trevor and Eliza kissed slowly, sensually. Will felt the need to avert his eyes, an unwelcome voyeur in their moment of intimacy. But when he crossed glances with Indy, seeing the hooded gaze, the heat in her eyes as she watched the two lovers kiss, was like a punch of lust directly to his groin.

'I asked her to marry me—again,' Trevor said, bringing Will back to the conversation. 'And finally she said yes. Do you know what it is to wait for a woman for nine months, Lieutenant?'

'Uh, no,' Will answered and dared another glance at Indy. 'But I can imagine.'

He didn't want to imagine it. The agony of having to wait nine months for Indy wasn't a thought he should be entertaining. They were not compatible, as Eliza and Trevor so obviously were.

'You're a hard-won woman, Miss Eliza.'

'To be sure she's been harder on me since,' Trevor said, his deep and booming laugh one of true contented happiness. 'It's a tough life we've made for ourselves here, Lieutenant, and it gets tougher by the day.'

'Please, call me Will,' he told Trevor and the man nodded and tipped more whiskey into Will's pannikin before he could stop him. 'Forgive me for asking but why do you stay in Ballarat if it's the—what did you call it?'

'Arse-end of the world,' Indy offered, taking a bite of lamb off the bone. She had the meat in her hands and was gnawing on it. Will could only marvel at her unladylike table manners, but the meat was so good he could see himself doing the same thing to ensure he got every morsel.

'I stay because I got the fever too,' Trevor said sighing heavily.

'Are you ill, man?' Will asked concerned.

Trevor leaned forward as though he had a deep dark secret. 'I got the gold fever!'

He slapped his thigh and laughed raucously, his mates joining in.

Rolling her eyes, Eliza stood from the table. 'Now, Mr Hennessy, you'll dance with me if you know what's good for you.'

'Sure, I know what's good for me,' Trevor said. Standing from the table, he took his wife's hand and led her away to the small clearing nearby. 'Strike up the band!'

And with that, the little troop of musicians, made up of two bodhran drums, a guitar, a banjo and a fiddle, began a polka.

No slow romantic waltz for the Irish, Will thought with a grin, as Trevor took his wife in a strong hold and they proceeded to trample the dry grass beneath their feet.

Will turned to Indy. 'Come, milady. I believe I owe you the first dance.'

'Are you sure?' she asked, her expression a picture of mock horror. 'You saw what I did to poor Mr Lawrence's feet at the ball.'

'You did not step on my feet at the ball,' Will pointed out.

'Yes, but that was a slow dance,' Indy said, suddenly looking shy and unsure of herself.

Leaning closer he stared deeply into her eyes. 'I am willing to risk it, Indy. Are you?'

It was a rare thing to see the strong, independent Indigo Wallace lost for words, and he was enjoying having the upper hand with her for once.

'Yes.' Her reply was a quiet squeak and she cleared her throat. 'Yes, I'm willing.'

Standing, he took her elbow and lightly lifted her from her seat, directing her out to join the flock of dancers.

He enjoyed seeing Indy in movement. Yes, he had danced with her at the ball but she had been in his arms. Now, in this lively dance, he could admire her in motion from a distance as she moved from partner to partner. She could be surprisingly graceful considering she was like a bull in a china shop a good portion of the time.

Mesmerised, he followed her movements in and out of the circle of dancers, lifting her skirts so as not to trip. And her smile when she looked at him, filled him with a euphoria so heady, he lost his breath through more than just the exuberance of the dancing. He'd thought she was a pretty girl, but when she smiled like that, just for him, it was like the sun coming out. Seeing her naked in the river that day had proved to him she was indeed a woman in body, but her actions since had proved her a woman in mind and spirit as well.

Dammit, he never should have thought of the river again. He'd done his best to put the vision of her perfect naked body out of his head. But on lonely nights in his tent at the government camp, her image came to him and kept him warm. Warm? The thought of her sweet, pale breasts had his body nearly setting fire to the sheets.

Shaking his head to clear the image, he watched her dancing and laughing with such joy. The indigo dress she wore was dusty at the hem, her straw bonnet long since discarded, and tendrils of blonde curls were already falling out of their pins. And watching her, he felt the fist tighten around his heart. His rough Indy; how she made him laugh. How she made him feel alive. Whether she was arguing with him, or looking at him with such unashamed want in her eyes. He enjoyed both sides of her. The prickly and the passionate. He had never had such a feeling before. A feeling he could find no words to describe. Could this be what it was like to be in love?

He stopped dancing, stopped smiling. *Love.*

The thought was so frightening to him, he walked away from the dancing and sat on a nearby log to catch his breath. Was the liquor befuddling his brain? It had to be the liquor, for him to be thinking himself in love? He'd stayed away from love deliberately, and had been helped along by the fact that he rarely remained in one place long enough to form attachments. The army had seen to that. The army was his life. He would not stay in Victoria forever. One day, not too far in the future, his regiment would receive new orders and he would be taken away from this land and on to another. Away from Indigo Wallace.

'Lieutenant, are you unfit to dance like the Irish?'

Indy was standing in front of him, smiling cheerfully and flushed from the dancing. The song had ended without him realising and the musicians had begun yet another spirited reel.

He tried to smile. 'I fear I am unfit.'

She laughed and sat herself down beside him on the log.

'Do they not make a lovely couple?' she asked. 'Are they not glowing with all the love between them?'

Will followed Indy's unusually dreamy gaze towards the happy couple. Trevor and Eliza sat alone at the huge table of food; not eating but kissing as though no one were watching.

'I suppose,' he said, still shocked at his own recent thoughts of love.

'You suppose?' Indy asked, fixing him with a mocking glare. 'Last of great romantics here, folks.'

Will stood up so suddenly, the imbalance nearly caused Indy to slide off the other side of the log.

'I must get back to camp,' he said, as she righted herself.

'But there's still cake to be had. You can't leave before cake,' Indy said, frowning at him. 'What's the matter, Will?'

Her frown deepened and he wondered what she read in his expression. But before he could speak or make a move to leave, the bride approached, seeming to have finally come up for air.

'May I have this dance, Lieutenant?'

He was trapped. How could he refuse the bride?

'Of course, madam. It would be my honour.' He bowed and offering his arm, he led her back to the dancing.

***

Bewildered, Indy gazed after him from her seat on the log. He'd been cheerful one moment and then become so sullen the next. She'd never understand the capricious moods of men.

The ladies liked him—that was evident. Caroline Chesser had been doing her very best to flirt with him all day. But then Caroline Chesser flirted with all men, married or not. Some of the men were less than thrilled to see a member of the regimentals amongst the wedding party, but most had heard the story of how Will had saved Trevor's life, and for that fact alone they kept their concerns to themselves and accepted him, at least for one day. But Indy could see others, outside of the

Irish settlement, looking in with disgust and disapproval. She couldn't blame them, but she also didn't believe a man should be judged by the company he kept. From what she had seen so far, Will Marsh was a decent man. He was more than a decent man. He was a good man.

She watched him dance with the bride, and then Annie. And when his eyes met hers across the dance floor of spring grasses and wildflowers, she felt that tug in her chest once again. She'd never felt anything so strong. It both thrilled and unnerved her. She'd had her fair share of male suitors. Since she and her mother had landed in Melbourne she had been made offers by men five, ten, even fifteen years older than herself. Her mother, thank God, had refused to let her go into a marriage until she turned eighteen. And when she had come of age, Indy had chosen instead to stay single and to take care of her mother.

She was at the table ravenously forking a piece of delicious wedding cake into her mouth, when Will finally found her again. The sun was beginning to set, casting a golden hue over the fields that turned the dull brown dirt into a blaze of reds and oranges. A cooling breeze set the tall grass in the nearby fields swaying in time to a slow tune only it could hear.

'It's been a wonderful day,' she said, smiling up at him contentedly.

He reached out and with a finger removed some leftover cream from the corner of her mouth, popping it into his own. She licked her lips, thinking the gesture incredibly intimate and seductive.

'I really must go now, Indy.'

She nodded slowly, resigned that he would have to leave her eventually. 'I'll walk you out.'

'No, you should stay here. It's not safe for a lady to be walking around after dusk.'

'Step one foot out of here alone and you'll be dead before your boots hit the road to the government camp.'

'They do like their guns, don't they,' Will said with a disapproving frown.

'Come along,' she said looping her arm through his. 'I'll protect you from the big, bad diggers.'

***

They walked through the rest of the Irish section of camp, the safest for him since he had saved a countryman. He even got a few head nods of gratitude from Trevor's mates on the way out to the main road.

Reaching the rear of the stables, where he had tethered his horse, it was significantly quieter. Only the occasional horse's snort or the stomp of a hoof could be heard.

'This is as far as you go,' Will said, turning to face her.

The warm glow of the setting sun cast a halo around her dishevelled blonde hair. An angel she wasn't. But right now, oh, how he wanted to kiss the devil out of her.

Instead, he dipped his head in farewell. 'Miss Indy. Thank you for a lovely day. I bid you goodnight.'

But before he could move, she looked up at him from beneath her long dark lashes. Her eyes were his undoing. Such wide, bright orbs of blue. He'd seen sunsets over oceans on his travels that had less lustre than Indigo

Wallace's eyes. She could be so soft when she wanted to be, and dangerously appealing with it. And the look on her face left no doubt that she wanted him to kiss her.

He knew it was a mistake, even as he took her face between his hands and lay his lips to hers. Softly, lightly, he let his tongue trace her full upper lip and thrilled at her gasp.

Fire ignited within him as he leaned away, leaving only a breath between them.

'Indy.' He groaned, part agony, part ecstasy.

'Yes?'

Her fingers splayed against his chest, grasping at his coat, giving him no chance to escape. Then her mouth captured his. She took control, and he was lost. Lost in the sensations of her warm mouth, her warm skin. Reaching up, he removed the last remaining hairpins, so that her hair fell in untamed curls. His hands followed their movement as they cascaded down her back to her waist. He urged her body closer to his, as her arms went up and around his neck. Electricity shot through his entire body at the touch of her fingers to his nape. His kisses became more impassioned and he knew he was losing the strength he needed to remain a gentleman.

A gunshot broke the air, and loud cheers floated out of the campsite. More boisterous wedding celebrations he assumed, but it was all the distraction he needed. He pulled back and her wide, pleading eyes nearly broke him again. She licked her lips.

'You should go back.' He spoke the words, but didn't believe them. 'Enjoy the rest of the party.'

Indy just smiled and took his hand in hers. She led him deeper into the stable where the horses were stalled, sheltered for the night. 'Not yet.'

'Indy, please,' he heard himself begging. 'This isn't a good idea.'

'Shh,' she said, and turning she kissed him again.

He had no fight left in him. He pushed her up against the stall door and kissed her hard and fast. But sense prevailed and he stopped himself just as quickly, removing his hands from her body to grip the wood of the stall behind her, his fingers digging in. He dropped his forehead to hers.

'I find it very hard to behave myself when I am around you.'

'And why do you need to?' Indy asked, her deep quick breaths drawing his eyes to the golden skin above her bosom.

'Don't go yet,' she pleaded. 'Kiss me again.'

He couldn't deny her and no longer had the desire to. Leaning in, he kissed her, enjoying the warmth of her tongue as it met his. His fingers travelled lightly down her throat, across her shoulders and her torso, making her gasp as he brushed past the side of her breasts.

'Touch me, Will,' she said, the desperation in her voice singing to him.

'God help me,' he said through gritted teeth. He wanted to lay her down in the straw-covered ground of the stables and take her body, let his be taken by her. His mouth found the skin at the top of her breasts and he tasted, thrilling at the little moans and sighs he coaxed from her. He brought his mouth back to hers with a powerful kiss.

'Indy this is dangerous for you. It's not safe for you to be seen with me, but if they find us like this, with me taking advantage of you, they will kill me.'

'Perhaps it is I who is taking advantage of you,' she said with a quiet chuckle.

'Perhaps it is,' he answered, for he wasn't a hundred percent sure he held any power over the situation anymore. 'But others will not think the same.'

She reached out and gripped his waist, pulling his hips against her and kissing him harder before she suddenly stopped and let him go. 'You're right, dammit all to hell. You should go.'

He chuckled at her sulky face and lifted her chin to stare into her eyes one last time, to take one last look at her ripe lips, swollen from his kisses. Sighing heavily, he stepped away and moved out of the stables to his horse. He mounted quickly before he could change his mind.

She walked slowly back out of the darkness of the stable and into the last rays of sunlight. A smile of pride and pleasure crossed her beautiful features.

'I told you that you would kiss me one day.'

He closed his eyes and tilted his face up to the sky. 'And God help me for it. I'll never be peaceful again.'

Her grin broadened with her obvious delight at his words and, taking one last long look, he turned his horse, let out his frustrations with a loud 'Yah!' and sped away.

***

As Will disappeared with the setting sun, Indy took a moment to catch her breath. Thank God she'd seen sense. A fling with a soldier in a stable? Was she no smarter than all those silly women who got themselves into trouble? At least now she understood the loss of modesty and intellect they must have felt in the arms of a beautiful man. His kisses had affected her brain as though she'd had too much whiskey. It was like a fog had settled over her mind, blocking it from all conscious thought, and all she'd wanted was the exquisite pressure of his lips on hers. Her hand went to her mouth to recall the firmness and the softness, the warmth and the taste.

And her body ... She let her hands run down her ribs where his had been. What thrills had coursed through her system at the touch of his hands when they'd drawn her closer against his strong and solid body. She'd felt his arousal against her when she'd pulled him in. Her heart leapt at the feeling, her belly had quivered and it quivered again now. No man's kiss had ever felt as wonderful, and as perfect, as a kiss from William Marsh. She had tasted a small, sweet slice of the passion the man had inside him. Now she wanted the whole cake.

Chapter 17

The early onset of nasty summer heat had tempers near boiling point as the licence raids went on five days a week. It seemed to Indy there was a meeting on Bakery Hill every second day now. Thousands of miners travelled in from surrounding goldfields to join with the Ballarat miners and make their pleas for social and moral rights as citizens of the colony of Victoria. Indy went along to the meetings occasionally, but the preaching would often go on for hours. It was easy to tell those who had serious intent of trying to abolish the licence tax, of continuing to push for justice for Scobie, and of ensuring the basic rights of miners in the land they had travelled thousands of miles to in hopes of finding a better life. But there were also those who postured and preened, looking for a place in politics should the miners' case for representation in the legislature ever be approved. They were mostly businessmen, many of whom had been wealthy gentlemen back in their homeland of England, Germany or America.

One man caught Indy's attention each time he got up to speak. Peter Lalor was a quietly spoken young Irishman, who was clearly well educated, and apparently came from a family with a long history in politics. She knew him a little because he was courting one of the school teachers Indy was friendly with. When Lalor spoke, the miners listened. He also spoke good sense and peaceful resolution and Indy decided he would be a strong ally in parliament, should anyone other than the landowning gentry ever be admitted. Those with no interest in or understanding of politics simply bypassed the large gatherings, and went about their day as usual, more occupied with trying to keep food in the bellies of their families.

Not unaware of the unrest around them, but more consumed by the change in their relationship, Indy and Will did their best to meet as often as they could. But the divide between miners and the government camp grew wider every day. The soldiers and police were never welcome when they chose to venture out of their camp and into town, and were often verbally abused. They rarely travelled about Ballarat alone anymore for fear of retribution. Indy couldn't blame the miners. Why would they welcome the very animals who would take any opportunity to beat a man simply for not having paid his taxes?

Unfortunately, Will's short reprieve from the miners' anger had well and truly been forgotten. Not by Trevor and Eliza though—they assured Will they would be fast friends forever. But for Indy and Will it meant meeting in secret was their only option. Days would go by before she would be able to see him, to touch him and kiss him, and her frustration was palpable. She was becoming tired of herself. Since when was she the type of woman to turn sullen and dreamy over a man? To not be able to hold a coherent conversation with someone because she would see something that would remind her of Will and completely forget what she'd been talking about. She thought of him during the day at work on the mine, and she thought of him at night in the quiet of her tent.

Sean often caught her daydreaming or staring off towards the government camp.

'What the bloody hell is wrong with you, Indy?' Sean asked when he'd climbed, yet again, out of the pit, when she'd not been there to take the bucket of dirt he'd sent up.

Feeling foolish, she walked back to their mine. 'There's nothing wrong with me.'

Except that a few moments ago, she'd all but raced across the goldfields when she'd seen a blond soldier emerge from Spencer's Confectionary. She was losing her mind.

Handing Sean a drink of water, she sat beside him.

'Indy, can you do me a favour?' Sean asked.

'Of course.'

'I want to go and see Clarissa,' Sean said.

Indy took a good look at Sean. He wouldn't meet her eyes and she could see there was more colour in his cheeks than just from the sun or hard work.

'Sean Sheridan, you sneaky bugger,' Indy said, elbowing him in the ribs. 'Has the love of a good woman found you?'

He shrugged, going even redder if that were possible. 'Dunno, never been in love have I. And don't you go telling Ma. She'll have me married off before Christmas.'

Indy chuckled. He was right about that.

'What's it like?' he asked, drawing lazy circles in the dirt with a stick. 'Being in love.'

'What are you asking me for, boyo?' Indy said with a scoffing laugh.

He shrugged. 'So then what do you think it's like?'

Indy took a deep breath and thought on it for a moment.

'I suppose it's when you can't live without someone,' she began. 'When your every thought is of them. You can't eat. You can barely sleep for dreaming of them. And then there's the kissing.'

'Kissing?'

'Mmm,' Indy murmured with a dreamy sigh. 'The kisses are wonderful. They take you to a whole other place.

Your body heats up and your stomach flutters like a thousand butterflies have let loose. And you ache to hold him against you.'

'Him?' Sean asked.

Indy blinked her way out of her own fantasies. Sean was staring at her with the oddest expression and it was her turn to feel the warmth of a blush creeping up her neck and into her cheeks.

'Are you in love, Indy?'

'Don't be an eejit,' Indy scolded. 'Why would you ask such a thing?'

''Cause of all that stuff you just said. That's how you've been acting lately.'

Her mind went back over everything she'd told him. He was right. She had been talking about herself and hadn't even realised it. But was it love?

'No, I'm not in love,' she said, more to herself than to Sean. 'I can't be.'

Sean seemed to accept her answer. 'So will you keep my secret? About me and Clarissa?'

Indy smiled. She was actually envious of Sean's ability to see his girl in public, his only fear being that his mother would be thrilled. He didn't have to worry about being caught in the arms of the enemy. Why couldn't she have attached herself to a man who she could be with openly? Instead, she had to wait patiently for a time when she could see Will in secret. Indy was not a patient woman by nature. She would have to get creative if she wanted to be with him more than once a week.

But as Sean went back down the mineshaft, and Indy lowered the bucket on the windlass, she realised that finding time to see Will wasn't her biggest problem. Losing him altogether when the Fortieth regiment was inevitably shipped out was suddenly at the top of her list of concerns.

***

As more days passed without seeing hide nor hair of Will, Indy went to visit her mother to try and give her mind something else to do other than think about Lieutenant Will Marsh.

She worked around the house and in her mother's vegetable patch, but unfortunately the manual labour gave her too much time to think. Her mind would wander if she didn't rein it in and suddenly she would find herself in a daydream about her and Will living at the little cottage with her mother, away from Ballarat and all its problems. She chastised herself for dreaming of something that just could not be. They couldn't even speak to one another in town for fear of reprisal on both sides of their camps. But as she pulled carrots and radishes one afternoon, Indy hit upon an idea.

'We should have some company for dinner now that we have all these wonderful vegetables you've grown.'

'The vegetables are for selling at market,' her mother responded.

'Yes,' she tried again. 'But we'll save some for ourselves, will we not? Must make sure they're good enough for market. And we should share our vegetables with a friend.'

'Indigo Wallace, you're about as subtle as a licence raid,' Mary tossed back without even pausing the arc of her hoe in the ground. 'If you want to invite the Lieutenant for dinner you've only a need to say so.'

Indy stood and stretched her aching back, frowning at her Mother's ability to read her so easily. 'I wasn't going to suggest that.'

After a few more moments of silent work she spoke again. 'Perhaps we can invite the Lieutenant back for dinner one evening.'

Mary chuckled. 'What a good idea.'

***

Indy went back to town the following morning with bags full of vegetables to sell to the stores and a heart full of joy. Now she just had to find a way to see Will so that she could convince him to come to her mother's for dinner.

She delivered one bag of vegetables to Grayson's grocery store and collected the shillings in return, and then proceeded up the hill to the government camp. She wasn't a hundred percent sure this plan would work, but she could think of no other way to get to Will.

Meeting the sentry at the gate, she smiled prettily.

'I bring vegetables for the cook,' she said, fluttering her eyelashes like she had seen Elena Gibson and her friends do when they were flirting.

The sentry moved to take the basket but Indy held it back. 'I was asked to deliver it personally to a Lieutenant Marsh. Would he be here?'

'No idea,' the sentry replied looking her over. 'There's so many buggers living 'ere now. I can't be expected to know 'em all.'

'Well, perhaps I can go in and have a look for him.'

'No one is allowed into the camp without authorisation from the Commissioner.'

Indy bit down on her anger. Most days the guard at the gate was so drunk she would have been able to walk right by him. She had to get the one sober sentry in all of Her Majesty's army.

'Very well,' she said, raising her chin defiantly. 'I shall take my delicious fresh vegetables, meat pies, cheeses, bottled fruits and pickles and deliver them elsewhere.'

'Meat pies?' the sentry asked and Indy knew she had him. She could all but see the man's mouth fill with saliva.

She lifted the cloth from the top of the basket to show him.

'How about a little morsel for yourself?' she said, offering him a wrapped portion of her mother's tiny meat pies. 'How can you be expected to stand post on an empty stomach?'

His stomach rumbled loudly, and she grinned as he took the little round pastry from her.

'Very well,' he said, already shoving the pie in his mouth as he waved her through the gates.

She was glad he'd taken the food. Her next plan had been to show him her breasts and the thought of that didn't thrill her.

Wandering across the compound, she tried her best to look like she belonged there as she searched out Will. The sentry had been right. The camp was overflowing with soldiers. The garrison was clearly not large enough to accommodate so many bodies. The men she passed looked tired, gaunt and dishevelled. Hardly the pride of Her

Majesty's military. They barely had the energy to take note of a woman passing them by. She had no idea how she would find Will before someone realised she shouldn't be there.

As she neared the jail, she frowned, concerned at the men who languished there. A well-known thief and several miners unable to pay their taxes, or the resulting fine, sat on the dirt covered floor inside the hot and vermin-infested prison. Looking around to ensure no one saw her, she tossed a few of the vegetables and fruits through the timber bars. The men dove on the food and she hoped there wouldn't be bloodshed as they fought over the scraps.

'Bless you, girl,' one of the men called out, and her heart sank again for the abuse the poor men had no doubt been subjected to.

She was about to turn away when she heard a voice behind her.

'You there!'

Blast it all!

She'd been caught. Turning slowly, she instantly recognised the soldier. He'd been with Will the first night she'd met him behind the Eureka Hotel.

His eyes narrowed as he tried to place her. 'I know you.'

'Yes,' she answered quietly. 'I'm Lieutenant Marsh's friend. Do you know where he is?'

'I'm right here. And just what the bloody hell do you think you're doing?'

She spun back to see Will stop just in front of her. 'Timmons, what is she doing here?'

'I had nothing to do with it. I just found her here feeding the prisoners,' Timmons said, leaning forward to see what else Indy had in her basket.

She lifted the cloth and held it out to him, urging him to take what he wanted.

'Ooh! Strawberry jam!' he exclaimed and gleefully took the little jar.

'Eat it in good health.'

'Indy!'

'Good luck,' Timmons murmured to her and made a hasty retreat as Will continued to glower at her.

'Prunes?' Indy asked, holding out the little bottle and giving him a sweet as sugar smile. 'You look a little constipated, Lieutenant.'

'God, you're a pain in my arse,' Will muttered exasperated. 'You really don't understand the concept of your own safety, do you?'

'No more than you it seems,' she tossed back. 'Why is my walking into the government camp any more dangerous than you spending time in the Eureka camp?'

'Because I am a man. I can take care of myself.'

'Well, oh great and mighty man. If you are so able to take care of yourself, you won't be requiring the lovely food basket my mother sent you.'

'Stop twisting my words, Indy, you know I hate that.'

He moved closer to peek into the basket and she saw the desperate hunger in his eyes.

A troubled frown touched her brow as she examined him. His red coat seemed to hang from his shoulders. Had he lost weight since last she saw him? She recalled how lean the other soldiers had appeared on her walk through camp. There'd been rumours throughout Ballarat that there was a boycott on deliveries to the government camp.

Local merchants were delaying food supplies for the nearly three hundred members of the police and military, and deliveries from Melbourne were intermittent.

Knowing Will's pride, Indy didn't mention it, instead moving on to the reason she had come in the first place.

'Mother also wanted me to invite you for dinner tomorrow,' she said, covering the basket again to show he would get nothing. 'But since you take such pleasure in annoying me, I may have to rescind the invitation.'

'You really do have the most wretched wild temper, Miss Wallace.'

'Those with wild tempers make the best lovers.'

'Indy, you shouldn't say such things,' he said lowering his voice. But his expression was now one of a different kind of hunger.

'So, dinner?' she asked, the picture of innocence.

'How can I deny your mother after the help she rendered me,' Will said, running a hand across Indy's hair. Her heart did a little leap at his touch.

'When did you see her last? Is she well?'

'I was at her house yesterday as a matter of fact. We have a wonderful vegetable patch and we've been busy harvesting as you can see.' She held out the basket for him to take. 'Do with this what you like. Share it or don't. But tomorrow night we'll have fresh sweet potatoes and carrots, and Ma is baking a pumpkin pie.'

His stomach grumbled in response and Indy chuckled, even though it made her heart ache to know he was probably surviving on very little food.

'I will meet you at the river,' he said, his gaze nervously sweeping about the camp. 'Now get out of here before they arrest you for a spy.'

With an exaggerated curtsey, she took an apple out of the basket he held and walked quickly to the gates.

Taking a bite of the apple, she tossed the rest to the grateful sentry as she left the camp.

Chapter 18

The sight of Will riding towards her the next day as she waited for him by the river sent Indy's heart galloping faster than the speed of his horse. Standing in the stirrups, he cut a fine figure leaning forward over the neck of the animal.

Smiling broadly, as he slowed the big black animal to a walk, he dismounted with an agility that thrilled her to the bone. Opening her mouth to say something smart, she was silenced abruptly when he took her in his arms and kissed her so strongly, so passionately, that all thought, other than the exquisite feeling of his warm lips on hers, left her brain.

They separated after a moment and Indy's head took a moment to stop spinning.

'Good afternoon, Lieutenant,' she said, surprised she had breath left to speak.

She never knew how he was going to react when they were together. Sometimes he was hesitant with her, as though he were still questioning their new arrangement. Other times, like this moment, it was as though he had not seen her in a year and had missed her dreadfully.

'I've been wanting to do that ever since you came to the government camp,' he told her, his voice gruff with his desire.

Although he had ridden his horse neither of them was keen to rush their time alone together, so they set off on foot towards her mother's house.

It was a blessing to be in the shade of the trees in the heat of the late afternoon and they walked in a companionable silence for a while, listening to the horses slow clopping against the hard, narrow road and the parrots' incessant chirping overhead.

'Indy, we haven't had much chance to talk since our relationship changed,' Will began.

The tone of his voice had her self-protection senses tingling. She liked him. More than she had expected or even wanted. But that didn't mean she was about to lose her pride and fawn all over him like some silly schoolgirl.

At least, not until she'd heard what he had to say about their 'new relationship'. So she went on the defensive.

'Will, I understand,' she said trying to sound more confident than she felt. 'You're a soldier. You will leave Ballarat eventually.'

'That's very mature of you, Indy.'

She studied his expression closely. Was he mocking her? He wore no smirk. No smile at all. In fact he was frowning quite vehemently.

'Did I say something wrong?' she asked, confused by his suddenly stormy countenance.

'No,' he answered but offered no more.

'You agree then? That there is no future for us?' she asked. Was it possible he had begun to think they could have something more? She did her best to quash the traitorous bubble of hope that rose up into her chest. Dreaming would do her no good.

'I do,' he said with a nod and a sideways glance at her. 'I'm glad we're of the same mind.'

The bubble of hope burst.

They said no more on the matter and thankfully reached her mother's house shortly after.

***

Mary was thrilled to see Will and even more thrilled when he handed her a posy of wildflowers he had collected on the walk into the bush.

'You are looking well, Lieutenant,' Mary said, but gave him a second look. 'A little thin perhaps. Do they not feed you at the government camp?'

'Not a lot,' he answered. 'I fear the inhabitants of the government camp are becoming as frustrated and aggrieved with their own lot in life as the miners. Desertions are becoming commonplace. Those who don't desert spend much of their time slobbering drunk and often end up on suspension or locked up until they are sober again. There are so many soldiers in the camp now that rations are becoming meagre. I am beyond grateful to be eating one of your delicious home-cooked meals tonight, Mrs Wallace.'

'More soldiers?' Mary asked and looked at Indy with concern. 'Are things getting so precarious in Ballarat that the entirety of the Queen's Army will soon be descending upon us?'

Will laughed to set Mary's mind at ease but Indy stayed quiet. Unusually quiet. He could see by Mary's frequent glances at her daughter that she had noticed Indy's solemnness too.

'The fillets of kangaroo will be ready soon,' Mary said. 'Why don't you two go and sit out on the porch? It's cooled down now that the sun has gone.'

Mary handed them both a beaker of cold tea and shuffled them out of the house.

The evening was calm, and with a strange new unease between them, Will sat on the top step while Indy chose one of the little wooden chairs on the other side of the porch. They watched the stars beginning to wink into sight through the tops of the tall stringybark gums. Birds were singing their last songs of the day and crickets and other bugs warmed up to conduct the night symphony. But between Will and Indy, the silence was deafening.

Will had never seen Indy so subdued and wondered what was going on in that head of hers.

'Indy.'

'Mmm? What?' she asked smiling weakly down at him.

'Is everything okay? You've been so quiet since we arrived.'

'I'm just relaxed. Mother's house does that to me.'

It was obvious she was lying to him, but knowing of the secretive ways of women he decided to err on the side of caution and leave her to her thoughts.

Throughout dinner, Will kept Mary and Indy entertained with stories from inside the camp.

'So Timmons pretended to be sick—dying of cholera or some such terminal disease,' Will continued with a story he was telling about his tent mate and friend. 'Turns out he was helping a young medic soldier named Briggs who is in love with a pretty nurse living in the Canadian camp. The young lovers had hatched a plan. Briggs was sent to care for Timmons in his terrible state, and called for the nurse to help out. Of course, when the nurse arrived Timmons made himself scarce so that the pair could have their time alone. Only while Briggs was entertaining the young lass in our tent, Timmons was sitting beneath a tree in the compound scoffing down that strawberry jam you gave him, Indy. Captain Wise comes along—'

'Oh no!' Mary exclaimed but then laughed, clearly knowing what was coming next.

'Oh yes! Wise says, "I say, Timmons, I thought you were on your deathbed",' Will mimicked in an over-exaggerated voice of authority.

'Timmons looks up at him, completely lost for a good excuse and with a face covered in strawberry jam and says "I got better, sir".'

The ladies laughter filled the house.

'Poor Briggs has been on latrine duty for the last week,' Will said shaking his head.

'And what of Timmons?' Mary asked.

Will sighed largely for effect. 'He lost his stash of strawberry jam to Captain Wise. The poor man is devastated. I think he'd have preferred latrine duty.'

'Oh, Lieutenant,' Mary said, wiping her eyes that had teared up with her laughter. 'You do tell a good tale. We'll have to send Lieutenant Timmons some more strawberry jam. And what of the young couple? The Canadian nurse and Briggs?'

Will cleared his throat, his jovial mood gone. 'I believe her father has banned her from ever seeing Briggs again. We soldiers are the enemy.'

And there was no more laughter.

He crossed glances with Indy. Her eyes were dull in the candlelight. The light they'd held and radiated throughout his story seemed to have been snuffed.

Mary's movement to the kitchen bench broke the locked stare between them.

Will stood. 'I should be getting back to the camp.'

'Are you staying here tonight, Indy?' her mother asked.

'No,' she answered, standing as well. 'I should get back too.'

The three walked outside to where Will's horse was tied to a hitching post.

'Farewell, Lieutenant,' Mary said. 'Take good care of yourself.'

'Thank you for dinner, Mrs Wallace.'

'William Marsh, we both know I am not a Mrs anything to anybody,' Mary said sighing.

He smiled and moved to kiss her forehead. 'Goodnight, Mary. Take care.'

She laid a hand to his cheek and smiled contentedly.

Will mounted his horse and then helped Indy swing up behind him.

'Bye, Ma,' Indy said as Will steered the horse into the darkness of the bush.

***

Only the pale moon peeking through the treetops lit the way along the road back to Ballarat. They rode in silence for a while, both lost in their own thoughts as the horse walked slowly.

'I've missed you,' Will said suddenly and lifted her hand from his waist to kiss her palm.

'Have you?'

'Of course. Have you not missed me?'

She stayed quiet. Her brain was full of his story about the Canadian nurse and her soldier. And all she could think about was that no matter what happened, whether they were caught fraternising or Will got his marching orders, this thing between them had no future. Any small admission of her feelings seemed fraught with danger for her suddenly very female heart.

Will twisted in the saddle and put his hand to her cheek. Then his lips were on hers, soft and warm and able to set fires burning low in her abdomen. He had a gifted mouth and she squeezed her arms about him, to hold him closer.

But he pulled his mouth away too soon and turned back to the road ahead. And her heart sank.

'Have you missed me?' he asked again, his deep voice sending shivers through her entire body.

She sighed, glad he couldn't see her face and the tears that shimmered in her eyes.

'Far too much for my own good,' she mumbled, putting her cheek to his broad, warm back and inhaling his wonderful manly scent.

She felt his body relax and they walked the horse in silence back to Ballarat.

As they reached the edges of town, Indy could see Miss Margaret's tent city.

'I think it would be smarter for us to part ways here,' Indy said.

'But it's dark,' Will argued.

'You are so clever, Will Marsh,' she teased him. 'You know we cannot be seen together.'

'I know.'

Reining in his horse, he once again twisted in the saddle to kiss her. It was a long, soft kiss and when he ended it, he dropped a light kiss on her nose too.

'Stay safe, beautiful girl.'

She hooked her arm through his and swung down to the ground.

'You too,' she said and continued to watch him as he urged his horse forward and away from her. Taking a deep breath, she left the road and disappeared into the bushland that would put her on a shortcut to the Eureka camp.

***

The man behind the tree no longer hid the glow of his cigarillo.

He watched the girl disappear into the darkness of the bush. His darling daughter, he thought grinding his teeth with disgust. When Sergeant Donnelly turned back to the horse and its rider, Will's red coat caught the light of Miss Margaret's as he passed by on his way back to the government camp.

Donnelly's grin was venomous. So his girl was bedding a soldier. Seemed little Miss High and Mighty wasn't so innocent after all. Like mother, like daughter.

Her mother had been just as willing as he had when he'd taken her into the shed all those years ago. She'd been flirting with him for weeks. He knew when a woman wanted him and when she was only playing coy just to get him even more excited. But then she'd acted as though he'd forced himself upon her. What rubbish! She'd been smart enough to stay silent on the matter. But then she'd announced she was with child and, although she'd never accused him, he knew the kid was his. Unfortunately, his friend, having seen him flirting with the kitchen maid, had also become suspicious. At that point Donnelly figured it was safer to keep his distance from everyone concerned.

Even after Mary Wallace had left the employ of his friend, he saw her and the baby out in London occasionally. He was close to being nominated for parliament and something had to be done to ensure the bastard child never came back to haunt him. Watching from the street, he'd seen the fear in Mary's expression as she'd read the anonymous note he'd left on her doorstep. He knew the threat alone had been adequate when news reached him that she and his illegitimate offspring had left England for Australia.

Before seeing to his political aspirations in London however, his own move to this horrid land became unavoidable when another woman, a business colleague's daughter this time, had accused him publicly of assaulting her. It was flee the country or be arrested and quite possibly sent to Australia on a very different part of the ship.

The last thing he'd expected was to run into Mary and the girl in Melbourne. It had been over ten years but he'd recognised her out at the market one day. She was still a beauty. He'd followed her home and the look on her face when he knocked on her door was priceless. She'd been terrified. And after a short discussion he'd had no qualms that she would continue to keep her silence on the child's paternity. What he didn't count on though, was her telling the girl who he was. He'd passed her on the way out of Mary's house. No longer a girl, she was closer to a woman, and just as beautiful as the mother. And he hated her for everything she stood for her—the death of his goals, the smothering of his ambitions.

A bitter taste filled his mouth and he spat at the ground. A miner girl whoring herself to a soldier. That little bit of information could be quite useful. His smile came slow and lecherous. Yes, quite useful.

***

'You got in late last night,' George said to Will as they strode across the compound to the mess hall.

'I was on a patrol,' Will entered the large tent to join the other soldiers and police.

He made a face at the sight of the runny oatmeal, the stale bread and the concoction that looked similar to what they'd had for dinner in the mess two nights ago. Even the blowflies that usually gathered en masse didn't seem interested in the day's offerings. Oh, how he wished for some of Mary Wallace's home cooking.

'This food is unfit to be given to the dogs,' Will said.

His friend stared back at him with a look Will couldn't discern.

'What? Am I wrong?'

'You've never lied to me before, Will.'

He closed his eyes. George was right. In the nearly twelve years they'd known each other, he'd never lied to his friend. Not once.

After his unusual evening with Indy the night before he was feeling out of sorts in so many ways. Telling George he had been out on patrol had seemed the simplest explanation for his disappearance, but he knew he owed it to his oldest and closest friend to be honest.

'I'm sorry. Please understand, I am trying to protect you. The less you know, the better off you are.'

'You were with the girl,' George said with a hint of a smile. 'I'm not an imbecile. But you might just be. Did Briggs's little love affair teach you nothing? He'll be lucky if the father of that girl doesn't find him in the night and put a bullet in him.'

'Indy has no father,' Will shot back a little too loud. He looked around and lowered his voice. 'At least not one we need to be worried about. At least, not in that way...' He stopped. He wasn't making any sense.

'Why don't you just find a woman at Miss Margaret's like the rest of us, Will?' George suggested. 'This girl from the Eureka fields will give you nothing but grief, in one form or another.'

'On that we can agree,' Will said with a knowing grin.

'But you'll continue to see her anyway.'

'Was it not you who told me I did not need to marry a girl to have a good time?'

George's gaze narrowed. 'Sounds like me.'

Will loaded some of the bread onto his plate before heading across the mess tent to find a table.

'What happens when we get orders to ship out?' George went on, following him through the maze of soldiers and police who sat and ate in segregated groups.

'Then we ship out,' Will answered.

'Is it that simple?' George asked, brightening suddenly. 'So, you have no real feelings for this girl? Well, that's splendid. Take what you please, enjoy her and all her amusements then cast her aside when the time comes. I underestimated you, Will.'

The anger Will felt towards George was misplaced and he knew it. He was simply being the voice of reason. But damn it if Will would have his friend talk about Indy as though she were one of his whores.

Before he could give George a piece of his mind though, he heard another voice raised louder than the rabble of the full mess tent.

'When you tire of the girls in the brothels, boys, there are plenty of women who work the mines who would be glad of some company.'

Will's teeth ground as he spotted the owner of the voice.

Donnelly.

'Those who work the mines are not ladies, you see,' Donnelly continued. 'They may still wear skirts but they do enjoy riding with one leg on either side of the horse, if you get my meaning.'

The police officers around him laughed at the suggestive jokes Donnelly made.

'I know a young Irish lass who seems happy to accept a soldier in her bed,' Donnelly said, his eyes landing directly on Will as he passed by.

'And here comes one such soldier,' Donnelly called out, gesturing in Will's direction. 'Still playing with the little digger girl, Lieutenant?'

Will froze in place, a few feet from Donnelly. Did Donnelly have specific information that he and Indy were together? How was it possible? He inhaled deeply and exhaled long, doing his best to keep his building rage under control. He ought to keep walking and ignore him. But his temper was already high with George's comments and he shook with his fury as he tried to bypass Donnelly.

'No doubt she likes it rough and tumble,' Donnelly called as the other police officers at the table laughed along. 'The mother liked it well enough.'

That did it.

'You bastard!'

The chain broke and tossing his breakfast tray aside, Will launched himself across the table between them and landed a fist to Donnelly's jaw.

George was in there just as fast trying to pull Will from the fray. The other police officers had jumped in to help their sergeant and George found himself fighting as much as Will just to survive it.

It wasn't long before soldiers came to assist in the fight that seemed unfairly leaning two to five in favour of the police.

Bodies were thrown across the mess tent, tables and chairs broke and scattered across the dirt floor. The men rolled and punched and kicked. Grunts were ejected from the writhing mass and yells and cheers went up from those on the sidelines just happy to watch until...

Bang!

The gunshot was so loud the soldiers and police instantly stopped their battle, grabbing at their ringing ears and searching the tent for the offending shooter.

'Get off the ground and stand to attention!' Captain Thomas yelled. Beside him stood Police Inspector Evans.

Will struggled to get to his feet and stood beside Donnelly in front of their respective commanding officers.

'Who was the instigator of this embarrassing brawl?' Thomas asked.

No one spoke but all other men took steps back leaving Will and Donnelly standing alone in the centre.

'Surely not. Lieutenant Marsh?' Captain Thomas was clearly shocked and appalled and a flicker of shame infiltrated Will's anger. He'd never been in trouble with his superiors in his entire career. 'To the Commissioner's office with both of you.'

Sending each other venomous glares, Will and Donnelly followed Evans and Thomas out of the destruction and across the compound to the Commissioner's tent.

The two men, still fuming and sporting the superficial wounds of their battle, fronted Commissioner Rede.

'Explain yourselves gentlemen,' Rede demanded.

Neither Donnelly nor Will said a word.

'Speak, Lieutenant,' Captain Thomas shot out. 'Or risk court martial and a flogging.'

Will swallowed hard. The flogging of soldiers may have been reduced from three hundred down to fifty lashes but that was bad enough.

'Just a difference of opinion, sir.'

'Well, unless you can give me a better reason as to why you attacked Sergeant Donnelly, Lieutenant, I'll have no choice but to reprimand you,' Rede said.

Will kept quiet. He had no better reason to offer.

'Four days confinement, Lieutenant,' Rede said. 'Robertson will see you to your tent and stand guard the first watch.'

'Sir, I have no intention of fleeing—'

Rede halted Will's argument with a stern countenance. 'Be thankful I'm feeling generous and will hold off on the lashing Captain Thomas seems so eager for you to have.'

'Yes, sir.' Will cast his eyes to the ground.

'And you can thank the unlicensed miners you're so sympathetic to for saving you prison time, Marsh,' Rede added. 'There's no room for the rats in that place. You'd think by adding more licence checks the miners would toe the line and pay the fees, but it seems to have increased their delinquency.' Rede seemed to remember himself. It was a rare outburst in front of subordinates. 'Get out of my sight. Dismissed.'

Will turned, gave Donnelly one last glowering look and followed his guard out of the tent.

'What the hell happened, Donnelly?' Rede asked.

'I was making a joke about a woman in town,' Donnelly said, lightening the facts in his favour. 'The Lieutenant took offence. I think perhaps she is his bit on the side, sir.'

'Well, regardless, his behaviour is unbefitting an officer,' Captain Thomas said.

'Yes, sir,' Donnelly agreed with a small satisfied grin.

'Don't look so smug, Sergeant,' Rede tossed in. 'I'll be garnishing your wages for that ridiculously immature display. You are also an officer and are supposed to be setting an example for the other troopers, not leading them into brawls.'

Donnelly crossed glances with Evans whose expression left no doubt of his annoyance that Rede was doling out punishment to one of his men. But everyone knew that thanks to Hotham's latest decree, Rede now had the run of things at the camp.

'Dismissed.' Rede waved Donnelly and Evans out of his office.

Outside, Donnelly leaned against the wall of the Commissioner's hut and lit a cigarillo. The docked pay was bad enough, but it was the humiliation of it, once it got around camp, that had him fuming. How had he sunk so low in life? He'd been a man of means and good breeding. Even upon his arrival in Australia, he'd been treated like the gentleman he was and had been accepted easily into Melbourne's polite society. However, after a few social indiscretions and some dreadful gambling debts, his chances of a career in politics in the new colony of Victoria were greatly diminished, and the highest position of authority he'd been able to acquire was that of a sergeant in the new Victorian Police Service.

The service had been in need of educated gentlemen who could control the motley crew of ex-convicts and black natives that made up the constabulary. And they had desperately needed someone to lead the troopers sent to watch over the rabble in the overpopulated township of Ballarat. Donnelly found the lawlessness of the goldfields agreed with him. He was able to dole out punishment when it suited him and had made himself a good income on the side by charging local businesses protection money. Granted, the protection required was mostly from his own troops, but supply and demand was a code to live by on the goldfields. Still, the monetary surplus did not make up for the loss of a prestigious career and a life of social prosperity. The way he saw it, the blame for his downfall fell squarely with his daughter who somehow kept turning up like a bad penny. It hadn't taken long for the gossips to uncover the truth that the miner girl Indigo Wallace was the Police Sergeant's illegitimate child. Secrets in Ballarat didn't remain secrets for long.

Letting his gaze wander to the soldiers' tents he smiled. The dig at the soldier, her lover, wheedling him into attacking him, had been worth the lost wages. It was a shame about the flogging, and the lack of space in the jail. He'd have enjoyed seeing the arrogant, interfering lieutenant flayed and bleeding against a whipping post. But the man was under house arrest, it would injure his daughter to know so, and that was what had him smiling.

Chapter 19

The moment the sun rose over Mt Warrenheip, Indy knew it was going to be another scorcher. The air was dense with humidity, making even the act of breathing a chore. The flies were thick already, swarming around leftover food and dirty dishes or simply attaching themselves to any sweaty human.

She was desperate for a swim in the river and due to the oppressive heat she and Sean decided to pass on opening their mine. They weren't the only ones.

Another meeting had been called and miners began the short walk up to Bakery Hill. Indy had stopped to read the agenda posted on the notice board by St Alipius inviting all miners and business owners to attend the meeting and sign the document of grievances.

DOWN WITH DESPOTISM the sign had said. DOWN WITH THE LICENCE FEE.

Indy figured if there was going to be something to sign, then she would be there to sign it.

Three men Indy only knew because of the long-winded speeches they had given over the last months had been chosen to go to Melbourne, to deliver the petition to Governor Hotham. After explaining the document to the thousands strong crowd, the call was put out.

'If you will come forward and sign the petition of grievances on behalf of the Ballarat Reform League.' The men began to step forward and Indy stepped up to follow them.

'Ladies, you may return to your children and camps.'

Indy stared at him, shocked at first but that was quickly overtaken by outrage.

'Wait!' Indy called, storming to the front of the line, ignoring the complaints of the men. 'I have no husband, no children to go home to. Are you saying that we women who are allowed to stake a claim and dig just like you, and are forced to pay the licence fees, just like you, are not allowed to join this Reform League? Are not able to sign the petition of grievances that we most definitely share?'

'That is correct, Miss Wallace,' the man she knew only as Mr Hummfray returned.

'So the Commissioner deems that we women have the right to dig for gold and run businesses, open hotels and stores, but you do not believe that women have any right to an opinion, a vote or essentially to gain the same rights that you are asking for?'

Indy wasn't the only woman who was incensed by this latest slight. Other women began to toss their two cents' worth in as well.

'Stop causing trouble, Miss Wallace,' one of the other delegates called back.

'Why should I? You're causing trouble to get what it is that you want,' Indy tossed back. 'Manhood suffrage indeed.'

'I'll be showing you manhood suffrage when you get home, Ian Murphy,' a woman called out to her husband.

'And what of the Chinese in all this?' Indy argued again. 'Do they get a right to vote? A right to land? You barely treat them as human. Poor buggers are one step lower than us ladies.'

'We only fight for the rights of British citizens,' Hummfray returned and cheers of agreement rang out.

'Britain lost the Americas a long time ago.' Indy stared down the Americans in the group. 'You're worse than those bastards up at the government camp! To hell with the bloody lot of you.'

Indy stormed away with a horde of women following indignantly behind her.

'You'll be making your own dinner, John Carr,' a woman told her husband as she scooped up her child and followed Indy. 'And don't be thinking you'll be sharing a bed with me tonight.'

***

Days passed and Indy saw nothing of Will. Perhaps he was on another gold escort to Melbourne. She was sure he would have told her if that had been the case. Unless it was a sudden thing and he had not been able to get word to her.

By day three, she was going crazy. And she was driving Sean crazy with her questions and theories on what could have happened to Will.

'He's probably just on a supply run for the government camp,' Sean told her.

'He would have said so, wouldn't he?'

'Maybe he didn't have time.'

She'd thought as much herself.

'Indy, if you are so concerned for his welfare, go up to the camp and ask.'

'Are you mad?'

Sean just rolled his eyes at her. 'I've never been so happy to go down a dark hole in the ground as I am right now, Indy. You drive a man to drink.'

'Drink?' Indy latched onto his last word. Maybe Will had gone on a bender with some soldiers. Maybe he was passed out somewhere in one of the bars.

'Right,' she said, dusting herself off with determination. 'See you later, Sean.'

'Not if I see you first!' he called back out of the mine but Indy had already headed off in the direction of the first hotel.

Three pubs down and still no sign of Will. Public houses numbered in the double figures in Ballarat these days and she'd never entered most of them before. It was quite the experience moving about areas of town she hadn't been aware had grown so dramatically over the months since winter. Life had been simpler in the beginning of the gold rush. Now the rush seemed to be in the building of wooden stores and housing and the canvas city was disappearing before her very eyes. Would everyone pack up and move back to the city once all the gold was gone? Would the thriving city of Ballarat with all its new buildings become a ghost town?

It took her all day to work her way through the bars, hotels, gaming rooms and theatres. There was only one place she hadn't looked.

Walking the distance to Miss Margaret's establishment—truthfully just a grouping of tents a mile outside of the town limits—Indy questioned the sanity of her actions. Darkness had fallen and she'd missed dinner, but she wasn't too concerned about that. Her hunger had long since left her, replaced by her fear for Will. Now that she stood in front of the tent brothel, her fear took a sharp turn. What if she found him with another woman? A woman of ill-repute at that. How would she react? She couldn't honestly say she wouldn't string him up by his private parts and hang him from the nearest tree. But she had to be prepared for the fact that she just might find him there. She could hear the music and screaming laughter pouring out of the biggest whorehouse in Ballarat.

Lifting the calico flap, cigarette and pipe smoke poured out of the enclosed tent area. Stepping through, immediately her eyes began to sting from the smoke, and in the dim lighting it took a moment to focus. Once her eyes had adjusted she saw soldiers, police officers and miners alike sitting and standing about in various states of dress.

No animosity between the government and miners here.

Women in even more varied states of undress straddled knees or sat in laps. In dark corners, men's mouths were attached to the lips or necks of working girls, their hands roaming over intimate places or, worse, disappearing beneath petticoats. Guttural grunts and groans, both male and female, could be heard and Indy did her best not to imagine what was going on behind thin canvas walls. Several beady-eyed, drunken men gave Indy lecherous looks as she walked through the tents, looking for one man amongst the many. Confident in most situations, it was rare for her to feel out of her comfort zone, but she was certainly beginning to feel so now.

Tamping down on her nerves, she searched for his face, his blond hair. She thought she spied him once until the man turned and she saw the face of another soldier. She asked some of the working girls if they had seen him. She'd known some of these women for years. Had even come out on the boat from England with a couple when they were children. On the odd occasion she saw them in town, she always said hello despite the looks of disgust they received from other womenfolk. Indy didn't care a tot what they did for a living. It was all about choices. It wasn't Indy's choice of occupation, but she wasn't about to ignore a woman or berate her for doing what she must to survive. That didn't mean she wouldn't scratch the eyes out of any woman who should be attached to Will if she found him here.

'I had a soldier last night. Might've been him,' one of the ladies told her. 'Blond hair and dark eyed?'

Indy felt sick.

'Can't trust these soldiers, love. They're not the everlasting lovin' type.'

She shuddered at the thought of Will here in this den of iniquity.

About to give up and leave, she saw a face she recognised. Not Will, but a soldier friend of his: George.

Rushing across the open air space between tents towards him, she ignored the looks and lewd suggestions from other soldiers and women.

'Miss Wallace,' George said, looking up at her from his seat. He shifted his ample bosomed companion slightly to the left so he could see Indy properly. 'What brings you by?'

'I inquire about Lieutenant Marsh,' she said. She could feel her face reddening. Chasing after men was not her default behaviour. She began to realise what a fool she was making of herself.

'Do you?' George asked. His expression was serious for a moment. 'I'd say he'd be safer away from the likes of you, but he'd be unhappy about that so I won't.'

Indy blinked, taken aback at George's opinion.

'Well, look who's come a callin'.'

Indy turned to face the Madam herself. A tall woman with voluminous red hair, Miss Margaret had probably been beautiful in her younger years, but being overly made-up did nothing to hide that time had marched an entire regiment across her face—and the rest of her body no doubt.

'Looking for a job?'

'No, thank you,' Indy said, again feeling out of her league.

'Come now, sweetheart,' Miss Margaret shot back. 'Giving it away to soldiers for free is plain silly, it is.'

'Thank you for the offer. I have no issue with what you and your ladies do. I just have no desire to take up the business.'

Miss Margaret simply shrugged a shoulder. ''Tis a pity.' Indy steeled herself as Miss Margaret studied her in a way she'd only seen men do. 'You'd bring them in, my lovely. Yes, you would.'

And with one last wink she walked away, leaving Indy to exhale her nervous breath. She wanted out of this place and quickly. But not without knowing where Will was first. Either way, she had to know. Men had needs and since it was near impossible for him to find a time and place to be alone with her, she almost couldn't blame him for turning elsewhere for release. If he had succumbed to the temptation of this place then she would deal with it—and then she'd shoot him later. But either way, she had to know.

'He's been confined to quarters.'

She stared down at George. This was not what she'd expected. 'Is he ill?'

'In a manner of speaking. He began a brawl with Sergeant Donnelly.'

Indy's mouth fell open before she snapped it shut quickly.

'Your father, I understand.'

'An accident of birth,' she tossed back, her chin going up in her usual defiant way whenever anyone challenged her on the matter.

'What was the fight about?'

'What do you think?' George asked with a huff. 'You, of course.'

'Me?'

'Donnelly was giving you a less than stellar review. Will took offence to his manner and decided to slap the smug grin right off the man's face.'

Indy grinned, not bothering to hide her admiration for Will. 'Good.'

'You're trouble in a pretty package, Miss Wallace,' George said, shaking his head. 'The police came to Donnelly's defence, and of course I had to help Will, so it ended in an all-in kafuffle. It had been coming for some time I might say, and for my part it felt good to get a few licks in against our brethren in blue. However, as Donnelly is considered a superior officer under the new regime that the Commissioner is now in control of, Will was reprimanded and confined to quarters in lieu of jail time. The jail is currently overcrowded with miners, you see.'

'And Donnelly? What of him?'

'Reprimanded as well. His wages garnished.'

'That's it!?' Indy was fuming. 'Will gets confined to his tent and Donnelly walks away?'

'Be thankful that's all he got, little girl,' George said with a wry grin. 'My friend is a man who would gladly lay down his life for you.'

This bit of news surprised and delighted Indy. 'Was he injured in the fight?'

George gave a light shrug. 'A blackened cheek and jaw. Knuckles with split skin. Hardly anything to a soldier who's seen more vicious battles and had life-threatening injuries.'

'I need to see him.'

'Miss Wallace—'

'I need to see him,' she repeated. 'With or without your help, I will see him.'

George sighed. 'Very well. I'll find a way. Come to rear of the camp nearest the bushland after curfew tonight. Our tent is nearby. I will find a way for you to see your man.'

Indy nodded and turning away she headed out of the maze of tents. As she reached the entrance, a tall shadow stepped in front of her. With only the dull light from campfires and lanterns, she couldn't make him out. But as he lit a cigarillo, she was unable to stop the gasp that escaped upon seeing his face illuminated. Donnelly.

'Well, well,' he said, his teeth holding onto the cigarillo as he blew smoke directly into her face. 'Hello, daughter. Finally come to realise your station in life.'

'Get out of my way,' Indy said, schooling her features to boredom, which belied the nervous hammering of her heart. No matter how much she hated the man, he also frightened her. Though she would never give him the satisfaction of letting him see that.

'I suppose you've heard by now that your beloved soldier is under house arrest.'

'I have no idea what you're talking about,' Indy feigned. She wasn't about to admit her relationship with Will to anyone. Let alone the devil himself.

'I've seen you together,' Donnelly said, menace dripping from his voice. 'Don't play the innocent child with me. Your handsome beau met his match with me. I had to teach him a lesson. I'm not to be trifled with.'

'I don't give a disease-ridden rat's arse for anything you have to say. Now get out of my way,' Indy demanded.

Any attempt by Donnelly to be genial, however false, was gone in an instant. 'I ought to sell you to the highest bidder right now. There would be plenty of men here who would pay to see your pretty face in the throes of passion.'

A trickle of fearful sweat ran down her back. 'That will never happen.'

He just shrugged a shoulder. 'You don't have to enjoy it. As long as they get their money's worth they'll be satisfied. Nor do you have to consent, given the right circumstances.' He leaned in, his breath reeking of liquor and stale tobacco. 'You always did think you were better than everyone. But I know the apple doesn't fall far from the tree. I know your mother, and you are just like her. Once a whore, always a whore.'

Indy shut him up with a slap, impressive even by her standard. Donnelly staggered back two full steps. Her hand stung from the force of it, but, oh, she felt good.

She took her opportunity to move by him and out of the calico compound. But before she could get out the doorway, he grabbed her arm, wrenching it so hard she feared her shoulder would pop out of its socket.

'Sergeant Donnelly!'

The shout was fierce, and Indy turned to see Miss Margaret walking towards them. All pleasantness vacated from her expression, she now carried the air of a frighteningly capable business owner.

'If you strike, injure or even grab a woman like that in my place again, I shall ban you for life.'

'She is not one of your women,' Donnelly insisted.

'That makes no never mind,' Miss Margaret returned. 'Strike *any* woman, Sergeant Donnelly, and you will be thrown out of my house. Now, let her go.'

He did as ordered and Indy was surprised to say the least. Then it dawned on her: Donnelly was bedding Miss Margaret herself.

'One day,' Donnelly said through gritted teeth before Indy could move. 'One day, you and I will have our meeting and there'll be no one around to stop me from giving you the hiding you deserve.'

Refusing to show him any fear, she gave Miss Margaret a nod of thanks, left the tent and made her way back into town.

***

A few hours later, in the deepest dark of the night, George led Will out to the rear of camp.

'I can relieve myself without a guard, George,' he told his friend, who seemed to be directing him a long way further than was required.

'You are confined to quarters, are you not?' George answered, causing Will to look quizzically at his friend.

'I am. But it's not as though I will run away. So why am I coming all the way out here just to take a piss?'

'Because a lady waits, my Lord,' George said, gesturing to where Indy was now scampering over the lowest part of the picket fence.

'Indy?' Will squinted into the half-light. 'What the hell are you doing here?'

He glared at George.

'Don't look at me, old boy,' George said, holding his hands up in defence. 'I am but an unwilling accomplice.' And with that he stepped away, making himself scarce.

'Indy, what are you thinking?' Will's voice was a gruff whisper. His eyes darted about the compound. 'If they catch you scrambling over the fence like that, they'll shoot you on sight.'

'They won't see me,' she assured. Taking a step closer she put her hand to his cheek. Even in the low light he knew she would see where the bruises bloomed.

'Oh, your pretty face.'

He smiled at the warmth of her touch and the concerned expression on her own lovely face.

Then he watched that expression darken as her legendary temper took hold. 'I heard what happened. Donnelly. I'll kill the bastard myself.'

'You'll do no such thing. Stay away from him. The man is not worth hanging for.'

'I wish I could stay away,' Indy sighed. 'It seems we are destined to run into one another. Even tonight—'

'You saw Donnelly tonight?' Will interrupted, fear gripping him. 'Indy—'

'I didn't go looking for him. I was looking for you. I went to Miss Margaret's and he happened to be there.'

'You went to Miss Margaret's?' Will asked. Shock was replaced by bewildered amusement. 'Why did you think I'd be there?'

She shrugged embarrassed.

'But you found Donnelly instead?'

She nodded. 'And George. We need to find your friend a decent woman, Will.'

He just smiled, pulled her into him and kissed her forehead, her nose and then her soft lips.

'I was worried,' she said, leaning in to his body as his arms enveloped her. 'I thought perhaps ... perhaps you'd become tired of me and went looking for more excitement.'

'More excitement than Indigo Wallace? I'm not sure I could cope with that.'

Will gave her a grin and tapped her nose before kissing her again. His body, tense for three days from sitting idle in his captivity, suddenly felt very alive. Especially when she pressed herself harder against him.

'I'm sorry I didn't get word to you,' he said between kisses. 'But, Indy, you must go before someone sees you here.'

'I know.' Resignedly, she rested her head against his chest. 'I know.'

Her arms tightened around his waist and something shifted in him at her rare display of emotion. His heart lurched and fell and he closed his eyes and returned her embrace, taking a deep inhale of her wonderful scent.

'I'll see you as soon as my punishment is over,' he promised, with one last kiss to her forehead.

'Goodnight.' Moving out of his arms, Indy climbed, agile as a cat, back over the fence.

'Stay safe,' he whispered out into the night air.

George joined him again and they watched her disappear into the scrub. 'I hope you know what you're doing.'

Will exhaled heavily. 'Not a clue, old friend. Not a damn clue.'

Chapter 20

Finally released from his canvas incarceration, Will knew exactly where he would find Indy on a beautiful day such as this. When he arrived at the waterhole, Indy was dangling her feet in the bubbling creek. The temperature was beginning to soar as the sun hit the top of its daily climb and the water looked so refreshing to him. But not as refreshing as Indy as she turned her head and smiled up at him.

'Well now, here comes my convict hero.'

Without a thought, he knelt down, took her face in his hands and pressed his mouth to hers. She tasted like sunshine and raspberry.

'Mmm.' He licked his lips. 'You've been eating raspberry drops from Spencer's again.'

She held up the little bag. He took a sweet and popped it into his mouth as he sat beside her.

Amused, he watched as she leaned over, took hold of one of his boots and pulled it off, tossing it over her shoulder. Then she took the other boot and tugged at it until it gave, and it met the same fate as the first. His socks followed and she rolled up his pant legs so he was able to dip his feet into the cool water.

He sighed and closed his eyes. 'This feels wonderful.'

A strange warbling sound alerted Will and he turned to look for the source.

'What is that?' he asked. 'I keep hearing that strange noise all over the place. Is it some sort of monkey?' He reached for the sweets.

Indy chuckled. 'There are no monkeys in Australia.' But she hesitated a moment and seemed to think about it. 'Not that I am aware of anyway. It's a bird. Whitey calls it a kookaburra, or something like that.'

'Monkeys were everywhere in India,' he told her. 'Wretched little beasts. Skilled thieves they were too. Always running off with food and property. Often trained by human masters to do so.'

Indy picked a raspberry drop from the bag in Will's hand.

The warble turned into a cackle.

'That's never a bird,' he argued.

She pointed up into the treetops where the unusual-looking bird sat with his mate and squawked.

'He laughs at me.'

'He laughs at everyone,' Indy said, laughing herself as she pushed him onto his back and lay beside him in the soft grass beside the creek.

Leaning up on one elbow, she looked down at him through eyes that sparkled. He smiled serenely. God, he'd missed those eyes. Concerned with where his thoughts were taking him, he closed his eyes against the blinding sun and the brightness of Indy. He felt her finger trace his cheeks and jaw before she ran it lightly across his lips, sending delicious electric shocks to every nerve in his body.

'Indy.'

'Yes,' she answered, sounding more like an innocent child than a seductress.

'You're playing with fire.'

His eyes flew open again as she suddenly straddled him on the grass.

'Indy, someone could see!'

'Nobody here but us kookaburras.' She bit his lip lightly and his thin grasp on control snapped. As she took his mouth, he felt all the blood in his head rush immediately to the lower half of his body.

When she sat up, looking satisfied with herself, he threw an arm across his eyes.

'What's wrong? Do I not kiss well?'

He groaned. 'Indy, you drive a man to insanity. Your mouth is an addiction. I want to kiss you and make love to you so badly I can barely sleep at night.'

'And who says you cannot kiss me and make love to me?'

He lifted his arm again and looked at her warily. 'I'm a man, Indy. A man who has been locked away in a tent for the last four days with nothing else to do but dream of a certain pretty Irish lass. You shouldn't say such things.'

'Aw, poor soldier boy.' She gave him a fake pout before leaning down to whisper in his ear. 'Did you miss me, Lieutenant?'

'It was like losing the sun for four days.'

She sat up and her face held the softest expression before she placed her mouth against his again.

As she nibbled lightly at his lips, he slowly lifted her skirts and ran his hand up underneath, thrilled to discover no long pantaloons, no stockings—just skin. Soft, smooth and all Indy. Unable to stop himself, his hands floated higher from behind her knees, up the back of her thighs until he finally met cotton.

'For the first time, I am sorry to discover you are wearing your undergarments, Miss Wallace.'

She chuckled. 'Sorry to disappoint you, sir.'

He frowned as he felt the unusually short pair of pantaloons.

'Um, exactly what are you wearing?'

'Oh, I fashioned them myself,' she said. 'I took a pair of bloomers and cut them up until they were very short. Still decent you see, but not so bloody hot.'

'Oh, Indy,' he said chuckling and pulling his hands out from beneath her skirts.

'They can be removed quite easily.'

He sat up and lifted her from his lap to the grass beside him with ease.

'You don't want to?'

'I want to,' he said. Oh Lord, did he want to. 'I just want to have you in a real bed, with real sheets. A place where we can take our time and not be concerned about who might see, or what deadly snakes and spiders might be crawling up my arse while I'm too lost in you.'

She gave a frustrated sigh. 'And just how do we find a place with a real bed with real sheets in Ballarat?'

'We'll find a way, Indy. I promise.'

She nodded.

The steam whistle announcing the arrival of the Geelong coach rang out from town and Indy jumped to attention.

'Is that the time?'

Will watched surprised at her sudden action. 'Late for something?'

'Yes,' Indy said pulling on her boots. 'A meeting with the ladies of the Ballarat Reform League.'

'The *ladies* of the Reform League?'

'Yes, we went to the meeting last Saturday expecting to be included in the establishment of the Ballarat Reform League, only to be told that as ladies our services and membership were not required. Manhood suffrage. What the bloody hell does that even mean? Men wouldn't know real suffering.'

Will chose to sidestep that open mineshaft. 'Indy, you shouldn't get involved in the politicking of these men.'

'Why? Because I'm a woman and women don't have a part to play in decision making? You're as bad as they are.'

'They're asking for trouble.'

'They're asking for equal rights,' Indy shot back. 'That politicking as you call it is a simple request for justice. We pay our taxes, yet we get nothing in return. There's no infrastructure, we cannot vote, we cannot own land...'

'You have land,' he pointed out. 'Anyway a moment ago you were annoyed that they weren't treating women with equal rights. You've changed the tune of your song.'

'That's beside the point. I have a house on land that the Crown can take away from me and my mother without a second thought and there is no recourse for us,' Indy told him. 'I pay taxes, Will, but I have no right to buy the land that my mother's house is built on. Land on which I could plant crops or run sheep. Is that fair?'

'What would you know about running sheep?' Will asked with a snorting laugh. 'And fair doesn't come into it. It's the law.'

She stared at him stunned for a moment. 'You can't really be that obtuse.'

'It's not obtuse to uphold the law of the land.'

'Even when that law is wrong and one sided?'

'Indy—'

'These are hardworking people, Lieutenant.'

God, he hated it when she reverted to calling him Lieutenant that way. It showed her irritation with him more than yelling ever could.

'They deserve respect.'

'Respect has to be earned, Indy.'

'Really? Do you expect the Commissioner to be shown respect? And Hotham?'

'Of course.'

'And just how is raiding and arresting hardworking people deserving of respect?'

'Those who are licensed have nothing to worry about. And there are better ways to get a point across than reverting to hooliganism.'

'We tried democracy, tried to talk to Hotham,' Indy argued. 'We've been rebuked.'

'We?' Will asked. Now it was 'we'.

'Just whose side are you on here?' she asked and stood to straighten her dress.

What the hell had he been thinking starting a quarrel with her? She was so obstinate about these things. He pushed himself up off the ground, dusting the dirt and grass from his trousers.

'That's just it. I can't take sides, Indy. I can only do as I'm ordered.'

'Don't you have a brain in that ridiculously handsome head of yours?' she asked. 'Don't you have a conscience?'

'You know I do,' he reasoned, trying to be calm in the face of Indy in a swelling rage. 'But I'm a soldier first and foremost, and I must do my duty. Without it I'm nothing.'

'Well, your duty is a load of bollocks,' she said. And clearly done with him, she stormed away.

***

Indy was fuming.

She barrelled down the hill towards town at a cracking pace, spurred on by her righteous anger.

Duty. Duty? Who talked like that?

He could be so frustrating sometimes. How could he not see that the duty he was so bound to was upholding unjust laws that kept good people from having a real life here in Victoria? The very reason so many left England and Ireland was to find a place less constricted by the codes and rules of richer men. Okay, the gold was a big draw card too, but even the guidebooks for emigrants touted a world of freedom.

Exhaling some of her frustration, she groaned out loud. The time she and Will spent together was precious and rare. She didn't want to spend it fighting with him. But it seemed he disagreed with her ideals and was only too happy to tell her so. One minute they were having a wonderful sensual moment together and the next they were on opposing sides of this ongoing conflict.

She'd felt the desire in him as she had straddled his legs. His hands had sent delicious vibrations direct to her core as they had crept higher on her thighs. They'd been talking of making love. Of finding a place and a way to be together. And then the real world had crept in and ruined everything.

Reaching the edge of town Indy sighed, horribly deflated all of a sudden. Her temper always left her feeling flat. She really had to learn to get a hold of it. She wondered how it was possible that a man as intelligent as Will could blindly defend the unjust laws of a totalitarian government. Still, she wished she were more mature in her discussions and less inclined to fly off the handle whenever someone didn't agree with her. Her silly female emotions always had her speaking without thinking and often got her into trouble.

Well, there was no time to think now on the hurt feelings of Lieutenant Will Marsh. He was a man. He would survive. She had work to do. She arrived at Mrs Murphy's tent store and was thrilled at the number of women who had turned out for the inaugural meeting of the Ladies of the Ballarat Reform League.

Taking a deep breath to cleanse the last of her temper, she followed the ladies into the tent, ready to use her righteous anger for the good of the fairer sex.

***

That evening Will and George watched the huge contingent of the Fortieth Regiment march into camp.

'Lord almighty,' Will murmured, staggered by the number of the latest arrivals. 'They're not pulling any punches.'

'Bring in any more soldiers and we'll be sleeping standing up,' George added. 'We're already cheek by jowl. Where do they think these poor blighters are going to bunk down?'

'I think they're past caring,' Will said scowling. 'It's a show of strength. Rede copped a slap on the wrist for his dealings over the Eureka Hotel fire.'

'He blamed the police for that,' George added. 'Inspector Evans was well annoyed.'

'Yes, but now Hotham has given Rede carte blanche. He has the ultimate say over everyone and everything in the government camp. The civil commissioners, the traps and now even the military, which of course is causing no end of irritation for Captain Thomas and the other regimental commanding officers. Rede was humiliated after the hotel fire. He is not about to allow another show of mob rioting happen on his watch.'

'Can you blame him?'

'No, but it's getting out of hand.'

'The miners have brought it upon themselves,' George said with a shrug.

Will's head jerked to look at his oldest friend. 'Do you really believe that this stockpiling of soldiers and weaponry is the answer to the requests of a bunch of immigrants?'

'From what I hear they demand, they don't request.'

'They're tired,' Will said, rubbing his neck, feeling somewhat weary himself. 'The gold is running out, yet they still have to pay for a licence regardless of whether they find any gold or not. Hotham doesn't listen. He makes promises he doesn't keep.' Will stopped abruptly. Where the hell had all that come from? All of a sudden he could hear Indy in his head speaking the words that were coming out of his mouth.

'You've been getting about with Miss Wallace too long, old friend,' George joked as though reading his mind. 'You're picking up her political tendencies.'

He thought about that for a long moment, watching George light a cigarette.

'She's not wrong,' he said finally.

George choked out smoke, 'Excuse me?'

Will could barely believe it himself. The more he thought about things, the more he began to agree with Indy's summation of the situation. He'd never questioned the reasons behind the orders before. He was a soldier and it was his job to do what he was told. But this situation felt different. And although he'd argued with Indy, and she'd stormed away from him, he'd thought a lot about what she'd said over the past week. She'd been so angry with him she'd made no attempt at contact in almost ten days. It had given him plenty of time to rehash their conversation.

'She's not wrong,' he said again as the latest arrivals dispersed to find accommodations and food. 'Regardless, this is not how you put down a simple civil disturbance. This is excessive.'

But it concerned him more than a little that his own political views were becoming so closely aligned to that of an uncontrollable girl with shining blonde hair and a wicked temper.

'Is it not?' George asked seemingly more amused than alarmed by Will's speech.

'Are we not fighting right now in Crimea against the Russian Empire who will oppress democracy? Are we not seeing here democracy and independence on fledgling legs being requested...' Will rolled his eyes at George's look, 'demanded then—by immigrant miners who just want to see some results from the taxes they pay. A right to vote in this country they live in, a right to have a seat in the legislative council regardless of whether they own land or not and the right to purchase that land should they wish to and have the means? Land they could sew and reap, land on which they could raise livestock. Would this country not be a better place if more industry could be found other than at the end of a pick and bucket of dirt?'

'Careful, Will,' George teased. 'Your words smack of dissent.'

Will blinked and scanned the area around him. He had been speaking at a normal volume but there were so many bodies in the government camp now a private conversation was near impossible. And there was Indy's voice again in his head. She had planted the seed of doubt and it had grown.

'Is it dissent, George?' Will asked thoughtfully. 'Or decency?'

Chapter 21

Indy left her mine earlier than usual to seek out a game of cards or dice. It was another stinking hot day and she wanted to plant herself in a nice cool hotel, be out of the sun and maybe, just maybe, she'd have a pannikin of beer or two.

She set off down the main road towards the Duchess of Kent Hotel, one of her favoured pubs for a good and fair game of poker. She'd refused to patronise many of the other hotels since they had introduced cock-fighting for sport and gambling. As she was about to turn up the alleyway beside Mr Diamond's home store that led to the Duchess of Kent, she heard hoof beats behind her.

Shading her eyes against the strong afternoon sun, she spotted Will riding towards her. He stopped but didn't dismount.

'Good afternoon, Miss Wallace,' he said smiling down at her.

His smile soon faded when she didn't respond.

'Can we talk?' he asked. 'Or are you still upset with me?'

Truth be told, she had been angry with Will. But she'd been angrier still that it had taken him ten days to come and find her. Ten days she had waited for him to apologise. She could have gone to him but she had far too much pride for that. And besides, she'd been in the right.

He finally dismounted to stand beside her.

'You really are an idiot, aren't you?' she murmured.

'Are we talking about our last argument or something else?'

Her eyes scanned the busy street around her. As Will had ridden up to her, miners had stopped to watch him with suspicious glares. Women who walked along the veranda in front of the Criterion store stopped to gawk and whisper behind their hands, gossiping no doubt about the miner girl and her soldier.

Over the last month, Indy had begun to notice a change in how people treated her. She'd never had many female friends. Without a husband or children she was on the outer circle of most groups of women, but in the last few weeks, even the ladies with whom she was friendly had become standoffish or hurried away whenever she was in their vicinity. Several of her students had failed to show for classes in the week past too, and she occasionally came across people talking about her when they thought she couldn't hear.

She knew it was because they thought she was sleeping with a soldier. The story of the young Canadian nurse, whose father had all but locked her away after she'd been caught cavorting with a soldier, had been fodder for the gossips for weeks. The rumours about Will and Indy had mostly been speculative since Trevor and Eliza's wedding, but having Will ride directly up to her in town would have the rumours cemented as truth in the minds of those who had witnessed.

'I'm sorry we quarrelled,' he continued, seemingly oblivious to the stares and whispers going on around them. 'Shall we go to the river? I have a keen desire for a swim.'

'You go on ahead,' she told him. 'I'll meet you there.'

As she watched him mount his horse again and ride away, Indy knew it was probably a pointless ruse to travel separately. But she'd still prefer to keep some doubt in the minds of the townsfolk.

Turning her back on the gossips to begin walking towards the river, she saw the teenaged paperboy rush out of the *Ballarat Times* building holding a pile of fresh copies of the newspaper.

'Bentley and Co convicted of the manslaughter of James Scobie!'

Indy stopped dead at the announcement and watched as townsfolk descended on the poor lad, fighting for a copy of the paper. Bentley finally convicted? Could it be true? She joined the scrambling crowd and managed to snatch the daily sheet before another woman could get it.

Moving out of the crush of people, Indy began to read the front page story. It stated that Bentley, Hance and Farrell had been retried in the city and sentenced to hard labour. She could scarcely believe it. Melbourne justice was clearly less biased than Ballarat justice. As she read on though, it also reported that miners Westerby, Fletcher and McIntyre had been convicted and sentenced to jail terms in Melbourne for the burning of the Eureka Hotel.

'Oh!' a woman exclaimed. 'But Catherine Bentley was found not guilty.'

'It doesn't matter,' another woman answered. 'She is a fallen woman now. A husband convicted of murder? She'll never be accepted in polite society again.'

Indy stared at the women as they passed by. A fallen woman? Was that where she was heading too? The miners could be unforgiving. Whether her relationship with Will had an end date or not, they would ostracise her for her involvement with him.

She folded the paper under her arm and started walking quickly towards the dense bushland on the town outskirts. Meandering through the scrub, she thought about what it might mean to the miners now that Bentley had been found guilty and finally convicted of the murder of Scobie. Would this calm the unrest that had plagued Ballarat since the fateful night, so long ago it seemed to her, that Scobie lost his life? Or would it urge the reformists on, giving them the support and energy they needed to continue with their fight for equality? She'd lay money on the latter. They would see this as a result of their petitions and protestations and be spurred on by it.

It was a blessing to find the shade of the trees in the heat of the day. The temperature dropped a little and as she arrived at the river, she found Will pacing impatiently.

'I thought you wouldn't come,' he said, looking more unsure of himself than she'd ever seen him.

'Bentley's been convicted of murder,' she blurted. She must still have been in shock for that to be the first thing that came out of her mouth.

'What?' He walked towards her as she held out the paper to him.

She watched his furrowed brow as he scanned the words.

'Well,' was all he said.

'I'm as surprised as you,' she answered, and walked to the small sandy beach by the river. She remembered the last time they had been here together—it felt like an age ago. Though less than two months had passed since he'd caught her bathing naked in the river. When she felt him behind her she had to try hard not to lean back against his broad chest.

'I'll apologise for my temper the last time we spoke,' she said, staring into the cool depths of the river. 'But I won't apologise for the content of it.'

'Understood,' he said, the reassurance of his deep voice spreading warmth throughout her body. 'It might be best if we keep our discussions to safer topics. Let's leave politics and religion to the politicians and the priests, shall we?'

She turned and smiled up at him. 'Agreed.'

'How did the inaugural meeting of the Ladies of the Ballarat Reform League go?'

Her smile faltered. 'I thought we weren't going to talk politics.'

'Pardon me, you are correct,' he acquiesced.

Indy sighed heavily and gave in. 'It was a complete waste of time. Here I was thinking we would talk about what we would do to get the men to see us as equals and all they wanted to talk about was babies and sewing patterns.'

She narrowed her eyes at Will as he stifled a laugh and pretended it was a cough.

'It's not funny,' she said, but she couldn't help the smile that touched her lips. 'There I was standing on my proverbial soapbox talking about rights for women and they wanted to know whether they were still allowed to wear their dresses if they wanted to be equal to men. That descended into a full out argument over bloomers and petticoats versus the latest in crinolines.'

'Change takes time, Indy,' Will offered, still trying not to laugh.

Indy pouted.

'You are so different to them,' he said, lifting a curl from her cheek and placing it behind her ear. 'Different to anyone I have ever met. They just want to make the world pretty, to make a home for their men and their children. You want to make the world a better place.'

She shrugged, 'What's wrong with that?'

'Nothing,' he said. 'Nothing at all. But, my courageous little warrior, the world is yet to catch up with your ideals. I am struggling to keep up with them. You can be a little intimidating.'

'So I should stop having an opinion? I should simply put on a dress and a bonnet and marry the first man who asks?'

'Tame the untamable Indy Wallace?' he asked, wide-eyed with mock horror. 'Never in a million years. And I do not wish you to marry the first man who asks,' he said moving closer to her. 'If you did that, I would not be allowed to do this.'

He kissed her cheek lightly. Then, pressing his body against hers, his tongue traced the curves of her ear and her breath caught.

'And I wouldn't be able to do this,' he whispered, before dropping warm kisses along her jawline until he reached the very corner of her mouth.

'No, I imagine my husband would be quite upset if you did that,' she said, her breath catching when his hands went to her ribs.

'Then I imagine he would kill me for this,' he said, his thumb moving up to caress a nipple.

'Will?' she pleaded.

'Mmm?'

'Kiss me.'

She didn't need to ask again. She was yanked against his body and his mouth descended to hers in a crushing kiss that made her head spin and her belly liquefy.

'I'm sorry we quarrelled,' he said between kisses.

'You said that already. I'm enjoying making up.'

Tired of his gentle teasing, she gripped his hair to pull his mouth back to hers.

After a few moments of breath-stealing kisses, she leaned away to let her spinning head and heart settle.

'I thought you wanted a swim.'

'I do,' he said, and grinning with a deviousness she'd not seen on his face before, he swung her up off the ground and into his arms before walking knee deep into the water, boots and all.

'Join me, will you?'

'Don't you dare!' she yelled before he tossed her into the river and dove in after her.

Chapter 22

The upbeat jaunty strains of a brass band marching through the town drew the attention of everyone on the Eureka goldfield. Standing up from the cradle and pushing her hat back on her head to wipe the perspiration away, Indy watched as the Stars and Stripes of the American flag was paraded along the streets and through the diggings, led by its musical escort.

She cringed and made an unladylike guttural groaning noise.

'Turkey Day,' Sean said, taking a mouthful of water as they watched the Americans trudge through town and camp singing 'The Star-Spangled Banner'—again, and again and again. Indy was so sick of the damn song.

For three years, they had endured the American miners celebrating Thanksgiving Day. And as the day wore on, the drinking got heavier, the gunfire exploded into the air with frightening regularity and fights would break out. Mostly between the Americans and the English as historical tensions from years of war between the sovereignty and the once British colony reared their heads on the back of a nobbler or ten of Kentucky bourbon.

The children of the goldfields loved Turkey Day. They followed the Americans about, as they seemed to have an endless supply of firecrackers as well as chocolate and candy imported specifically for the event.

A party was always held in honour of the day and the American consular Mr Tarleton was travelling up from Melbourne this year to attend the extravagant dinner at the Victoria Hotel. Commissioner Rede would also be in attendance along with many of the other top government officials from the camp.

Back at the campsite with Annie and Sean that evening, Indy listened with ever rising aggravation as the music poured out of the Victoria Hotel in the near distance.

'Christ almighty!' she yelled to the sky. 'Shut the bleeding hell up!'

'Don't you take the Lord's name in vain, young lady,' Annie scolded. But

Indy's call was soon seconded by other members of the camp.

'I'm sorry, but if I have to listen to this much longer I won't be held responsible for what I might do.'

A guitar played quietly nearby and Indy looked about for its owner. She spotted the Kennedy brothers, well-known musicians in the Irish camp, and standing from her seat she walked with purpose across to their tent.

'Come on, lads!' she prompted. 'Play us a tune, and play it as loud as you can to drown out those blasted Yankees!'

Taking up their guitar and fiddle, the brothers began a fast and popular Irish folk song and cheers went up all around the Eureka camp. The previously subdued tenants suddenly came alive with the urge to show the Americans that they had nothing on an Irish céilí. More musicians joined the Kennedys with drums, accordion, tin whistle and even a set of spoons for percussion and the music grew louder, drawing neighbours in. The whiskey was passed around, couples danced and soon enough they had drowned out the noise of the American celebrations.

Thrilled with the impromptu party, Indy took a break from the dancing, sitting down with Sean and Annie on a long log a short distance from the frolicking crowd.

''Tis a fine thing to remember your roots, Indy,' Annie told her as she clapped along. 'That's all the Americans are doing too.'

'I know,' Indy conceded. 'But do they have to be so unholy arrogant about it?'

Annie laughed heartily and as the music played on, no one at the party paid much heed to the small group of soldiers that marched down the main street past the Eureka camp. But Indy did. She kept one eye on them as they walked quietly by. They were only a small troop, guarding a wagon of supplies just come from Melbourne no doubt. A young drummer boy led the convoy but kept his drum silent as they passed by the camp. Had they been warned of the dangers for soldiers here in Ballarat?

Indy was about to turn her back and ignore them as they went on their way to the government camp when something else caught her attention. From a tent nearest the road, a group of men crept out and ran stealthily towards the soldiers' procession. The men wore kerchiefs across their faces and even in the dark she could see they brandished weapons.

Indy stood up. 'What in the bloody hell are they about?'

'What?' Sean asked, as he and Annie followed Indy's movements.

'Bushrangers!' Annie exclaimed, but her voice was drowned out by the band that had decided to up the tempo of their tunes.

'Not bushrangers,' Indy said, shaking her head frustrated. 'It's those brainless O'Toole brothers. They're after getting themselves killed.'

She took off across the camp towards the road with Sean hot on her heels.

'Don't!' Annie called after them. 'You'll get hurt. Indy! Sean! I'm telling you to stop!'

But Indy kept going.

Fireworks exploded into the sky, heralding the finale of the official Thanksgiving Day celebrations. The loud explosions and bright colours pulled the attention of everyone in the nearby campsite away from the passing soldiers but Indy saw none of it.

'Stand and Deliver!' One of the O'Toole boys called to the soldiers. The youngest of the five O'Tooles Indy realised. He was only sixteen.

The soldiers stopped walking and circled the wagon, aiming their rifles at the boys. Indy watched on with equal parts of fear and irritation. The foolish lads were going to find their way into an early grave.

Two of the O'Tooles crept from beneath the wagon and jumped the soldiers from behind. A mad wrestle for the guns ensued, but Indy's attention was dragged away as another of the brothers climbed up onto the wagon to battle it out with the driver.

'What are you doing, you bloody eejits?' Indy shouted, but there was no way she was about to get herself into such a fight.

She held Sean back too.

'We're getting our money's worth from our taxes,' one of the O'Tooles called back.

'This isn't the way.' Indy tried to make them see sense, but their blood was high.

'Talking about it at meetings on Bakery Hill every other day ain't the way neither,' Pat, the oldest brother said, stopping beside her. He was twenty-two and likely to be dead before his twenty-third birthday with such a taste for trouble. 'Face it, Indy. This is a war. Choose your side. You're either Irish or you're English.'

'I'm Australian, you great git,' Indy tossed back, frustrated. 'I thought that's what we were fighting for. Independence. You want to bring all that Irish against the English rubbish with you to this new place? What was the bloody point in us leaving?'

There was a loud explosion and a flash of light. Louder and closer than the fireworks from the celebrations. Indy's heart leapt into her throat and she quickly looked at Sean who was equally as stunned. One of the soldier's guns had fired and everyone seemed to stop, frozen in place.

'Are you shot?' she asked Sean.

'No,' he returned, looking himself over as though to be sure. 'You?'

'No.'

He was fine. She was fine.

Soldiers and bandits alike checked themselves and each other for gunshot wounds, before the fight for the wagon and its cargo began again.

Indy's eyes were drawn to something lying on the ground a short distance from the wagon. Moving closer she saw it was the drummer boy. He was holding his leg and groaning.

'Shite!' she said and ran across to the boy, Sean hot on her heels.

Sure enough, he was bleeding from a gunshot wound to his thigh. Indy quickly pulled Sean's kerchief from his neck and tied a tourniquet around the drummer boy's upper thigh to try to stem the bleeding.

'You're a brave lad,' she told him as she worked. He must have been no older than fourteen years old. Dressed in a red coat that looked much too big for his slight build. 'Is this your first battle wound?'

'Yes, m'am,' he answered in a small and shaking voice.

Spooked by the shot, the horses were now trying to flee, and she and the boy were directly in their path. Indy dragged the boy to safety and watched horrified as the wagon was overturned, taking horses and men with it. Two of the would-be bushrangers continued emptying the wagon of whatever they could get their hands on—food, weapons, baggage—while the others fought off the soldiers.

Cheers went up and the battle went on attracting nearby diggers who came to help loot the goods, until finally the pack of thieves disappeared with their ill-gotten booty. The soldiers were ordered by an officer not to give chase, leaving them nothing to do but to clean up what was left of their cargo.

Indy was helping the soldiers lift the drummer boy onto the righted wagon when Commissioner Rede and a contingent of soldiers rode towards them.

'What happened here?' Rede demanded.

'Ambush, sir,' one of the soldiers replied.

Indy took Sean's arm and was about to lead him away when she heard the Commissioner call out.

'You there, girl!'

She stopped and turned slowly to face the most powerful man in Ballarat.

'Did you see the perpetrators of this?'

'No, sir,' Indy replied. 'They were masked.'

Rede stared at her a moment before turning his back on her.

'The boy there is shot, sir,' she called out. 'He needs medical assistance.'

'We'll see to it,' Rede responded barely sparing her a glance.

Indy and Sean moved back to where Annie had been watching worriedly. A single slap across the back of the head greeted both of them.

'Getting involved in a gunfight?' Annie lashed out.

'Ma!' Sean complained, rubbing his head.

'Wasn't us who had the guns,' Indy disputed.

Annie walked back to camp with Sean following behind her, his head hung low from his scolding. Indy took another look at the soldiers as they struggled to move the now righted and half empty wagon along the road. The horses were injured, as was the driver.

She frowned, feeling real apprehension for the first time. Until now, the aggression shown by the miners towards soldiers had been mostly vocal. While the diggers had taken to calling abuse at the military and police if they were ever in town, no one had ever purposely physically assaulted anyone from the government camp. Yes, miners had attacked Bentley's Hotel and soldiers had been caught up in that, Will included. But no digger had ever stolen from Her Majesty's supply before. They left that up to the bushrangers or highway thieves.

The ruckus had caused severe injury to soldiers and government workers, and Indy knew the authorities would not stand for that. It was like a red flag to a bull. There was bugger all chance of peaceful resolution now. No more petitions would be heard, Indy knew. There was no undoing what had just been done.

***

The story of the attack on the government wagon by the O'Toole brothers spread around camp faster than a dysentery outbreak. Naturally, the story was embellished with every telling. The number of soldiers had gone from eight to eighteen, the drummer boy was barely clinging to life—even though he'd been seen walking about on a simple crutch.

The following evening, spurred on by the story of courage and daring, a huge crowd gathered on Bakery Hill and Indy, Annie and Sean watched on with trepidation. A makeshift flagpole had been erected. While the Union Jack was flying, it was soon lowered and another flag was raised in its place. Indy had to admit it was impressive. The five white stars of the Southern Cross constellation, connected by white stripes on a field of deep blue—it was a symbol for the people of a new Australia. A defiant departure from the tyrannical rule of Her Majesty under the Union Jack. 'The Australia Flag'. It was clear the miners had been planning this revelation for some time.

'We shall no longer live under the oppression of the Union Jack,' Lalor preached. 'Who will stand with me?'

A cheer went up in the affirmative. Lalor walked towards the large fire in the middle of the massive crowd. He took a piece of paper from his pocket and held it aloft. His mining licence, Indy realised. She watched in disbelief as he purposely dropped it into the fire. Gasps of surprise were soon drowned out by cheers of exultation. One by one, men followed Lalor's lead and threw their hard-earned licences into the fire.

'Oh, Lord save us.' Annie said, concern etching her brow. 'Indy, what does all this mean?'

'It's okay, Ma,' Sean told his mother and put an arm around her as she wrung her hands anxiously.

'Don't you go burning your licence, Sean,' Annie demanded quietly. 'I'll not have you getting caught up in this.'

'He'll not burn his licence,' Indy insisted giving Sean a firm 'I dare you' look.

'I won't,' he said, but Indy could see the admiration in his eyes as he watched miner after miner step forward to turn their thirty shillings into ashes.

***

'The camp is becoming stifling,' Will told Indy as he walked back and forth along the water's edge.

The natural spring had become their most beloved secret meeting place as it was far too dangerous for them to be seen together in town or the camps. Luckily, they could both use the excuse of going to get water for their respective camps if they were caught.

'Since that band of diggers attacked the wagon, Rede has doubled the guard around the compound. I can hardly take a piss without a sentry watching on.'

Indy happily watched him pace off his frustrations from her position on a flat rock. Each time he walked away it gave a good view of her most favoured part of his anatomy tucked tight in his trousers.

'I hear all the diggers burned their licences last night,' Will said in passing.

'Not all,' Indy responded. 'I didn't. Most just went to hear Peter Lalor talk and to figure out the next move.'

Will stopped pacing and stared at her, his mouth moved in shock and he blinked erratically but no words were forthcoming.

'You were there?' he finally asked.

'Of course I was there,' she answered with a casual shrug. 'Who wasn't there?'

'You shouldn't be so glib about this,' he said, staring fiercely into her eyes. 'Rede was there last night. He saw everything.'

Now it was Indy's turn to stare with her mouth open. Rede knew miners had burned their licences. That changed things. A raid would surely follow. She had to warn the miners. But would they be afraid? Or would they welcome the challenge? Her brain was working at a hundred miles an hour when Will grabbed her arms, lifting her to stand.

'Indy, he heard everything.'

'Will, you're hurting my arm.'

'They suspect something is brewing. Something bigger than just burned licences. The government camp is like a fort. More soldiers come from Melbourne every day. Rede thinks the diggers are planning to attack the government camp.'

'Don't be ridiculous,' Indy said with a laugh of disbelief as she pulled out of his grip. 'They may be hotheaded and impulsive but they're not stupid enough to attack an entire garrison of soldiers.'

'Aren't they?'

Stepping to the edge of the spring, Indy chewed on a thumbnail as she stared at her reflection in the calm, flowing water. There'd been no calm at the meeting last night. There'd been hotheaded calls for action. The burning of licences had given her an uneasy feeling, to say the least. Miners talked of paying no more fees until some concessions were made by the Governor. Top of that list was being allowed to have a representative in the newly formed Victorian Government. Someone who would speak for the people. Even gentlemen miners who had erred on the side of talk rather than action seemed to have given up hope of a democratic resolution, and many of them had dropped their licence into the fire just as Lalor had.

Would a few thousand diggers be reckless enough to take on the might of the British infantry? Until the attack on the soldiers' wagon she would have said a resounding 'no'. But patience was wearing thin and the ill winds that blew through Ballarat were testing even the calmest of temperaments.

'Indy, the newspapers are calling anyone who was at that meeting last night a rebel.'

He took her hands in his, snapping her out of her thoughts. 'I don't mind admitting I'm afraid for you. I don't want to see you get caught up in something you can't get out of. I don't want to see you arrested or injured.'

'Lalor is a level-headed man. He will keep them in check,' Indy said, but uncertainty had taken root.

'We both know he can't,' Will argued. 'Look at the burning of the Eureka Hotel. Isn't that enough proof that despite Lalor's best intentions, if there's enough grog and enough outrage in a large crowd, no one will be able to talk them down? And from what I hear, Lalor himself is now talking revolution not peaceful solutions.'

'He's doing what's right,' Indy insisted, battling her frustration. On one hand she agreed with what Will was saying. He made sense, damn him. But on the other, she was a miner and she knew that what they were asking for was justified.

She paced away a few steps, kicking at gumnuts on the ground before turning back to face him.

'Listen, I'm not about to get caught up in the ranting of a bunch of chest-banging men. But neither am I opposed to the reasons for their dissatisfaction. You have fought in wars to save foreign countries from dictatorial rule. Yet here, the Queen's own countrymen are the enemy. But how are these men any different in their quest for freedom from oppression?'

She braced herself, fully expecting him to launch into his usual rant about her crazy ideologies, but instead he simply smiled at her.

'What are you grinning at?' she asked, confused by his calm expression.

'You're magnificent, Indy Wallace. If I was not attracted to your beauty, your brain would have me spellbound just the same. How do you do it?'

'What?'

'You live with such passion, such determination.'

She blinked at the compliment, then shaking her head clear, she took a step back to put some distance between them.

'Stop changing the subject. I'm mad at you.'

'Of course you are,' he said, moving into her again and running his finger across her jawline.

'I ... I can't think when you touch me. So cut it out.'

'You're exquisite,' he continued, and dropped a kiss on her cheek.

'Don't flatter me, Lieutenant, I have things to say.'

'Then say them, Indy.' He kissed her other cheek, taking his mouth on a journey along her chin to her ear. 'I'm not stopping you.'

The whisper against her ear sent shivers down her spine and warmed the lowest depths of her belly. She fisted her hands at her sides to stop from grabbing him and pulling him closer.

'Um, um, I ... see now you've distracted me and I can't recall exactly what I was going to say.' She couldn't stop the quiver in her voice as his hands trailed up her ribs to settle beneath her breasts.

'I'm sure it was good,' he murmured against her ear before sucking the lobe into his mouth. 'You'll remember it later.'

'I will,' she nodded, trying to access her brain through the fog of arousal as his talented hands moved up to claim first her left breast, and then her right. 'I will remember ... later.'

Giving in, she wrapped her arms about his neck, bringing his mouth to hers.

Soft and warm, his kisses sent delicious tingles through her entire body. She wanted him here and now. She wanted him to touch her in places that would incite and excite.

'I can't wait much longer for you,' she said between kisses.

'Nor I for you, Indy,' he said and kissed her again. 'But what can we do?'

She sighed heavily. 'Our time is running out, Will. Do you feel it?'

He put his forehead to hers and closed his eyes. 'I do. We always knew it would.'

She leaned back to look into his beautiful eyes. Searching, delving into their depths to find some inkling to his real feelings. But he was a closed book. An expert at masking his emotions. How would she ever say goodbye when the time came?

'I can't bear the idea of you leaving ... without us having been together, I mean,' she added, covering what she had truly wanted to say—that she could no longer bear the thought of him leaving. Still gazing into his eyes she saw the heat and the desperation. She felt it too. Along with the first cracks of her heart breaking.

Chapter 23

'Conditions in the camp are deteriorating, sir,' Johnston told Commissioner Rede at their daily meeting. 'If we keep bringing in more redcoats I'm not sure where we'll put them.'

'Understood. But we must protect the camp, Johnston,' Rede maintained. 'I've petitioned Hotham on many occasions over the last six months about the upgrade to the amenities. But even if we have the new barracks I requested, we still wouldn't fit them all in.'

Johnston followed Rede outside of the command tent to survey the compound. From one end of the government camp to the other, soldiers and police filled almost every square inch. The men were sleeping in shifts. While their colleagues took the watch, they had their turn under canvas and at shift change they would swap out. Some police officers had found respite in the shade of the few buildings in the camp. While others simply found a patch of ground, hopefully not too hard or wet if there'd been rain, and caught whatever shut-eye they could get in the swelter of the day. All of the men looked undernourished and demoralised.

'There are just so many of them,' Rede said, a small measure of despondency creeping into his voice.

'Hotham continues to order more soldiers to Ballarat since word reached Melbourne about the latest attack on the supply convoy,' Johnston said.

'It is justified,' Rede agreed. 'But how do we house and feed them all appropriately? Morale is plummeting and there is unrest and unease between the police and soldiers like never before. I feel as though we are fighting a battle on two sides now. We must protect the government camp from the growing instability on the goldfields. My spy in the diggers' camp says that although no outright declaration has yet been made, he believes an attack of sorts by the miners is forthcoming.'

'Do you believe them foolhardy enough to attempt a run at the camp itself?' Johnston asked with scepticism.

'I'm not going to sit about on our hands and wait to find out,' Rede insisted. 'Perhaps it is time to go on the offensive instead of waiting for the rebels to make the first move. Show them that any uprising will be dealt with by the harshest of penalties. Call the commanding officers in here please, Johnston. It's time to act.'

The Commissioner moved back into the tent and a soldier was sent to find the officers of the government camp. Moments later, Captain Thomas was entering Commissioner Rede's tent followed shortly afterwards by Police Inspector Evans.

'I want to run a licence raid today. The likes of which they have never seen before. We know for a fact that many of the diggers burned their licences last night. I want to ensure they know we won't stand by and take that lightly. Send a message. Send a large party of soldiers with the police. Arrest as many diggers as you can.'

'It's a swift and decisive response,' Captain Thomas agreed. 'May I make a suggestion, sir?'

'By all means.'

'Put Lieutenant Marsh in charge of this raid,' Thomas said.

Rede eyed the Captain curiously. 'To what end?'

'The men talk, sir,' Thomas told him. 'I hear tittering in the ranks that Marsh is courting a digger. A young girl.'

'Men have been known to fraternise before, Captain,' Rede said, shrugging it off. 'It's not uncommon.'

'True, sir. But I believe her to be quite the troublemaker. It was over her that Marsh and Donnelly fought. And she was at the meeting on Bakery Hill last night.'

'From what I saw the whole damn town of Ballarat was at that meeting,' Rede said frustrated. 'As well as a few from Creswick and Bendigo. Did she burn her licence?'

'I'm not sure, sir.'

'Well, she'll be picked up in the raid if she did,' Rede continued to brush it off.

'Sergeant Donnelly tells me the girl is one of the main instigators of the uprising,' Inspector Evans added.

'Indeed?' Rede said, taking more notice now. 'Donnelly said that?'

'He was quite adamant, sir, before he left for Melbourne this morning,' Evans responded.

Rede leaned back in his chair thoughtfully and turned his attentions to Thomas. 'You're his commanding officer. Do you believe Lieutenant Marsh would be tempted into desertion by this girl?'

'I couldn't say, sir,' Thomas said honestly. 'He has always been one of my finest officers. But he has been challenging authority lately. He questions the manner in which the licence raids are delivered and was overheard saying that we are not at war and therefore should treat these civilians with more care. He and Sergeant Donnelly have traded insults, and fists I believe, more than once.'

'It hardly makes Donnelly a reliable source then does it,' Rede countered. He steepled his hands, put them to his lips in thought. 'Very well then. Send Lieutenant Marsh to lead the licence raid. Ensure he knows he must go in with them and not just stand on the sidelines. That ought to put paid to any allegiance with the miners.'

'Yes, sir.'

***

Assembled with police and soldiers by the now heavily guarded entrance to the government camp, Will's senses were on high alert. Commissioner Rede and Assistant Commissioner Johnston sat mounted on their horses, watching proceedings as Captain Thomas announced the coming raid.

'Commissioner Rede has requested a contingent of soldiers lead the next licence raid on the Gravel Pits goldfield. We need to show a strong united front and prove to the rebels that we will not sit idly by whilst they burn their licences in protest.'

He walked down the line. 'Lieutenant Marsh.'

'Sir!' Will stood to attention at the end of the row of soldiers who seemed all too eager to be included in some action for the first time.

'Lieutenant Marsh shall lead the raid alongside Assistant Commissioner Johnston,' Thomas said.

Will blinked. 'Captain Thomas, is it not the jurisdiction of the local police to—'

'Are you questioning my orders, Marsh?' Captain Thomas barked, spinning on his heel to glare at him.

'No, sir.'

'Good,' Thomas said. 'I'd hate to see such a fine officer written up for insubordination twice in as many months.'

Will was trapped and he knew it.

'Assistant Commissioner Johnston will take the raid to the Gravel Pits with the police,' Thomas instructed the troops in a loud commanding voice.

'Lieutenant Marsh will call for the licences to be shown and then take the mounted troops through the fields and into the camps to chase the runners. Commissioner Rede and I will lead the foot soldiers down the hill to the plateau to the south. We must show the rebels they cannot win this game. Move out!'

Will's gut churned as police and mounted soldiers moved out of the camp. He had to lead the soldiers and police into the Gravel Pits section of the goldfields. Indy worked the Eureka lead. His only hope would be that she didn't see him and that she would never find out. But well aware of the phenomenal speed in which gossip travelled around the diggings, he knew he had more chance of striking gold than word of this raid not reaching Indy Wallace.

***

The small contingent of soldiers joined the larger troop of mounted and foot police that marched down the hill, with Will in the lead, Johnston beside him. The only blessing Will felt was that Donnelly wasn't amongst the police raiders.

When they arrived at the Gravel Pits mining lead, the diggers stopped working, eyeing with confusion the unusually large contingent of soldiers numbered in with the police. The miners crossed glances with one another, unsure of what to do.

Will took a deep breath. 'Gentlemen! Present your licences please.'

The diggers didn't move forward as requested, but instead joined together in a line, hands in pockets, a united front.

Not good.

'Present your licences,' he called again.

Still nothing. A nervous sweat trickled down his back. He was a soldier and had been into battle more times than he could count, advancing on a foe without a second thought. But this felt different. These men, these miners, were not his enemy. They were not the enemy of Britain. He refused to sound an advance without provocation and even then he swore he would keep the raid controlled and efficient without need for brutality or bloodshed.

'Gentlemen, we do not want any trouble. Present your licences and disperse this assembly.'

Move, dammit, Will urged in silent desperation. *Don't make me do this.*

He was about to move his horse forward to talk with the men in the hope of keeping the peace when one shot rang out, then another and another as the police began firing above the heads of the crowd that had gathered.

'Joe! Joe!' came the familiar yell from miners.

Suspicion and confusion had turned into panic. Despite Will's best efforts to contain the raid, all hell broke loose as miners and onlookers ran from the gunfire and the mounted police who now stormed unchecked through the diggings. He spun his horse and glared back at the line of soldiers and policemen.

'Who fired?' he yelled but it was too late. Another shot rang out and diggers who'd burned their licences, or didn't have one to begin with, hid in mineshafts and tents to avoid arrest. 'Hold!' he yelled, watching the chaos from his position on his horse.

He hated himself. All around him police and soldiers were attacked with bottles and rocks. Will ducked a flying liquor jug just as a large and furious miner reached up to grab at him, but he managed to kick him off.

Commissioner Rede, who had come down from the camp to watch, moved in quickly and read the riot act as if it would make any difference to the mayhem.

'Present arms!' Rede called.

Soldiers took up position on one knee and aimed rifles into the scattering crowd.

'No!' Will yelled and rode quickly over to where Rede stood. 'Sir, they are surrendering. Look. There's no need for more guns.'

Thankfully, he was right. A group of miners who'd been rounded up were tied together and led away. Others stood by, fuming, but no longer attacking the police who raced by.

'Stand down,' Rede called to the soldiers and police.

Will heaved a sigh of relief. The situation could have escalated, but thankfully the miners had seen sense and desisted once the riot act had been read. He surveyed the group of arrested men. It was a large catch. He'd done his job. Bully for him, he thought sardonically as the prisoners were led away towards the government camp and jail. He wiped the sweat from his brow and slumped in his saddle, suddenly drained of all energy. And then, from behind, he heard the voice of the one person he had hoped to avoid.

'Enjoying yourself, Lieutenant?'

He closed his eyes and swore.

Almost wishing someone would shoot him then and there, he turned his head slowly, finding her standing on the road between the Gravel Pits and the Eureka Lead. He steered his horse in her direction and as he got closer, he could see that she appeared uncommonly calm. If she yelled and screamed, hit him perhaps, he would be able to deal with that. But this look of stone cold disappointment—it cut him damn near in half.

'Of course I'm not enjoying myself,' he said, keeping his voice low so his troops wouldn't hear. 'I'm under orders.'

'Where have I heard that before?' she queried, sarcasm dripping. 'Oh, of course. Donnelly.'

Will's breath caught. She'd compare him to Donnelly? A man she hated with every part of her. 'I'm a soldier, Indy. I have to do as I am instructed to do. Do you want me to choose you and your principles over my allegiance to the Crown?'

'It's not about me,' she shot back, some of her well-known fire leaking through. 'It's not about choosing me. It's about choosing to do what is right. Not blindly following orders.'

'You really don't understand, do you?' he snapped, feeling acutely his irritation over the whole situation. 'I have a duty to uphold. Why can't you see that?'

'All I see is a grown man cuckolded by an autocratic world bully.'

'Christ,' he said through gritted teeth. 'Everything is black and white with you. You haven't been out there in the world enough to see that life isn't that simple. You don't always get to do what you think is right. Sometimes you have to do what you must to survive.'

He was well fired up now. His adrenaline was still pumping from the raid and while his temper didn't loosen often, when it did he had a hard time reining it in again.

'Oh, that's a load of bullock shite if ever I heard it,' she said, the Irish in her words showing just how angry she really was. 'And don't talk to me like I'm a child, Lieutenant.'

'Well, you're acting like one,' he shot back. 'It's true I did not want to lead this raid but I don't answer to you, Indy. I can do no right by your lofty standards and I am tired of defending myself to you.'

Her eyes went wide with shock. Her mouth dropped open but nothing came out. He could see the effort it took her to hold back her emotions. Knowing Indy like he did, he knew the tears that welled were more likely from fury than distress but all the same he felt wretched for having put them there.

He followed her gaze to where the group of arrested miners were being dragged away. Her pretty face, usually so lively and animated now appeared tired and worn down. Her bottom lip quivered a little before she bit down to stop it.

'How could I have been so wrong about you?'

The smallness of her voice tugged at his heart.

'Indy...' he started, finally getting a hold of his temper. 'Please. I had no choice.'

Her eyes slid to his but she stayed quiet for the longest time. The betrayal, so evident in the dark blue, would haunt him forever.

'There's always a choice,' she said and he heard the sadness beneath the anger. 'And clearly you have made yours.'

With that she turned and walked slowly away from him.

'Indy,' he called after her.

'Lieutenant!'

Captain Thomas's call had him turning away from Indy for a moment. The officer waved for him to follow him back to camp. Faltering, Will turned back to watch Indy retreating from him. Another choice. Follow her and try to make her understand? Or continue to do his duty and complete the raid? It was the proverbial rock and hard place.

'Yah!' he yelled in frustration as much as to spur his horse into action. He'd have to deal with Indy later.

At a dangerous speed he rode out of the goldfields. He'd almost made it to the road when a shot rang out. He heard the bullet whistle past his ear.

His horse spooked, but being an excellent horseman he stayed seated.

He wheeled the horse in a circle, searching for the culprit, waiting for the next bullet to hit its mark. He saw no one with a weapon aimed at him, so set his horse off down the road again. People jumped out of his way as he galloped furiously to catch up to the raiders and their unlicensed catch of the day.

***

Indy turned back once. Allowing herself just one last look at Will riding away from her. Back to the government camp. Back where he belonged.

'They've gone and done it now,' an old fellow Indy knew only as Samson stopped beside her. His pipe hung out the side of his mouth while he lit it. He exhaled a puff of smoke. 'You'd do well to stay away from that soldier boy, Miss Indy. There be trouble waiting there for ye.'

'Don't worry about that. I'll not be seeing the likes of him again.'

A heaviness overtook her as she stood by the side of the road. It squeezed at her lungs until she struggled to breathe. Her eyes stung as for the first time in years she felt the prick of tears threaten.

Diggers in the Gravel Pits gathered to deal with the wounded from the raid. No one had been shot, thank God, but there were still minor injuries to be seen to and bail to be raised for the poor unlicensed miners who'd been carted away. Indy saw none of it as she walked in a daze back to the Eureka fields.

When news got about that the soldiers and police had fired at the diggers there was uproar. Rede had read the riot act. Next would be martial law. Gossip spread like wildfire and more and more people converged on the Gravel Pits goldfields. The tides were turning and the time to act was fast approaching.

'To Bakery Hill!' someone called, and the group swarmed to the usual gathering place. More miners and townsfolk fell in to the procession as they passed.

Still caught up in her anger and desolation over Will, Indy followed Sean to Bakery Hill. The noise of the crowd was incredible and Indy gazed about her, overwhelmed by the shouting and the fury. In the midst of the yelling and demands for vengeance, someone climbed upon a log and the crowd hushed momentarily—such was the charisma of Peter Lalor. He couldn't have been much older than Will she guessed, but he had a commanding way about him that drew people in.

'Liberty!' he called and the roar of the crowd was deafening.

Not in the mood to join in with the jeering and jostling of the angry mob, she sat at a distance. She was stunned by the attendance. They had to number ten thousand by now. Diggers were coming in from other leads in other towns. Creswick, Bendigo, even Castlemaine. They talked of the delegation Lalor had sent to Melbourne to speak with Governor Hotham and their failure to get a decent response from him. Decent response? Lalor would have been better off going himself, since it was no secret the men who had been sent had all but been booted out of Government House for their lack of decorum and respect.

Several men took to the tree-stump platform to speak but it was Lalor who held the audience captive with his calm manner and sophisticated way of speaking. The diggers thought Lalor to be Jesus, but Indy knew, in the end, he was just a man. A man who would get them all killed if he continued to rouse them with words like 'independence' and catchphrases such as 'freedom from tyranny'.

She listened to him speak but couldn't concentrate on what he was saying. She still felt Will's betrayal deeply. He'd not only been a part of the last raid, he'd been its leader. Shots had been fired. Had he ordered the troops to shoot into the crowd? She could scarcely believe it. Orders, he'd said. Bloody orders! Blindly following the direction of supposedly superior men regardless of whether it was right or wrong. Just like these men here listening to Lalor now asking them to swear an oath, allegiance to the cause and the new flag. The diggers would blindly follow Peter Lalor to their deaths if they weren't careful. The latest licence raid on the Gravel Pits had been the catalyst they'd needed to get the unprecedented numbers Indy now saw gathered before her. Unprecedented numbers.

A thought struck Indy. She remembered the conversations she'd had with Will in the last month. *More soldiers were arriving every day. The government camp was becoming more and more like a fort.* Indy frowned, trying to block out all the talk around her. Had Will been right? Was it possible Commissioner Rede now believed these miners would attack the government camp? What could possibly be gained by miners attacking a virtual fortress of heavily armed soldiers and police? There was no resolution to be had on the other side of such an act of violent anarchy.

She contemplated the huddle of men who were cheering again and raising cries of rebellion. Battle cries. She'd told Will he was being ridiculous thinking these men would be stupid enough to take on the might of the British

Infantry. Suddenly it didn't seem so ridiculous.

These men and women were not soldiers. They'd be lambs to the slaughter. Especially if the army knew they were coming. The men were discussing erecting a barricade. It was tantamount to poking a bear. And not even a sleeping bear. She had to say something.

When a lull fell between speakers she took a deep breath and called out, 'Do you think it's wise to provoke the Commissioner with such a show of force and defiance?'

Silence fell as people scanned the crowd for the owner of the voice.

Indy stood reluctantly.

'What are you doing?' Sean hissed.

The men who held the high ground in front of the meeting exchanged glances. She could see what they were thinking. A woman was questioning them?

'Young lady,' one of the leaders called back, Hayes she recalled was his name. 'We must do what we can to protect ourselves from the violence of the licence raids.'

'And do you really believe you can beat back the Queen's infantry by building a barricade?'

'She's a spy!' someone yelled.

'Yeah, I seen her talkin' to that redcoat,' another called. 'Same one who led the raid today.'

'And she's Sergeant Donnelly's daughter!'

Those who didn't already know Indy's family situation yelled accusations and pointed fingers and suspicious glares in her direction. She felt the humiliation as people sent her looks of disgust she'd dealt with all her life.

'Yes, he is my father,' she admitted, her chin jutting out. 'And anyone who knows that is aware of just how much he hates me and how I return the sentiment tenfold.'

'Easy to say...'

More grumbles of agreement.

'Indy.' Sean took her hand and tried to get her to sit again. She resisted.

'The Army is reinforcing. More soldiers arrive every day. Can't you see what's happening?'

'It's all for show. To scare us into submission,' Lalor said and he was quickly backed up by calls from the crowd.

'Yeah, it's just trickery!'

'Falsehoods!'

'Do you not wonder why the government camp now stands as a military stronghold instead of a simple gold commissioner's compound?' Indy asked, stunned that they couldn't see what was right before their eyes. 'They suspect you are going to attack the government camp.'

'That's a good idea!' someone yelled.

'Aye, let's storm the fortress!'

There was laughter and there were calls of affirmation.

'Let us have calm,' Lalor called and the rabble settled down again 'We shall take a stand. We have burned our licences. Most of us anyway.'

'And they know that,' Indy added. Another thought struck. 'The raid today was in retaliation of that. They know just how many of you are unlicensed. They were there last night.'

'And how, pray tell, do you come upon that knowledge?' Hayes asked, suspicion written all over his face. 'We have often wondered if there was a government spy amongst us.'

'She's the spy!' someone called out again.

'I'm no spy,' Indy said standing straight and proud. 'I'm a miner. Just like you. I believe we deserve the right to make a home here. To get more for our taxes than a few pieces of wood and a tiny patch of dirt to dig—even if you believe females are not worthy of the same rights as men.'

That brought more grumbles which were drowned out by the cheers of agreement by women. Once again she felt Sean tugging on her hand, trying to get her to sit down.

'I will fight for my rights until I too can own land and have a say in this new Australia. But I don't believe building barricades and tossing out threats is the way to go about that.'

'If you are not a spy, then take the oath!'

'Yeah!'

'Make her take the oath!'

'Aye, let her prove her loyalty to the miners!'

Peter Lalor stepped forward, the unfurled blue flag with the white stars of the Southern Cross held out to her.

'The time for talk is over, Miss Wallace,' Lalor said. 'It's time for action. Will you take the oath and stand by your fellow miners? Your fellow Australians?'

Indy felt trapped. If she didn't say the oath, they would all think her a spy or a traitor. But if she swore the oath, she'd more than likely be signing her own arrest warrant.

She was a woman without choice.

In that moment she understood what Will had been trying to tell her. The Army was his home, just as this band of rebel miners was hers.

Life isn't always black and white, his voice rang in her head.

Will had been forced to run that raid, she realised with a heavy stab to her heart. He would never have chosen to do it but he hadn't had that choice. He would have been arrested, flogged, or whatever they did to soldiers who disobeyed orders. Having already been confined to quarters once, thanks to her, she doubted his superiors would be as lenient a second time.

But more than that, he would lose his family. The only family he'd ever known. To an orphan, she imagined, that would be harder than the arrest and punishment.

'So you gonna say the oath or not?'

Indy had heard the oath read in groups all day long but now they expected her to say it alone.

Despite Sean's murmured warnings, she pulled out of his grasp. The crowd parted as she walked towards Lalor.

She looked all four men who stood on the makeshift platform squarely in the eye. Lalor, Black, Hayes and Hummfray. Then she reached out and touched the wool of the dark blue flag. It was coarser than she'd expected.

Taking a deep breath, Indy turned and faced the crowd.

'"We swear by the Southern Cross to stand truly by each other and fight to defend our rights and liberties."'

A deafening cheer went up. At Lalor's signal, the crowd moved in a wave of humanity down the slopes from Bakery Hill to the Eureka fields following their leader and the flag he carried aloft. When they reached the Irish section of the camp, Indy turned and walked away from the mob.

For the rest of the day Indy watched with growing trepidation as all around her men worked, not on their mines, but at building what could only be described as a stockade. Wood from mineshafts, or anywhere else it could be taken from, was repurposed into a crude fence around a small patch of land that backed onto the scrub of Brown Hill. A few mines and at least ten tents had been encompassed within the stockade either by accident or plain bad luck as they had the poor fortune of holding good ground.

Anxious and irritated, she watched as groups of miners trawled the goldfields and the camps requesting, or demanding, that diggers and their families hand over all guns, weapons and anything else they wanted. Determined now that when the next licence raid came, they would be ready to fight back with force equal to what had been doled out to them. Try as she might, it was impossible to ignore the fortification being built not two hundred yards from where she and Sean continued to work their mine.

Indy found it hard to concentrate on the work at hand. All she could think of was that regardless of whether or not she joined the hundreds of rebelling miners behind the barricades, having taken the oath, she was now a sworn enemy of Her Majesty the Queen of England.

Chapter 24

The dark clouds building overhead matched Will's mood perfectly. He was angry with himself. He was angry with Indy. How could a man be expected to live up to such high moral standards as held by Indigo Wallace? She was by no means perfect. A gambler, he thought, ticking off her flaws one by one in his head. She stuck her nose into things that didn't concern her on a regular basis, and that temper of hers was legendary. Everything she thought came straight out of that smart mouth of hers. Not to mention the stubborn streak broader than the Yarrowee River that ran through her.

It was probably for the best that they went their separate ways now, he decided as the first fat raindrops began to leak out of the menacing clouds. He'd said it before: he and Indy were different creatures from different worlds. Wild and determined, she knew exactly what she wanted out of her life and, no doubt, she expected to get it. He was a soldier. A military man who had been taking orders for so long he scarcely knew how to think for himself anymore. She'd been right about that, and it irked him.

Sitting just inside the open flap of his shabby tent, Will took a good look around the camp. It was not yet three in the afternoon but the severity of the approaching storm descended the day into an early twilight. Timmons grumbled behind him as the hole in the roof of their tent sent small rivers of water flooding onto his cot. But Will was past listening and certainly past caring.

Soldiers and police scattered as the rain fell in torrents now, seeking out shelter wherever they could find it. Turned out of the stables in favour of the soldiers who had arrived that afternoon with Major General Nickle, the police huddled beneath their horses to try to stay dry. Those soldiers unable to leave their posts, guarding the perimeter of the compound, folded into themselves against the weather, looking weary and quickly becoming saturated in the heavy downpour.

Captain Thomas had been keeping them up for twenty-four hour stints on sentry duty. The soldiers were unwashed, unfed and antsy. Many of them were young and bored and everyone was irritated at the state of the camp. These men were spoiling for a fight. Any fight. Soldiers and police were kept at the ready as they waited for the rumoured attack by the rebel miners. But by the time the rain had stopped late in the evening, the expected attack had not yet transpired.

With cabin fever setting in, Will decided to go for a walk about the camp. He came upon George in the mess tent playing cards with several other officers. Gentlemen of the same ilk as George, from wealthy families who had bought their commission, unlike Will who had earned his in battle. George would be promoted to Captain soon, Will was certain of it. He also knew that he would never move higher up the ranks of the military than Lieutenant. His upbringing and parentage were too questionable. It had never really concerned him since he was a soldier for the adventure. He was not attracted to the posturing and pretentiousness that so often went with the higher ranks of the British Army.

Leaving George to his cards, Will wandered along the perimeter of the compound. Part of him wanted to jump the fence, go to Indy and finish explaining to her his role in the Gravel Pits raid that morning. Could he make her understand? He doubted it. The woman was immovable when she dug her heels in.

As he neared the front entrance of the compound he could hear shouting, and curious, he moved towards the gate.

'You'll not cross! Come any closer and I'll shoot.'

Fearing the itchy trigger finger of a tired sentry, he rushed towards the two soldiers pointing their rifles at a contingent of three miners. He recognised Father Smythe and the Italian he'd seen a few times around the goldfields named Carboni.

'These rebels are trying to enter the camp,' the soldier relayed as Will made his presence known. 'It's a ploy to get into the compound. Captain Thomas said an attack was coming and to shoot any miner who tried to cross.'

'Lower your weapons,' Will told the soldiers. 'You can see these men are unarmed.'

He turned to the three men who stood warily back from the armed soldiers. 'What business have you here, gentlemen?'

'We demand to speak with Commissioner Rede,' one of the men said.

'Demand?' Will asked, rubbing the bridge of his nose wearily. They really had no idea of negotiations. If he took these three men into the camp and they went down their usual path of making 'requests', Commissioner Rede would toss him out with them.

'Father Smythe may enter,' Will said, noting that the young priest seemed much less antagonistic than his two counterparts. 'You two can stay here.'

Father Smythe placated the other men who complained at being denied access and said he would try to bring Rede back.

Will took the young priest to Rede, who did indeed follow him back to the entry to the compound.

'You must listen to reason, sir,' the man named Black insisted.

'I must not do anything of the sort,' Rede countered. 'A rebellion uprising is hardly appealing to my good faith, gentlemen.'

'But no one is listening to our concerns,' Carboni added. 'We have petitioned the Governor time and again and have not had the response we require.'

'Then what do you expect me to do?' Rede asked. 'The Governor's word is final. I answer to him. If you insist on barricading yourselves behind that stockade you have created, I cannot guarantee your safety.'

'Reduce the severity of the licence raids at the very least,' Father Smythe tried.

'They are necessary,' Rede said. 'It is my duty to ensure that licences are held by those who wish to dig for Her Majesty's gold. Otherwise we would be even more overrun on the goldfields than we are now. It is the only way to keep order.'

'But, sir, it is the manner in which the raids are carried out—'

'I am done with this line of discussion,' Rede interrupted. 'It seems we are at an impasse. But let me warn you, gentlemen. If any of the rebels attempt to infiltrate or attack the government compound, we are ready and will strike with fatal force. Do you understand me?'

As the three men turned away from the gates of the government camp, the Italian let fly with a host of words Will didn't understand, but his temperament gave him the gist of the man's sentiments.

***

The noise of the storm made it impossible to sleep. Or perhaps it was her fight with Will that had Indy tossing and turning in her cot. Sean didn't seem troubled by the thundering downpour as he snored on behind the sheet that separated his bed from hers and Annie's in the tent.

When the rain finally abated, Indy crept outside and sat by the waning fire. Despite the rain it was a warm night, though the events of the day left her feeling cold. The chill, which ran deep into her bones, was more a feeling of dread that time was fast running out. For her and Will, for the unlicensed miners, and for the men and women ensconced inside the now completed stockade.

For the hundredth time that day her eyes were drawn across to the northern border of the Eureka camp, towards the crudely constructed barricade. Campfires burned low inside the stockade grounds. The large dark flag, now hoisted high upon a makeshift flagpole, waved in the light breeze—the white stars and stripes glowing ominously by the light of the bright moon. Some men had gone to sleep inside the small area of fortification, others sat around a single fire while two men stood guard at the small entrance.

Not a hundred yards from the stockade, just down the Melbourne Road, Indy could see the burned out shell of the Bentley's Eureka Hotel. It stood as a sad reminder of how rapidly a peaceful protest could get out of hand. McIntyre and Fletcher languished in jail for their part in the burning of the Eureka Hotel. Possibly in the very same area of the prison that Bentley, Vance and Farrell were all serving time for the murder of James Scobie. What a ridiculous, futile waste.

Indy poked absently at the sodden coals in the fireplace with a stick, staring blindly into the glow as the flames struggled to reignite after the rain. So much had happened in just a few months. Letting her gaze fall back on the stockade, she wondered what would come of this latest outlandish defiance. Hearing a twig snap, Indy twisted quickly in her seat to check behind her. But seeing no one she turned back to her fire. It was probably just a fox picking up dinner scraps or more rats on the move spreading disease through the camp.

For almost three years she had lived in this camp with Annie and Sean. It was miraculous how fast it had grown from a small temporary tent settlement of only a few thousand miners to a bustling town with wood and brick buildings. Small businesses thrived as demand necessitated supply. Industry may have been booming but the alluvial leads of Ballarat were beginning to run dry. More mines duffered out, but people still needed to eat. They still required doctors and blacksmiths and tinsmiths. Not to mention the all-important enterprise of liquor and beer.

Glancing back at the stockade, she sighed. She'd had enough. Enough of living side by side in over-occupied camps with hundreds of other people. Enough of digging her mine every day—she didn't need to, she'd found enough gold. But if they didn't dig, they would lose the claim to someone else. Did she even care anymore? Someone else could have it if Sean didn't want to continue to work it himself. She wanted out. She could move in with her mother, find occupation that meant she didn't need to stay in the camps or in town.

Together they could turn her mother's small vegetable patch into a proper farm. A good living could be made from what they grew and sold to the stores in town. Especially if they sold to the hotels for their restaurants, or to John Alloo for his popular Chinese restaurant. She would learn how to grow the foreign vegetables he no doubt paid a fortune to import.

Excited at the thought of a new challenge, her clever brain began to put it all together. And none of it would include having a man around messing with her head or her heart. Life was simpler without men. Life had been simpler before she'd ever met Will Marsh. With his sunny blond hair and his warm, dark eyes and his hands ... his hands. Her stomach flipped as she recalled the pleasure he could incite within her body with only the softest caress of those hands.

The dig in her ribs had her jumping sky high, spinning at the same time to aim the stick she held at her assailant.

'Sweet Jesus, Mary and Joseph!' she exclaimed as a grinning Jack Fairweather stepped into the light. She exhaled a gust of relieved breath. 'Jack, you scared the typhus out of me.'

'And I am glad of it,' Jack said. 'You're so easy to sneak up on. What were you thinking about sitting here alone looking all forlorn like a puppy?'

'None of your beeswax, bushranger. And shush,' she scolded him. 'Annie and Sean are sleeping. You shouldn't be here, Jack. It's not safe. There are traps about, and soldiers.'

'I know,' he said and looked towards the stockade as Indy had done only moments before. 'I had to come and see for myself this fort the miners have built.'

'Fools,' Indy grumbled.

'Aye,' Jack agreed, unusually solemn. 'Can't fault their commitment though.'

Taking out a liquor flask, Jack handed it to her before he sat beside her on the log. She eyed the shiny and expensive-looking flask before she gave him a look of censure. It was no doubt stolen from some rich fellow. But needing the hit of calm the liquor would give her, she took the flask and drank long and deep.

'Will you join them in their stand?' he asked her as she handed back the flask.

She shrugged. 'I took the oath.'

She watched him take a long swig of the liquor himself before he spoke again. 'And what does your boyfriend think of that?'

She narrowed her eyes at Jack but said nothing.

'Indy Wallace, I've known you a long time,' he said smiling a crooked smile. 'I can see you're crazy in love with the soldier boy.'

'Bollocks.'

Jack hesitated a moment before speaking again. 'I believe him to be a good man.'

Indy's eyebrows went up in surprise.

'I know I don't say that about soldiers as a rule,' Jack added defensively. 'But I can see he is a gentleman and I'd wager he is quite smitten with you too.'

Shyly lowering her eyes, she sighed heavily.

'It doesn't matter now. Our paths are divided by all of this.' She waved a hand towards the stockade. 'We had words. A disagreement. I was mercilessly vicious. He thinks himself well shot of me now I imagine.'

'Not possible. You're a pain in the arse a good portion of the time, but I for one know it's impossible to stay mad at you. Talk to him.'

'Oh, to be sure,' Indy huffed. 'I'll just wander over to the government camp, knock on the gate and ask to see Lieutenant Marsh.'

'And why not?'

'The diggers already think me a spy.'

'So I'll go to him for you,' Jack offered with an easy shrug, like he was offering to go to the market for her. 'I'll get him a message that he must come to meet you.'

'We can't be seen together.'

'So meet somewhere privately,' Jack said and added a lewd smile that had his brows dancing above his honey-coloured eyes. 'Do I have to think of everything?'

Indy turned it over in her head. Could she dare to hope that Will might forgive her?

'Use the widow Barnett's boarding house,' Jack suggested. 'She owes me a favour since I handed back some goods I appropriated on the highway that were meant for her. We have an agreement. I don't steal her deliveries on the road from Melbourne and she allows me to stay in the boarding house rent free when I have a need.'

Indy frowned into the glowing red coals of the campfire. 'He wouldn't come probably.'

'Won't know less you try.'

Regret filled her as she thought back to the last time she'd seen Will. 'I said some awful things to him.'

'Then say you're sorry before you bed him,' Jack said and laughed loudly again.

'Shh,' Indy reprimanded. She sat quietly for a moment as she churned over Jack's proposal. He made it sound so easy. But if there was even the slightest chance Will would come to her, she should try shouldn't she? She could explain, tell him she understood now, tell him that she was sorry for the horrible accusations she'd laid against him. But how could Jack possibly get a message to him? It was a stupid idea. 'You can't get into the government camp any more than I can.'

'Don't worry about me,' Jack said with a devious wink. 'I have my ways. I'll talk to Mrs Barnett. I'll talk to the Lieutenant Handsome and get word to you when it's all arranged.'

Indy's eyes met his, but she couldn't read him. 'Why are you doing this, Jack?'

'What can I say,' Jack said shrugging. 'I'm a hopeless romantic. That and I want you as far away from that blasted stockade as possible, for as long as possible.'

She kissed his cheek and drank more of his liquor and they sat and stared into the fire in a companionable silence.

Chapter 25

Two days later, Will was a reluctant traveller on an errand to Creswick. The supplies in the bullock dray they guarded were being taken to the small garrison of soldiers in the goldfields at Bendigo. They would only escort the dray as far as Creswick before turning around and doing the return trip to Ballarat, this time with their wagon full of weapons and ammunition. It should have concerned Will the amount of weaponry that was being stockpiled at the government camp, but his mind was elsewhere.

He knew he was being punished for his continuous questioning of his superior officers, and being relegated to supply detail did not help alter the bad mood he'd been in since the raid on the Gravel Pits.

Thankfully, he had been allowed to request a soldier to accompany him and he had selected George.

'You may as well have chosen to take this trip alone for all the company you've been,' George's voice broke into the myriad thoughts scattering through Will's brain.

'Sorry,' Will mumbled, but still made no attempt to converse.

'Uh oh,' George started. 'Do I detect trouble in the love life of William Marsh?'

He merely grunted and scowled even deeper than he had been.

'Did you quarrel with your love, my Lord?' George continued to tease.

'Must you harass me?'

'You brought me on this trip, old friend,' George said, tossing roasted nuts in the air and catching them in his mouth with ease. 'Therefore, you must deal with my tormenting you, should it please me to do so. And just now, it pleases me.'

Looking over at his friend, he couldn't help but laugh at the goofy grin on George's face. Nothing ever bothered the man. He was lighthearted in the face of whatever was thrown at him. And just now, Will envied him that ability.

Taking a deep breath, he exhaled with a frustrated growl.

'That bad?' George asked.

Will gave him a shortened account of the raid two days before and Indy's reaction.

'She can't seem to grasp that I was only doing my job,' he said, finishing the story. 'The woman is impossible. She's stubborn and hardheaded and nearsighted.'

'And you love her.'

Will's head snapped around to stare wide-eyed at George.

'What? I never said that.'

The corner of George's mouth kicked up in a half grin. 'You didn't have to.'

It shouldn't have surprised him that his friend knew him so well. They rode without conversation for a moment or two. Only the rhythmic plodding of horse and bullock hooves on the hard road, and the occasional native bird cry, could be heard as Will mulled over George's keen observation.

He'd suspected his strong feelings for Indy were what people described as love. Even as far back as Trevor and Eliza's wedding the idea had been playing in the recesses of his mind. But he had managed to keep it locked back there safely. That was until she'd put herself at risk and come to see him at the government camp during his confinement to quarters. Seeing her climbing over the fence of the camp in the moonlight had simultaneously thrilled and terrified him. Three days confined to the camp, without being able to see her had been agony. The past few days without her—knowing she was angry at him, probably despised him—was a new type of agony.

'And despite knowing you were only doing your job, you feel guilty,' George spoke up again.

'I have become exactly what she hates. I am now most definitely the enemy. But what am I supposed to do? If I don't follow orders, I am an anarchist and a deserter. But to her that's the better option. She's impossible.'

'Yes, you said that already.'

At a loss to explain to his friend how he felt about Indy, Will fell into a melancholy silence and was thankful that George seemed to be done with his teasing for the moment.

At about the halfway point between Ballarat and Creswick, the horses became agitated and skittish. Will looked to the trees.

'Be aware, George,' he said, the hairs on his neck rising. 'I'd say we have company.'

'The last supply coach that had "company", as you say, did not return with all men alive,' George added, his keen eyes also scanning the brush beside the road.

From behind several large bushes, three men rode out halting the forward motion of the dray. Their faces were covered in black kerchiefs and their guns were out and pointed at Will and George.

'Throw your weapons over there,' the masked man who appeared to be the leader called out. One of the bushrangers kept the bullock driver busy, the second moved in to sort through the cargo. The bushranger who had spoken stayed alert on Will and George.

George looked at Will questioningly.

'Don't try to be a hero, soldier boy,' the bushranger called back, reading them easily. 'I am fast with a gun and it's not my wish to take your life today, only your goods.'

Both men removed their guns and threw them across to the tree the man had motioned to.

'You,' the man pointed at Will. 'Lieutenant of the fair hair. Dismount.'

Will frowned. Not because of the request, but when the bushranger had spoken there'd been a twinkle in the highwayman's eyes that somehow seemed familiar to him.

'Will,' George said, anxious for his friend.

But curious, Will did as asked and dismounted before putting his hands in the air in surrender.

'Now, sir, if you would be so kind as to lead the way into the woods,' the bushranger requested.

Noting George's nervous movements on his horse, he gave his friend a quick shake of his head. 'It's okay. Don't do anything stupid. Just wait till I return.'

George, unsure and on edge, sent a warning of his own. 'Be careful, bushranger.'

'Don't worry, I'll return your man in one piece,' the bushranger tossed back with a teasing wink.

The highwayman stayed mounted and followed as Will walked into the scrub until they were far enough from the others.

'Stop here.'

Will obeyed and turned to face his foe. The highwayman lowered his kerchief and his gun, and Will exhaled loudly with a combination of relief and annoyance.

'Jack. I thought it was you.'

'Now, what sort of rubbish is that?' Jack asked, tossing his hands in the air. 'How is a highwayman to make a living these days if he is so recognisable? You've met me but once. It's my pretty eyes isn't it? They give me away.'

Will merely rolled his own eyes. 'Yes, Jack, it's your pretty eyes. Men on the roads will fear Jack Fairweather the bushranger for his pretty eyes. Now, why the hell am I here?'

'Sorry, old chap,' Jack said, grinning as he dismounted. 'Only way I knew how to get you alone.'

'And just why do you need to get me alone?'

'Indy.'

The panic was immediate. 'What is it? Is she hurt? Is she ill? Speak man, has something happened to her?' He grabbed Jack by the shirt and shook him but Jack only smiled his crooked smile.

'So, you do care about her.'

Will dropped his hands and stepped back.

Jack straightened his shirt and waistcoat. 'Knowing that makes this a lot easier for me.'

'Makes what easier?'

'I come to you with a message from a lady,' Jack announced, then chuckled. 'Well, a message from Indy anyway.'

'A message?'

'She wishes to see you?'

More than surprised, Will leaned heavily back against a tree. 'Why? To tell me again what a terrible and pathetic excuse for a human being I am? That I am cuckolded by the army?'

'She said that?' Jack snorted in amusement but then whistled low.

'Ouch. She has a way with words, that girl.'

Will just grunted and dug the toe of his boot into a patch of mushrooms, watching the brown dust cloud waft away in the breeze.

'What she wishes to discuss with you is her business,' Jack said. 'I will never understand the vagaries of the fairer sex but Indy is special to me, so heed me, Lieutenant.'

He glanced up at the warning in Jack's tone.

'If you hurt her in any small way, shape or form either by design or by accident, if you so much as cause one tear to fall, I will see to it that pain will be your constant companion. Your internal organs will become my personal punching bag...'

Will held up a hand to stop him. 'I get the picture. You too have a way with words, Jack.'

The two men stared each other off, and Will couldn't help himself. 'Do you love her, Jack?'

Jack's honey-coloured eyes softened for a moment before the bushranger's grin was back in place. 'Meet her tonight at nine at the Barnett Boarding House. The widow is expecting you and shall remain tight-lipped.'

'The Commissioner has called a curfew at eight pm. And just how in the hell am I supposed to move about the town after dark? We soldiers can barely leave camp in daylight for fear of getting our heads knocked in or blown off.'

'So tonight you are not a soldier,' Jack said, and pulling a duffel bag off his horse he tossed it at Will.

He caught it awkwardly, glancing into the bag quickly as Jack mounted his horse again. 'Thank you, Jack. I don't know how to repay you.'

'Just take care of her,' Jack told him. 'This world is about to collapse and I don't want her anywhere near it when it happens.'

'You're a good man, Jack Fairweather.'

Jack baulked. 'Christ, don't let that get about. I have a reputation to uphold. Now, I must bid you good day. I'm afraid I will have to liberate you of some of your goods however. Can't have people thinking that Jack Fairweather has gone soft.'

He positioned the kerchief over his face again and with a wave of his gun directed Will back to the road.

***

When Will and George returned to Ballarat, rumours were spreading throughout camp like the plague. Rede was sure an attack on the camp was imminent. Sandbags, bales of hay, sacks of flour and wheat were carted out of the stores and piled in front of the most important buildings and along the fenceline facing the diggings.

The women who had somewhere else to go had been moved out of the government camp weeks ago but those who had stayed were set up in the sturdiest buildings for safety. At eight pm the announcement came that all tents near the camp were under a curfew.

'Lights out!' the soldiers shouted as they made rounds of the tents closest to the government camp. Darkness fell quickly as the order was obeyed on threat of summary fire.

Will glanced up at the full moon shining brightly. It would be tantamount to suicide to attempt an attack on the government camp. Anyone making a run on the camp would easily be spotted by the many sentries standing post around the picketed fence. Occasionally, a handful of clouds would cross the white orb blacking everything out. But when the clouds rolled away, it was almost as bright as the sun rising. The trees beyond the camp and the tents nearby were easily seen and that meant Will had to choose his moment carefully.

His eyes swept up to the heavens again and when he saw a large clump of clouds drifting towards the moon, he made his move. Casually, he sidled up to an unmanned area of the fence, pretending to relieve himself in case anyone saw. It was a low fence and easy to jump, and less than fifty yards away was the edge of the scrub leading to Black Hill.

As the clouds moved in again and moonlight dimmed, Will hurdled the fence. His heart racing, he ran full speed across the clearing to the safety of the trees. Once under cover, he removed his red coat, and pulled on the blue miner's shirt Jack had given him. As he stuffed his uniform coat into the duffel bag, he half expected to hear the crack of a rifle or the whistle of a bullet by his ear, and more than once he asked himself what the hell he was doing. He'd get himself killed before the night was over, either by his side or by the rebels. And all for a woman. All so that he could spend five minutes in Indy's company again.

Is she worth it? his practical brain asked as he ran in the dark, dodging tree branches as best he could. Soon he was far enough away from the camp that he was able to slow to a walk. In cover of the bush, he changed out of his uniform trousers to complete his disguise. The moon came out again to light his way to the rear of the township.

Is she worth it?

'Yes,' he said out loud.

She had asked to see him he recalled, still a little baffled as he followed the Yarrowee River towards a small cluster of buildings that made up the Eureka township. Why? What else could she possibly have to say? She'd been very clear in her opinion of him after he'd done his duty and led the licence raid. He had almost accepted that he would never see her again. But she had planned it all through Jack, and the bushranger had done her bidding. A trustworthy man? Hardly. It had crossed his mind several times that it could all be a trap set by the miners to get a soldier out of the camp. But Will dismissed it when he recalled the sincerity in Jack's usually laughing eyes. And there was no denying the seriousness of his colourful warning should Will do anything to hurt Indy either physically or emotionally.

As he slipped between the buildings and reached the front door of Mrs Barnett's boarding house, he had no exact idea of the hour. Would Indy be there already, waiting for him? Or was he early? He felt the thrill of anticipation run through him. Not unlike the feeling he got just before he went into battle.

Stopping on the porch, he realised he could easily see the now completed stockade from here. It was his first close-up look at the stronghold the miners had created for themselves. A few tents were inside the lines of the barricades. By happenstance or by design he couldn't tell. It was strangely quiet and only two men seemed to be posted as guards. They leaned against a post, smoking and chatting as though they were enjoying a drink at the pub. Other than that it looked like any other part of the goldfield's camps, except for a few upturned wagons and some oddly shaped fencing made from lumber probably stolen from mineshafts.

As far as defensive fortresses went it was a pretty sad sight. It would serve no hindrance to the licence hunts that were bound to happen the next day. Sunday or not, Rede would not let another day go by without asserting his authority by the arrest of more miners. Shaking his head at the futility of it all, Will slipped quietly into the boarding house.

**

The evening was warm and a light wind blew as Indy ate her dinner with

Annie and Sean. The moon rose as a giant gold nugget, creating an almost false daylight across the canvas city. Many of their neighbours commented on the stunning beauty of it. Others were more apprehensive and the superstitious amongst them saw it as a bad omen.

The rice and beans dish Indy swallowed was good she was sure, as it was one of Annie's signature meals, but she couldn't taste it thanks to her nerves that intensified as the hour ticked by.

While Jack had been waiting to direct Will to stand and deliver, Indy had already been up and working her little mine for hours. There had been a lot of enthusiasm on the goldfields that day. Men who would usually be down their mineshafts had gathered in little groups to talk in hushed tones as though it were all a grand game to them.

Throughout the day, her emotions were as up and down as the little bucket in her mineshaft. She'd count the slow minutes, excited that she would possibly see Will that night. Then a great depression would come over her that Jack wouldn't be able to get to Will. Or that if he did, Will wouldn't come. Or if he did come, it would only be to say farewell. Occasionally, movement in the stockade would distract her from her obsessing about Will. Some men left the barricades in shifts to work their mines, largely unlicensed now of course, taunting the soldiers and police who made occasional sojourns to town in small groups. But no raids came. No effort to break the stockade was attempted by the government forces and the inaction only added to Indy's apprehension.

More diggers had arrived from surrounding goldfields at midday, boosting the rebels' spirits. Women could occasionally be seen delivering food to the miners inside the stockade and as the afternoon wore on, the mood at the barricades was jovial. Indy, on the other hand, left her mine with a horrible sense of foreboding that stayed with her as she headed back to camp.

Having helped Sean clean up after dinner, Indy made her excuses to Annie that she was going up to the Gravel Pits to check on one of the German children who was ill with the measles. It was a good plan and easily believed since she'd been teaching English to many of the children in the camp over the last year. She pulled a straw bonnet over her head. The December evening was warm and with many people still milling about, Indy needed to keep her identity covered for as long as possible. The less people who saw her entering the widow Barnett's establishment the better she figured, since there was no real reason for her to be there.

Passing by the stockade on her way to the boarding house, she noted that quite a few of the miners who had been there earlier in the day had now obviously decided to go back to their own tents to get some sleep or to spend time with family. The men who remained, sat around a fire, drinking and laughing as though it were a normal Saturday night in the camps.

When she arrived at the boarding house, she quickly ducked behind the door as two women she knew were residents came out gossiping.

'They ought to close the grog tents beside the stockade,' one woman was saying. 'The men will become inebriated and then what good will it do them when the troopers come down to check their licences again.'

'But there has never been a licence hunt at night,' the other woman responded. 'They may as well all go back to their tents. Go back to their wives and children. This is all so much a storm in a teacup.'

The voices faded away into the night and Indy ducked into the house behind them. She was relieved to find Mrs Barnett just inside the door. The austere-looking widow, in her plain black dress with dark hair bundled up in a tight bun, had Indy cowering a little as she waited for a lecture about cavorting with soldiers, or bushrangers for that matter. But the widow Barnett simply tilted her head, urging Indy to move upstairs.

'Room two,' she said, her lips pursed in disapproval. But Indy knew those lips would remain tightly closed if she wanted to keep her goods from being waylaid on the trip from Melbourne.

Standing at the door of room two, Indy's heart raced, her breath quick and shallow. Not from the brisk walk or the short climb of the stairs, but because she knew for certain that Will was on the other side of the door. He had come.

Did she knock?

Did she just enter?

She decided to do both. She knocked on the door and opened it just as she heard him call out, 'Come in.'

Inside, she quickly shut the door behind her and leaned against it for support. Thank God she did. The sight of him made her legs weak. He wasn't clad in his usual uniform of red coat and buff-coloured breeches. He wore the uniform of a digger—the blue shirt and rough corduroy pants—and he had never looked more handsome. And he was barefoot. Oh, how she loved his bare feet. Looking around the room she saw that his soldier's boots sat in the corner by the door.

Shyly, she met his eyes again and for a moment they just stared at each other. Neither speaking, both unsure of what to say.

Digging for strength she surveyed the room. It was nice, as boarding houses went. One small double bed, a side table with a ceramic water pitcher and bowl, a rocking chair in the corner and ... she was stalling. When she slowly brought her eyes back to Will, his expression was unreadable.

'Jack said you wanted to see me.' His voice held no emotion, no inkling of what he might be feeling.

She became enthralled by the bob of his Adam's apple as he spoke. She stared and stared but she still couldn't find her voice.

'Why am I here, Indy?'

Her eyes flicked up to his again. All day she had thought about what she would say and now that she was faced with the reality of him, all her words, her eloquent speech so well-rehearsed, fell out of her head and what came out was something else entirely.

'I love you.'

He blinked, surprise now evident across his beautiful features.

A nervous laugh escaped her lips and she dropped her eyes to the floor.

'I'm sorry, that was abrupt.'

When she lifted her gaze again, he had taken a step closer.

She tried to smile, tried to make light of her clumsily blurted admission. 'I probably shouldn't have started with that but...'

There was no time for more because he had crossed the room in two long strides, his hand clasping the back of her neck, the other going to her cheek and his mouth was on hers, desperate, urgent, seeking and giving at the same time.

He pulled back long enough to look into her eyes.

'I love you too, Indy,' he said, putting his forehead to hers. 'Beyond reason.'

A relieved breath whooshed out of her before he kissed her again. His mouth found her cheek, her ear, her neck, and her back found the door once again.

'I've missed you so much these last few days,' he said, whispering into her ear. 'I thought I'd lost you. It felt like a lifetime. It's a kind of madness to be with you and yet a keener madness to be without you.'

'Then we're both mad,' she said, her breath coming quickly. Her hands shook as she began to unbutton his shirt. She tugged the hem from his trousers and he gasped when her hands met his skin.

'Where did you get these clothes?'

'Jack,' he answered. 'He is a resourceful gentleman. And frightening too.'

'Jack's frightening?' She snorted out a laugh, followed quickly by a gasp as Will's hands slid up her torso and his thumbs rested across her nipples, now hard and aching beneath her dress.

Will's mouth was on her neck as he spoke. 'He threatened to cause my internal organs substantial discomfort should I hurt you in any way.'

Indy dug her fingers into his shoulders as he pressed his lips to her cleavage.

She lifted his head so she could look into his beautiful eyes when she asked him. 'Make love to me, Will?'

Chapter 26

Will stared, mute and spellbound, at the pure want and love he saw swimming in Indy's eyes. Swallowing hard against the lump that had formed in his throat, he slowly leaned in to take her mouth with his.

She tasted so sweet and his mind and body were filled to overflowing with the scent and flavour of her. He used his lips to coax hers open, his tongue sweeping against hers, enticing a soft moan from deep within her that reached deep within him.

Keeping her in his arms, he turned her towards the small double bed in the middle of the room. The full moon filtered in through a tiny window and bathed the bed in pale light. But before he could lay her down, she urged him to sit on the side of the bed. Although he was confused at first, he stayed where he was and stared, captivated, as she began to undress herself for him.

More often than not she was dressed in men's clothing, or the wide-legged bloomer trousers that had become so popular with the working women of the goldfields. But tonight she wore a dress the colour of ripe apricots. She unlaced the threads at the front until she was able to drop the fabric from her shoulders and he was mesmerised as it fell in a swirling heap around her feet. There was no corset—that was no surprise to him—but there were no undergarments at all. He had seen her naked at the river all those weeks ago, but modesty and propriety had forced him to look away. He wasn't looking away now. His eyes took in every beautiful inch of her body.

She was no porcelain doll. The skin on her arms and neck were tanned from hours in the sun, but the rest of her body was pale and looked soft and sweet and he ached to taste and touch every morsel of her.

Her small hand reached out and he took it and pulled her gently to him. His eyes were level with her navel and he kissed it lightly. She smiled shyly down at him as she reached for his shirt, lifting it over his head and tossing it aside. When he stood, her fingers came to his chest and she feathered them through the light smattering of hair between his pectoral muscles, sending sparks of electricity through his system and straight to his groin. Following the line of hair down his flat stomach, she reached for the waist of his trousers.

His hand caught hers and she looked up at him, surprise and confusion on her pretty features. 'Let me undress you,' she said, her voice soft and pleading.

Helpless against her big blue eyes, he slowly removed his hand from hers and let her continue. As she undid the buttons on his trousers he ran his hands first down her arms, then around and down the soft, smooth skin of her back.

'You don't mind a woman taking control, do you?'

'I don't mind *you* taking control,' he said, his voice gruff and affected by his arousal. 'I'm not going to argue a woman's place in sex when every touch of you,' he leaned down and kissed her lightly, 'every taste, has me wanting you more and more.'

He felt his pants give way and she pushed them down so he could step out of them. Now they were both naked and he took her in his arms and held her against him.

'Indy,' he whispered worshipfully. 'You feel like heaven to me. You're a revelation. You love as you live, Indy. With passion and purpose and I adore you and love you as I have never loved anyone.'

Gazing down at her again, he kissed her lips softly. Gently, he lay her down on the bed but knelt beside her for a moment, taking in the naked length of her as she glowed in the moonlight that bathed the bed and her.

Reaching out, he covered one breast with his hand, his thumb teasing at the hard bud. Her breath caught and she arched into his hand. He leaned down and took her peak in his mouth. Her soft sigh urged him on. He moved his attentions to the other breast and while his mouth was busy his hand slid down her soft skin to the apex between her thighs. She arched again and he felt just how ready she was for him.

'My beautiful Indy.'

Taking every care not to hurt her, he covered her body with his and she wrapped her legs around his waist. He entered her slowly, carefully and watched her eyes change as they joined together. But as they began to move, Indy rolled so that he was beneath her. She rose up above him, giving him the most glorious view of her bare breasts, before she leaned down to take his mouth again in a passionate kiss that emptied his mind of anything but her. Her long curls curtained his head in spun gold, surrounding him in her scent and he buried his hands in the thickness, pulling her closer as she moved against him.

The beauty of her face in unabashed ecstasy as she rode him broke his thin grasp on restraint and he fought his passion, fought not to grip her too hard. His wild Indy. His beautiful, untamable girl. How would he ever live his life without her? He pushed aside the thoughts of desperation and drew her down to ravage her mouth as they came together at the peak of their passion.

***

Dozing on a wave of sex-induced relaxation, Will finally opened his eyes. Indy lay across his chest staring at him. Her fingers were interlaced and her chin rested on her hands. She smiled in that devilish way of hers.

'Why do you stare?'

'I can't help it,' she said. 'You are too beautiful not to stare at.'

'Men are not beautiful. Men are handsome, striking even, but not beautiful.'

'You are,' she said, running a finger lightly across his lips. 'The most beautiful man I have ever seen.'

He threaded his hand through her long curls again. Moving her so that she was lying beside him, he continued to play with her hair. It was so soft, so lustrous. He wanted to hold her like this for the rest of their lives. He closed his eyes. That was a dream he could not hope to entertain. Stopping the thought before it took hold he changed the subject.

'I saw the stockade as I came into town.'

'I've been watching them all day,' she said, taking her finger down his jawbone. 'I'm worried.'

That surprised him. 'I didn't think anything worried you.'

'This does,' she said, a small frown crinkling between her big blue eyes. 'Where will it all end?'

'I don't know. But it won't end well if the diggers continue to rebel. Commissioner Rede grows tired of them. And that stockade they've set up is a show of aggression that won't be tolerated. Just today more soldiers arrived from Melbourne.'

'How long?'

He knew what she was asking.

'A day. Two at the most, before the army will act with force.'

She propped herself up on her elbow to look down at him. 'What amount of force?'

He didn't answer her, couldn't look at her.

'I have to get them to stop,' she said, sitting upright in the bed. 'I have to get them to see reason.'

'You can't. Indy, It's too dangerous for you to try and stop them now. They've dug a hole too deep.'

'Then I'm in that hole with them. I took the oath to stand beside them.'

He felt the fear envelop him as he pushed himself up in the bed to look her in the eye. 'You did what? Indy, please, tell me you won't do anything stupid. Stay away from the stockade.'

'Trying to tell me what to do now that you have had my body, Lieutenant?' she asked, one eyebrow raised in challenge.

'I know better than that,' he said, annoyance flaring. 'And don't throw our lovemaking back at me as though I would ever use it as a weapon against you. Do not insult me that way.'

Indy fell back against the pillow heavily. 'This may have been our only chance to be together, Will.'

'What do you mean?'

'How will we ever meet up like this again?' she asked. 'This was a stolen evening. Even if we weren't on opposite sides of this conflict, where would we be able to meet?'

Propping himself back against the iron bedhead he sighed, 'I don't know.'

'We could leave.'

She'd said it so quietly he wasn't sure he had heard her.

'Leave?'

'Leave Ballarat. Leave Victoria.'

'Where would we go?' he humoured her.

'Queensland,' she said, sitting up again and pulling the bedsheet up to cover her breasts, which only drew his attention to them more. 'I hear it's warm all year round as it's in the tropics. We can lay on the beach, swim in the ocean.'

He let out a soft laugh. 'How can we? We have no money. I have nothing to give you, Indy.'

'I have plenty of money.'

She'd said it so matter-of-factly he almost believed her.

'Unofficially, I have the third largest chunk of gold found in any lead in the Ballarat Goldfields.'

'What?'

'I kept my find quiet,' Indy explained. 'Should any of the men find out, it wouldn't be long before one of them robbed me of it. Only Annie and Sean know it's real. Others who saw this huge chunk of gold think it is pyrite—fool's gold. There have only been two other finds that big before. I've kept it hidden. Kept it safe.'

'How big?'

'Ninety pounds,' she answered and watched his eyes widen. 'And that's only the one chunk. Since 1852, my mine has produced over a thousand pounds of gold. Sean has half of it, of course, but it's still more than we need.'

'Good Lord.' He ran a hand through his sex-rumpled hair.

'So we can go away,' she said again, becoming more excited. 'I have enough money for the both of us.'

'So I'm to be a kept man?' he asked, a small frown marred his features.

'Is that a problem?'

He shook his head. 'No, not at all. I've been working for nigh on twenty years. It's time I had a break.'

She snorted out a laugh and he joined her. 'You won't be resting. Not once we set up the sugar plantation.

I'll work you so hard you will wish you were still in the army.'

'Sugar?' he asked, grinning.

'I hear there is a burgeoning sugar cane industry in Queensland,' she went on, her voice full of excitement. 'My gold will buy us land enough to start a farm of sorts.'

'Why have you not exchanged your gold already? Why are you still here?'

Indy shrugged. 'My mother loves her house. But I can't sit around and do nothing so I continue to dig and help out at the fields. Besides, I adore Annie and Sean. I couldn't just up and leave them alone. But I admit, I have been thinking about giving up the mine for a while now. Sean can work on the mine alone if he wants to.'

He stared at the amazing woman before him. 'You are indeed a rare creature, Indy. You put the needs of everyone ahead of yourself.'

She shook her head. 'I don't. I can be selfish when I want to be. I'll be selfish when it comes to you. Things have changed. This place is a barrel of gunpowder ready to blow. You said so yourself. We could leave, Will. Leave all this behind. We should go now, before it's too late.'

'You just said Annie and Sean need you. Your mother needs you.' He lay back on the bed and exhaled heavily, hating the look of disappointment on her face. 'But you're right.' Hope flashed in Indy's eyes, her smile instantly brightening her features. He hated to quash it. 'You should go. Take your mother and get far away from this place.'

Beaming, she leaned down as though to kiss him. He stopped her with a hand to her shoulder, a shake of his head. 'But I cannot desert the army. It is my home. My only home.'

She sat back, lifting her eyes to stare wistfully out the window towards the moonlight as understanding began to sink in.

'Indy, I...' He tugged on her hands to make her look at him. 'I love you. But I can't go with you.'

***

When Will finally fell asleep, Indy lay awake for a long time watching him breathing deeply in slumber. Her head and her heart were torn as she gazed upon the beautiful man before her.

One minute they'd been planning a future together. A mere moment later, the joking, teasing, lighthearted lover had been replaced by the level-headed soldier once again. Her mother had been right. His life was with the army. He would never give it up to stay with her. Her heart was crushed, broken. She didn't like the feeling at all.

She could take her mother and leave. Just leave Ballarat and all its troubles behind her. And if Will didn't want to go with them? Well, then she would leave him behind as well. Just the thought of that had her chest constricting all over again.

Where had all her strength gone? Six months ago she would never have thought twice about doing what she wanted to do. She most certainly would not have let a man dictate her actions. But Will was not just any man. She loved him. If she stayed in Ballarat, what good would it do her? Her mother had said he would probably be gone by year's end anyway. He'd said he loved her. But not enough. Not more than he loved his army.

She hated being this woman. She hated this feeling of desperation now that she was in love. Love was surrendering control wasn't it? So why wouldn't he surrender to her? She hated that she couldn't control what he did. But even worse, she hated that she wanted to. She would never allow him, or any man, to control her. There was nothing left to do. They had reached an impasse. Their fledgling relationship was over before it had even begun.

Decision made, she climbed carefully from the small bed and dressed quietly so as not to disturb him. Taking one last look at the man who had shown her so much love and kindness, she crept from the room and out into the night. Calculating the angle of the full moon, she decided it must have been about two in the morning. Listlessly, and with her heart aching, she meandered back towards the Eureka camp.

***

Will dreamed of Indy. Dreamed of her lying beside him on warm tropical beaches. Queensland, she had said. His subconscious mind conjured up soft, fine white sand and they swam together in the clear, warm waters. Naked. He dreamed of her naked.

Aroused by his dreams, Will rolled over to pull her closer to him in the small bed. But when his arm found nothing but cool sheet, he opened his eyes. She was gone. Back to her tent in the campsite before morning broke he guessed. It would do neither of them any good to be caught here together. He had to protect her reputation, but more importantly, he had to protect her from the dangers of being found sleeping with the enemy.

The light from the full moon brightened the little room and made it easy for him to see the furnishings, the small chair by the door where his miner's costume had been carelessly tossed in the throes of passion. Beneath it, lay his soldier's red coat.

It was probably time for him to get up too and head back to camp before dawn. It would be the last straw for him to be caught outside the government camp after curfew. He'd switch back his miner's garb for his officer's uniform on the road, as he neared the camp. If caught by the miners in his red coat, he'd more than likely be shot or lynched. If he was caught by the government camp he might just get that flogging Captain Thomas had threatened him with the last time he'd stepped out of line.

He heard what he thought was a gunshot and frowned. It was the middle of the night, but that didn't mean anything. Miners protected their claims with gunfire at all hours of the day and night. Drunks often set off a volley of shots just for the hell of it.

But then he heard the call of the bugle, and his blood turned cold.

Chapter 27

Will sat bolt upright in bed.

A second, louder volley of multiple simultaneous shots rang out. He knew it already without having to look outside. The Army had attacked the stockade.

The miners would have been sleeping, unprepared other than the two sentries he'd seen posted on the front entrance. It was the perfectly strategised dawn offensive so successful in war.

But this wasn't a war.

He recalled the tents unlucky enough to be positioned so that the stockade surrounded them whether they wanted to be included or not. Simple men, women too, had been taking refuge behind the flimsy barricades.

Women.

Indy!

In seconds he was out of bed and getting dressed. He grabbed whatever was closest and ended up with the miner's trousers and his uniform coat. Without bothering to fasten the brass buttons he was out the door and flying down the stairs, almost bowling over the widow Barnett and other guests, as in their nightclothes they too ventured out.

'Lieutenant!' the widow called after him. 'What goes on?'

Ignoring her, he barrelled out the door.

The streets of Ballarat were in chaos. People, many still in their night garments and wrapped in blankets, alternately congregated on verandas of stores or ran from the gun battle blazing around the nearby stockade.

The unholy noise of the skirmish had woken everyone. In the distance, Will could see the flashes as the gunpowder exploded, sending lead balls out of the barrels of the military rifles.

At first he was stunned. There were so many soldiers, so many police surrounding the stockade. There had to be well over a hundred infantry in the first offensive line alone. And he knew enough of Captain Thomas's strategising to be assured a second wave of mounted soldiers waited in the east and west flanks. It was the perfect storming formation. They were taking no chances. This uprising would be put down tonight. And put down fast with force unmatched.

People rushed passed Will, screaming and crying, frantically trying to escape the gunfire that was now being returned by the men in the stockade. Will was the only person running towards the battle. He fought his way past the soldiers waiting in reserve, rushing to get to where Captain Thomas sat on his horse overseeing the conflict.

'Present arms!' came Thomas's call. 'Fire! Reload!'

Will had to cover his ears with his hands, such was the noise of fifty rifles in chorus.

'What are you doing?' he yelled at Thomas.

'Marsh?' Captain Thomas looked down at Will with obvious surprise. 'We received orders to storm the stockade and break the rebellion. The Commissioner agreed we could no longer sit back and wait for the miners to attack the government camp.'

'It's not yet five in the morning!'

'I'm sorry, Lieutenant Marsh, did we wake you?' the Captain asked sarcastically, eyeing Will's shabby state of dress.

'There are women and children in there!' Will yelled, horrified as he watched a woman fleeing the stockade only to be shot in the back.

'You are out of uniform, Lieutenant,' Thomas scowled. Will looked down at his mismatched clothing. Was he a miner, or was he a soldier?

As though reading his mind Thomas demanded, 'Decide where your loyalties lie, Lieutenant Marsh.'

Will stared at his superior officer, then turned to look back across to the frontline of the battle. The military had the upper hand. They hardly needed his help. But what else could he do to try and halt the fighting before anyone was killed or injured? He was just one man, and his only priority was to find Indy. He had a choice to make and he had to make it quick.

'I said, take up arms, Lieutenant.'

'No,' he defied. 'I will not be a part of murdering innocent women and children.'

'Innocent!?' Thomas said glaring back at him. 'Like that woman you've been cavorting with? She's hardly innocent. Gambling, fights and sharing herself with officers. Fall in, Lieutenant Marsh, or face the consequences.'

Will hesitated. It would do him no good to get fired up over Thomas's appraisal of Indy. The battle continued through the thick gun smoke that hung heavy in the air, obscuring the aim of the military rifles. Unable to see their mark, the soldiers were ordered forward and ran towards the stockade, clambering over the low pikes, attacking miners with bayonets. Random shots still rang out, echoing in the haze, blocking all other sound.

Another man fell as Will watched. A few minutes more and he wouldn't have to choose. This battle wouldn't last much longer, and he had to find Indy.

'Fall in, Lieutenant. That's an order!'

Making the only decision he could make and still live with himself, Will turned and ran. The gunfire swallowed his superior officer's shouted demands to return and he made his way around the soldiers and the local troopers, being sure to steer clear of the firing range. There was nothing he could do to save the poor blighters in the stockade. And even if there was, nothing mattered more to him than getting to Indy, than making sure she was safe in all this madness.

He ran until he felt his lungs would collapse. Smoke wafted into his eyes, stinging, burning, as he bolted into the trees. He circled around through the tents where the diggers and their families watched in horror the battle for the stockade.

Forgetting he still wore his military red, he was spotted by a miner just outside the Eureka camp.

'The bastards are sneaking up on us!' the man yelled.

Will was set upon by a group of men, armed with whatever they could lift and hit him with, or their own fists if they could find no weapon.

'No!' Will fought back as best he could. 'I mean you no harm.'

'Like hell you don't!'

He went down hard, and once down it was impossible to get back up again no matter how hard he fought.

'Please! I need to find Indy Wallace!' he shouted desperately to no avail.

'You need to be dead,' someone yelled back. He lost his breath and his ability to speak with the kick landed to his stomach. A blow to his head came a moment later, grogginess enveloped him and he fell into the black.

***

Will heard voices as though from under a deep, deep ocean. He tried to swim to the surface, tried to open his eyes. When he finally managed it, the bright light sent searing pain into his skull and he slammed his eyes shut again. Slowly, he eased them open again and was eventually able to keep them open, although his left eye felt swollen and partially pasted closed.

The voices became clearer and then a woman appeared in his blurred vision.

'He's awake is he?'

The Irish brogue was unmistakable.

'Annie?'

'Aye,' she answered, and he felt a cool cloth over his damaged eye. It soothed and he sighed at the instant relief. When she pulled it away, he saw the red of his own blood by the bright light of the lantern as she continued to wipe at his battered forehead and face.

He tried to sit up, pain ricocheting through his ribs.

'Stay down, you fool!' Annie scolded. 'They did a good job of you before Lenny here managed to pull them off.'

Will's good eye focused on the big black man he recognised as Lenny the American.

'I'm indebted to you, sir,' Will said and slowly pushed himself up again, wincing at the pain.

Outside the tent, it was still dark so he couldn't have been out for long. Dawn had not yet set in.

'I said stay down,' Annie instructed.

'Is it over?' he asked. He could only hear the occasional gunshot now.

'I'll say,' Annie said, anger and frustration in her voice. 'One sided fight that it was. The rebels didn't stand a chance after the surprise attack. The battle didn't last much longer than twenty minutes, but those bastards are still out there now rounding up miners.'

'Indy?' he asked through his pain. 'Have you seen her?'

'Not since the shooting started,' Annie said, gnawing in her lip. 'Only Indigo Wallace would run into a gunfight.'

Will's eyes were wide open now as he stared at the woman's anxious face.

'She ran towards the stockade? During the attack?'

'Aye, she did.' Annie gave a curt nod. 'Foolish child. Her poor mother will be broken in two if she's gone and got herself killed.'

Annie's wrath was replaced by a sudden sob and she turned her back on him. Will waited for her to collect herself. He knew how much Indy meant to Annie and it wouldn't just be Indy's mother who would be broken.

Refusing to think the worst, Will stood despite the flare of pain that rolled along his chest and into his gut making him nauseated and dizzy. Taking stock, he was quite sure one or two ribs were broken considering the pain that flared each time he took a breath. His leg ached as well, but severe bruising was the extent there he determined when he was able to put some weight on the limb.

'Sit back down, you great eejit!' Annie reprimanded, her usual iron lady disposition back in place. 'You're badly injured.'

'I've had worse,' he muttered. 'Annie, please. I can't just sit here. I have to find her. I told her not to do anything stupid. She has no sense of her own safety.' He was rambling, probably still a bit dazed he realised, but he needed to go. He looked determinedly into Annie's eyes. 'Please, Annie. I beg you. Let me go. I have to find her. No matter the consequences. I need to find her.'

Annie hesitated a moment. 'Lenny, will go with you.'

'No, really, I'm fine. Lenny will be more help here.'

'It's for your protection,' she added. 'You'll not get five yards out there without him. They'll leave you alone if you have Lenny alongside.'

He agreed, more to save time in arguments, but as it turned out he couldn't walk easily on his bad leg, so having Lenny supporting him helped immensely.

The scene that greeted him outside the tent was one of devastation and grief. The sun had not yet risen and the blue haze of pre-dawn, and the setting moon, released only shadowy figures as everywhere he looked women were crying over their injured men. Babies wailed. Gun smoke still hung in the air, acrid and bitter. He could smell the blood, could smell death. It was a scent a man of war never forgot and so at odds with the sweet, fresh, perfume of dew on the eucalypts. It was a blending of scents to make a man nauseated. It was impossible to miss the hatred aimed his way, even with his bung eye. But Annie was right. No one came near him while he had his six-foot-seven guard beside him.

He searched the Eureka campsite first, looking for Indy, asking anyone if they'd seen her. He came across the newly married couple, Eliza and Trevor. They had been smart enough to stay out of the stockade and promised they would keep an eye out for Indy.

As he neared the now dilapidated stockade itself, he had to cover his nose. The rank odour of death was everywhere. Bodies were being removed by friends or loved ones under the keen eye of the contingent of soldiers who remained. The walking wounded helped those who were not ambulatory. The looks he got from the diggers were vicious. A woman spat on his red coat as she walked beside a stretcher carrying a man—her dead husband.

'It was a bloodbath,' Will murmured.

'They say the soldiers didn't just shoot,' Lenny spoke for the first time. 'They chased down the wounded and bayoneted them until they were dead.'

Will was sickened by what he saw. By what Lenny was telling him. Had he been there at the government camp, could he have stopped it before it began? Could he have done more? These were civilians. They weren't soldiers. They were simple people looking for a better life and fighting for their rights in the world. They had built the barricade in defence, not offence. A wave of anger began to overtake his fear and weariness. At the edge of the ruins of the stockade, he spotted a group of three soldiers kicking over the bodies of fallen miners, ensuring they were dead. He saw their delight as they came across a wounded man and began to taunt him and poke him with the ends of their rifles and bayonets.

'Stop that!' Will yelled. Lenny helped him hobble as quickly as he could towards the men. They regarded him suspiciously, wary of the injured man in half an officer's uniform.

Finally seeing the ranking on the epaulets of Will's red coat, the soldiers quickly stood to attention.

'Lieutenant, sir,' one of the men spoke.

'What are you doing?'

'We were ordered to ensure the rebellion was dead, sir,' the soldier responded a little wild-eyed.

'Stop. I am ordering you to stop. Let the dead alone and let the wounded be returned to their loved ones. They'll give you no trouble now. Fall back.'

'Yes, sir.'

None of the men looked overly happy about the order but with a salute they turned to head back out of the barricades.

'Lenny, help me with this man.' Will moved towards the wounded digger.

But Lenny didn't follow.

'Lenny, please,' he asked again. Looking up into the big man's dark face he saw shock in the whites of Lenny's widened eyes as he stared, frozen in place, past Will.

Will turned to follow his stupefied gaze and his eyes fell on a mass of long blonde hair.

She was face down in the dirt. Blood matted one side of her head, and on her back bloomed a dark wet stain.

'No.' Will's voice came out in a hoarse whisper. 'Indy!' He willed her to move as he began to stagger towards her. 'No! No!' he was yelling now as he ran, forgetting his pain as he scrambled around the fallen bodies, the fallen barricades, to get to her. 'No! Indy!'

He fell to his knees beside the body. Lenny was there beside him in an instant.

There was no question. She was dead.

He let out one guttural, devastated moan and reaching forward, he moved her hair aside to see her pretty face. The face of the woman he loved and adored so much. His tears blurred his vision and the pain from his own injuries was flaring, making him dizzy again. Fighting the pain and nausea, he rolled her over onto her back. Yes, she was most definitely dead. The bullet wound to the side of her head would have killed her before the bayonet had been speared into her back.

But he let out his breath on another cry. This time a cry of relief.

'It's not her,' he said, wiping the tears from his filthy face. 'It's not Indy. Thank you, God.'

He'd never felt such relief, but it was short-lived since he still didn't know where Indy was.

Ignoring his own pain, he carefully lifted the woman into his arms. She was so light, so small. On second glance, he realised she could be no older than sixteen. He felt ill. His own regiment had done this. This despicable act against humanity. And for what?

He shouldn't have been surprised. He'd come to learn that the wars he had fought in were never about the righteous saving of civilisations as his superiors in their rallying induction speeches had led him to believe. Wars were about money and about greed and about power.

Lenny helped the other wounded man, carrying him out of the stockade. Just as they reached the Eureka camp they heard the yell.

'Fire!'

Will turned with the girl in his arms to see the soldiers he had just left setting fire to the tents and buildings inside the stockade. Will knew there were still wounded men, possibly women, inside the stockade. Only God could help them now.

As he was about to turn away he saw, through the mist and smoke, a figure inside the stockade. Will watched the policeman release the ropes so that the blue flag with the white stars of the Southern Cross fluttered slowly to the ground. No man of uniform—police or soldier—worth his salt would let a standard hit the ground. But this flag was the symbol of rebellion, the very representation of all that the British Government wanted quashed. Independence and freedom. It put a lump in Will's throat.

Having obtained the flag, the policeman ran across the stockade out of the range of the now spreading fires. Cheers rang out from other policemen who saw the man dragging the flag along the ground. They jumped on it, tore at it, before handing it up to a policeman on a horse who held it aloft to the crazed cheers of the soldiers and police, united for the first time in their lunacy. The mounted policeman turned his horse in a circle and looking up from his cheering fans, stared directly at Will, a sort of maddened, victorious grin lit his face.

Donnelly.

Will's heart stopped. He had to find Indy. If Donnelly found her first in this mess ... He cleared it from his mind. Thinking that way would only make him crazy. He had to find her.

Will moved back into camp where the unclaimed wounded were being gathered. A woman's cry broke the sombre silence as she rushed towards him. A man followed closely behind.

'It's my Cora,' the woman cried, inconsolably. 'She only went in there to take food to the men in the stockade. She should never have been there.'

'I'm so sorry,' Will said, knowing an apology from him would be hard taken.

The father took his daughter from Will's arms and, with a look of hatred unlike any Will had ever seen, he and his wife carried their dead child away.

In his numbness, he didn't even realise when Annie took his arm and led him to sit outside her tent. He felt the blessed warming from the campfire as she handed him a cup of billy tea and threw a blanket around his shoulders.

'I can't find her, Annie.' He put the tea down and dropped his head into his hands, his blond hair falling across his face to hide the despair and hopelessness he felt.

'Don't you give up on her, boy,' Annie demanded. 'Our Indy? She's resourceful. Got nine lives that girl. She's a survivor. She probably got out of there and went to her mother's.'

He felt Annie's soothing hand rubbing his back. She talked tough but he knew Annie was just as worried about Indy as he was.

'She could have been arrested,' Lenny threw in. He'd arrived back at the tent from handing the wounded man over to his mates. 'I heard they're arresting anyone involved in the rebellion and taking them up to the government camp.'

He knew he should go back to the soldiers' camp himself. Maybe he would find Indy there in the small jail with hundreds of other stockaders.

Another hour passed and Will sat where he was, staring out at the miners as they collected their dead and brought them home. It was Sunday. There would be no church today for many of the faithful. Only funerals to prepare. Those who had no family to claim them were hastily being readied by soldiers for burial in mass graves.

'Thirty,' Will overheard Lenny say to Sean. 'I heard them say thirty miners dead and only three soldiers.'

'Who can be sure that's even right?' Sean asked. 'It's bad odds either way. Bastards didn't give them a chance.'

Will had seen some of the wounded. The count of the dead would rise in the coming days.

Dawn finally broke over Mt Warrenheip and brought with it the scale of the devastation. The occasional gunshot could still be heard as soldiers and police chased down fugitives who had fled into the scrub to hide.

Will looked up from the second cup of tea Annie had given him and stared into the mist, dissipating now as the sun fought to burn through the haze. All around him people worked on the wounded, moving slowly, beaten, their spirits broken. He'd never heard the place so eerily quiet before.

Shadows crossed through the fog, diggers and families made faceless by the backlight of the rising sun. Staring so hard into the swirling mist, shapes blurred and Will wondered if the pain was beginning to make him hallucinate as an apparition appeared in the distance. The silhouette of a body walking towards him with hair wild and untamed.

'Indy,' he whispered.

Was he seeing a ghost?

'Indy?'

He'd been mistaken before. Perhaps his mind was playing tricks on him.

'Oh! Sweet Mary and Joseph!' Annie was suddenly beside him and Will looked up at her stunned expression. She stared, wide-eyed, into the mist as she crossed herself.

'You see her too?' he asked her.

'As plain as I see you,' Annie said, relief and happiness in every word.

He stood on unsteady legs and staggered towards the apparition that apparently wasn't an apparition. He could see by the smile on her lips that she had spotted him too, and she picked up her pace.

'Indy,' he said her name like a prayer, and a moment later she was in his arms. He gripped her to him tightly, never wanting to let her go.

'Ouch. Will, you're crushing me,' she said, her voice muffled into his coat.

'Sweet Indy,' he said leaning back and taking her face in his hands. She was filthy. Her teeth and the whites of her eyes shone in the dawn light against the dirt and blood smeared across her face.

Blood.

'You're injured?' he asked, panic overtaking his relief. His hands fluttered over her face, down her body as he searched for bullet or bayonet wounds.

'No,' she said looking down at herself. 'It's not my blood. Some of the miners ran into the bush to get away from the soldiers, but with injuries they didn't get very far. I helped those I could. Others weren't so lucky. They'll need proper burials later.'

She looked him up and down for the first time and frowned. 'But you are wounded.'

'I'm fine now you're here.'

He simply leaned his forehead to hers and closed his eyes, saying another little prayer of thanks. He kissed her, not caring who saw. The soldier and the miner. An unacceptable coupling to most. But she was his miner. And she was alive. That was all he cared about.

'Come, soldier boy. Let's have a look at you.'

With her arm around his waist and his over her shoulder, she moved him back towards Annie's tent to sit him down.

Annie took Indy in her arms and squeezed her tight. 'Thank God, you're alright.'

'I'm fine, Annie.' She knelt down in front of Will who sat again by the fire. 'What happened to you? Were you at the stockade when it happened?'

'No, I was still at the boarding house when the first attack was called. I came looking for you and was set upon by diggers. It was my own bloody fault. A red coat in the stockade is akin to a fox in the henhouse.'

'You idiot,' she reprimanded, but there was no heat in her scolding.

'I had to find you,' he said and taking her face in his hands once more, he leaned forward and kissed her lips. Kissed her eyes, her cheeks, her nose. 'My beautiful, uncontrollable, indestructible, Indy. I thought you were dead. I should have known better.'

'How badly damaged are you?' Indy asked and looking him over she was suddenly incensed. 'Who did this to you? Tell me who it was and I'll kick their bloody arses.'

Will could only smile and kiss her until he felt her tense body relax and her temper drain away. 'Will you avenge me, my love?'

She sighed. 'No. I'm too tired for vengeance just now. I'll go after them tomorrow.'

'Is there a tomorrow?'

His question hit home as they gazed wearily around the campsite.

Her hand on his cheek forced him to meet her eyes again. 'Just kiss me again and everything will be alright.'

He did as she asked. Taking her lips in a crushing kiss as though it was the last time he would touch her.

'Missed me did you?' she teased, but he could see the affection in her eyes. The love.

'There are things to discuss,' he said shaking his head, shaking away the sleep and the fatigue that went bone deep.

'You need to sleep first and heal a little,' Indy said, examining his wounds beneath the bandages. 'They opened up that thick head of yours again.'

Obviously satisfied that Annie had already tended Will's injuries, she stood. 'Annie, help me get him inside.'

The two women walked him carefully into the tent and lay him on the bed.

'Sleep.' Indy kissed his lips as Annie left them alone. 'We'll talk again when you're awake.'

'Indy,' he murmured through exhaustion.

'Will?'

'Don't go doing anything stupid.'

She grinned and winked. 'Me? When have I ever? Sleep now.'

Chapter 28

The sun was sitting high in the sky when Will managed to lift his aching body out of bed. Moving slowly and gingerly, he stepped out of the tent. It was late morning. He'd slept for hours. Annie sat by the fire with Walter O'Shanahan drinking tea and talking in hushed tones.

Looking around for Indy, and not finding her, panic set in all over again.

'Indy!' he called.

'Alright, alright, settle down.' Annie stood from her seat at the fire, taking a cup of water from Walter and handing it to him.

'Where is she?' he asked shaking his head at the water.

'Drink, lad,' Walter instructed. 'You must be parched.'

'She's out with Lenny,' Annie said. 'She'll be safe with him.'

'Not from a bullet she won't,' Will argued. He sipped the water and found he was dreadfully thirsty so drank the whole cup in one large gulp. Walter quickly poured him another.

'All the soldiers and police have slunk back into their hole at the government camp,' Annie told him. 'And good riddance to them.'

'Good riddance to who?'

Will turned at the sound of her voice and relief filled him. Dropping the cup, he went to her, pulling her against him. He just had to touch her, to know she was safe.

'What have you been doing?' he asked, leaning back to look down into the sapphire of her eyes. The sparkle was gone. Replaced by weariness. The weariness of someone who had seen too much.

He watched her glance around before she spoke, as though spies were everywhere.

'Lenny and I collected dresses from the ladies in camp,' she started, in a low voice. When Annie and Walter left their fire to render assistance to their neighbours, she sat Will down again and took a seat beside him. 'We delivered the women's clothing to miners hiding in the bush behind Black Hill. They—reluctantly I can tell you—surrendered their manliness and put on a dress in order to save their lives and escape to Geelong and Melbourne. I believe they are safely on their way.'

'If soldiers catch you aiding fugitives you'll be arrested or shot, Indy.'

'I'll not sit back and do nothing.'

And there, in her eyes, was the fire he admired so much. It warmed him to see it again. 'Of course you won't,' he said, dusting a curl from her forehead. 'And that's why I love you. Dressing as women. It's a clever idea. How can I help?'

'I think we've done all that we can,' Indy said, gazing desolately around the campsite before turning back to him. 'I heard you helped carry the wounded back to camp from the stockade. They're calling you the Red Coat Miner.'

Will shook his head sadly. 'I only carried the dead.'

Looking down at his red coat, he slowly removed it and tossed it over a log. He no longer felt pride in wearing it.

'You were right,' he said, taking her hand as they solemnly watched the wounded being patched up while the dead were shrouded and mourned.

'It's rare, but it happens,' Indy said, with the faintest of laughs. 'But what was I right about this time?'

'We need to leave.'

Her mouth fell open, before she snapped it shut. 'You said you couldn't leave the army.'

'I know that's what I said, but I can no longer be part of this life, *this* army,' Will said, his eyes scanning the landscape of death before them. 'You showed me it is better to be a good man than to be part of something so vile and wrong, blindly following orders simply because I have nothing else.'

'You have me,' Indy said, softly laying a hand on his injured face.

'I know that now.' He pulled her in for a strong kiss then just held her to him, relieved in the feeling of her heart beating against his. 'I know that.'

He leaned back and gazed down at her. 'Come away with me, Indy.'

'But my mother...'

'She'll come too,' he added. 'Of course she'll come. I could never ask you to leave her behind. We'll go north, follow the sun. I'll build you and Mary a house.'

They should have gone last night when she'd first suggested it, he thought, but hindsight was a wonderful thing. She didn't have a price on her head as so many of the other miners did, but Will knew the police would come after her if they found out she was helping the fugitives escape.

'We'll build a house together,' she told him and he grinned at her.

'Stubborn to the end.'

'Naturally,' she said with a wink. 'When shall we go?'

'As soon as possible. We'll go to your mother's tonight, help her pack her belongings, and leave in the morning if we can.'

'That soon? What about Annie and Sean? I can't just up and leave without telling them what's going on.'

'I'm not sure it's safe for us all to travel together,' Will said with a troubled frown. 'I'm deserting, Indy. We need to leave as lightly and as quickly as we can. I disobeyed orders again last night. Once things have settled down at the government camp they will reprimand me.'

'You mean you'll be flogged and court-martialled.'

He nodded solemnly. 'I may not have a chance to get away after today.'

A sadness came into her eyes as she glanced across to where Sean had now joined Annie and Walter in delivering food to families of the injured. 'I'll leave them a note. It'll hurt to just walk away, but Annie will understand. And now they have Walter. He'll take care of them.'

Will brushed a curl from her forehead and kissed her there. 'Tell them we'll send for them when we get settled and they can join us if they wish.'

'You are a good man, Will Marsh.'

Picking up his red coat, he kissed her once more before embracing her. The thought of leaving her alone again had him tightening his hold for a moment before he found the strength to let her go. 'I'll see you at your mother's later.'

'Be careful.'

***

Once out of the miner's camp, Will pulled on his slightly damaged red coat. He slipped quietly into a group of soldiers who were returning to the government camp with a collection of prisoners hobbled together. It pained him to see these simple men in chains, many of whom were carrying injuries so severe they should have been going to a hospital, not prison.

As he walked across the compound, still limping a little with his own injuries, he spotted Captain Thomas outside the Gold Commissioner's hut. The man gave him a look of suspicion as Will pretended to be amongst the soldiers ferrying the prisoners.

'Good to see you made it back safely, Lieutenant Marsh,' Thomas called out. 'And with a haul of fugitives. Fine work, Officer.'

'Thank you, sir,' Will called back through gritted teeth. There was nothing he could do for these poor blighters. Any show of opposition now would see him in leg irons shackled together with them.

Out of the line of sight of Captain Thomas and the command, he veered off towards the tent he shared with George, who just happened to be there when he arrived.

'Christ almighty!' George blurted on seeing Will. 'Are you wounded, man?'

'Just a few bumps and scrapes,' Will played it down. 'I had a run in with some miners after the attack.'

'Where have you been all this time?' George asked, helping Will to sit on his stretcher bed. Will hissed through his teeth at the ache in his ribs.

'Trying to find a safe way to get back.' He could see George's doubtful expression out of the corner of his eye. 'Were you not there this morning? In the attack against the stockade?'

'No, I was put in charge of the brigades here, tasked with protection of the camp,' George said shaking his head. 'Thomas came looking for you late last night. I had to cover for you. I told him you were preparing the men to protect the rear of the camp. I watched them sneak down the hill towards town at half four this morning.'

Will nodded, exhaustion threatening to swallow him again.

'I thought you'd deserted. Where were you?'

Will hesitated on whether to tell George that he'd been with Indy last night. It would definitely be safer if George was unaware that he'd been helping with the wounded at the camp after the attack.

'Where's Timmons?' Will asked, looking for their other tent mate.

George's whole body sagged. He couldn't meet Will's eyes.

'No,' Will said, his shock forcing the word out in a gasp.

'A small number of soldiers lost their lives on the field,' George said, his usually cheerful expression replaced with one of dismay. 'Timmons was one of them.'

'There are several others seriously wounded,' George went on. 'But Timmons ... he took a single gunshot wound to the throat.'

They spent a moment in silence, remembering their fallen comrade, their lost friend.

'George, you and I have been friends a long time.'

'We have,' George agreed sitting across from Will on his own cot.

'Brothers even,' Will added and George nodded. 'If I were to tell you something ... something that would surely get me killed or court-martialled should you share it, can I trust you to keep it to yourself?'

'I would take it to the grave, Will,' George said insulted. 'How can you ask me that?'

Will shook his head. 'I'm sorry, old friend. It's been a dreadful night. I wasn't thinking straight.'

'So?' George asked. 'What is it then? What's this big secret?'

'I'm leaving,' Will said quietly. 'Today.'

George just stared at him unblinking for a moment and Will wondered if he had made a mistake. But then his friend took a deep breath and exhaled as he smiled wistfully.

'I think I knew that already. Is it the girl?'

'Partly. I love her.'

George grinned. 'Told you.'

'Yes, yes, you were right as usual,' Will conceded.

'Then I give you my fondest wishes for your happiness, Will,' George said. 'But why must you leave for love? Many officers are allowed to have their wives along for the campaigns.'

'It's not just her,' Will said shaking his head. 'It's this.'

He waved his hand towards the opening of the tent where they could see prisoners being transferred to larger holdings.

'This?'

'You don't think what happened here this morning was an over-reaction? An abuse of power?'

George took a deep breath and exhaled in a gust. 'It's not up to us to think, Will. We have orders.'

'And if those orders are wrong?' Will asked. 'If they kill innocent women and children? Innocent men come to that? Is it right to send a battalion of hundreds of armed soldiers and policemen to attack a group of civilians armed with nothing but a few rifles and handmade pikes? Do the ends justify the means?'

'I feel we have had this conversation before.'

Will nodded. 'Yes. And you were right. My words smack of dissent. And that is why I am leaving. I no longer believe in the greater good of the British campaign here. I was there, George. It was a massacre. And even after the stockade was taken and so many men killed, those boy soldiers were allowed to run riot attacking men and women who were already wounded. They ran them through over and over with bayonets. I saw the carnage for myself.'

George said nothing, but Will could see by the tensing of George's jaw that he was unhappy with what he was hearing. 'Is your girl alright?'

'She is uninjured,' Will said. 'But she helped the fugitives escape, and she is a miner herself. If they catch her—'

'Yes, yes.' George stopped him with a raised hand saying he understood. 'Where will you go?'

'North. That's all I know and I think it's best if I don't tell you anything else. It's for your safety as much as mine. You know they will question you after I am gone. I don't want you in any trouble.'

'If they catch you, you will be court-martialled,' George reminded him.

'It's a risk I am willing to take.'

George studied Will closely and gave a sad smile. 'I will miss you. We have grown up together in the Fortieth regiment. Seen much of the world together.' He stood and held out his hand to his friend.

Will took George's offered hand and let him help him up. Then he pulled George into a one armed embrace with a slap on the back for good measure.

'You are the best of men, George Preston. I will never forget you.'

***

Will showed his face around camp a little more to ensure people knew he was there. He found his horse in the line-up of animals tied to the fence and casually packed things into his saddlebags for his departure later that evening. The soldiers were drinking heavily now and despite the Commissioner's concerns about a counterattack, the spirits of the men were high. Even the sentries were partaking in the rum that was being handed about. It would be easy for him to make his escape in the twilight.

As he finished loading his gear into his saddlebag that afternoon, he noticed another Lieutenant standing beside his horse. He was from the Twelfth regiment, Will believed. He didn't know the man well but he could read easily the expression on his face. Guilt.

Will didn't wish to appear suspicious himself so he nodded at the Lieutenant in greeting. 'Hell of a morning.'

'Hell is a good word for it,' the Lieutenant replied gruffly.

'You do not think it was a good victory then?' Will asked, still wary.

The other Lieutenant scanned the vicinity as though checking no one could hear. 'I do not. The act that took place this morning was murder, plain and true.'

Will took a breath. 'I agree.'

'I cannot stay in Her Majesty's service,' the man lowered his voice further. 'I am a God-fearing Christian man with a wife back in England and a child I have never met. Four soldiers are dead, nine wounded and countless of those poor miners lay festering in their own blood and muck. I must do what I feel in my soul to be right.'

Will nodded. 'As must I. This was a disgrace what happened here.'

'It was,' the Lieutenant agreed. 'When do you plan to go?'

'Tonight. At sundown.'

'No. The men shoot at anything that moves after dark. A woman was shot early this morning as she passed by the government camp. The ball went through her and then through the babe in her arms. Both dead.'

Will felt sick. Even after everything he'd seen, the more stories he heard, the more horrifying it all became.

'You must go now, while the men are still celebrating and drunk. Go while confusion still reigns. They will be expecting a counterattack tonight and they'll rally the troops. You won't get five paces past the fence. You have your belongings there in your saddlebags?'

'I do.'

'You must go now,' the Lieutenant said again, mounting his horse.

Will took one long study of the camp, its inhabitants still in disarray dealing with prisoners and the wounded. The young boy soldiers were high on the adrenaline of battle, toasting their victory with grog Captain Thomas himself had handed them.

'I thank you, sir, for your counsel and your discretion,' Will said and mounted his horse. 'Good luck on your journey back to England.'

The two men rode out of the camp acting for all intents and purposes like two soldiers on a patrol. Once they reached the Melbourne Road, they shook hands and parted ways and Will watched the Lieutenant kick his horse into a gallop and head for Melbourne. He was sorry he had never thought to ask the man's name. Then he turned his own horse and headed for Mary Wallace's cabin.

Chapter 29

Gum leaves crunched beneath her feet as Indy walked through the bush. The aroma filled the air and lightened her heart. It replaced the smell of blood and gun smoke that seemed to have permanently attached itself to her since this morning's massacre. The small duffel bag she carried held everything she owned of value from the campground in Eureka. She'd left a note for Annie and Sean. Her heart was heavy that she couldn't have told them more and she wished they could have travelled together. But Will was right. It was better for all of them if they went separately. And safer for Annie and Sean that they didn't know about Will's desertion.

Will.

Her heart fluttered. So much had happened since they'd held each other, loved each other, in the small bed at the boarding house. Had that really only been last night? When she had left him sleeping at the widow Barnett's, he'd been determined to stay with the army.

But then he'd seen the horror of the attack on the stockade. It had been the last straw for him. He was too good a man with too big a heart to be party to such brutal tactics.

As she came to the road, her daydreams were interrupted by the sound of horse's hooves.

'Dammit,' she swore.

Lost in her thoughts, she'd heard the sound too late to hide. All she could do was prepare herself to act as though she were just on an afternoon's walk. Pasting on a smile, she turned to face the traveller. But her smile faded rapidly at the sight of a policeman riding towards her. Her concern turned to fear in a heartbeat as she recognised Donnelly. She also saw the moment his face registered her, too, as he rode closer.

'Well, well,' he said, pulling his horse up in front of her as she tried to dart into the safety of the scrub. 'Uh, uh, uh.' He shook a finger at her as he manoeuvered his horse, blocking her path as though he were herding her like cattle.

He dismounted and she took the opportunity to make a run for it. But he was faster. She felt the sharp pain in her skull when he yanked her by her hair. Losing her footing and hitting the ground heavily on her back, she let out a pained cry. He quickly dragged her to her feet, again by her hair, and finding strength in her anger she fought back. She dug her short nails into his hands making him curse and let go of her momentarily.

'You little bitch!' he yelled and slammed his fist in a backhand against her cheek.

Indy fell to the ground again with a thud, her hands grazed painfully along the rough dirt of the dry road. She shook her head to clear it and tried to get up but Donnelly shoved his boot into her back, pressing her down.

'Stop fighting,' he told her as she struggled against him. 'You, my little daughter, cost me a comfortable and wealthy life as a gentleman. I should be in England now, instead of this cesspool of a colony.'

'Nothing could make you a gentleman,' Indy shouted back, twisting and turning as she fought to escape from him. 'And you're delusional. I cost you nothing. We left England without anyone knowing what you had done to my mother. You must have raped someone else. Someone who didn't stay quiet about it. No doubt you've spread your disgusting seed across half of England. If your career was ruined, you did it all by yourself.'

He leaned down so close to her face that she could smell the booze on him.

'I could kill you and say you were a fugitive from the stockade running from the law. Do you think anyone will care, or even notice for that matter, with everything else that's going on in Ballarat just now? I'd probably get a bloody medal.'

Real panic soaked Indy in a cold sweat. He was right. No one would blink an eye should a miner girl go missing or suddenly turn up dead. She thought of Will and her mother, and it gave her fortitude. No. She wouldn't die now. She refused to die. Not after all of this.

He stood upright and she took the opportunity to scramble away from him. But before she could find her feet, she watched horrified as he removed the whip from the horse's saddle.

'You are nothing but a bastard rebel and a soldier's whore,' he said and raised the whip to bring it down on her.

Indy covered her face, waiting for the snap of the whip and the certain agony that would follow. She heard the crack but felt nothing.

Donnelly's horse spooked at the sound, and the thud of something landing near her had her lifting her head. Donnelly lay beside her, his face contorted as his surprised eyes fixed on hers. His breathing was quick and laboured, and she was confused until she saw the blood seeping through his blue uniform tunic, spreading across his chest as the life leaked out of his body. When her stunned gaze travelled back to his face, it was relaxed—his eyes cold and dead.

Panicked, she scrambled away from him and stood up to stare down at the unmoving corpse of her father. She should feel something she supposed. But there was nothing. No grief. No relief. Nothing.

A footfall behind her had her swinging around quickly, knowing now that the crack she had heard was a gunshot. She was surprised to see a woman walk towards her, a gun hanging loosely in her hand. Indy didn't know the woman and watched warily as she moved in and looked down at the body of Donnelly.

'Thank you,' Indy said still shaking. 'I'm sorry, but you have killed a policeman.'

'I don't care,' the woman answered, her voice hollow and emotionless. 'This man killed my husband. I stood in front of my Kenneth at the stockade after they had shot him. He was wounded. Wasn't that enough? They kicked me out of the way and this man, this animal, he took that knife in his pocket there and slit my husband's throat.'

The woman met Indy's gaze for the first time. Quiet tears had fallen down her cheeks as she'd spoken. She must have been no older than herself.

'Why?' the woman asked.

Indy shook her head. A dull ache was beginning to set in. 'I don't know. I'm sorry.'

Wiping the blood from her cheek where Donnelly had struck her, she remembered Will and her mother.

'I'm sorry,' she said again. 'I have to go. I suggest you do the same. Run. Go back to the camp as though nothing happened. Thank you. I wish you well.'

'And you.'

Indy began to move as quickly as she could through the scrub. As the shock subsided, the pain began to set in. She turned back once and was glad to see the woman had moved on, away from the dead body of Sergeant Donnelly.

When she arrived at the cabin, Will rushed out the door to greet her, but the relieved smile on his face was quickly replaced by alarm.

'Oh my God, Indy. What happened?'

Gently he took her now swelling face in his hands and wiped at the drying blood on her cheek. Mary rushed out too, having heard Will's raised voice. They led her into the house and sat her down in the chair by the window. Mary wetted a cloth to put to her daughter's injured face.

'Were you attacked on the way here?' Will asked, kneeling in front of her and taking her hands.

'Ow.' Indy hissed at the pain that flared.

He turned her palms over and saw the scrapes left by her desperate scramble across the road. Small pieces of stone and dirt were etched into her skin and Mary moved the cooling cloth to her hands. It felt heavenly and Indy closed her eyes for a moment.

'Indy, who did this to you?' Will asked.

'Donnelly.'

She heard her mother's squeal and opened her eyes again. Or tried to. One eye was beginning to swell shut where Donnelly had smacked her. It was making it hard to keep it open. It watered mightily.

'I'm alright, Mother.'

'But did he follow you here?' Mary asked, her eyes darted to the front door, still wide open to let the fresh air in. 'Is he coming after us?'

'That would be some feat considering he's dead.'

Both Will and Mary stared at Indy, their faces frozen in shock.

'Oh, Indy, you didn't,' Mary said, sinking into a chair.

'No, Mother, I didn't,' Indy replied. 'A woman came along just in time. She shot him. He apparently killed her husband at the stockade. Slit the man's throat even after he had been wounded by gunfire.'

'Oh, will this nightmare ever end?' Mary cried.

'Yes,' Will insisted. 'It will end tomorrow when we are far away from here.'

'He's really dead?' Mary asked, a tear running down her face.

Indy stood and went to her mother, pulling her in for a comforting hug despite her own pain.

'It's over, Mother. Warren Donnelly will never bother us again.'

They moved quickly once Indy's eye had been patched up, packing everything they could possibly carry, ready to load onto the small wagon that Indy had purchased a few weeks before. It had originally been bought to carry vegetables to sell at market in Ballarat.

Now, it was loaded with their most treasured belongings. The largest of the furniture, the beds and the dining table, would have to be left behind and that upset Mary a little but Indy promised she would buy more when they got to where they were going.

Will helped her dig up the vegetables in the garden so that they would have food for the trip, and he stared amazed when she unearthed a wooden box from beneath the garden bed and opened it. The size of the gold nugget in the box was incomprehensible.

She laughed at the look of comical astonishment on his face.

'Didn't you believe me when I said I had the third largest nugget?'

'I thought I did but...' he couldn't finish his sentence as he ran his hand over the smooth, dull nobs of the nugget. 'I thought it might be shinier.'

Indy just laughed again and they packed the box with its valuable cargo safely in a bottom compartment in the wagon.

They would spend one last, nervous night in the cottage before loading the wagon at dawn. Will stayed awake throughout it, expecting soldiers or the police to come looking for him or Indy.

An hour or so before the sun was due to rise, Indy woke. Leaving her mother in the bed they shared, she joined Will on the front porch where he had sat watchful all night.

'We have a long journey ahead of us,' she told him. 'You should try to get a few hours' sleep. I can take the watch.'

'I'm sure the officers will be too busy just now, dealing with fugitive miners and their own wounded, to be concerned with a missing lieutenant,' Will said staring out into the night. 'But they'll notice I'm gone eventually. And I won't relax until we are well away from this place.'

Taking her bandaged hand, he pulled her into his lap, nuzzling into her ear. His nose was cool and she squirmed a little.

'Mmm, you're still warm from your bed,' he murmured against her neck, taking a long inhale. The exhalation of his breath against her skin filled her belly with butterflies.

'I wish you could have been in it with me,' she answered, winding her arms around him and holding him close. He tipped his head back and took her mouth with his, strongly, desperately, as though all his fears and worries for her were pouring out in the kiss they shared. Leaning back to offer a quick kiss to her injured eye, he hugged her tightly against him.

'It would have been crowded with your mother in there too,' he said, taking his clever mouth and tongue to her earlobe.

'Ha, ha.' It was all she could manage as his kisses were making her weak.

'There'll be time for sharing a bed when we are married.'

Pushing him back, she stared at him. 'Married?'

'Of course.'

'And what if I don't want to be married?'

That deep line between his eyebrows was back. 'Why wouldn't you want to marry me?'

'Perhaps I like being my own woman. Perhaps I don't want some man telling me what I can and can't do.'

Will laughed, 'And what manner of fool do you think I am to believe I could ever tell you what to do, Indigo Wallace?'

She had to grin. 'Well, then. If you are willing to concede that I shall never honour the "obey" portion of the vows, then I guess I can agree to marry you.'

'The British Army is willing to concede,' he said with a rich chuckle and kissed her again.

Her heart soared. She was engaged. Engaged to be married. She never thought she would see the day. She never thought she'd wanted to. But when they parted his smile faded.

'What is it?' she questioned.

'I am no longer British Army.'

Regret crossed his features. He was a deserter, and she knew it didn't sit well with him. Smiling sympathetically, she ran a hand down the tan-coloured shirt and the dark brown vest he wore.

'But you look so handsome in civilian clothing, Will,' she said, gazing deeply into his eyes.

Thankfully, his beautiful smile returned and he kissed her again. Would she ever get enough of his kisses?

'I shall miss the uniform though,' she said with an exaggerated sigh. 'You did look so lovely in it.'

'I still have it.' He raised his eyebrows suggestively. 'Perhaps I can put it on for special occasions.'

Her laugh was smothered as he captured her mouth in another heart-melting kiss.

'I'll marry you, Will Marsh. I never thought to marry, but that's because I have never known love until now.'

'I've never known love before you, Indigo Wallace,' Will said and kissed her injured eye lightly.

The eye hurt more than she let on. But while the physical wounds would heal, the memories of the horrors that went on at the stockade on that December dawn would stay with them forever.

Epilogue

Four days had passed since the 'massacre at the Eureka Stockade', as the papers and gossips were now calling it. Jack thought it was probably safe enough for him to head back closer to town without being arrested just for being.

He rode up to the little cabin in the woods, his two fellow highwaymen beside him.

'Hi ho, Mrs Mary Wallace!' Jack called out his usual greeting as he neared the house nestled amongst the tall stringybarks.

There was no movement from the house. No one rushed out to meet him.

He called again.

Nothing.

Dismounting agilely from his horse, he stepped up to the door and knocked. His mates stayed where they were on their horses, eyes sharp as always for signs of the troopers. These were still dangerous times for bushrangers as much as they were for rebel diggers. Still there was no noise from inside the house. Jack peered through one of the small windows. He frowned at what he saw. Or rather, what he didn't see.

Warily, he opened the door and stepped in. It took a moment for his eyes to adjust to the darkness from the bright summer sun outside.

He blinked. Blinked again. A wave of shock enveloped him as he looked around at the shell of the house.

His eyes had not deceived him. Almost everything was gone. The dining table remained but Mary's comfortable chair by the fireplace, the small end table where he'd shared many wonderful cups of tea with the Wallace women were all missing. Mary's prettily sewn calico and lace curtains and all the feminine touches that had made the little cottage a home—they were all gone.

He peered into the small bedrooms. The beds were still there, the mattresses stripped of their sheets and covers. The shelves stood bare on Indy's prized bookcase.

What had happened here? A moment of fear overwhelmed him. Had they been taken away by soldiers? He'd heard that Indy had assisted fugitive miners; had given them her own dresses to see them safely on their way to Melbourne or Geelong. Had the military found them out?

He was about to rush out of the house in his panic when something on the fireplace mantle caught his eye.

Mary's ceramic biscuit barrel.

Everything else in the house had been stripped. Why leave one biscuit barrel behind? He lifted the little ceramic pot from the shelf and taking the large cork lid out he peered in. The mouth of the container was just wide enough to fit his hand—he ought to know, he'd slipped his crafty fingers into it to steal a biscuit often enough.

He found biscuits—as you would expect in a biscuit barrel—but his hand also brushed against a piece of paper. He tugged it out and unfolding it he read:

'To Whom it May Concern,

Should you be rebels or miners, use this cottage with our blessing, we've no need of it anymore.

We leave this place, Ballarat, which was once a place of hope but is now stained with the blood of so many who, like us, only wanted a better life.

We shall find our better life elsewhere.

Should you be the British Army, a soldier gives back his Queen's shilling. He thanks you for his home and begs your forgiveness for his desertion. But he must take his leave from a military so lost in its mission to protect against tyranny that is has become tyranny itself.

PS: Jack, enjoy the biscuits as they will be the last you will see from us you mooching bushranger, xxxx. Indy.'

Jack let out a snorting laugh. He bit into the sugary biscuit and sighed. The last of these delights. 'Twas a crying shame. And a shame the Wallace women, with their soldier it seemed, had headed for greener pastures. He shoved the note into his pocket and, taking the biscuit barrel, he walked back out into the bright sunlight.

'So do we get tea or what?' Bobby called out.

'Not here we don't, lads.'

Mounting his horse, Jack took one last look at the empty little house, smiled a small, melancholy smile, then turning his horse he kicked it into a gallop and followed his mates into the bush.

Author's Note: The Facts

In the early hours of 3 December 1854, the British Army attacked the Eureka Stockade in Ballarat with almost three hundred soldiers and police. It has been widely argued as to whether the army or the miners in the stockade fired first. The conflict lasted no more than thirty minutes, but in that time it is said (although there is some discrepancy in the reference books as to definite numbers) that approximately twenty-seven civilians and four soldiers were killed. Nine more soldiers and countless other civilians, including women and children, were wounded. Over a hundred diggers were arrested and eventually a group of thirteen miners were charged with treason including the Italian Raffaello Carboni and Timothy Hayes, and many others who had fled Ballarat to Geelong or Melbourne, who had prices on their heads. They were eventually acquitted of all charges and cheered on by thousands of Melbourne residents who had come to watch the trials and to condemn the actions taken by the British Government and military in the taking of the Eureka Stockade in Ballarat. The diggers' commander in chief, Peter Lalor, was shot and severely injured in the stockade battle and eventually had his arm amputated. In November 1855 he was elected to the Victorian Legislative Council as Member for the new district of Ballarat, a role he stayed in until March 1856. The original Eureka Flag, damaged by the policemen who tore it down, is on loan from the Art Gallery of Ballarat and can be seen at the MADE Museum (Museum of Australian Democracy at Eureka) in Ballarat, which sits on the site of the Eureka Stockade. Some say the constant petitions and battles by the immigrant miners were Australia's first step towards an independent democracy. As for the soldiers, who have often been portrayed throughout history in film and literature as the villains, twenty-two soldiers of Her Majesty's service deserted between December 1854 and the early months of 1855. In total, one hundred and sixty-five soldiers threw back the Queen's shilling in Victoria alone. Their living conditions in the government camp weren't much better than the squalor of the diggers' camps. I have tried to show the facts of one of the most significant moments in Australia's history but, as with all fiction, a little artistic flair is sometimes required. In 1854 the town of Ballarat was actually spelled Ballaarat. The word originated from two Aboriginal words *balla* and *arat,* meaning 'resting place'. The town eventually came to be known as Ballarat. To save confusion for readers I used the modern, and more commonly known, spelling. While the main characters of this novel are fictional, to retain some authenticity some of the people depicted in the story were present at the events that happened during the time period. Extensive research allowed me to find their roles in the events that transpired in Ballarat in 1854. However any dialogue, description and action taken by those real persons in this novel are purely fictional.

Thanks for reading *The Girl from Eureka.* I hope you enjoyed it.

Reviews can help readers find books, and I am grateful for all honest reviews. Thank you for taking the time to let others know what you've read, and what you thought.

If you liked this book visit my website at cheryladnams.com

Sign up to our newsletter romance. com.au/newsletter/ and find out about new releases, must-read series and ***ebook deals*** at romance.com.au.

Share your reading experience on:

Facebook

Instagram

romance.com.au